A Thin Veil of the Cosmos
A Case of High Strangeness and Alien Abduction through the Eyes of a Goth Teen

I0667255

A novel
Thomas Michael Thomas
www.thomasmichaelthomas.com[1]

---

1. http://www.thomasmichaelthomas.com

Thank you to Elyse and my cats.

A special thank you.

Linda & Dave Price, Douglas & Jerlin Ford, Derik Cavignano, Christina Persaud, Josh Strnad, Matt and Lori Massuci, Mike & Becky Schuller, Rebecca Rowland, Kenzie Jennings, Ed Morales, Michael Tyger, Albert Mudrian, Dave Couillou, Keith Bynum, Jesus Orduno, Darren Garoutte, Sam Peterson, Bryan Nastanski, Ross Purvis, Brandon Legion, Brandon Fair, Scott Zientek, Tyler & Sara Gingery, Erica & Tyler Caswell, Johnny Wolfman, Mike Murphy, Grayson Kirkham, Terri Bricker, Robynn Kelly, "Mac" McMillan, Nathan Andre, and Michael Brown.

Dedicated to Mr. Ed Domrzalski

Within the boundaries of this work of fiction, you and I are standing on an obsidian plateau, witnessing millions of stars in the Milky Way change their course over the span of eons, a place where men's hearts could be overwhelmed by the infinite beauty above us. As you were someone who understood the concept of a heavenly place, where our spirits do not die; and in that steadfast faith being held as truth, then the God you believe in must shine upon us all, and in that warmth, I hope to see you again.

About the author: Michael is a rabid fan of 70's horror movies and old books that most people have never heard of. He lives happily in Florida with his wife and cats.

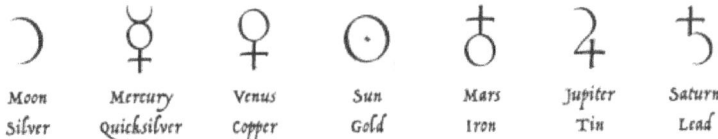

Moon	Mercury	Venus	Sun	Mars	Jupiter	Saturn
Silver	Quicksilver	Copper	Gold	Iron	Tin	Lead

"I WAS BESIDE MYSELF for some time, as I had all of the proper elements in place for communicating with the cosmos, more than just looking up at the stars, sifting tea leaves, or utilizing tarot. In this process, my birthstones were in my hand, my chakra was right, and I had chanted in the proper tones, until it dawned on me, in a drunken stupor of course, that I needed to be sitting in a chalk circle, with my astrological symbol drawn, along with Saturn's. In this incompetence, I laughed and laughed, then I spoke to the universe and heard back."

   -Famed Mystic/Astronomer/Professor Francis Truelove, 1866

"IF WE WERE VISITED by aliens from another world, bringing us technology capable of modern-day miracles: with the knowledge to yield crops a hundred-fold and the eradication of disease and machinery beyond our comprehension, would we meet them with a handshake, while the other hand was formed into a fist? And If we, the human race, with our prejudices and limited wisdom, spit in the face of furthering the advancement of our civilization, not be expectant of the wrath from celestial beings?"

    -A statement taken from a man who lived in his car, while folding tinfoil and placing it in his baseball cap.

"Ninkaḷ ninta ayulai allatu celvattai tervu ceykirirkala?"

1
May 1974

The pre-summer humidity caused a diffraction of yellow halos around the lamp posts on the old Pennsylvania state road; moths flocked to them in a frenzy. The quiet ride home from a Saturday evening church revival held a hypnotic schizophrenic buzzing, a hum felt deep within the regions of the Earth, matching vibrations of habitable planets throughout the expanding universe. A dormant schizophrenia that dwells within all of our minds, broken out of the hallucinations of old age alchemy, tying the inner workings of our primitive self, sinewing into the lesser brain, into the core of basic electric impulses that harbor both the wars and lusts of humankind. Most of those dark passages are never noticed, but in our weakness, we are at our most diabolic.

An old hymnal was on the truck radio. Young Helen Beaumont sang along like a mindless bird; floating on a spiritual high, a residue left over from the revival service. Her husband, Jerry, a man only in religion because his wife forced him to, had questioned the hymnals to their core. He questioned the preachers' words and didn't take them as God's. They were just a man's interpretation being twisted to scare a sheepish congregation. He wondered if the chills he felt on his arms and neck were a good or bad reaction. If an outsider didn't know who was singing the hymns, or the words being uttered, how could one discern if it was good or evil? Could hymnals themselves be neutral until meaning was placed behind them? Was he wired to feel something, anything at all when an atmosphere of that type was present? Would his natural reaction be the same if he heard the hymnals and just stared at a blank wall?

At tonight's church service, the guest revivalist, S. W. Grantly, seemed to think the Devil was everywhere in the state of the world: in the government, in movie stars, and even in the radio waves. Grantly's words echoed, "All the crevices and darkest parts of men's minds are threatened by the powers of Satan."

A terrifying thought came to Jerry's mind, *What if an evil person had his own channel for his own hymnals to be broadcast, and without deciphering the words within the long dramatic aaaaaaaaahs, who would know any different?*

A hiss of static hummed, followed by a pulsating reverberation. Jerry furrowed his brows and thought it sounded like a sick man breathing into a greasy paper bag. The static cleared and the hymnal continued, but it was strained and devoid of warmth. He drove slowly as the visibility was poor. Words replayed in his mind from that night, and they didn't sit well with him. Grantly claimed he was an end-time prophet, sent by God to reveal to his chosen people how to survive in the last days prior to Christ's second coming. A series of self-published paperback books were brought with him as well. Books that held the exact answers to the very questions that only the revivalist brought up. He sold his grandiose fear and his absolute solutions to the parishioners, who were willing to please a deity, who should have been pleased with them already. This troubled Jerry even more. Grantly reminded him of a game show host, only on drugs. Contrary to Jerry's concern, his wife Helen thought the revivalist was wonderful. She purchased one of his books. She clutched it in her hand as she held her daughters with the other. The book was titled: *The Forthcoming Doom: A Devil Among Us.* On the cover, a man's hand held the Devil's hand, the red hand indicated that it belonged to the Devil. *Why would a so-called man of God focus on so much darkness and evil?* Jerry thought. He saw through the façade as fear was a motivator. It did nothing good for a small congregation that was supposed to be in the grace of God.

Between them sat Nova, their four-year-old daughter. Nova had a special condition that the doctor called "hyperactivity". She needed medication to keep her regular. If not for the medication, Nova would become so erratic that she would vibrate like an overwound spinning top.

"I thought he was delightful," Helen said. "The way he explained things, it was like scales fell off my eyes. I never realized how awful the state of the world is. I almost feel dumb for not noticing sooner."

"I am sorry, my dear?" Jerry asked. His mind had been blanketed by layers of thought and the drone of the night.

"I can't wait to discuss everything with the others tomorrow," Helen said.

"Doesn't a Saturday evening church service, with people flailing about and passing out on the floor under the power of God, count as a checkmark for attendance this weekend?"

"What?" Helen smiled. Her left eye fluttered. A perpetual eye tic had occurred after Nova was born. "Of course not. I want more of that very thing. I think I want to bake Mr. Grantly and his wife cookies. Do you think he would like cookies?" She looked out the window. "I am certain he would."

Helen squeezed Nova's hand, "Honey, do you want to go to church tomorrow and see your friends?"

Nova nodded her head.

"See Jerry, Nova wants to go to church tomorrow. We can't tell her no now."

"You don't want to watch cartoons instead?" Jerry asked.

Nova enjoyed mimicking her mother, both of them shook their head at the same time and smiled.

"I see," he said. He sat in silent frustration.

"Stop at the grocery store; I want to get some ingredients."

"Mmmm hmmm."

Cautiously, he slowed down in the dewy stretch of the night. Static pierced through the speakers. Quickly, he reached for the knob and turned the dial to the next AM station, leaving it barely audible.

"Why, look at all those fireflies in the parking lot," Helen exclaimed.

"Those are moths," Jerry said. He pulled in.

"No, in spattered color. Reds and greens and blues. Don't you see them?" She took off her glasses. "And their butts are glowing. Do you see the glowing butts, Nova?"

Nova laughed, "Glowing butts."

Only two other cars were in the parking lot. When he turned off the engine, silence pulsated between them. Jerry looked out at the moths. They were more sparse than they were on the main road.

"I don't see any fireflies, dear."

"Well, they are there," Helen said.

Jerry shook his head, "I will be back in a minute. Nova, do you want to come in with me?"

Nova shook her head and held her mother's hand.

"Chocolate chips, flour, and butter."

"Got it," he said.

"Fireflies, Jerry. I am telling you they are fireflies."

"Yes, Helen. Greens and blues."

He opened the door and stepped into the parking lot.

"Fireflies. Aaaaaaaaaaaaaaaaaah," Helen hummed.

"What?"

Jerry looked over his shoulder. Helen's head was tilted back, mouth agape, like she was stuck in a terrible yawn. Her eyes bugged out and her tongue stretched out over her bottom lip. She stared at the roof as if she was gazing at the stars.

"Helen, are you all right?"

Her face was frozen.

"Helen!" He reached over Nova and touched his wife's hand.

Her face turned to him warmly, as if the action did not happen. She smiled, "Yes dear?"

"What the hell was that?" he whispered.

He looked at Nova, who did not notice.

"That sound?" Jerry asked.

"I didn't make any sound." She opened her mouth wide and held it, like a snake about to unhinge its jaw.

"Aaaaaaaaaaaaaaaaaaa," she hummed again.

"You just..." Jerry said.

Helen snapped out of the mini trance, laughed, and pushed on her husband's arm, "What is with you? Go get the eggs."

"What?"

"Eggs, little round things that come out of a chicken's butt," she said.

"Glowing butts," Nova said.

"I heard you, I just... well, you are acting weird."

Helen looked at Nova, "Honey, am I being weird?"

Nova shook her head, "I want chocolate chips too, Daddy. I want my own bag."

Jerry sighed; he messed up Nova's hair. "You don't need any chocolate chips, but I will get two bags. He shut the door and walked across the parking lot. Before he entered the store, Helen rolled down the window and yelled to him.

"Jerry!"

He turned around, raised his arms slowly above his head, and flashed a tired smile.

"Tan makalukum avvare ceyyvarkal!" she said. "Margaret is going to break her hip and jaw."

"What?" His voice echoed through the parking lot.

"Tan makalukum!" Helen's eye twitched and closed completely.

"I will check if they have that by the dairy section," Jerry said.

He dismissed her last sentence as an attempt to be funny. Or maybe it was a forced moment of speaking in tongues. A common practice that occurred in their church, a practice that he never understood. He wondered if Catholic people acted that crazy in their services.

As he walked down the refrigerated aisle, questions stirred in his mind; the faith he had in God was faltering. What he didn't understand about the world was supposed to be found through faith. But the church they went to, which was supposed to provide answers, often went into the deep end. He made up his mind that he didn't want to go to that church anymore, and he didn't know how to tell his wife. All he wanted was for his weekends to be boring.

When he checked out at the register, the young cashier had a knife scar across her face. The scar from the stitches were crude. The white zig-zagged lines made him think about a moment in Vietnam. It was just two years ago when he witnessed men in his squad being torn to shreds by machine gunfire. Jerry survived without any injuries, at least physically. This gave him a feeling of invincibility and that was where his faith was. Aside from the survivor's guilt that weighed on him, he felt he was built for something more.

The pastor of his church told him this at least once a month. He didn't like hearing his words, as the pastor seemed ingenuine, or as Jerry would like to tell him, that he was full of shit.

"Are you okay?" the cashier asked.

"I forgot the second bag of chocolate chips."

Jerry went back to the aisle, retrieved a second bag, paid for them, and left. He opened the bag in the foyer of the store and picked out a few for himself. Nova would eat the whole bag before they got home if he let her. She had more than enough energy already.

When he exited the store, he was alarmed to see Helen standing in the center of the parking lot. She stood dumbstruck at the sky, twirling slowly as if a marionette's strings were controlling her. A flicker of light flashed through scattered clouds. A solid dark shape could be seen hovering within them.

He dropped the bag of chocolate chips onto the asphalt when he saw the shape. It was not a plane. It was not a helicopter; this was something foreign to this world. A red circle of light illuminated Helen. A deep rumble shook the ground. Jerry felt it in the depth of his soul. The red light brightened. He shielded his face with his arm. Nova's screams could be heard from inside the truck. It was lifting off the ground. Helen held out her arms, towards the light and levitated.

"Itu Maranata? Nan eppotum kanavu kantatu itutana!" She screamed with a face of delight.

As she continued to levitate, she looked like a bird that was struck by a pellet gun.

"Helen!" Jerry yelled.

"Mama!" Nova screamed.

Helen continued to ascend hundreds of feet above the ground.

"It is Maranatha!" she cried. Then she disappeared. A flash ignited across the sky, and the hovering shape in the clouds was gone.

Jerry dropped the grocery bag. An egg hopped out of the Styrofoam carton, rolled onto the pavement, and spun haphazardly, landing in a pothole, without cracking. In disbelief, he muttered curses and begged for God's help as he ran to where his wife had stood.

"God, please no." His voice became hoarse.

"Daddy, where did Mommy go?" Nova asked. Bitter confused tears streamed down her face.

"I don't know, honey." He hugged her. They both looked to the space in the clouds where the strange shape had been.

"I think something took her."

He sat in the passenger seat with his legs hanging loosely and held his daughter. Nova started to flail her arms and legs and jumped out of his arms. She stood in the parking lot and hopped erratically.

"Nova, it's okay," he said. It wasn't true, but any good father tells their child it is okay, even when it isn't, in a poor attempt to string together stability.

Nova's shrieks were deafening.

Jerry wanted to call the police, but he was a smart man, and he knew that no one would believe that his wife was taken by an object in the sky. Stories like this have been told before, alien abductions and UFO's were regarded as nonsense. The people who told them were viewed as crazy. Jerry thought they were as well. He wanted to tell the truth, but he couldn't. So, he made up his truth right then and there, and he told Nova what to say as well.

"Nova! Look at me!" He held her shoulders. She stared at him intently. The strong little girl inside of the trembling one recognized her father's strength.

"Get a hold of yourself!"

Her jumping came to a halt. He told her what she would say when anyone asked. The truth was altered. From Jerry's perspective, it would protect both of them, and they had to lie.

When the police questioned him, Jerry claimed his wife wasn't in the truck when he returned. When Nova was asked the same question, she answered as her father had instructed her, that her mother got out and went away. Nova didn't mention the circle in the clouds, or that her mother levitated in the air. As she had done this, she made shapes with her fingers, like she was doing sign language, although she did not realize it.

That week, the police began searching the forest and surrounding areas; Helen was not found. For a few days, her picture and story were on the news. A vicious rumor had spread that Jerry murdered her, but that was only said by cruel people. It was enough to make Jerry feel less invincible; it was enough to make him move.

They left Pennsylvania and headed to Illinois with his older, unmarried sister, Ruth. She was a plain woman, with a disposition of an old, damp mop leaning in a pantry corner. Even though she opened her home to Jerry and Nova, it bothered him that she was heavily religious as well. To her credit though, she looked after Nova like she was her own.

Helen's disappearance transformed Jerry into a reclusive alcoholic, but he worked to keep his mind busy. Driving a tractor-trailer seemed to match his love for isolation. Sadly, Nova was affected far worse than her father understood. The lie she told the police at a young age had warped her reality. The shape in the sky and the red light that it cast haunted her dreams. Her twisted sense of truth tweaked her view of the world. A world that looked similar to S.W. Grantley's book cover, one which a red-handed devil was going to destroy. As she recalled that night, even at the age of four, there were a few chosen, who would answer to the calling of God, as part of his army, those that were set apart, to prepare the world for the tribulation and Armageddon.

Nova hid her mother's paperback book. Her father never thought of it again. It was hidden under her bed and admired often. Poorly drawn scenes of the forthcoming apocalypse, the mark of the beast and the rapture, and ultimately the return of Christ, remained part of her fragile psyche.

While her father was away, she opened the windows at night, even when it was cold, and whispered to herself in the dark corners of the house. The whispers were names of angels and demons, spiritual soldiers, specters between worlds, that would be part of an upcoming transcendent war between good and evil. The names came to her at random. Her aunt Ruth took notice but never corrected her. Ruth bought into the same line of thought little Nova had. She wished she too would be utilized as an instrument of God, one that could help shape and mold the future world against its impending doom.

2

When Nova attended grade school, her hyperactive delusions of grandeur fell into a mild hibernation. Being raised in a sterile environment chiseled down her unpredictable behavior and made her a rabid voyeur of the world around her, always looking outward. It wired her to become a people watcher, and she observed them ignorantly through the small looking glass of her religious perception.

In her time alone, she still whispered to herself, repeating things she heard throughout the day, imagining interactions she had with people that never happened. Conversations were held, picking up where they left off from the previous day. Aunt Ruth's sheltered lifestyle kept Nova in a protective bubble, but in some cases, when a person with no life experience takes the wrong path, it can cause unwanted tragedy.

As Nova grew older, she developed into a pretty young woman but was often ridiculed by boys for the way she dressed. Belonging to an old country church that flexed drab fashion standards for women to adorn themselves in ankle-length jean skirts and head scarfs was the normality. It was commonplace for the ultra-conservatives to downplay anything to not be alluring to the male gaze.

Sadly, her father was not home enough to give good guidance or be the protector he always wanted to be. The demons that followed him home from the war and the gaping hole of his wife's unexplained exit from this world never allowed for mental rest. The demon of uncertainty and hellish nightmares was his drunken companion, who sat next to him on his long rides across the country. The horned apparition reminded him of the violence he saw, and his alcoholism fed the timeworn ghosts daily.

Despite her social awkwardness, Nova became favored at her church. Her Aunt vouched for her, and she got a job after school. A church family owned a corner store/gas station adjacent to a well-trafficked state road. She took initiative, worked hard, and became trusted. The owners allowed her to work alone at the cash register. She was responsible enough to open and close the shop and remained there for some years.

In all this, Nova kept her eye on the fragments of the world that passed by. Most were lost sinners of the world, directionless and without God. Yet, there were a few who came into the store, from another town, or city that did not think of religion, and they seemed to hold a purpose. In admiration, it made her wonder, as in the slow days, time passed like watching paint dry.

At the age of eighteen, her dormant spirit of wonder awoke. Repression loosened its strangling grip when an attractive face entered the landscape. The needle of temptation had burst the protective bubble, and the catalyst was an English goth rock band called The Cure.

It was on a warm Saturday afternoon when foot traffic was intermittent. A young man, with a teased-out rats' nest of hair, pulled to the front of the store; his car stereo blasted. The windows were down in his rusted Saab, and a voice of beauty and tortured sadness filled the parking lot. The man left the car running, so the world around him would revere how cool he thought he was. In a cinematic stance, he finished a drag of his cigarette, crushed it under his black dress shoes, and entered the store, with his sunglasses still on.

Nova was mesmerized by this image. For all she knew, he could have come from a distant world. At that moment, Nova was mesmerized by the music of The Cure, as Robert Smith's voice held a newfound magic. A sound like this was forbidden. It was a fruit of the world that she was warned about, as plain hymnals and worship music were the custom. Nova came from behind the counter and stood in the doorframe to listen better.

"Um..." Nova smiled, "...who is this band playing?"

Walking in an overconfident stride, he flipped hanging beef sticks with his black fingernail, sneered, and said, "This is The Cure."

"I think I love them." She pulled on her braid and hopped playfully.

He was fascinated by her wild-eyed interest in the music, which didn't seem fitting for a girl whom he had mistaken for being Amish. He went out to his car and got the tape. When he came back inside, he sneered at her and placed it delicately on the counter. It was a dubbed copy of their new album *Disintegration*.

"They might fucking change your life," he said.

"Oh," she smiled. She was taken aback by his language.

Fuck was a word she rarely heard and never used. Once two truck drivers pulled into the gas station at the same time. They said it to each other. She couldn't tell if they were happy to see each other or angry. A man once used it to describe how good Ms. Yoder's fudge was. Its multiple uses confused her.

The man chose a pair of silver aviators off the spin rack and put them on. He looked over at Nova, then took them off and put his glasses back on. He smiled at her flirtatiously, paid for his gas, and left. He was right, The Cure did change her life. Obsession set in. The Cure was a secret that she hid from her Aunt. She bought a Walkman at the convenience store and absorbed their sound on long walks. When she got the courage, she rode her bike to a record store and bought anything she could find by them. In the times she frequented the store, a college girl, Marcy Collins recognized her. Marcy nicknamed Nova the weird church kid who liked goth music. Marcy was the local rebel. She took no shit from anyone. She was an unfiltered pack-a-day smoker with a nose ring, who wanted to drop out of college and work on a cruise ship so she could see the world. Nova's timidity attracted her; it was a personality type that fed her ego. Marcy loved it when women who were prettier than her continually expressed how *cool* she was. This was a mind game that she played with everyone, and those who were wise to it, usually made themselves scarce.

"Do you know The Cure is doing a US tour? They are playing in Columbus soon," Marcy said.

When Nova heard this, her mind went supernova.

"When?" she screamed. A stick of teenage dynamite exploded.

"August."

"Are you going, can I go? We should go. Holy shit! Sorry Lord for cursing. I will give you gas money!" Nova jumped up and down.

Marcy eyed Nova and hated how immaculate her complexion was. She hated that someone could seem so happy about a band that embraced being sad. She bet Nova was a virgin.

"Sure, I think we will have fun, but..." she leaned over the counter and pointed her black fingernail at Nova. "... you aren't dressing like that."

It was a dig, but Nova didn't care. Experiencing a concert in a big city would be worth putting up with anything. Marcy had to endure Nova as part of the undertaking because Marcy was a drama queen and didn't have anyone else to go with. Any other mild acquaintance she would ask would not have gas money to contribute.

In this adventure, Nova concluded that lying to her Aunt, to see a band she adored, wasn't wrong. If her Aunt understood how much it meant to her, and if Nova stayed out of trouble, then how could it be iniquitous?

On the day of the concert, Marcy pulled up in the driveway and waited for Nova. Aunt Ruth saw her through the lace curtains and didn't like her one bit. As Marcy ashed her cigarette in the driveway, Aunt Ruth shuddered. She was worried that she would never see Nova again. Nova lied and said that they were going to the movies and dinner afterward. Knowing her aunt wouldn't be aware, she made up a movie name and explained how boring it would be. Aunt Ruth was full of dread. She got on her knees in the kitchen and prayed for Nova's safety.

Marcy surprised Nova and brought clothes for her to wear.

"You aren't going to see The Cure looking like a nun, hon," Marcy laughed. She blew cigarette smoke as she said it. A social cue lacing her dialog with piss and vinegar.

The statement was a stab at Nova's fragility. Nova responded with a smile, "Nuns wear habits and look like penguins."

"Well, no guy is going to want to be with you if you are dressed like that."

"Do you mean fuck?" It was the first time Nova said the word. It was the proper usage.

Marcy smirked in surprise.

As they neared the city, they pulled off at a gas station. Marcy did Nova's makeup in a filthy bathroom that smelled like motor oil and animal feces. The bubbly, plain-faced, gangly teen, with a voluminous jean skirt, emerged from a 7/11 off Route 80 in Ohio in a low-cut black blouse, short jean skirt, tights, and a pair of scuffed Doc Martens. Her eye makeup was thick and dark like all goth girls. Both girls looked like raccoons attending a funeral, fitting in perfectly for the crowd they would attach themselves to. Nova loved her new image. She never thought she was pretty, only because no man had ever told her so. For the first time in her life, she thought she was.

They parked in a lot a block away from the concert. Nova paid for it. Marcy lit a joint and handed it to Nova, who took a puff and coughed violently. Marcy took a fifth of Fireball out of her purse and took a swig. She winced and laughed.

"Security won't let us bring this in, so we need to get our buzz on now."

Nova took a swig and gagged. "Gross."

Marcy grabbed it out of her hand, took another swig, and handed it back to Nova.

"I don't know if I want anymore," Nova said. Her stomach was becoming knotted.

As all pillars in the world of peer pressure do, Marcy pushed, "Come on, already."

Nova took a long sip and coughed some up in the parking lot. They both took another hit from the joint and Marcy ashed it on her boot. Nova's head was spinning. She smiled with fiery excitement and fear as they headed to the concert in inebriated anticipation. Marcy grabbed Nova's hand as they cut through the crowd, and they found their place, becoming one with the crowd. When The Cure played, the girls were caught up in the wave of ecstasy that can encompass a young person's mind and soul as they are blasted with waves of light and sound. During one song, the stage lights dimmed only to red. The band members' pale faces were illuminated by the hot color. As her mind was swirling, Nova looked at Marcy, who swayed side to side with her eyes closed; it was then that a dark and painful thought, hidden by an old lie, burst up from the depths of her subconscious.

What is this sick familiarity? she thought.

It played out as she witnessed it when she was just four years old. Her mother was lifted off the ground in a circle of red light, taken upwards into the clouds, never to be seen again. The repressed recollection was buried under heavy scrutiny from her father. The darkness was unearthed from her subconscious and was revealed in a crowd of strangers. As she recalled every detail, she screamed at the top of her lungs at a perfect place in between songs. The singer of The Cure, Robert Smith, looked at her in goth god glory and thanked her, but she did not hear him as she was miles away on a string of electrons that cut through a repurposed childhood story whose harsh truth was being uncovered.

Retching overwhelmed her. She ran to the bathroom, forcing her way through a clan of goth women applying extra layers of makeup who were there for the fashion show, more than the music. She vomited a mixture of old gas station taquitos and Fireball Whiskey. Her throat was torn and burned. She got a Coke at the bar and stood against the wall, hoping her stomach would settle. It was fourteen years ago, that the echoed shouts of her mother rang out, and the words became clear in her mind now.

"Itu Maranata?" she whispered.

As much as she wanted to enjoy the rest of the show, she felt disconnected from reality. If someone told her she was in her bedroom and that this was a bad dream, she would have believed them. Her only defense was to sway side to side with the hope of slowing the tempestuous reflux within her.

A handsome goth man, in his 20s, emerged from the smoky shadows of the club and headed toward her. He smiled at her, turned around to watch the band, then turned back to her, trying to catch her gaze. It was the first male attention she had received when she wasn't dressed in her normal attire. With a burning throat and dark memory attached, she flirted back with a smile. He stepped close to her and said something, but she could not hear him. Moving within an earshot, he asked if she was having fun. She sipped on her straw and nodded her head. He was taller than her, and his purple velvet shirt was unbuttoned to the middle of his pale, hairless chest. Nova didn't think he was particularly attractive, but she was attracted to the attention he gave her. He went on a long diatribe about society, music, and culture while sipping from a can of cheap beer. She didn't understand a word he said. The music was too loud, and her head was not in the right space. In between his pausing to search for the next thing to make himself desirable, she had flashes of her mother floating into the air and leaving Earth.

She pulled on the lapel of his velvet shirt and kissed him. The forced spark had led them into a corner, and they proceeded to kiss further. The desire to see her favorite band perform at the end of their set took second place as a rush of repressed sexual energy flowed through her body. They left the concert, holding hands, and headed to his car in a parking lot two blocks away. It was Nova's first time for everything with him. His attempts at passion were weak and unimpressive by any woman's standards, but Nova wanted more than just him.

The yearning abyss of her womb opened, sucking the life essence from the emaciated vampire in the backseat of a dirty Cadillac Cimarron. A terrifying force was connected to the memory of the disappearance of her mother as her fragile virginity evaporated and welcomed a seed that would take root and eventually blossom.

Afterward, he spoke to her softly, but she did not pay attention to him. Perhaps her disconnect from the regular way people spoke affected her comprehension, or was it that the pale goth man was really just an idiot? Regardless, she felt adored. He walked her back to the concert, but the security guard told them there was no reentry. When the concert ended, Nova and the young man stood quietly and watched the crowds of goths pass, each one looking more like Marcy than the next, until they found her.

Marcy spotted them and waved. Nova waved while holding the hand of her new, nameless lover. Marcy pieced together what had happened, as she had done the same herself at concerts, hence her lack of friends. They walked through the crowd together, and Marcy turned to ask Nova's new lover his name, but he was gone. The young vampire disappeared back into the crowd, blending in with a thousand other faces that looked like his. Nova stood on a bench and searched for him, but he could not be found, nor did he want to be.

If he said his name, Nova didn't catch it, or maybe he never said it at all. They walked back to the car. Heartbroken, Nova returned a changed woman from a world her aunt had tried to protect her from. Marcy was jealous that Nova, in her naiveté, was able to hook up with someone easily. They drove home in silence. The friendship between them never blossomed. Marcy viewed Nova's weirdness as high maintenance. Nova had too much on her mind to find a way to reconnect again. The carousel of emotions was too much for her. A country girl, who spent the best of her days in and around church, did not have the emotional capacity for a one-night stand with a nameless man, while her levitating mother kept vanishing before her. It was a Missing Person's Report never solved, and resentment for her father immediately formed in her heart.

Nova reverted to her subdued ways, casting aside all that she had learned in the few hours that night. What had been prohibited was displayed before her like a buffet that only a few could dine at, and she renounced all of it, vowing never to return. Only she carried something that night that changed her life. Nine months later, on June 20th of 1990, her daughter Abagail was born; a Gemini under the waning crescent moon.

Being an unwed teen mother weighed heavy on Nova. Aunt Ruth and her church treated her with pious cruelty. The elders delivered a harshness equivalent of being shocked with electricity. Nova underwent deep spiritual counseling daily as she confessed her sinful ways of careless casual sex and drunkenness. It was easy for a young vulnerable woman to allow the noose of guilt to tighten around her neck. Due to the conflict between her pregnancy and her status at the church, she lost her job at the corner store. But being a punctual hard worker and determined, Nova was able to find another job, at another corner store, owned by a Jewish family.

They saw a spark in her eye, despite the sadness in her face and gladly worked around the young mother's schedule.

When Jerry discovered that Nova was with child, he wasn't just angry, he was disappointed. Thankfully, his disappointment wasn't cruel but when he was home, the tension was felt throughout the house. Nova resurfaced the old story, and anger burned in her like acid. She questioned her father about what happened the night her mother disappeared and how she believed in a lie so much that it changed her feelings toward everything.

He wept and told her exactly what happened and why he told her to lie. Even as she heard him tell the story, as it matched the image in her mind, she had a hard time believing it herself. Nova held him and cried, then she called him an asshole and punched him in the chest, and slapped his face. He stood in front of her—broken—and wanted to say something that made sense. She hugged him again, apologized for cursing but not for hitting him, and ran off.

It rained that night, and she ran through the dark wetness, saying the names of the imaginary angels that she made up when she was a girl. They were to protect her and be part of the army of God when the final apocalyptic battle would take place.

"Seraphim Jodine, Cherubim Azael, Thrones of Might and Mercy!"

She slid on the wet grass and fell in the front yard. The lights from inside her house looked like a face, and it mocked her. She spat at the house and slept in the garage that night.

The next morning, her father went back on the road. Nothing was resolved. As neither of them at their most calm could ever match the other at their most angry. Yet, a small thought snuck in. It warmed Jerry's cold heart as he traveled. He was going to be a grandfather. As he cut through the landscape of the country, he wore a smile, it was broken, but it was a part of himself that he never thought would ever exist.

When Abagail was born, Nova tried to raise her under the strict thumb of Godly rule, but Abagail was different from her mother. Her perception was sharper. Abagail did not take in everything she heard easily and questioned everything. Whenever she was told to do something, she responded with difficulty. Aunt Ruth said it was because there was no husband in the picture, which was a blueprint to have an unruly child. Jerry laughed and said that Abby took after him—only part of this was true.

As Abagail grew, she sensed her mother's jealousy of her. She felt the competition between them. Part of her church's testimony of faith was a public confession, and Nova mentioned week after week how she had her poor rebellious daughter out of wedlock. Abagail heard *time* and *time* again that she was conceived in the back of a dirty car in a parking lot during a rock concert, with a nameless man as a father. If it was a means for her mother to keep Abby in the shadow of guilt, it didn't work. Instead, Abagail took it as an edge, it made her different than all the other perfect church girls. They always looked at Abagail scornfully and whispered behind her back. She wondered what it would be like to have two parents and a solid home. But if it would be at the cost of her being like them, she was grateful without it.

Abagail took to books. She read everything and anything she could find that was not related to the Christian faith. Her Aunt Ruth, who homeschooled her said that those books would warp her mind. Abagail apologized for her fiery desire to learn more but continued to add to her arsenal of books that challenged the world.

Nova regressed as Abagail developed, and she expected her calling from God to be answered. And again, when Nova was left alone with her thoughts, she whispered to herself the names of angels, hoping they would remember who she was.

"Seraphim Eli, Cherubim Sarthos, Thrones of Might and Mercy," Nova whispered.

An old paperback book from Nova's youth that was nearly forgotten was re-discovered. Images of demons and angels fighting for humankind and heaven's reign on Earth became a new reality. A dream came to Nova, light filled her room and hymns were sung, some distorted and some clear. A voice spoke, at first, it was her father's, then it changed, as if a lion spoke as a man. The voice told her there was indeed a calling on her life, but she had to wait for the right time, as pieces on the chess board of the world were still moving. Nova told no one of this and took it as the absolute truth. She thanked God in small whispers in the corners of her house, and on the edges of her yard. Once she danced in the road in the middle of the night as a speeding car approached and nearly hit her. The driver called her a *crazy bitch* as it passed, but she smiled and waved as she felt the invincibility of her newfound calling, set apart from others, expectant of grand things to come.

3
June 2008

ON THE SLANTED ROOF outside of her bedroom window, Abagail laid upside down and stared trance-like at the infinite night sky; hair spread out like a black smattering of ink, arms stretched, cheap headphones buried deep within her ears. From above, she would look like a squashed black dragonfly. The star map she read online said that Spica, the brightest star in the constellation of Virgo would be visible tonight. It was a special star for her, as her eighteenth birthday was around the corner; it was a connection to her life and the grand cosmos. To her, the bright star meant there could be another version of her in another galaxy. There was a minute possibility that the other Abagail from another habitable planet, was on her slanted roof, looking up at *her* sky, wondering the same questions all teenagers had: *is life shitty, and is it normal to feel out of place?*

The near-endless space in between the worlds that divided her from this other Abagail was an infinite gorge of separation—a boundless void. Could a simple hello be heard beyond the comprehension of lightyears and modern communication? Could a psychic reverberance in her mind be felt elsewhere in the seemingly infinite cosmos?

Her stomach growled. Abagail slapped the outside of her belly to calm it. There was no science behind the action to subdue her hunger, but it was a psychological hush to her cravings. It would only be crackers tonight, and her salivary glands were working in excess; peristalsis in overdrive. In her headphones was the swooning voice of Robert Smith, oversaturating her occipital lobe. The Cure's vocalist was helping her burn out the day's anxiety.

Sadly, she had incorrectly convinced herself this month that she was fat. This morning, she ate a small chocolate torte cupcake and thought it put three pounds on her by this afternoon. In frustration, she closed her eyes from the night tapestry and grit her teeth at the images of skinny bitches at her school, bragging about eating anything they wanted while still having the confidence to post bikini pictures of themselves on social media. To get her mind off such thoughts, and to find her center, she focused on the stars and the astronomical units in between planets, warmed by the thought of the other Abagail's that existed elsewhere.

The scrutiny she inflicted upon herself was triggered when her best friend Rose moved to Miami. It caused a tear in Abby's soul. The move happened nearly overnight when Rose's father was caught cheating on her mother. The breakup was violent, and immediate separation was integral to the family's survival. Rose's older sister in Miami offered for them to live with her. A rental truck was packed haphazardly. Abby and Rose hugged and cried in an emotionally fragmented rush, and she hadn't seen her since Thanksgiving of last year.

Like all best friends, some may place the other on a pedestal for the support they are always looking for. In Abby's obsessiveness, she placed Rose as an idol in her heart, to such a point not even Rose could fulfill her expectations. Oddly, when Abagail told Rose this, she seemed to become distant, and that was before she moved away. At low points, in the middle of the night, Abagail would whisper to Rose, in the dark corners of her house, hoping that Rose could feel her desperate yearnings for their strained friendship. When they would catch up for lost time on the phone, Rose would say things that made Abagail wonder if she heard her whispers, but she was filling in the blanks of how she saw it to fit the pieces she was always looking for.

With her best friend absent, Abby unwillingly dove into a dark phase. The bright girl in school, who kept good grades and stuck to one friend, morphed into an unhealthy dose of fly-on-the-wall stoicism. Common open laughter melted into a macabre sarcasm. The normally dressed, natural-looking girl transformed herself with funeral chic clothes, heavy make-up, and dyed hair. The catalyst for this was an unearthed record in the basement, kept in a milk crate by the English goth-rock band The Cure.

Abby gravitated to the allure of the band's image and dressed like them and those who worshipped them. All of which was a cry for attention. The exact same record had once done the same to Abby's mother, who watched in astonishment, as a reflection of another eighteen-year-old girl half a lifetime ago walked through her home.

Abby realized how important Rose's friendship had been to her sanity as the days within her home were growing less sane. Her stepfather Richard was a drone that yielded to her mother's spiritual proclamations. And her mother's recent church promotion was to a prophetic speaker of the end times. It meant nothing more—to Abby or any other non-religious person—than an entitled person yelling wild statements from behind a pulpit with hyper-emotionalism. Nova claimed dramatically that she was a mouthpiece of spiritual wisdom and warning for the people of God to adhere to before the forthcoming apocalypse. With that mindset, the house was filled with doom and gloom. Nova's spare time, when not selling cheap make-up as part of a pyramid scheme, was filled with endless searching for articles relating to global catastrophes connected to the Book of Revelation.

As the threads of Abby and Rose's strained friendship grew thin, she still reached out to her in vain. The last time they spoke, Rose's twin nieces were crying in unison at the pitch of two tea kettles in the background. Their one-on-one time was constantly interrupted and the need that was usually fulfilled was dissipating. To Abby's surprise, Rose suggested that she visit after she graduated. Only Abby did not have enough money to fly, and her old Honda, which her stepfather Richard bought for her late last year, would struggle on a cross-country trip. Blueville, Tennessee to Miami was over 900 miles, and a bus trip would be hell.

After graduating, Abby planned to move out and go to beauty school. Cutting women's hair and doing make-up was soothing to her. Bringing extra beauty out of already beautiful women made her feel like an artist. Only the internal conflict at home, from her mother's bat-shit insanity, put her future in disarray. Going to school in Nashville and living on her own or with a roommate, was a cost that she couldn't afford. Her mother didn't have the common sense and foresight to see that far, nor did Abby communicate well with her stepfather Richard. They never struggled, but they didn't seem to be well off. Abby thought Richard must have put his money away for retirement, or he didn't make much at his job, despite him having a good one. She suspected that he secretly gambled since most of his time at home was spent in his man cave on his computer playing video games. They had gone on vacation only once in the four years since Richard's arrival into their lives. It was to a bunch of parks in Orlando, and most of it was spent standing in lines and getting dehydrated.

A black wire frame on her wall held a picture of the three of them half-smiling and sunburnt with red eyes glaring, with stupid mouse ears on their heads. A few months later, they were a different family. Abby wasn't thrilled about the picture being taken then, but she missed the time when the family appeared normal. Even though Richard was as exciting as a stale pretzel wearing a polo, he brought some stability to the landscape for a moment. That was before her mother went off the deep end.

It was when Abagail disappeared for a week, and her Missing Person's Report ended up on national news, that the people in the small town of Blueville lost their minds. Never had they experienced the disappearance of one of their young people before. During Abby's absence, the police and the citizens combed the forest looking for her. Most thought she ran away or committed suicide given the way she dressed and skulked around town. Some thought she was dead, and her remains had been dragged off by animals, and she would never be found. A few thought she joined a cult and was sacrificed. Her mother falsely believed she would return on a specific day and claimed God told her so.

From Nova's perspective, she thought Abagail opened a doorway to Satan, brought on by an occult book she found in Abby's room the night before her disappearance. Nova flipped through the pages of the old book and saw circular patterns and astrological symbols. It mentioned incantations to connect with the universe, all of which were beyond her comprehension, and she thought it was devilry. Nova was overwhelmed with body chills, raised her arms out, bent like birds' wings, and spoke glossolalia. In a standing convulsion, she waited on a message, as if she were a lightning rod awaiting a random current to electrify her next holy vocation.

It was the bizarre way in which Abagail returned to the center of town. Some people still speak of her reappearance in disbelief. With just the mention of a UFO, the town seemed to lose credibility in her statement as most of the town was aware of what kind of church Nova attended, which was rumored to handle snakes. But to hear such an outlandish statement mentioned by Abby made people question who her family really was.

In the end, the house they lived in was left empty, which rested like a sun-bleached cow skull in a desert. Its empty shell echoed the memories of that time. It is now a place where kids ride by on their bikes and claim that it is cursed or haunted. It is a place where light does not catch well in the windows. A place where the once flowery bushes just die; where the rain pools in front and floods the street.

"It was different..." the next-door neighbor Mr. Robinson said. "...after those hooded figures showed up with those sacrificial knives."

4

Scowling at the disarray in Abby's bedroom, Nova stood in the archway and asked Abby the question a second time. Her words simmered into a whisper.

"Abagail, I asked you if you were a witch?"

Abby was applying black eyeliner wings to the corners of her already darkened eyes. Earlier she had taken a photo and updated her Myspace profile picture. Each time she had done so, she would acquire more followers, which she felt would raise her visibility to gain clientele. This culminated her desire to become a successful beautician. However, it felt dichotomous, because the online attention consumed a lot of energy which she felt could be spent elsewhere. Living in a small town would never attract proper responsiveness from near-Neanderthals, so she allowed herself to suffer, by uploading one of her favorite dozen selfies.

"I want to say *yes*, just to piss you off but it isn't true," Abby said.

Nova gripped the wood frame of the door. Dario, Abagail's black cat, sensed the tension rising in the room. He jumped off the bed and hid under it.

"I want to believe that my little girl is still good, but I fear you are on a dark path," Nova said.

Abby didn't respond, as anything she said would be wrong and laced with sarcasm. It was easier for her to bite her lip and hope that her mother would become bored and find another piece of *spiritual warfare* on TV and leave her alone.

"What are those awful-smelling leaves? I read about witches burning such things."

Sage leaves smoldered in a mason jar on the windowsill.

"That is white sage, it is supposed to have cleansing properties and negate bad energy. Plus, Dario doesn't bathe himself properly and I don't want to smell like a cat every time I put my clothes on."

"That sounds witchy to me."

"Sage has been used for this purpose for thousands of years."

Nova picked up a book off Abby's dresser. It was a paperback on meditation. The book underneath it was about chakras and psychic energy.

"Well, perhaps it's pagan then, and I don't approve of this reading material." She looked at the back of each book and read the synopsis. The books that Abby read intimidated her, as Nova never sought education beyond what the church had taught. Nova's head started to wobble. It was an action that surfaced when she was trying to comprehend something.

Abby looked at her through the reflection of the dresser mirror.

"Do you think Jesus meditated?" Abby's lighthearted question, trying to diffuse the situation, hit a wall.

"He meditated on God. He heard the voice of God!" Nova yelled.

"Well, I think Jesus might have meditated. I mean if I were him, I would have. You know? He does all this cool stuff, healing and feeding people and then he gets in trouble for it."

Despite Abby's witchy leanings, she didn't mind the concept of a man claiming to be a prophet while getting in trouble for doing good things for the disenfranchised. It was heroic to her. But since her mother had to have the last say in everything, no matter how Abby worded it, the conversation always spiraled back to how her mother was now an appointed prophet of God and the whole world is going to shit.

"Well, Jesus wouldn't befriend witches."

"Are you sure about that?" It was a choice of words Abby shouldn't have said. She was still seventeen for the next week and had to play her cards right. Grounding could still happen, even though it hadn't in a while. Her mother had the ferocity to confiscate the car keys or throw away or hide things from Abby.

"How dare you question me? Do you know what my place is at the church?"

It was the ignorance that made Abby cringe. Going out tonight, was important to her, but winning this argument would be epic, and she was already two Red Bulls in. Abby closed her eyes, took a deep breath, turned around, and smiled. Her mother's hair looked like a rat's nest. The unflattering dress was large and wrinkled. Before she dwelled on the apocalypse, her mother used to carry herself better. That was before she thought of eternal damnation and judgment on an hourly basis.

"Mother, would you like for me to do your hair or make-up? Do you remember the way I used to do it when you first met Richard?"

Four years ago, their relationship was as good as any teenager and a single mother could be. Now both of them could not be alone in a room for a few minutes without an argument. Tension was always present, and proper love was an emotion that was rarely shown. Lately, Nova wanted to win any dispute, especially when it came to anything religious. It was Nova's way to flex her faux spirituality over the knowledge that Abby had about the outside world.

"I have had it with you looking like some sort of dead whore. You are my daughter, and you will not embarrass me in front of our church this weekend."

"A whore?" Abby stood up. Her voice shook.

"Yes." Nova glared with wild eyes.

"How could you say such a thing?"

"Because I had a dream about you and another woman."

Abby gasped. "Well, that is a dream, that you had. I had a dream that I won the lottery, and I bought a rocket ship, but that doesn't mean anything."

"So, you are not indulging in the ways of a lesbian?"

"Mother, listen to yourself. That sounds ridiculous." Abby wanted to leave her small, cluttered room. Her mother blocked her way. Her purse was downstairs in the kitchen, and her Doc Martens were on the back porch. With how the conversation was escalating, Abby considered climbing onto the roof and jumping into the backyard. The drop was at least fifteen feet and even though she wanted out, she didn't want to risk breaking her ankle.

"May I get through please?" Abby passed by her mother. Nova grabbed her wrist.

"Your silence makes you appear guilty."

Abby pulled her wrist away. Nova's hand snapped. Abby stepped out of the room and made her way to the top of the stairs.

"You know..." Abby paused, "...we live in a big universe, and if God exists, I don't think he is limited to the small churches with white folks in America, who get so damn offended at gay people."

Her mother stormed out of the room clutching the two paperbacks. "How dare you!"

"I can see you aren't ready to have this conversation with me. If you wouldn't mind, I would like to leave."

"Oh Abagail, my defiant daughter! I knew a woman who was in a place like yours."

Nova's head shook erratically as she raised her voice. "She was at our service, and she left her penitence in anger and died in a car accident that night. Her body flung from the car and laid in the road, like a dead animal. I did not carry my daughter this far to be lost in hellfire!"

Abby turned to her mother, "Oh shut up with the woman in the car accident story. I heard that one so many times at the church. Every month, there is a damn woman dying in a car accident when a stalemate happens with a..." Abby made quotes with her fingers, "...non-believer, the car accident story surfaces. That is the insurance salesman trick."

As good as Abby's defense was, there was only one play left that a Pentecostal newly promoted prophet of God could do. Nova raised her right hand like she was pulling lightning from the sky and placed it on Abby's head, "I bind you Satan, and your powers over my daughter's life!"

It was the final act of every Sunday service at the church she attended. Parishioners usually broke out in elaborate displays of emotionalism, which brought on hysteria. People in her church lifted their hands high and shook them into erratic trembling. They screamed passages from the Bible, and spoke in tongues, often outdoing one another, like glass soda bottles popping in the heat. If a random passerby peeked their head in, they would be concerned if the attendees were maddened lunatics or babbling drunkards. Abby's mother kept her trembling hand on her daughter's head and let loose a spring of glossolalia.

"Shundacomoshakadeshunda!"

Abby said calmly, "Mom, please don't."

"Shakalashokadeshunda! Oh, Devil, you get your hands off my daughter!"

10

"Mother, please!"

"Loooooooooooosen your grip, demons!"

Abby stepped backward and turned around.

"I am not done!" Nova yelled.

Abby wanted to cry but didn't. She wanted to tell her mother to shut the fuck up but wouldn't give in. She didn't want to out-crazy the crazy person.

"I am an elder of God's Tabernacle and you will yield to the spirit of fire of which I speak!"

Abby ran down the stairs and out the front door. She had no shoes or purse. If her mother broke the boundary of coming outdoors, in her tirade, Abby would have to run down the street in her socks. Inside the trails of "shondashakas" and "heed my warnings" were in full effect. If only Richard was home, he would be enough cannon fodder for her mother to chew through and keep Abby safe. But this night was special, her mother wanted to be heard.

Nova burst onto the porch in a blaze. Her frayed blonde hair looked white and wispy, in the evening light. The terrible gaze she cast belonged to a Greek monster, rather than a religious woman.

"You will not run from his will. You will yield to that which I hold!" Nova yelled.

Abby backed to the edge of the porch. Her mother was blocking the stairwell to the front yard.

Across the street, sat the Robinsons, an old couple who had been here since the sixties. They raised children who had children, all of them were churchgoers as well, but none of them acted like this. Nor had they seen such a thing. They were concerned with Abby's mother's actions. Old Ms. Robinson told her husband, that she thought Nova must have been stung by a bee or burnt herself. Mr. Robinson nodded his head in agreement.

"Perhaps both," he said,

"Mother, you need to chill the fuck out!" Abby said.

It was then that the invisible bee that tormented her mother stung. The self-propelled spiritual flame that followed her had taken full ignition. Nova swung her arm rigidly as if it were on the end of a string and slapped Abby across her face. Then her left arm swung harder, but Abby blocked it.

11

Her mother intended to say her famous words, *how dare you*, but all that came out was a long shriek. Abby grabbed the chair behind her and put it between them. Like a lion tamer trying to keep distance, she backed to the edge of the railing. Her mother raised both of her hands above her head and laughed. It was a guttural laugh that a medieval torturer would use in a prison cell of chained thieves.

In the annals of religious tyranny, there are some cases noted of an unstoppable force versus an immovable object. Some of those scenarios resulted in governments and churches being overthrown, but in all of those cases, good people died. As Nova stood in witch-burning delusion, with her Medusian gaze, hoping to petrify her innocent daughter, Abby had a correct thought, she stepped over the banister and jumped into the yard. She landed in the dewy grass and slipped. Regaining her footing, she opened the front gate and ran into the street. Mr. Robinson stood up; his jaw hung in shock. He was going to ask if she was okay but was without words. Abby saw the concern on his face, but she did not think that his home could be a refuge from her mother. On impulse, she ran down the street. Nova stumbled, opened the gate, and continued in her verbal outburst.

"Your actions are not becoming of a young woman of God! Derelicts on the street act no different than you. What you value is all bland in God's eyes! You are blackened tissue, and your tongue is damning! Your generation holds no sweetness. It is saccharine, and it is lukewarm. As a dog returns to its vomit, it is all the same!"

Abby was not a runner, but she ran as fast as she could. Tears blinded her, her chest tightened, and her lungs burned. As her mother's voice faded in the distance, she looked back and saw light ribbons of pinks and magentas losing their fight against the coming darkness in the sky.

An approaching car was at the far end of the street. Abby passed it as she continued to run down the center. The driver honked the horn at her, but she paid no attention to him. She continued to run passed the stop sign and onto the next road. The desire to drink chocolate milk became overwhelming. The only place she could get that now was at the gas station by the highway. The young man inside the car didn't understand what he was seeing. A woman who looked like she worked at a Halloween store full-time was running full speed passed the illumination of his headlights and back into the darkness.

He was shipping off for boot camp at the end of the school year. A hero inside him was trying to awaken. A woman in distress needed his help. He stopped the car, got out, and yelled.

"Ma'am, are you all right? Do you need a ride?"

Abby heard his beckon. His accent was thick. A true Tennessean. *Perhaps a gentleman,* she thought. Through countless hours of watching and reading true crime stories, this is how young women disappeared. But her desperation was louder. Was the woman who chased her out of her house more insane than the consideration of seeking shelter in a strange man's car?

Abby stopped running. Her feet hurt from the pavement. She knelt over, put her hands on her knees, and breathed heavily. The thought of drinking chocolate milk became secondary. *What if this guy is cute?* she thought.

The young man did a k-turn in the middle of the street. Slowly, he pulled up alongside Abby. He wore GI glasses that framed his thin face. His cheekbones were high, and he had a thin mustache. His mouth moved in slow motion; the words were not audible. On the horizon, Abby saw a flash in the sky. It was a white streak, and it moved faster than anything her eyes ever witnessed. It was probably a meteorite, perfectly timed for this moment. But when discussing cosmic things, Abby always thought it was something bigger. She pointed in the direction to which it went.

"Was that a UFO?" she said.

The young man looked in the direction she was pointing. He stuck his head out the window and saw nothing but the darkening sky rolling over a faint remainder of dusk.

"Did you hear what I said?" he asked.

"No."

"You look like a chubby Bettie Page," he said with a grin. His attempt at being a hero stumbled on words that were not flattering. He was just a young man still learning how to speak to a woman.

"Well, you look like a serial killer who hasn't found his first victim," Abby said.

He smirked at her surprising remark. "Where are your shoes?"

"Back at my house, with my psycho mother."

"Do you need a ride?"

His car was clean. It was a classic Oldsmobile, navy colored, with silver rims. The best response would be to run in any other direction and head back when the alleged prophet of God calmed down.

"I would like a ride to the gas station, but I have to warn you, I will rip that crooked nose off your face if you try anything funny. So, swear to God you aren't a creep or a psycho."

"Well, I am not a church-going type, so I ain't going to swear on anything."

This was a relief, but she had nothing else to gauge him by. Her raw nerves were just going on impulse.

"Swear on your grandmother then."

"How do you know I even have a grandmother?"

"In this part of the country, everyone has at least a half dozen grandmothers"

The young man looked down. He closed his eyes and recalled all of his grandmother's names.

"I swear on my Grandmother Matilda that I won't try anything funny with you."

Abby went around the front of the car. The young man leaned across and unlocked the door. In any other instance she would have told him to leave her alone, but his concern, despite his stupid comment on her weight, was consoling.

Abby got in. She eyed him up. He might have been 120 lbs. She squinted her eyes at him.

"You, okay?" he asked.

Abby opened his glove compartment. Inside of it were neatly organized car-related papers.

"What are you looking for?"

"To see if you have a weapon or handcuffs in here."

"Why would I have that?"

Abby reached under the seat. There was nothing. Not even an empty soda bottle or fast-food wrapper. She looked in the back seat and frowned.

"Why is your car so clean?"

"I don't know. I guess I like to be clean. What do you want to go to the gas station for, you don't have a car?"

"I want chocolate milk."

"You don't have a purse either."

"Well then you're buying," she laughed.

"I can do that," he grinned.

He stepped on the gas and saw in the rearview mirror a figure in the middle of the street; it was a long-haired woman in a gown. He pieced together that the *psycho mother* comment may be the same person behind them, but it was too bizarre of an image to mention to his new awkward acquaintance. He kept it to himself.

He turned the radio dial from a country station to another country station. One man sang about a horse and then the other sang about fishing.

"I didn't catch your name."

"Abagail, but friends call me Abby."

"Am I your friend yet?"

"After you buy me chocolate milk, yes."

"Okay, Abagail, my name is Sutton."

"Sutton?"

"Yes ma'am"

She reached out her hand and they shook. She grinned at him; his nervousness kept his eyes forward. Both hands remained at ten and two on the wheel.

"Sutton and his mustache and clean car, picking up a goth girl at dusk."

"That is not an average day, but yes it looks like that."

"Well, thank you for your chivalry."

"My dad taught me to be this way," he half smiled and then hid it with his hand.

"Do you always listen to your parents?"

"My dad yeah, until the day he died."

The scorched feeling of her mother's outburst forced Abby into a scattered rambling with her new friend. It caused her to say things, anything to make conversation. In times similar to this, she was too sarcastic for her own good.

"I'm sorry," she said.

"It's okay, you didn't know."

She reached out her index finger to him and held it. He looked at her and frowned.

"Do the same," she said.

He raised his finger, and she poked the tip of his with hers.

"E.T.," she said.

He laughed awkwardly. "My dad gave this car to me. He kept it in good shape. It is nearly twenty years old but there are only 80,000 miles on it. It was his pride and joy, so it is *my* pride and joy."

Sutton pulled onto the on-ramp. There was enough time to accelerate in front of an oncoming tractor-trailer. Cautiously, he waited for it to pass.

"My dad was a decorated vet, then he became a fireman. He breathed in some shit he wasn't supposed to in the war. Or maybe it happened over here in one of the old buildings, who knows? Cancer got him, though. So, yes. I did what he told me. I still hear him from time to time. Like a voice, I guess."

"I believe in things like that. Hearing voices from the beyond; psychic energy and reverberations," Abby said.

"I don't know what any of that means, just my dad's voice is all that I know."

When they arrived at the gas station, Sutton pulled up to the pump. They walked together side by side. Abby wasn't concerned about the *no-shoes sign*, as she had never seen it enforced before. When they entered, immediately she headed to the cooler in the back. She grabbed a chocolate milk and a bag of pretzels. Sutton was at the register paying for the gas. He turned to look at Abby.

He was smitten by her warm smile under the scattered darkness of her hair and make-up.

Abby caught Sutton's gaze. He was tall, muscular, parted hair, showing an early widow's peak. His stance was intense, it was obvious that he had a father in the military.

"Out and about in dirty socks," the clerk said. She was an old woman who had the face of a Shar Pei dog.

"I left them at my house with my purse."

"No purse either?"

"It's okay," Sutton said. "She's with me, ma'am. I am sorry."

16

The woman said nothing and charged him for the gas and Abby's items. They walked outside; Abby opened the chocolate milk and consumed it in a few gulps. The rush of sugar was soothing. She tossed the bottle in the trash as Sutton pumped gas. He spoke about how many miles per gallon his car got, and how he changed the oil himself. Abby was fading out of the conversation; she felt her cheek and it was tender from where her mother struck her.

Sutton continued speaking with little fluctuation in his voice. He wasn't particularly interesting, but he got her mind off of things. Reality set in. This guy wasn't bad. No different than any other guy she saw around town. The only difference was he really liked an old car instead of an old truck.

He put the hose back into the pump and wiped his hands on his jeans. Abby walked up to him, touched him on the chin, leaned in, and kissed him. It was the third time she ever kissed someone; it was the second time it was a man.

"What was that for?" He smiled and wiped his mouth.

"Because you came into my life at the right time."

"Hmm."

Sutton looked out into the empty parking lot.

"Just so you know, I am going to boot camp in July. I plan on doing four years in the Army, maybe eight, depending on how I like it."

"Nice."

"Does that bother you?"

"Why should it?"

"I don't know. Some women don't like military guys."

"I like nice people. Most people aren't nice."

He opened the door and was about to get in. Abagail did not move. She leaned against the hood and ate her pretzels.

"Are you coming?"

"I don't want to go home yet."

"Well, I got school tomorrow."

"So do I."

"My mom needs help getting some stuff done around the house. I need to head back."

"Where do you go, Lincoln?" she asked.

"Yep, let me guess, you go to Dermot?"

"Yep."

"Figures."

Sutton was aware of how people from different schools saw each other, he had seen it before. But Abby didn't seem like a girl who would be concerned with that.

"Let me take you back home. If you want, we can hang out sometime."

She nodded her head in agreement.

On the ride home, Sutton spoke about his family and what he thought the Army could do for him. He made an odd comment about a future with him and how it would be difficult when he was away. He mentioned how other military men got married early, so their wives could visit the base if they were overseas. She didn't think the kindness of buying chocolate milk deserved that deep of a conversation so early. But he did help her, and he wasn't a creep.

"What do you want to do with yourself?" he asked.

She was surprised, most men never asked a question like that.

"Cut women's hair. Make pretty women, even prettier."

"Really?"

"Yep. I have some money saved up for a beauty school in Nashville. I think my parents, well at least my father, actually my stepfather, but he isn't so bad so I think of him as a father, might help me. I just have to figure out if I drive to Nashville in an old car every day for a few months or if I live down there. Both could be difficult. I don't know yet. I can't figure shit out until I graduate next week."

Sutton didn't comment on what she said. His brain didn't seem like it had the bandwidth to comprehend it. He just nodded his head and said what all teen guys say.

"Cool."

When they arrived near her house, Abby made him stop halfway down the block. She wanted to explain why she ran down the street, but she didn't know how to process it herself. The front porch light was on. She could see Richard's car in the driveway. Abby could only imagine what her mother told him and how she spun the story, how God said *this,* and the Devil did *that.*

The lights were off inside the Robinson's house. She wondered what they thought about her mother's actions earlier. They were her only witnesses to the insanity that unfolded.

She didn't want to go inside. But she couldn't remain in Sutton's car, or he would be asking her to fly over to Afghanistan with him and be his bride in a few months. He was the opposite of everything that she wanted for her future. It was his fault for being so kind to her, at a time when she was desperate.

He asked for her number, and she gave it to him. Since Abby changed her image, no one had asked for it. Either they were too scared of her, or they thought she was dreadful. He texted her and smiled.

"Sorry, my phone is in the house. I swear that is my number."

"With your shoes and purse, I understand," he laughed.

She thanked Sutton by kissing him on the cheek. She shouldn't have, but she wanted to feel the warmth of another person who wasn't going to hit her or tell her she was going to hell. At that moment, she understood why some women get stuck in certain relationships. Sometimes when a woman does not have any ground of her own to stand on, she has to pick the next best thing, even if it has uncertainties, because at least it is something.

5

No matter what Abby's mother said, it would be unlike Richard to have an outburst, as he was mild-mannered about everything. His personality was like a warm glass of milk on a hot day. If a photo of him was taken at his happiest and saddest points, it would be hard to discern the difference. The concern was, what would be the aftermath of tonight's episode? If Abby was made into the villain, days before graduation. The outcome of the summer; moving out and going to beauty school, would be in jeopardy.

As Abby opened the side gate, she walked up the pathway. The TV was not on in the front room and the kitchen light spilled out into the backyard. Either both of them were in the kitchen preparing for witch trial dialog or it was only Richard. With a quick peek through the kitchen window, she was relieved to see Richard by himself. He was just a boring man making a boring sandwich. Surprisingly, a bit of sadness settled inside Abby. It was one of her mother's worst episodes, and she would get away with being a lunatic. Even though the Robinsons saw what happened, they wouldn't get involved. When Abby first got her car, the Robinsons scowled at her if the music was too loud, and the mild *hellos* they usually exchanged faded.

Slowly, Abby entered the kitchen. Richard looked at her with a blank expression, then smiled. The delayed reaction was alarming. His rosacea made him appear more flushed than usual. His faded red t-shirt said *I am technically a tech guy*. Abby had seen it before and in a moment of sass, she said it might as well say *I am a big dork* instead.

Abby once saw a nature show where a starving cheetah devoured a rabbit. The rabbit screamed; its eyes bulged out of its skull as it was being consumed. Abby always thought Richard was a half-human-cyborg with the soul of a devoured rabbit while wearing a nice pair of pleated pants.

"Hello, young lady, how are you?" he asked.

"Fine," she muttered.

She wondered how much he knew. If he was unaware, she wouldn't be able to tell, and if he did, then he was just being very Richard.

"I just went for a walk to clear my head," she said.

"Your mother was upset when I came home. She is in bed resting."

Abby was silent.

"We just finished praying for you."

And there it was. That meant poor Nova had done what she needed to do to make herself a persecuted hero. She was the apostle who was being stoned for preaching the truth in front of the deniers of faith.

It was selfish of Abby to think a line of concern would be next, but it wasn't like him, and she didn't want to instigate. As always, Richard was under the spell of the great prophet from Blueville.

He placed potato chips in a greasy half-ring around his sandwich and pickles on his plate. In his pigeon-like awkwardness, he held the plate like a little kid holding a catcher's mitt, waiting for a baseball to hit him in the forehead.

Without responding, Abby leaned her back against the counter with her arms folded. Her hair covered the side of her face, where her mother had slapped her. Dario ran into the kitchen to greet her. Many times, his big personality would fill the room and break the tension. She leaned down and petted him. Dario spun in a circle and meowed. Abby opened the cupboard for food and filled his bowl.

"Well, I am glad you are home and safe."

He stood in the hallway of the kitchen with his plate tipped. A spatter of pickle juice dripped onto the linoleum. Abby spoke softly to Dario and didn't respond to Richard.

"Did you hear me?" he asked.

"Yep."

Abby wasn't intimidated by his glare, and if she made eye contact, she would have cursed at him for being a coward.

It was four years ago, when the flimsy computer nerd, Richard Gibson, came into their lives. He was passing through the back roads of Illinois, hunting for a meatball sandwich at a famed deli he heard about on a famous diners TV show. By chance, he stopped for gas at the same station where Nova worked, and he was smitten by her. That was when Abagail and her mother were close. It was a time when Abagail was allowed to do her mother's make-up and hair before she went off the deep end. That day, the sun hit the highlights in Nova's hair like glistening rain beads on a stained glass window. It was enough to lure a thirty-something, balding man with a Gap-clearance ringer t-shirt into her world. He said, *Hello, I play video games.* Nova said *Hello, I believe in Jesus.* Two months later they were married.

Their wedding was small, as Richard had no family. His parents died in a car accident on black ice when he was in college. He had distant cousins in some part of the country that he hadn't spoken to anymore. In his twenties, he was a partier and got a DUI. Since then, he kept his social circle to a minimum and didn't hang out with anyone outside of work. All of his friends were people he played online games with, most of whom were teens or directionless college students. Three of his gaming friends showed up to the wedding, two of whom Richard had never met in person before.

There was one person, who didn't take to Richard, who also stood in to be the best man at the wedding, and that was the truck-driving, Vietnam vet, and father of the bride, Jerry Beaumont. Jerry told Nova that he thought Richard looked like a bowl of tapioca pudding with a pair of glasses. Nova defended him and said he was a good man, who made a fair amount of money and owned his own home.

Abby and Nova said goodbye to Aunt Ruth, left their home, and migrated south, to Blueville, Tennessee. The first order was that Nova needed a church and hoped that they would be mindful of God's calling on her life. Richard never cared about church and didn't know there was a radical Pentecostal place just two miles from his home. They attended as a family; however, Abby flicked the autopilot button on, and all was well. That was before Rose left, that was before Nova was promoted to be an end-times prophet.

"Sorry Richard, I am not talkative. I just want to go to bed," Abby said.

Looking at the floor, she passed by him. If he was intuitive, he would have noticed she was upset. He acted indifferently as she went upstairs.

"Come on, Dario, let's go."

Dario looked up at her, licking his chops. He ignored her calling, as all cats do, licked his paw, and wiped his face.

"Typical cat," she muttered.

Richard went into the front room, sat down uncomfortably on the edge of the couch, and ate his sandwich. He thought what he accomplished tonight was enough to be considered a good husband and father figure. He turned on the TV and flipped through the channels. On a weird cable station, a show he had never seen before caught his eye. Two busty women were jumping on a trampoline discussing geopolitics, Richard smiled. If Nova caught him watching this, he would be skinned alive. He changed the channel and found an episode of *The Honeymooners* and watched that instead. It was more suitable to watch a classic show about a working-class man who berated his wife with physical threats, over a show that displayed intelligence and beauty.

Abby moved silently through the hallway and hid in the bathroom. She waited for the sounds of her mother patrolling; there were none. The pious sentry must have been recharging with lamentations and sackcloth elsewhere. Abby showered and headed to her room. When she entered, a display of malice was spread out before her, like a murder scene. A new boundary of cruelty had been crossed. The old vinyl records that she held so dear, unearthed from an old milk crate in the basement, the same records adored by her mother, ages ago, were slashed violently. The damage was made with a box cutter. Chills rose on the back of Abby's neck. The mindset that her mother was in, to do such a thing, was terrifying. To stand over her daughter's bed with a blade and destroy something simple yet considered sinful was vile. Imagining her mother spewing biblical verses mixed with her self-righteous banter, hacking each black disc in maniacal slashes, made Abby want to jump out the window.

If she had enough money, she would leave, and find an apartment with a roommate, anywhere but here. If her finals at school weren't so crucial, she would sleep at a truck stop, somewhere in the next state over, Kentucky or even fucking Duluth, Michigan. The temptation of calling Sutton and toying with his view of where he thought a woman belonged in his life became real. It would be a place better than here, but it would be a place where she would be unhappy as well.

No, she thought. *I am tougher than her, I will survive this. I will eventually get the hell out of here. Fuck her and her stupid church and to hell with Richard as well.*

To keep a feeble illusion of security, Abby locked the door and tilted the chair under the doorknob. Tears streamed. She didn't wince or make a crying face, though. They just rolled right out of her open eyes. Robert Smith's beautiful face, from the cover of her favorite record, *Disintegration,* was hacked with an X. A burnt CD of this album, with mild scratches, had been on repeat in her car stereo, endlessly. The songs had carried her through colorful levels of melancholy peppered with madness yet making her feel wonderfully alive. Abby tore the cardboard, spared the left half of Robert's face, and put it in her purse.

"Sorry Robert, emo chicks have been cutting themselves to your shit for years, and it takes a whack job who reads the Book of Revelation to disfigure you."

She picked up the destroyed records and placed them into a garbage can by her desk. Sleep wouldn't come easy. Abby opened the bedroom window and shuffled onto the slanted roof. This past year, it was her nightly habit. The June weather was mild, and the night air beckoned her. As her mind calmed, she wondered what she witnessed earlier. What was the mysterious light that shot across the sky? Was it a UFO? If it was, did they acknowledge her in their passing, or were they headed to the White House lawn to state Earthly dominance? Either would be fine for her. As her life was nothing more than her room and random occurrences that happened before she retreated into it again, and she didn't feel safe here anymore.

"She is such a bitch."

Abby stared into the night sky for some time. She wanted to see another meteorite but there were none. She hoped she would see a UFO of some kind, but none of those passed by either. She began to doze. It would be dangerous to spend the night on an angled roof, so she crawled back inside.

The next day at school was last-minute prep for Friday finals. It was the end of a difficult year for her. She hated high school and within a few days, she would never see this place again. All that was left was watching the clock wind down. Even though she was considered one of the smart kids, she didn't fit in. Too much of a dreamer for the serious and studious, too much of a goth fashionista for the pretty girls, and the jock crowd gawked at her like she was an exotic animal in a small cage. At least their sneers showed that they acknowledged her young prowess.

Next week, when she turned eighteen, she would attempt to lay down some ground rules for her mother and stepfather. As she would be an adult, they would treat her like one. The days of being forced to go to church were over. It would be the last of, "March yourself upstairs and put something decent on." The archaic thinking of her mother would not keep her from being an individual. Even though she lived under their roof, they could not force her to believe as they did. If it turned the house into a bigger warzone than it already was, she would leave. Sadly, she would have to make a sacrifice and put off going to beauty school, to escape her mother's craziness. Would it be worth it for sanity and safety?

Replacing the destroyed record was imperative. Abby wasn't certain if it conjured up old demons from her mother's past, or if she just saw the Devil everywhere. Acquiring another piece of treasured media so quickly would solidify the future of her independence. *Disintegration* would be displayed on a shelf in her apartment, for all to see. The only place that would carry such a classic goth record would be one of the music stores in Nashville. If she left when the bell rang after school, she could be on the highway in under ten minutes and in the city within an hour. As long as there were no hiccups, she could be back before seven and tell her mother that she was at the library.

Yes, Mother, she thought, *I will replace what you destroyed, tenfold. The ghosts of your past, that you considered idols, will be the temples in which I worship, and you can go to hell for taking them away from me.*

The next day, when she left school, she did as planned, hit the highway, and headed east. A long overdue call with Rose was needed. The girls used to talk a lot when Rose first left. As regular mundane high school days took over, the distance in their relationship became further. Communication boiled down into texts or emails, and sadly, there would be a delay in response at the fault of both girls. As Abby sped on the highway, she passed slow-moving cars and sipped her diet soda. After two calls, she finally got a hold of Rose.

"Hey, babe, what is going on?" Rose said.

Her voice was much-needed warmth that melted some of the icy edge.

"It's all fucked up. How are you? "Abby said. She tried to hide an immediate swallow in her throat. Tears were right around the corner.

"Wow, already cutting to the chase. Is your mom still a whack job?"

A baby screamed in the background. It was one of Rose's twin nieces. Abby wanted to have a therapy session, but she knew it would be interrupted by whatever was making the baby cry.

"Yeah Nova, went supernova. She slapped me, chased me down the street, and cut my records with a box cutter."

Before the sentence was even out of her mouth, she was weeping. Driving became difficult. She pulled into the right lane and drove below the speed limit, to remain safe.

"Are you fucking serious?" Rose yelled.

"Yeah, it got bad."

"Well, there is only one answer. Graduate, get in your crappy Honda, and get down here."

Abby liked the idea of leaving, but she didn't like the idea of living with Rose's family in a small Miami apartment.

"It's an option," Abby mumbled.

"That is what you said last time, and that was before this. Do you think there is only one beauty school in the country that you can go to, and there is only one Denny's in the world to work at?"

"I know. You are right." She wiped her eye with her sleeve. She looked at her eyes in the mirror and her dark make-up was smeared.

"You are mumbling again. I think I heard you say that it was a good idea, see you soon."

"I am not mumbling!" Abby yelled.

"Yes, you are!" Rose yelled.

Both girls laughed. The prior baby that screamed in the background was matched with another. It sounded like two birds fighting over a stray french fry in a parking lot. Rose's sister yelled something in Spanish. A door slammed and a man yelled.

"Abs, I hate to cut you off. You deserve more from me, but I have to be a super aunt right now."

"Comprendo," Abby said. It was common for Abby to loosely integrate Spanish into dialog with Rose however she wasn't fluent.

"Si, mamasita. Hasta pronto, te amo!" Rose hung up.

The emptiness of uncertainty settled. If Abby could transport her room and put it next to Rose's apartment, life would improve. Rose was right, there were other places to work and go to school. Even though Abby would be a legal adult within days, she sure didn't feel like growing up so quickly.

She reached inside her purse, took out the half-torn cardboard piece of Robert Smith's face, and put it in her dash console. He looked up at her, not giving wisdom or guidance, but wondered what move she was going to do next.

Abby turned up the volume on her stereo and sang at the top of her lungs.

6

Abby entered the mall parking lot and parked near the food court entrance. She got out and lit a cigarette. The few cigarettes she smoked a week were always borrowed from people at work. Next week she would be able to purchase her own. She walked to the foyer of the mall, took a drag, and watched people walk in, who looked at her quickly and then looked away. Even though she didn't stick out as much as others who dressed like her did, her image still caught attention in public. Behind her, two young, tattooed men, reeking of alcohol and juvenile detention, sat against a rail and heckled others. They were predators waiting for innocent prey.

"What's going on living dead girl?" One of the men said. He had bleach-blonde hair and a tattoo on his cheek. His friend wore a beanie and a gold chain. They eyed her up and made a crass comment that she didn't make out nor care to. She ignored them, ashed her cigarette, and went inside.

"Yo! You didn't hold the door open for me!" The man with the gold chain said as he pursued.

Without turning around, she picked up pace and continued through the mall. Foot traffic was at a minimum and there were no crowds for her to get lost in. The music store, which she frequented often, was around the corner, there were a few customers inside. She went in and ducked behind a t-shirt spin rack. At the counter was a skinny emo teenager. He looked up and gave her a head nod. Rock music was blaring from the speakers. Her two pursuers passed by, looked inside the store, and kept walking. Either they didn't see her, or they didn't want to be around that many people as they caused a scene. As they passed, she stepped outside and watched their backs. They looked inside a clothing store and then entered a lingerie store. Someone must have caught their eye and they changed their disruptive course.

A few stores down by a darkened hallway, Abby saw what looked like a pile of blankets move on the floor. Next to the moving mass was a wooden cane. Abby left the music store and hid behind a gumball kiosk. She watched the blankets move and realized it was a person.

A woman's voice groaned.

"Are you okay?" Abby asked the slow-moving blankets.

It was an old woman, she looked up at Abby. A white shawl was over her face. It obscured her features. She looked ghostly and out of place.

"Ma'am, are you hurt?" Slowly, Abby walked toward her.

Around the woman was a black circle scribbled in chalk. The circle's line was harsh and jagged, as if the old woman drew it with a hand stronger than hers, over a thousand times,

"Ha," the woman said. She looked into Abby's eyes through the shawl. Her eyes were the color of milk. The woman squinted at Abby. Abby felt faint as they made eye contact. She was frightened of the woman, but the concern for her well-being was stronger than her own fear.

"Here, let me help you," Abby said. She reached out her hand.

The woman grabbed Abby's hand and the mall went dark. All that was visible was a faint light from the circle around the old woman.

"It is something isn't it?" The old woman said.

"What is?" Abby asked.

"When you have an experience like this, astral or psychic, the moment you are in it, it feels right, and when you step out of it, you immediately deny it, some even forget about it."

"I don't think I will forget this, and I don't even know what this is," Abby said. She wanted to ask where they were. She wondered where the mall went. Or were they still there in some form but elsewhere?

"Other frames of dimensions in our universe often overlap, and at times people who are sensitive enough are in tune to realize it. But there are too many moments far and few between where we hit a dry spell and there is nothing. The universe and its wonder isn't here for our entertainment. It is good to be in tune with it but is also foolish to think one can wield it to their will. Not all of us though are aimless pieces of driftwood that float on a sea of nothingness," the old woman said.

"What do you want from me?" Abby asked. She was kneeling in front of the woman; her knees were on the outer edge of the circle.

"It isn't what I want with you. I am just a conduit. But something beyond us and our comprehension needs to tell you this. And it will stay there until you know what to do with it. In fact, I fear..."

The woman extended her finger. Her nail was brown and sharp as a razor. She opened up Abby's palm and scratched a small circle into it.

"Hmm." The woman grumbled.

"What is it?" Abby asked.

"It skips one generation and then goes on to the next."

"What does?" Abby asked.

"As I feared, the way you have developed, you will forget this conversation. At least the awake version of yourself will. However, your subconscious is more powerful than a young girl like you can even imagine. The hunger within side you will burst beyond the stars."

"Ma'am, I don't know anything about anything," Abby said. As she said it, she realized it was the smartest thing she ever said.

"Perhaps, you need to be as dormant as you are on the outside, to have the experiences that carry on through your dreams."

The woman spoke in a language that was beyond all of Abby's comprehension. Abby loved Italian horror movies and knew a few words in Spanish, but this dialect sounded otherworldly. "Cila porttalkalai avarkl parkkumpotu ullita ventum, avarkal unkalukkakak kattirukkirarkal, eccarikkaiyutan payanpatuttavum."

Abby was astonished at what the woman had said. Somehow she understood it and responded.

"Eccarikkai?"

"Yes," the old woman said, "Always use caution!"

The woman smiled at her. Her face changed to youthful beauty. The constellatory wonder spun backward within her eyes, which switched from the blank slate of pure snow to wretched blackness. Abby felt like her soul left the Earth. She transcended beyond the boundaries of the natural realm and laid upon the upper stratosphere of the Earth, witnessing specks of cosmic dust travel at a hyper-accelerated rate across space. With another blink of the fortune teller's eyes, Abby's emotions shifted as she saw the woman change from the beauty of what she used to be until seconds before her death. Abby's fear became understanding, then questions were raised again.

She wondered if she could learn anything, if each answer to life, was followed by another question.

"Is that all you are looking for?" asked the skinny teen boy.

Abby was in the record store. There was no recollection of what just happened with the fortune teller. She was in front of the cash register. In her hands was a vinyl record of *Disintegration, by* The Cure.

"What?" Abby snapped.

"You said that you wanted to get that record and something else," The clerk said. He was wearing a Ween shirt and continuously pushed his bangs down over his eyebrows.

She traced her finger over Robert Smith's pouty face, wondering how many other women from the 80's until this moment had done the same. She wondered if her mother ever adored Robert Smith as much as she did. The way her mother thought now, she would consider Robert to have climbed out of the pit of hell, if he did, Abby thought they would be the sad and dreary pits of hell.

One vinyl was enough for now, it would remain hidden, and one day be displayed in her future apartment.

"My mother would forbid this to be played in the house. But vinyl records are so damn cool."

"Then buy that and the CD and listen to it in your car."

"I already have a burned copy. It is all scratched up though," Abby smiled.

"Then it is time to get a new one."

There was no one else behind her. Abby put the record on the counter. The clerk ran to the CD section and within seconds came back with *Disintegration*.

"This record is a classic," he said.

"You like The Cure?" Abby said.

"Of course."

"You aren't one of those punk rock, spit at old people while you skateboard types?"

"I am a little bit of both."

"Tell me something, I don't know about them then."

"They are working on a new record now and it should be out at the end of the year."

"Get the fuck out of here!" she shouted. "How do you know?"

Two middle-aged women were in the Gospel section. They both glared at Abby.

"Because I work at a music store," he said. He rolled his eyes, and his eye roll changed everything for her. For a moment he was desirable. His attitude pushed him back into the caricature of how every high school music store kid acts.

"Well, I will be first in line to get it then," she smiled.

She paid, thanked him coolly, and left.

"Hey!" He yelled. "There is a party this weekend at my friend's house. I will give you my number if you want to come."

Examining him with caution, she wondered if he was worth the trouble.

"I mean, if you want," he said. "My name is Arn, by the way."

"Arn, short for Arnold? "Abby asked.

"Yeah, but Arnold is a stupid name."

"I guess. My name is Abagail."

She stuck her index finger out at him. He reciprocated and touched it with his index finger.

"That's a witch's name," he said.

"My mother would burn you at the cross for saying that."

"Is that why you can't play The Cure on vinyl at your house?"

Abby scrunched her nose, in agreeing disgust. He wrote his number down on a Post-it note and handed it to her. The soft exchange between them felt foreign to her. The weird experience she had with the old woman was deep in her subconscious. But the awake Abby was unaware of this. Although part of her knew something was different. It wasn't teenage emotions in a loud music store, as she dodged parking lot creeps. Because part of her felt like she had a foot elsewhere, a place that wasn't of this world.

She took the record out of the bag and stared at the cover as she walked through the mall. The temptation to get a cinnamon pretzel surfaced, but she fought the urge and left. As she exited, her two pursuers were back at their posts, leaning against the railings. They were laughing obnoxiously. As Abby walked by them, they stopped laughing and stared at her.

"What are you like a mortician or something?" The man with the face tattoo asked.

Do not engage, she thought.

They sought no purpose in life, but to harass and be seen doing it. It was a fuel they needed and lived for. They sold weed and pills to teens, scared old ladies, and hit on any woman who gave them a dirty look. The man in the beanie meowed at Abby. She lost her edge, turned, and gave them the death stare followed by the middle finger. Both men scoffed at her reaction and started walking towards her. Abby fed the hungry bears.

The man in the beanie called her a *bitch*. They walked after her, quickly. She moved between parked cars, going diagonal in an attempt to confuse them. She dug her hand into her clutch purse.

"Oh shit."

Today she carried the black clutch purse with the gold buckle. Yesterday, was the black clutch purse with the white trim. In it, was her pepper spray. Richard bought the pepper spray for her when she woke up from a nightmare after binging *Unsolved Mysteries.* The pepper spray sat safely in her other purse on a chair in her room.

As she approached her car, she looked behind and saw the stalkers trailing. Nerves took over. With shaking hands, she took out her keys, got in the car, and locked it. The man with the face tattoo stood in front of her car.

"Yo, living dead girl, we just want to talk."

She put the car in reverse and the man with the beanie was standing behind the adjacent car. He stepped out of the way as she backed up. In a flash of obstinance, she rolled her window down an inch.

"You fuckers like creeping on women?"

"Just women like you," he said.

"It's a shame I don't have my gun."

"A gun, why are you being so mean?"

"Maybe if you didn't smell like you just got out of jail you could find a nice toothless girlfriend."

He held his arms out like a matador with no cape, grinned, and spit at her. The spittle landed on the window; a small flick landed on her nose.

Abby stepped on the gas and sped through the parking lot. A pickup truck drove without caution and cut in front of her. She slammed on her brakes. The truck drove through the yellow light and exited the parking lot. Abby was stuck at the red light. She watched for her pursuers in the mirror. Gripping the steering wheel until her knuckles whitened, she waited for the light to turn. All year she thought of the liberties that she would have when she turned eighteen; get a credit card and purchase cigarettes. But now she did consider getting a gun. A black Jetta, set low to the ground, pulled out of a mass of parked cars. Slowly, it approached behind Abby's car. Across the street in a plaza was Dino's Pizza. It was a pizza place Rose and she had visited a few times. She could hide there, amongst the crowd, and call the cops if needed. The light turned green, she floored it, crossed the intersection, and parked in an open spot in front of a small bookstore called Above & Beyond Books. The Jetta entered the parking lot. Abby got out and went into the bookstore.

Behind the counter was a tall broad-shouldered man, with dreadlocks.

"Welcome, young lady," he said. His voice was deep, and he had a rich Caribbean accent.

"Hi," she said.

She stepped out of view of the open doors and walked against the furthest wall.

"I just opened this month. I deal mostly in old books. I do some trading for credit. Anything I can help you look for?" He stepped out from behind the counter.

"Oh, I like odd stuff: aliens, cults, serial killers."

"Ah, that is over here." He pointed.

Outside, she heard the voice of her pursuers. They were in front of the store. Either they didn't know she entered, or they were waiting for her.

"I think I might have something you will like."

Abby smiled at the store owner. He was nearly two feet taller than her. Confidence seemed to come from within him, rather than his size and height. He fit the ambiance of the ornately decorated and incense-infused store.

She looked toward the door but did not see anyone enter. The store owner matched her gaze and looked out towards the front. He handed her a book.

"Forgive me, I know it isn't good to judge a book by its cover, but I think this might interest you."

She looked down at the book he handed her.

"*Connecting to the Astral World*," she said. "It does sound interesting."

As she examined it, she turned the book around to read the jacket. Outside of the store, the presence of her pursuers were made known.

"I think that fucking bitch went in here."

The store owner looked at Abby, "Are those men bothering you?"

"Yes," she whispered. She was frightened at their aggressiveness. It was nothing for her to match wits with kids at school or a flirty truck driver at work. Those were on her level, these men were different, and they were a threat.

The store owner picked up his cordless phone, put it to his ear, and walked out the front door.

"Hello," he said.

Abby wasn't certain if he was talking to the men outside or someone on the phone. She peeked around the shelf and saw his back. His shoulders were as wide as the doorway. The phone was to his ear. He laughed with whomever he was conversing with on the phone. He was diffusing the situation without getting violent. She couldn't see if her pursuers were still out front or not. But as the owner remained guard, she felt safe.

Looking through old books would help settle her nerves. She scanned the shelf in front of her. A title of a book stuck out, *The Occult in Modern-Day America*. She read the back and saw that it was from some Christian Evangelist, warning parents about Satan and his grip on the youth in America. She put it back.

"A crock of shit."

Delicately, she touched the spines of paperbacks, allowing the titles to conjure an emotion in her that could spark interest and take her beyond the reaches of potential threats; it became trancelike. The act was soothing as it had been many times before. She felt this same way when flipping through old records, but books had a different personality. She would remain here as long as possible, until she felt safe, hopefully leaving with a few gems to dive into this weekend. There was a row that catered to cults. She picked up one, Charles Manson's crazed face was on the cover. Whenever someone wanted to sell their book on this subject, Manson was always the focal point. The book could have been about twenty different cults, but Manson was the spotlight, with a cheap price of 2.99. She put it back. The next one seemed more interesting, *UFO Cults and the Adoration of Other Realms*. Marshall Applewhite was on the cover. A little over ten years ago, Applewhite led a group into a suicide pact, with the intent of meeting a spacecraft behind the comet Halle-Bopp. This incident stuck out in her memory. Recalling footage of the crime scene with tracksuit-wearing dead bodies, covered in sheets shocked the country. How could a group, on their own accord, go that far into something so far-fetched? She picked it up and flipped through it, this would be a keeper. The subject interested her more than Manson. However, a book about Manson would piss her mother off. He was a household name. Her mother thought the 60's sitcom *Bewitched* was an evil show, then this would certainly cause a stir. Abby smiled at the thought of her mother throwing the Manson book out. It would be left in plain sight as bait for her mother to not dig anywhere else.

A peculiar title stood out to her, as it stood out to many others, but those who picked it up and flipped through it were never compelled to purchase it. *Channeling Your Conscience Through the Unknown Universe* by famed mystic/astronomer/professor Francis Truelove. It was written in 1866. The book's top and bottom spine were worn but the pages were white and intact. The artwork on the front cover had embossed gold impressions of alchemic symbols. She had read a few odd books before, mostly mainstream material about bizarre topics, from crystals to meditation or haunted houses and alien encounters; this was from an era beyond her understanding. Some would call it a stroke of fate that it fell into her hands. Francis Truelove didn't believe in fate though. His writings did not move on past two generations since his emergence, as the world had changed. The concept of Spiritualism and the connection with the cosmos fell away from modern thinking. With his works and findings, nearly forgotten, there were a few people from time to time, as curious as Abagail, who would stumble upon his work.

The person who owned this book prior was an old psychic woman named Shirley Walters, who died of pneumonia and never saw it coming. Shirley had the book in her possession for many years but never read it, she just liked the title and thought it looked nice on the bookshelf in her parlor, where she had done tarot readings. She wrote her name on the last page of the book. Abby saw it and wondered who she was.

Prior to Shirley's possession of the book, it was owned by a sickly boy, named Peter Kaminski. Peter read it from front to back twice and believed every word of it. He was encouraged to look up, and away from what plagued him. He chanted and channeled, just like the famed mystic/astronomer/professor had admonished that the readers should do. As Peter followed his words, he had dreams and visions. Some of which were brought on by the copious amounts of codeine that he took for his respiratory ailments. On one of his nights of chanting, the sky was peppered with a meteor shower. People then, spent time adoring the tapestry of the heavens, something so very few people do anymore. Regardless of what Peter saw in his dreams and visions, connected to his channeling, his health still suffered. He died a short time after, at the age of thirteen from tuberculosis. He scribbled the words, *Find my geodes* on the last page, and his name, was above Shirley's.

The owner of the book before Peter was a Catholic priest, named Nicholas Athernos. The book was given to him by a small print publisher, who was publishing the priest's book, about how the state of the church needed to focus more on helping the poor. It was a bold statement from Nicholas' viewpoint. He was a giving man and wanted to reach others through love and without harsh judgment. The publisher, who was an advocate for freedom of religion and expression did not realize the conflict he had caused by giving a Catholic Priest a book concerning channeling and chanting. As Nicholas read the book, he secretly started to chant in a way described by Francis Truelove. This act was heard by one of the visiting bishops in his church and he was heavily scrutinized. Nicholas lost faith in the church after that and quit being a priest. He took the book with him and left it at a chapel in a hospital. It sat untouched for three years until it was found again. The priest had written his name on the last page, with the phrase, "I believe in God, just not the one they do."

Abby opened it and read a random passage.

"I feel that in all I have researched and by what means are available, there is something else out there, beyond our comprehension, in the cosmos, that observes us. I believe that they are advanced beyond our scope of understanding, to such a degree that I think they visited us, and we have been unaware. In this thought,

it would only make sense that they would remain hidden; observing the human race, in all of our greatness and flaws. I think their intentions are to gather information, for themselves. I hope they will approach us and show us the error of our ways, or perhaps they are finding our weaknesses and will eliminate us from our beautiful planet and take it over. After all, our world, sitting perfectly in rotation around a perfect sun, far from the gas planets and far from the ice planets, is such a beautiful place."

The store owner came back inside, still conversing on the phone. He looked at Abby and looked behind him and swatted his hand slowly, signaling that the men were gone.

A high-backed blue velvet chair was in the middle of the store. At the top of the chair was a carved wooden ram head. An end table with a white marble top and glossy black wooden legs was next to it. She sat in the chair, pressed her back against it, and relaxed for a moment. The furniture had personality to it as if it belonged in a funeral home prior to occupying the store. The chair and table had a vibe that her mother would call evil, and that brought Abby comfort.

Abby flipped through the old book and read another passage at random,

"And in that practice is how I communicated with the cosmos, my voice, the fingerprint of my soul, reached beyond the realm of our world. I beckoned to others. Others who are just like me, sitting on their grassy hills, with the cool of the day blowing through oaks on the ridge, looking up at the stars and wondering just the same."

Out of all the odd books and articles that Abby had found in recent months, this was unlike anything she ever read. She would devour this when she got home. Closing the book, she placed it on the coffee table and put her hands over her face. In admiration, she rubbed her hand over the marble. She opened the drawer and looked inside; it was empty. She sat up and looked back at the register. The owner was taping a small box with a tape gun.

"That table isn't for sale," the owner said. He laughed warmly.

"Everything is for sale," she said.

"Not that one. It belonged to my mother, and she is no longer with us."

"Then why do you have it on display, tempting me to ask?"

"Because she would be proud of me for opening my own store. And I want it to be admired by people like you."

"People like me, or maybe just other people?

"Listen," he smiled, "Just because you look like a lone vampire in the Bible Belt, doesn't mean everyone is going to treat you like a freak."

"Hmmm."

The owner had enough energy to fill his store and go beyond the realms of the parking lot and out into the world with just a smile and laugh. She wanted to read more but the owner's presence was unintentionally commanding.

"What is your name?"

"Abagail."

"Tony," he smiled. "Nice to meet you, Abagail. I see you have a few books."

"Yes." She held up the book with Manson's face on it.

"Ah, you like him?"

"Not at all, this is just to piss my mother off. She is a mix between a witch hunter and a book burner. This will be my distraction book and this..." She held up the Francis Truelove book,

"...is what I will hide from her."

"A witch burner? You peacock around so proudly, while living with a pilgrim?" He laughed enthusiastically.

Abby smirked. She wanted to laugh with him, as it was contagious. Most reactions she gave to people were forcefully subdued, but Tony was a rare gem. She covered her mouth, looked away, and laughed quietly.

"You know..." Tony came out from behind the counter, he was twirling the tape gun in his hand. "...my mother said that deep down inside every good woman is a witch."

Abagail furrowed her brows. Tony's words were insightful; they pricked her heart, and the feeling of acceptance became soothing. Too many times this past year, she remained on the defense. This was the lowest she ever let her guard down with someone new. Most of her dialog with anyone was sarcasm or a challenging statement, but not with this man. Tony was being his genuine magical self, and without him realizing it, she learned a bit more of herself, just sitting contently in a fantastic chair, in the middle of a marvelous store.

She came to the register and placed the books on the counter.

"I want this place to be a hangout for people to talk as well. No politics, just people talking. Questioning the world around them and learning from one another," he said.

"I don't know about that; people can be assholes," Abby said.

"But we can teach them, to be better, *by* being better."

"That's easy for you to say, some people live with people who act like monsters."

"Hmm." Tony took her cash and gave her change. "Perhaps there are some like you say, but not all."

He slid a bookmark, with the store's logo on it, into *Channeling Your Conscience Through the Unknown Universe.*

"Oh, this book, came in with a weird lot. I have never heard of this author before. I love how you were drawn to such an obscure item."

He slid the books into a black plastic bag.

"Well, that's me, I guess," she grinned.

"Nah. You are good."

"And thank you for chasing my stalkers away."

Tony folded his arms like a proud shop owner in his first month of business should. He thwarted evildoers and gave advice to a young woman, all while maintaining his passion.

"Now those types of fellas can stay out," he laughed. "No conversations for them in here."

"Well, if that is the case, I will be back."

"If you see them again, sit in that chair and read, and I will take care of them."

"Thank you."

She waved and left. Tony was a gem. He made her feel normal. She stepped into the pizza place, ordered a slice and a soda, and ate with her back facing the wall. Her stalkers did not appear again. Her curfew wasn't until ten. Thankfully, nothing had changed, even with yesterday's fiasco. She texted Richard and said that she would be home soon. Sitting in the restaurant by herself was a little better than being in her room doing the same, at least for tonight.

While she flipped through her books, she would read a page, close one book, open the other, and repeat for the next few hours. Focusing was difficult. By next Wednesday she would be eighteen. She believed that her life would change for the better. Wherever she would move to and whenever she would go to beauty school, she would be the best version of herself. Hopefully alone, with no roommate, with her odd books, and records, and Dario as well.

7

The ride home was somber. The windows were down, and the stars permeated the night sky, like a legion of bat's eyes hanging in a cave. The Cure dominated the airspace, but she turned Robert Smith down. The plan was to scream every word of *Disintegration* until she pulled into her driveway. But her emotions were erratic from the mall hoodlum's chase to the insightful bookstore owner, and the heavy pressure on her soul about her future's uncertainty. This was supposed to be a victory ride home. The odd flash in the sky she witnessed last night could have been a meteorite or falling space junk. She hoped it was a UFO, and in that hope, she wanted to witness something like it again. Scanning the horizon, she saw nothing but the twinkling stars millions of miles away. Other Abby's from other solar systems were saying *hello* on their car rides home. But nothing in the Earth's sky flew by. To shake off the anxiety, she turned up the music and sang her heart out into sugary streams of wonder and sadness.

When she arrived home, she could not walk into the house so boldly, bearing the same record her mother just destroyed. This would have to be hidden carefully. Her mother didn't have the key to her car, and it would be her safe space. She opened the trunk. A box was in the back from the last time she bought old knick-knacks and picture frames from a thrift store. She placed the record in the box. Tomorrow would be warm, and she didn't want it to melt. In the morning, she would sneak it inside, while the prophet still slept.

The second priority was the book about channeling. She slid it into the back of her waistband and covered it with her cardigan. The book about cults with a wild-eyed Charlie Manson on the cover remained in the black bag. If her mother stopped her at the door, she would allow it to be confiscated, like a troll given a token to pass a bridge. Without hesitating, she walked inside.

Richard and her mother were sitting on the couch. Her mother had a blanket over her legs, and she was bent forward. Bags hung under her eyes and her hair was unkempt. Abby used to enjoy doing her mother's hair, but since yesterday's outburst, Abby didn't care if it looked like a bird shit on her head. Four years ago, her mother was in her prime, when she snagged Richard. Sadly, it looked like she aged ten years in the past few months. On the wall behind them, was a picture taken at her mother's birthday. Rose was with them and had taken the photo. Abby recalled the conversation that night not being good. Her mother went on a rant about a movie star who came out as a lesbian. She said that their filth would end just like Sodom and Gomorrah, and fire would rain down upon them in Hollywood. Richard agreed with her ludicrous statement and nodded his head. Abby pushed the envelope and said that Rose and she considered dating each other because all the guys in high school were stupid. Abby's mother looked like she was going to have a stroke. Rose being the buffer, calmed the situation and lied about a fake boyfriend and her doing something nice for Christmas. Shortly afterward Rose moved to Miami. Even though they fought that night, it was the last time Abby remembered her mother looked pretty.

"Abby?" Nova asked.

Abby was lost in thought. "I am sorry."

"I said, where were you?"

"I told you she texted me, Nova," Richard mumbled.

"I went for pizza after school with a friend."

"With whom?"

"A woman who is going to beauty school. She told me that I should enroll soon and consider going somewhere in Nashville."

Abby had a knack for laying bigger things in front of small arguments to distract or disrupt.

"Oh," Nova said.

Richard sensed the tension of an argument beginning to surface. He wasn't good for much in any dialog between the women of the house, but his presence and ability to interject another topic of conversation was welcomed. "So, Abagail, we were thinking, after next week, you will be coming and going as you please, given your new venture into adulthood and..." he looked at Nova and put his hand on hers, "...you have hinted recently that you wanted to move out, but we agreed that you can stay here, however, you will have to pay rent."

Abby shook her head in disbelief. "I am sorry, what?"

"You can pay us rent, instead of moving out," Richard repeated.

"How does that make sense?"

"Well, we thought you would want to leave as soon as you graduated."

"I would if I could, but I have nowhere to go, and I don't have much money saved. I don't understand why you would want to charge me rent?"

"Abby..." Nova stood up, "...listen, with my position at the church, I have to live under a certain light. I don't want anyone to say I have an unruly child living here. The old associate pastor; you remember Pastor Davis? His son used to do drugs and he had an awful time having the congregation listen to him because of it. If you are going to be living outside of the rules of our church, I want to be covered and say that you pay rent."

Abby had witnessed a lot of manipulative things from the people who attended the church. But this was a great display of doublespeak.

"So, for you to save face as a prophet of God, you want to charge me rent, before I can save enough money to move out. As if paying for my room, makes me exempt from the church's scrutiny on how I present myself?"

"Yes," Nova said.

"Y-yes," Richard stuttered.

"That doesn't make any sense," Abby responded.

Nova contorted her face, raised her hands like she was shooting blasts of light from them,

"The Bible speaks of an unruly child in a household, and who will listen to the voice of God.

As I am his mouthpiece for our church, and in the end times, prior to the return of Christ, we will be the bride of Christ, as the church needs to prepare...."

"Mother," Abby interrupted, "Do you realize, if you stood on the street and said this, you would look like an insane person? Someone would call the mental hospital and take you in for an evaluation."

Her mother's eyes bulged from her head. Richard, usually unable to produce extreme emotion, winced his face. Both parents' expressions looked like poorly done caricatures, rubberized and comically ugly.

"How dare you," her mother whispered.

Fighting the urge, Abby couldn't help but smirk, it was the subtle reaction that was the cherry on top of her rebuttal. With gritted teeth, a spit of saliva shot out of her mother's mouth, "Get to your room, now!"

Abby lowered her gaze. She climbed the stairs. Dario followed, meowing in short bursts, and passed by her. Dario ran down the hallway to the closed door of her room. Abby picked him up and kissed him on the head. Before she opened the door, she wondered what items inside would have been cut with a razor or what misinterpreted passages from the Bible would be written on the walls in lamb's blood. As she entered, she was relieved that nothing was out of the ordinary. She locked the door and moved her computer chair against it. The other purse was on it; the purse that contained her pepper spray. If it was with her when the men followed her, she would have sprayed them in the eyes and mouth and enjoyed the gagging sounds they emitted. It would have been a deserved reaction to their vulgar encounter. She wondered if her mother would ever barge into her room, wielding a boxcutter while she was sleeping. It was a terrifying thought. Would she be capable of pepper spraying her? Was her mother's unjust actions equivalent to mall thugs who terrorized teenagers? She waited to hear heavy footsteps, but there were none. When she looked in the mirror, there were black lines down the center of her cheeks. She wondered how long they had been there.

Ten minutes passed and her mother did not make another overly theatrical appearance; tomorrow would be another day for that. She put the pepper spray back in her purse.

Dario meowed and rubbed against her legs.

"Yes Dario, she is a bitch."

He meowed again, in agreement.

"By the might of Robert Smith's hand, I plan on being out of here by midsummer."

Abby put the Manson book on her dresser. If she survived next Saturday's graduation party, whatever money she would make, would be put towards an apartment. Only one month would be paid here, for their ludicrous new rules, and then goodbye Nova and your less-than-stellar explosions.

She went onto the roof and by cell phone light, she started to read *Channeling Your Conscience Through the Unknown Universe* by Francis

Truelove. Excitement gripped her, as she opened the book and let it part at random. The mystic/astronomer/professor wrote like no one she had ever read. Brilliant, bumbling, and full of charm.

"It was then that I drew a chalk circle on the ground, outside of my home. I suppose I could have done it in my study, but the eloquent and radiating tapestry above had beckoned me. I surrounded myself with candles. As a mystic, I have always harbored an overabundance, as such ceremonies could be spontaneous. I have noted before, that candles spark a mood that allows me to dig deeper into my troubled psyche. The alchemic symbols of Saturn and Mercury lay before me, as Mercury is my ruling planet, Saturn to my left and Mercury to my right. I sat appropriately in the center. Earlier I had tried this but felt that clearing my mind through the usage of white sage and rubbing the ashes on my forehead, made me deeply meditative. In my hands, I held my birthstones, in geode form, which I explained earlier the complexities of finding. And with this, I began to chant. The waves, and how they were formed were out of the diaphragm. As such a long 'A' sound flowed into an 'O'. Then 'A' led into an 'Um'. I did this for some time and felt my consciousness leave the boundaries of our Earth. It should be noted that any fool can AO and AUM all night and day and see nothing. It is safe to say that some can do the same and pretend that they are elsewhere, and I do believe that such fools exist, but a fool, or a charlatan, I am not. With that said, I transcended into another plane that left this Earthly one. My doublemindedness seemed to stabilize, as it has been a crutch in my life. My constant need for alcohol to quiet part of my soul wasn't needed either. As I had studied in some cultures in which the third eye could become clouded by the excesses of it.

I was in an ethereal state, and I saw lights, of different colors, and warmth, but I always assumed space would be cold. It was then I saw eyes observing me, but I did not cower. Because the one thought I had in my mind is, if this were my last moment, I will stand in the face of something unearthly and still be who I am."

Abby closed the book and wept bitterly. The concept of reaching into the unknown was overwhelming. Having her voice sent, like a letter to go beyond what she knew on Earth, and to be painted in the cosmos. The complex person that she was, had a voice and she wanted it to be heard in the universe, from a world that didn't seem to bring kindness to her. Improving

47

her life, by looking up and focusing on the well-being of her soul meant more to her than whatever the witch-hunting book burner she lived with ever said or did. If her mother considered her a witch for this, then her mother had always been holding the torch. For this, her mother would not triumph, and Abby knew what steps she had to take.

8

On a cocaine high, the three men drove in a black Chevy G30 van from Phoenix to the border of Mexico. Isaac had read on a 4Chan message board about a cult that was active in black magic, near Nogales. He mentioned this to Jericho, as a dare, hopefully pushing him further. That was a few hours ago at a dive bar. Jericho lost his mind when he heard it. He threw a freshly uncapped Rolling Rock beer bottle across the bar. It smashed behind a pool table and was followed by a wolf cry. The bar owner told them to leave, or he would shoot them, then call the cops after they bled out from gut wounds. Gentry, the more tame of the three, put a hundred-dollar bill on the bar and apologized for his friend's outburst. The bartender, who had the personality, of an abused Rottweiler, told them to get the fuck out and placed a 9mm handgun on the counter.

When the young men crept up to the Mexican border; the van idled, and exhaust fumes filled the guard's booth. The guard told them to shut the engine off. Jericho was driving, and he should not have been as he was drunk and high, and it was Gentry's van. The guard peered into the window with steaming judgment and said that they needed passports to enter. Jericho said he didn't know that was required, and asked if an allowance could be made. The guard told Jericho that even though he was too dumb to comprehend the clear words coming out of his mouth, it didn't change a damn thing. Jericho smiled and offered him 500 dollars. The guard took off his aviators and told him to get his white privileged ass out of his face. Jericho called him a racial slur and they headed east.

They drove to a small no-name town in Texas and bought peyote behind a Mexican restaurant from a one-armed boy with an eye patch across the street from a Motel 6. They rented a room, took the peyote, and walked out to the Chihuahuan Desert in their boxer shorts. Jericho wielded a moon-shaped blade that he found at a fortune teller's shop south of Phoenix, a place where he claimed he had dreamt of before seeing it.

Gentry was the diffuser of the bad situations amongst the small group. He only agreed on the cross-country trip because he felt horribly alone in this world. At twenty-two, with a bachelor's in business management, no ambition, and no significant other, he desired to see the beautiful landscape of America. Jericho went to college with him briefly before he got kicked out for stalking a woman on campus, who got a restraining order against him. Although Jericho treated him like shit, Gentry liked being around him. Simply because Jericho looked cool and didn't give a shit about the rules. It was a dark charisma that was hated by most people but admired by those who had a twisted view of what being *cool* meant.

Isaac being the instigator, loved to watch Jericho take things to the next level. Isaac was the only boy amongst two older sisters. They were spoiled rotten by his parents. To get attention, he shoplifted and allowed himself to be caught. His father's resources always kept him from serious trouble with the law, and Isaac hated him even more for that. He took great joy in the ability to see Jericho get triggered so easily. Jericho's temper was something that gave him the satisfaction that he was never able to get from anyone else.

What made the three men dangerous, more threatening than the drugs, and the constant dares, was they all came from wealthy families and somewhat decent parents who pushed the young men to apply themselves. They resisted any good guidance and met with one common desire; an oddity that wasn't found in the drive of men with their construct; they loved ufology and the occult. It came from an obsession with a late-night radio show they got into at college. All manner of paranormal and high strangeness was covered. In their yearning for the unknown, they wanted to find real evidence of aliens. Like all who seek out peculiar things, they discovered some theories to be proven untrue, while others only added more unanswered questions.

It was after Jericho got kicked out of college for the second time, that he made Gentry and Isaac make a blood vow, via palm and knife, that they would drive across America to find a piece of undeniable truth; something to solidify their hunger. Whether it be an alien relic, or a buried secret, shrouded by the government, he wanted it, and he swore he was destined for it. In his rants, he proclaimed that they had to push the boundaries of what fanatics had tried to accomplish before them. The near-endless stream of income, supplied by his father, and his lust for violence could push them beyond the limits where others have failed. It was his burning desire to go beyond the veil of the simulation that is unseen by most. It was a fire in him, that no one understood, in which he wanted to visit another dimension that called out to him since he was a young boy.

The fire in Jericho was sparked by an old book he stumbled upon when he was seventeen. It was written by a once-famed mystic/astrologer/professor named Francis Truelove. It was titled *Channeling Your Conscience Through the Unknown Universe*. It was a second-edition paperback, which was reformatted and pressed by a small and now defunct company, that specialized in obscure occult literature. Jericho liked the title and the artwork. However, he was never scholarly nor understood how to digest good reading material. He was either too high or ignorant to comprehend anything that held more depth than a high school poem. Upon his readings of Truelove, he misinterpreted what was written and in his twisted mind, he concluded that other dimensions and portals did exist. In his misconception, he was convinced that access to them was by human sacrifice and bloodletting. Francis Truelove *did* speak of dimensions and realms, but *not* once commended the drawing of blood. Truelove *made* mention of a witch coven that threatened his family. He was concerned by their bloodthirsty lust and feared they would kidnap and sacrifice his wife and son, as a means to acquire knowledge from him. As Francis had stated, he was able to keep his family safe, at least at the time of writing the book.

Jericho and his delusions of grandeur read a different story. He saw the words *portal* and *sacrifice*, and *blood* and *dimension*, and formed his own perversion of other-worldly travel.

When the three of them came to a place in the desert, at a moment when the tendrils of the evening hung onto the sky, the men drew circles with their fingers on the dry earth. It was a ritual they tried to practice but failed miserably at. A portion of Truelove's book mentioned drawing oneself, in a circle with the symbol of Saturn to the right and their astrological symbol in front of them. They had no geodes and did not chant. They sat in the pre-trance of psychedelia. Yet, the doors of their hearts were not opened. The portals of their minds remained closed. The universe did not speak to them, and they remained like unbaked masses of clay before the yawn of a fiery furnace but were not permitted to be molded into something enlightening. They sat in the ash of their selfishness and felt nothing more than the weight of reality; remaining as unchanged monsters.

The effects of the peyote took over, what was certain in and around them morphed. They drifted into a dark world, and that was their own subconscious.

Gentry had a vision of his dead grandfather, only more hulking and menacing than he ever was when he was alive. His grandfather huffed at him, shirtless and muscular, looking down as though he was going to destroy Gentry. His grandfather never held such a physique in his lifetime. He called Gentry a waste of breath and body. With his large soot-covered hand, he wiped his nose, called Gentry a pussy, and slapped him. Gentry cried out in the desert. He sweat and panted and gagged and retched and ran back to the hotel, bursting through the door and hid in the corner. His friends were not friendly to him. They let him work out his misery by himself, and it made him a much heavier, damaged person.

Isaac sat in the lotus position and stared at the stars. He watched them for hours. Two meteorites passed by. He drooled like a caveman and observed a universe of color, a spectrum of delirium, interchanging slowly in front of him. Deep inside, a tugging on his soul told him to be better and do better. The message came to him from an image of a beautiful woman, whose face was placed between two twisted cacti, ten feet in front of him. This made him angry. In his immaturity, he wondered if the woman was sent to torment him, only because he never had a good relationship with any woman. All women that knew him, ended up hating him. There are people in this world who could influence others to become better people and change the course of others' lives with wonderful words of passion and light. On the opposite end, there are some whose very speech could form a dark cloud above another enlightened being. Just their presence can withdraw warmth from a room. Some call them energy vampires, while decent people call them misguided. Isaac took pleasure in other people's misery. If a decent person had a worse day, because of him, he would smile, and his smile was vulgar, full of contempt. In his darkness, he sat on the dusty floor of the Earth, next to a more dangerous, treacherous person, who was having the time of his life on his spiritual journey.

Jericho's trip would give a normal person nightmares, but Jericho enjoyed what he was experiencing. A blue demon, with a horse-like misshapen face, and mismatched animal horns on its head, one belonging to a deer and the other to an antelope, spoke to him about the forthcoming apocalypse. The demon told him that he would be a rich prince in the next world after this. It gave explicit instructions, that drinking the blood of the innocent is what would give him strength and power and wisdom could be absorbed through the lifeblood of those he felt he could gain power from. The victims he would find were the fruit of this world and needed to be picked, sliced, and drained.

"Yes!" Jericho screamed. He spat in the sand and made a mask over his face. Isaac jumped out of his meditative posture and looked at him. He was confused and started laughing. Jericho thought he was being mocked and wanted his friend to respect him because he would soon rule a portion of the world. He slapped Isaac across the face. Isaac retaliated by slapping him harder and drew blood from Jericho's lip. Jericho frowned and spit blood on the ground.

"What the hell is your problem!" Isaac yelled.

Jericho lunged and bit Isaac on the shoulder. Isaac punched him in the stomach. Jericho cursed at him and scratched Isaac's chest with his fingernails. Isaac backed away slowly, turned, and ran into the desert, screaming the lyrics of a song he heard on the radio earlier. He replaced all of the words that were about *love*, with the word *hate*.

"Oh baby, I hate you. I need you and I hate; I hate, I hate!"

After a mile, into the horizon of emptiness, he became exhausted and fell over. Jericho walked back to the motel and sat on the curb. He watched cars back in and out and people walk by until the night grew quiet. He rocked back and forth and cursed to himself. People saw him and ignored him. He knew they were ignoring him, and this angered him. He remembered their faces, so when he ruled a portion of the Earth, he would find all of them and enslave them. When daylight came, by chance he remembered what room he was staying in, opened the unlocked door, and laid in bed until noon.

Gentry awoke in a panic. His nightmare had passed. He showered and got dressed, in nice dress clothes. Jericho was still asleep in his bed. Isaac wasn't to be found. Gentry learned not to worry about Isaac because he would always turn up. Gentry wanted pancakes and drove to a breakfast house. As he sat there and ate, he felt his psychedelic trip was wasted. He learned nothing and it made him depressed.

Perhaps, Jericho was right? he thought. Being the stable one in the group didn't get them far and since they started this trip, he felt unfulfilled. Gentry made up his mind when he returned to the motel, he would tell Jericho that he would do the first crazy thing that came to his mind. It would be their mission; whether it would be jail or hell, he didn't care. In doing this he hoped it would allow him to be able to feel something different than the pain of waking up every morning.

9

The old science room in Abby's high school was unlocked. The lights were turned off. The only time she could enter without being seen was during lunch. All of the students and expected faculty were in the cafeteria. She entered the dark classroom and illuminated her path with the light of her cell phone. All of the paraphernalia related to the high school science world resided in a long closet behind Mr. Carter's desk. She entered the closet and turned on the light. It was a year since she had been in this small room, and it was to return the Bunsen burners. That was the day that she saw them, in their unique beauty. To her knowledge, they were never used once during the entire time she attended high school. Their crystalline beauty always stuck out in her mind.

To her surprise, the glass cabinets had been replaced. She would have to check every drawer if they were still here. The time she had was minimal. She pulled out each drawer, from left to right in the closet, discovering nothing. Only unorganized papers from previous tests, scalpels for frog dissection, metal prongs and devices for probing and scraping, test tubes, measuring devices, and bottles were found. In the last drawer, she found a jade-colored glass smoking pipe in a plastic bag with charred resin in it.

"Looks like Mr. Carter likes to smoke weed. Well, Mr. Carter, where did you hide the geodes?"

Before she gave up hope, she looked up and saw white cardboard boxes lined on top of the cabinets. If they weren't thrown away, it was the only logical place left to look. Lunch was over by now and kids would be returning to their classes. She attempted to climb onto the cabinet shelf, but it was too narrow, and she slid off and stumbled backward.

If she were to continue this search, it would have to get noisy. And if she was caught red-handed, how would she explain herself? But she wondered, what her life would be like in a room, paying rent to the goblin woman and her faithful troll. The thought of living at home for the summer, dodging daily fights, as her mother's craziness fueled by her fanatic church sparked a bit of madness in Abby. She left the closet and pulled one of the desks inside. The metal legs screeched and left black marks on the linoleum. She pushed it against the cabinet, and recklessly stood on top of the wobbly desk, reaching into the first box. Inside it, she felt a rough organic hard surface.

"By the power of Robert Smith!"

Abby took the box down and looked inside. Halves of geodes, from fist to golf ball-sized rolled around. Gorgeous amethyst, emerald, and citrine colors sparkled at her. As a Gemini, her birthstone was a citrine. If a geode worked for the mystic Francis Truelove then it would work for her. She placed the box at her feet, climbed off the desk, and pulled a plastic bag out of her purse. She placed all of the geodes inside the bag. Today's purse was large and black with a silver zipper and a chain strap. The bag of geodes rested safely in the purse, and her last mission at school was accomplished. As she turned off the light, she heard someone open the door to the still-darkened classroom. Someone entered and shut the door quietly behind them. Whoever was moving so stealthily, certainly wasn't a teacher. Abby backed up to the desk behind her. She hoped it was students hiding, trying to make out while remaining out of view of others. Footsteps approached the closet quickly. A silhouette of a man wearing a letterman jacket stood in the archway. He reached in and turned on the lights. The man yelled and took a step back.

"What the hell are you doing here?" the student yelled. He flailed his arms as if a spider crawled down his back. It was Bradford Cummings. He was the blonde, muscular, and white-toothed football star. Most guys wanted to be him, and most girls wanted to be with him. His lawyer father bought him a new car two weeks ago, as a gift for barely passing. If Abby had a crystal ball, she predicted he would be a college dropout, divorced with two kids, and a regular at a bar eating an endless amount of chicken wings before he hit thirty. The typical life for a guy with a name like Bradford Cummings.

Abby was startled we he turned on the lights, but she held her composure.

56

Bradford pointed at her, "You know, looking the way you do, and hiding in the dark isn't good for anyone."

"Are you saying that I am ugly?" she smirked.

"No, but you are a little scary."

Abby wondered why someone like Bradford would be lurking in a science room closet. He was dumb as hell, and he only passed high school because he knew how to toss a football and made the school look good,

"So, what are you doing here, hiding in the dark?" he asked.

"I got lost."

"Lost? I bet you were doing drugs or cutting yourself," he laughed.

"I don't do either of those."

"I thought goth chicks were into that?"

"How would you know?" Abby folded her arms defensively.

"I don't know I saw it in a movie. Some girl looked like you and she killed people and ate them. Or maybe they ate her? Maybe I am thinking of two different movies at the same time, but I know someone that looked like you, did drugs, and cut themselves, in one of those movies," Bradford said. He looked confused and scratched his head.

Abby wanted to leave but didn't want him to figure out what she was doing or why she was here. "That sounds like an awful movie. So, Bradford is that your weed pipe that I saw hidden in the last drawer?"

"M-my what?" His face flushed.

"You heard what I said."

"I don't do drugs either," he said.

"Well, then we didn't see each other today."

It was the only way Abby could end the conversation, without him digging further. She assumed he was headed here to retrieve his pipe. For whatever reason he kept it here didn't matter. Maybe he hid in here to have a toke while no one suspected a thing or shared it with Mr. Carter, given it was the science room. But Brad knew that she knew, and he stepped away as she pushed by him.

"Hey, Abby, do you have any plans this weekend?"

She wondered why he would ask. He would only do it for two reasons: to make fun of her or wear her on his arm like a trophy. While her back faced him, she turned her head to the side, partially illuminated by the light from the hallway. The darkness of her features was enhanced by her essence. She smiled at him ominously. "I am joining a Satanic cult."

Brad's face went cold. "Oh."

She turned to leave with Brad never knowing why she was here in the first place.

"Why did you change?" he asked.

"I am sorry?" Her hand was on the handle of the door. She didn't turn around.

"You used to be, you know, normal and kind of hot."

It was a moment that every teenager wanted to be asked. It was that one specific question, to step to a microphone and say *who* and *what* they identify as in the face of the question *why?*

She did not have any poetic rebuttal. Her only response was, "Because The Cure changed my fucking life." She left the room and never saw Bradford Cummings again.

After school, she headed to work. Waitressing her ass off would be her main focus for the summer. In order to get the hell out of Dodge, she needed money. The creepy night manager favored her, and when she put the time in, she made good tips. After her birthday, she would be able to work later, and more importantly, she would be able to work Sundays. What prevented her from working that day up until now was her mother's strict rule that no one should work on Sunday, what she referred to as the Sabbath.

The Denny's parking lot was full, and the only space available was in the back by the dumpster. She pulled down her visor and looked in the mirror. There were times this year when she would get flashes of dark impulses. They surfaced when her mother took a turn in her pious madness. It took restraint but she hadn't acted out on any of them, but it bothered her when they surfaced. The thought occurred to her, to burn the skin on her thigh with a lighter. It was a gross feeling, but the destructive power felt romantic.

"No," she whispered.

She didn't want to fall into the trope of self-mutilation, as some goth women did. Applying heavy eye makeup was a two or three-times-a-day ritual. To her advantage, the way she looked, seemed to garner more attention from tipping patrons, or she surprised them for how warm her personality was, an unexpected contrast to her image.

With a few minutes to spare, she peeked into the mind of Francis Truelove and opened his book.

"The day after I went into deep channeling, I felt slightly different. There are claims by some who chant, of reaching enlightenment, or a higher consciousness. Have I attained it? Of this I am uncertain. Perhaps I have moments of enlightenment through daily meditation, but something was different. I had the overwhelming feeling of being watched; more so than usual. As if something from another world was peeking into my complicated life. In this, I became more conscious of my efforts, to represent myself as if I were on a stage. It should be noted that acting accordingly is not healthy for the mind to be intensely paranoid, as it can cause one to act odd, more than I already do, and that is my constant conundrum. To be and act as I should, but not be genuine or to be a sham, in order to convince others. I suppose most people who work a regular week at an office, within proximity of others, hone this skill daily. Therefore, I played as a sham. Late the following evening, I refrained from strong drink, as I had been busy in my study. A pulse moved through me. I was drawn to leave my room by an unknown force, and I could not help but look up and witness not one or two, but nearly a dozen streaks across the sky. They were diagonal, east to west and north to south. Were they meteorites? Were they chariots holding beings from another world? I do not know. So, I sat in a field by a tree and waited for the answer to come."

Abby connected with the mystic/astronomer/professor. He witnessed things, wondered, and questioned, and did not always find the answer. It was who she felt she was before she bought the book, and it was who she wanted to be, today and tomorrow as well.

The words of Francis Truelove would lay heavy on her mind, and she would let them take root in her. She hugged the book as if it were an animal that could understand her feelings and hoped for a better future.

Dante, the night manager, was standing by the back door smoking a cigarette. He slicked his hair, like a 50's greaser, and wore black and white wing-tip shoes. He used to play guitar in a dime-a-dozen type rockabilly band that toured and partied hard. It was rumored that while at the height of the band's career, Dante became a violent alcoholic and attacked his bandmates. He ended up in jail, and the band didn't post bail, as they were tired of his shit. They replaced him with another dime-a-dozen guitar player and left him somewhere in Michigan. When he dried up and had a moment of introspection, he claimed to have found Jesus. As he got cleaned up, his love for rock and roll music drew him to Nashville. The only other thing he was good at, with years of road experience was dealing with difficult people. To him, his calling was working as the late shift manager at a Denny's by the highway, dealing with drunks, truck drivers, and bitchy teens. This kept his cool-guy image carved out, as someone who had been *there* and done *that*. He made a steady paycheck, told embellished stories, and always acted like he had to be elsewhere.

He leaned against the propped-open door with his thumb in his pocket. Every pose he did, emulated a bastardized version of James Dean. Yet, Dante smelled of rehab and living off of the illusion of his best days being fifteen years ago. It was often if he was given the platform to mention how his time, back in the day, was great because of *this* or *that*. Usually, no one paid attention and smiled. The thing is, he worked hard as hell, and all of it was for his ten-year-old daughter who lived somewhere in Kentucky. He hadn't seen her in years.

"I heard some flighty keyboards and vocals that sounded like a dying bird coming out of your speakers. I guess you still listen to that goth shit?" Dante jested.

"You mean good music that doesn't suck on Elvis's fat tit? Yes, all the time." Abby said.

Dante laughed and clapped his hands.

"Can I bum a cigarette?"

"You are still a minor; I can get in trouble."

Abby wondered how many times he had said that in his lifetime.

"I will be eighteen on Wednesday."

He took his pack out of his back pocket and handed her a cigarette.

"You are telling me that after Wednesday you are old enough to buy your own cigarettes and work late shifts?"

Abby nodded her head. "And not be forced to go to church."

She held the cigarette between her lips. Dante lit it with a zippo lighter, with flames and dice on the side. She took a step back, a comfortable distance from him. Dante's posturing always gave off the vibe of a guy who could get the ladies, yet he forgot he was getting old. Grey hair didn't hide beneath the layers of cheap hair gel anymore.

"Well, not all church is bad. It helped me out some, at least when I needed it," he said.

"Yeah, but if you have your hand stuck to a hot iron and it's called Jesus, you tend to flinch when someone says religion."

"Fair enough."

A police car blazed by; its siren echoed. They both turned to watch it pass.

"So, you want full-time now, until you go to school in the fall?"

"That's the plan. I want to save as much money as possible this summer before I go off to beauty school in Nash."

He pointed at her with his cigarette hand, one eye closed as if he was shooting at a deer from a tree post. "Beauty school? I can see you working at a salon. That is the perfect job for you."

"I hope so. It is going to take a lot of time and money though."

He extinguished his cigarette into a green glass Sprite bottle.

"That's good, you sound like you got it figured out. I think you will do well on the late shift."

"Thank you."

"Just be overly nice to the other waitresses and don't let the customers get to you. Let your shit out in the back if you have to, but not on the floor. It can be a grind, especially if you are doing over thirty hours."

He looked down at his wingtips and noticed a blob of ketchupy egg on the toe.

"Son of a bitch."

He leaned down and flicked the egg onto the asphalt. The presentation of his rockabilly image was held higher than any conversation he could have with an employee, to the point where nothing else mattered. He went back inside.

Abby yelled a *thank you* to him again.

Dante grunted in frustration.

The night was a hustle. Every customer she encountered was mild to pleasant. Every tip she counted as a benefit for her future and soon-to-be freedom. The money she would make working late would forge a strong course towards that goal if nothing else went wrong. She did the math in her head and estimated she could pull in a few hundred a week. This kept her mood light.

At the end of the night, Priscilla, an abnormally skinny brunette waitress, met Abagail outside for a cigarette. Priscilla was a college dropout. She got pregnant in her first year, and the father of the child took no responsibility. Priscilla's grandmother stepped in and helped raise the baby while she worked her ass off for tips. On the side, she sold pills to truckers, who were making the long haul. At her most frustrated, she dreamt of going back to school but did not have the right encouragement to push further.

"I heard you are coming on full-time?" Priscilla asked.

"Yeah, I need to."

A light drizzle misted the parking lot. Hypnotic ovals of light formed around the lamp posts.

"Dante told me you were heading to beauty school."

"Making beautiful women, look more radiant is my passion."

"Well, you are a pretty girl, and I think women would come to you just for your energy."

Priscilla blew smoke above her. She reached into her pocket, took out a pill, and swallowed it dry.

"You don't think beauty can be drawn out of a woman?"

Priscilla laughed, "Not ugly women! I mean what do you do with a woman who has nothing to offer the world?"

"Everyone has something to offer." Abby was proud of herself for sounding like Tony, the bookstore owner.

"Well, my dear Abby, I beg to differ."

Abagail extinguished her cigarette in the Sprite bottle. "My dear Priscilla, this has been a night for me."

"Hey, Abs, do you want to go to a party tomorrow?"

It was another offer for a party she had for the weekend. For a girl who continually thought no one liked her, she was beginning to see it wasn't entirely true. Priscilla was different. She was a bit rude but more honest than anyone Abby knew; her abrasiveness felt refreshing.

Abby liked the idea of coming home late, on a Saturday before her last week of school, "I think I would like that, as long as I could get drunk or high."

"How about both?" Priscilla laughed.

"Okay then. After work tomorrow," Abby smiled.

10

Abagail was swimming underwater in a dimly lit room. The wall lamps cast green and blue hues, illuminating her way. Her first thought was that she was on a sunken cruise ship. Despite her not being a strong swimmer, nor having great lungs, she explored with no need to come up for air. She discovered she was in a library, ten times as large as the one in school. The end caps of the rows of books had placards displaying the subjects within each row. The library was filled with obscure subjects of the occult, and knowledge, that is rarely spoken of; Astral Projection, Cryptozoology, Dreams & Dimensions, and Demonology. The bizarre subjects seemed endless. The books should have been floating and bloated but were perfectly intact, sitting as they should. This did not concern Abby, as being able to breathe was more of a marvel to her. She wondered where she could find the writings of Francis Truelove, as he would be the only author she was aware of who dealt with these topics. The row titled *Channeling* caught her eye. She swam down the aisle. All of the spines were muted in colors; browns, greens, maroons, and tans, but nothing stuck out. Until she saw one book at the bottom, at the furthest corner, with a gold glowing spine. She opened it, and a ray of light came forth and touched her face. The first line of the book was in a different language. She did not know what it was, but somehow she knew how to say it.

"Nan natcattirankalaik katantu en ulakattai vittuc celven."

As the words were spoken, she was no longer in the library but was teleported to the top of a mountain. The night sky was clear above her; a heavy chill lay in the air. She looked up and said the peculiar phrase again.

"Nan natcattirankalaik katantu en ulakattai vittuc celven."

Tears streamed from her eyes. As if millions of photographs were taken from this position for the span of eons. She saw a shift in space through the arm of the Milky Way Galaxy. Flashing in a hyper-color phantasmagoria above her, she saw the clear tapestry of the cosmos; all that had been viewed from this point above the Earth before it had been habitable until its end was visible. It was a sight that no human on Earth should be capable of witnessing. Thousands upon thousands of meteorites flew by, some hit the moon, others hit the Earth as she stood untouched on an elevated piece of obsidian. Something or someone in the universe chose her to see this moment. She was elated but her heart was in pain. She wanted to yell but it could not escape her. Looking down at her trembling hands, she saw glowing eyes inside of her palms. She dropped to her knees.

"What is happening? Am I dying? Am I dead?"

She grabbed her chest and wondered if she was having a heart attack. This was too much for a human to experience. Despite her hunger for the unknown and the majesty of the universe, this was overwhelming. Whispering to herself, she wanted to be back home.

She awoke in her bed. Above her were white Christmas lights she had tacked to the ceiling; they were in a spiral. The goal was to make them look like a galaxy, so she could stare into it before she drifted off to sleep. They had been up there for months. It was unlikely this was the catalyst for her dream. It had to be from the writings of Francis Truelove.

The dream was overwhelming and too real. Her heart palpitated. There was no way to explain to a living soul and not be mocked for her out-of-body experience. Did Truelove experience these same things? Then she started laughing, and covered her mouth, in shock at her outburst. Moments like this would get her through the summer, they would help her from going crazy in a house run by a possibly insane person.

Dario meowed at her. He twirled in a circle on the floor. She scratched his back, and he raised his tail.

"I don't know. I feel different though." She answered him as if he understood.

Although she could not place it, there was a hunger inside her, that wasn't there before. She got dressed and retrieved the Francis Truelove book from under her bed. It was hidden in a paper bag with an old newspaper and a fashion magazine. She opened it, flipped through it, and tried making sense of what she had said in the dream.

"Nan natcattirankalaik katappen," she whispered. "What the hell could that mean?"

She opened the book and flipped through the pages. "It has to be an incantation."

Dario meowed again.

"Dammit Dario, give me a minute."

Conducting something of this nature couldn't be done within the walls of this house. If her mother even heard a whisper of this, all of the members of The East Holy Tabernacle of Blueville would be marching up the stairs screaming holy words of terror at her. It would have to be outside, and away from everyone, just as Truelove had said, "Under the tapestry."

She pondered for a suitable spot and finally thought of a place to do the ritual. It wasn't perfect, but it would do. The stolen geodes were hidden in a plastic bag in an old shoe box, with dirty Chuck Taylor's in it. She felt bad for stealing, as it wasn't her way. However, the geodes sat unused and forgotten for so long, that if Mr. Carter found out she stole them for something so grand, he may not mind at all. Also, she had good reason to assume he was a pothead.

Looking in the mirror, while holding the citrine geodes in her hand, she felt the hunger change within her. This was a different desire. It was the same feeling when she imagined herself elsewhere, working, and living on her own. It was a spirit of adventure. This feeling is what she would fight for, this would keep her from sinking into a depressed slump, and this would keep her alive.

To partake in the old ritual, she needed chalk. There was some in an old Tupperware container in the pantry.

"Well, Mr. Truelove, I am sure that I am not the first to do this, but I doubt there is anyone on Earth doing this exact thing today, so I hope I get it right."

Descending the stairs quietly, with Dario trailing behind her, she headed to the kitchen. Richard usually went to work a half day on Saturday for overtime. Even though he was culpable for the odd setting in the house, he probably needed a break from Nova as well. The house was oddly quiet. There was a fifty-fifty chance her mother was home. Either she was locked away in her biblical devotions or she was out in the world on a self-propelled mission from God.

Dario meowed incessantly as he followed Abby.

"Shut up, you might wake her," she whispered. "I don't want to hear any of her bullshit this morning."

As Abby entered the kitchen, she discovered her mother on her knees. A cup of tea was in front of her. She had a white veil over her face and was adorned in a loose white, long-sleeved dress.

"What are you referring to?" her mother asked. She was holding a teacup in her hand.

"Jeez, mother you scared me." Abby put her hand on her chest. "Why are you on the floor, and dressed like a bride going to a funeral?"

Her mother's head jerked like it was hit with a pellet. Her obscured gaze was intense. Abagail felt as if her mother was attempting to use some sort of mind control on her. Abby looked away and opened the cupboard to get Dario's food.

"In biblical times, women of the church, whilst in prayer wore veils. It has been a practice of the old Pentecostals to partake in. Some sects of the church had done away with it, to be more modern, but I feel it needs to be brought back, especially when I am waiting on the Spirit." Nova's voice held a vibrato tone like she was announcing a contestant on a game show to run through the audience.

Abby fed Dario. He crunched loudly and purred while eating. Abby petted him. He looked up at Abby and slowly blinked at her, then continued to eat. It was the affection between a particular cat owner that went beyond human emotion. The cat truly loved the owner, the owner truly loved the cat and they said so with their eyes.

Retrieving the chalk was vital. Abby wanted to do this ritual before work, and it had to be today. It would be out of the ordinary for Abby to just go in the pantry as her mother would question her. Abby opened the cupboard above the sink and took out a box of Pop-Tarts. She opened a package, put both Pop-Tarts in the toaster, and held onto the box. These past months, eating breakfast in the house had become a rarity for her, as sitting with a vicious jackal was never good company.

"So, will you go out in public like that? I mean, I know we are in the Bible Belt, but that veil is a bit much," Abby said.

Abruptly, her mother got up and tossed the tea into the sink. She put the cup on the counter.

"I can't have a minute of peace in this house with you, can I? The Devil seeks to rob God's people, and God's chosen daily, and here he sends my daughter, to play into his tricks."

"A rational thought is considered the Devil's tricks?" Abby asked.

Her mother pointed her shaking finger. "Abagail Gibson!"

"Mother, I am trying to bring reason."

"Get out!" Nova yelled. Her chest rose and fell erratically like a large balloon was inside of her.

"Mother, you need to calm down."

"Be gone!" Nova shouted again but raised her hands in the air, "I command you to be gone!"

Abby stepped into the pantry and put the Pop-Tarts on a shelf. She spotted the Tupperware container. She picked it up, held it on her left side, out of her mother's view, and walked passed her.

"Do you know how the Devil works? How he tries to lie, kill, and destroy every day! God's people, warriors for souls, do not stay the course. They backslide and give into temptation before they die. Yet, I am one of the few that are constant!"

The Pop Tart ejected. It was slightly brown and smelled of delicious fruit paste and high fructose corn syrup. Abby wanted it but it wasn't worth spending another second in her mother's presence.

Abby looked back at the cat dish and Dario was gone. He wasn't going to put up with her shit, either. He was probably in the front window, licking his chops. She grabbed her keys and Doc Martens and headed out. As she left, still walking in her socks, her mother continued to yell.

"You listen to me! Before we moved here, I raised you, not Richard, it was I who made the decisions to keep you alive, to keep you from iniquity, it was I who climbed the mountain of righteousness, with you clutching my hand, it was I!"

Hastily, Abby walked a few steps on the pebble path, stooped down, and slid on her boots. In their backyard, at the top of the hill was a metal gate that was never used. It led into a small road; so small it didn't have a street sign. It was just called Chuchi's Street. Chuchi was the old Polish lady who used to live there, and her house had the biggest lot on the road. Next to Chuchi's house, was an unkempt field with a netless tennis court. An anarchy symbol was spray painted on it. Everyone who saw this knew it was done by Billy Meyers, because next to the anarchy symbol, in the same color paint was the name, Billy, and Billy was dumb enough to do such a thing. This would be the place for Francis Truelove's ritual.

"Abagail! Are you listening!" Nova screamed as she was in mid-tirade, holding the screen door open with one hand. In the noonday sun, with the veil on her head, Abby thought her mother looked like a witch from a dreadful 70's horror film. The words that were spewed were far from Godly, but something that belonged to a person who missed theater class and missed their sedatives as well.

As much as Abby wanted to be meditative, as much as she wanted to survive the rest of her time this summer, she lost her cool.

"Mother, shut the fuck up and go stick that hot Pop-tart up your ass!"

Abby ran through the backyard. She cried and laughed. Her mother was more batshit than ever. She didn't mean to curse, *hell* would have been better than *fuck*, as there were known tiers in the realm of cursing, but to someone like her mother, words that weren't even curses were still curses to her.

As Abby ran to the top of the hill, she flung open the metal gate and headed into the open field. The weeds were tall, if she wouldn't have known of the tennis court, it would have been easily missed. It was just a 2000 square-foot piece of abandoned, graffitied slab. A place where people used to hang out, and eventually defiled. It was a perfect place for a chalk-drawn, old mystic ritual.

Abby sat down in the middle of the court, facing south, in the direction of her house. She could see the top of her house, and the slanted roof where she collected her thoughts. She waited a moment and did not hear her mother pursuing. Despite her mother's need to be heard, it seemed that the hill thwarted her conquest.

Since Abby read of this bizarre ritual, she couldn't wait for another second to try it. Her hands were shaking; a shaking greater than the jarring

70

moment facing her mother's outburst. She removed the geodes from her purse and placed the Tupperware of chalk next to them.

"Oh shit."

The Francis Trulove book was still in her room. She hoped she didn't leave it exposed on her bed. If records from The Cure didn't survive, then it would be certain that an old book with occult symbols would be torn to shreds.

There was no way she could go back now; not after that exit.

"Okay, it was a circle, symbols, geodes, chakra, and chant."

Her birth symbol was Mercury, and she knew what that looked like. Rose wanted to buy her a necklace with the symbol on it. Then, Abby thought it would be a bad idea. As astrological signs were forbidden in the house.

With chalk in hand, Abby drew two lines with an arched top and bottom to her right, and to her left, she drew Saturn's symbol; a tall cross with a hook on it. She got up, picked up some dirt in her palm and spit on it, made it into mud, and put it on her forehead, then sat back in the circle. Crossing her legs in a half lotus, she lifted each citrine geode in her hand and closed her eyes. Meditation was something she had done before. It was something Rose practiced and she tried getting Abby into it. Abby didn't mind meditating, but she was never diligent enough to build a regimen. Thoughts raced through her mind as she sat with her eyes closed. A light breeze blew and rustled the branches of oak trees behind her. Painfully, she realized in order to speak to the universe, to be heard through some obscure archaic practice, saying *fuck* to one's mother shouldn't have been the previous action, regardless of how irrational they acted.

"Aaaaaaaaaooooooooooo," Abby chanted. It sounded weird but it was unique enough that she welcomed it immediately.

"Aaaaaaaaaaaaaaaum."

The first thought that entered her mind, was the tension at home; her mind was not clear. She took a deep breath and focused. In the distance, kids were splashing in a pool. Birds chirped on a telephone wire. An air conditioner hummed in a nearby house.

"I don't want to hold onto anything. I don't want anything to hold onto me. I want to let go of everything; I don't want anything to bring me down. If I could leave this place, I would, and I certainly wouldn't look back."

The phrase she uttered in her dream came back to her. *Nan natcattirankalaik katantu en ulakattai vittuc celven.* She heard it in her mind but couldn't speak it.

"Aaaaaaaaaoooooooooo. Aaaaaaaaaaaaaaum," she chanted. Over and over, she hummed with echoes mimicking the slow reverberations felt deep within the Earth.

"Nan natcattirankalaik katantu."

She focused and hummed the syllables from what she recalled.

"Nan natcattirankalaik katantu en ulakattai vittuc celven."

As she uttered the words, chirping birds flew away. Miles from here, down by the train tracks, a freight train signaled its passing at a crossroads.

And then she understood what she was saying.

"I will cross the stars and leave my world behind," she said.

An old woman laughed out the window of a nearby home. A half block away, on the lower street, a boy fell on his bike. Abby heard the clatter of metal on asphalt. The boy cursed. A dog ran in front of a car and the car slammed on its brakes. The dog put his head down, went back on the sidewalk, and ran home.

"Nan natcattirankalaik katappen," she said. The bizarre language began to make sense. It wasn't what she was saying, it was what she was feeling. "I will cross the stars!"

Her mind wandered. She was in a cave, maybe from this time period or another; it didn't matter, except for being alone, and in that loneliness was solace. There was nothing to prove to anyone, no standing amongst others. All that was ever-present was the human mind bouncing resonances of the internal workings of a deep cavern in dim light, brought on by far away flame; crackling in the distance. Water was near and it came up from underneath the ground, bubbling, traveling, and pooling elsewhere, disappearing into cracks and fissures, further off in the darkness.

"Katantu celven."

A cloud passed in front of the sun. The shadow was sensed through her eyelids. Without any bearing, she believed the ritual was done. Aside from calming her mind, she didn't recognize anything different around her. The world still looked and felt the same, but she felt centered. It was time to head to work. She put the geodes and chalk in her purse, and walked alongside the outer part of her fence, through the Jackson's yard. Her car was parked in the port. She wanted to leave without being noticed.

Anxiety should have met her by the car, but it didn't. The odd meditation and magical incantation did something to her. As Abby sat in her car, in the dimness of the carport, she noticed something written on her windshield in soap. The writing had the same terrifying angles and cuts that the old records suffered from. Her mother did this. She came into the carport in the same fury she had the night of cutting The Cure records. Abby recognized the biblical passage in reverse.

It was a Bible chapter and verse: Proverbs 13:24

She started the car and turned on the windshield wipers. It smeared the soap and made it worse. For the sake of safety, she would have to stop at a car wash and spray the religious graffiti off. Just as Billy Meyers was known for spray painting an anarchy symbol on a forgotten tennis court, Nova Gibson, the end-time prophet was known, only amongst a few, as a religious zealot; one so bold to use an edge of a bar of soap to scrawl a warning on her daughter's windshield.

"Whoever spares the rod hates his son or daughter, but he who loves him or her is diligent to discipline him. Thank you Mother for the Bible lesson today," Abby whispered.

She drove down the street to the stop sign and put on her blinker. The driver in the other vehicle slammed on their horn as Abby didn't have the right of way. She did not see them with the white smear of soap across her windshield. She waved and mouthed *I'm sorry*, through the passenger window to them and headed towards the car wash on the outskirts of town. She wondered if the ritual did anything. Did she change something in herself and make her voice heard in the cosmos, or was she just as crazy as the person who raised her?

11

The shift that evening was demanding enough to keep her mind off the tension at home. Abby kept focused and the tips were good. It was a lesson to her, as part of the working class; work still needed to get done, regardless of what hell was waiting at home. But in the back of her mind, like a shadow standing in the corner, was the wonderful but odd feeling from the incantation she had done; she would revisit the ritual. It felt suitable to be part of something so archaic and unique, arising from a relic tucked away in a random used bookstore.

The other waitresses had always been friendly, but Priscilla had gravitated toward her. Part of it was because Abby felt comfortable enough to let her guard down with her. She admired Priscilla, a single mother, who held her shit together. As Abby would be putting in more hours this summer, she wanted to create an ally at work, maybe even call her a friend. It didn't take much coaxing from Priscilla to get Abby to go to a party later. It was in a shitty part of town where no one cared who or what you were.

After her shift ended, Abby changed in the bathroom. There wasn't a need to bring out both guns, in terms of how she preferred to dress, but if she was going out in a new social circle, even at a trailer park, she wanted to have her hair and make-up done. Her eye makeup was heavy and dark, and her hair was on par with an 80's new wave rock video.

When the shift was over, she followed Priscilla's car to the party. Abby was amazed at how far out she lived. They approached a trailer park called Heather Field Oaks. It was behind a partially abandoned strip mall across the street from a junkyard. Abby didn't judge people's class or living accommodations, but this place felt unsafe. An uneasiness settled in. Her desire to get drunk and high started to shrink as she passed dilapidated trailer after trailer. Car parts and rusted-out vehicles were in and around every yard.

A man and woman sat on a couch, that was placed on the roof of their double-wide trailer. They watched the girls' vehicles pass. The front of their short driveway had a row of old washing machines which were used as a gate to prevent other cars from entering their property. The headlights from the girls' vehicles were the only source of light, aside from the dim glow under tattered lampshades and TV's with muted colors from the interiors of thin shells called homes.

They pulled into an ash lot. A half dozen pickup trucks were out front. Two of them had the rebel flag as decals in the entirety of the back windows. Country music was playing from the inside of one of the two trailers ahead. It was obvious the party was between both places. A man laughed from the darkness and yelled that he was going to *kill someone* with his *fucking knife*. It was followed by more laughter from others. A shirtless man was lifting cinderblocks over his head and tossing them into a hole. One of the bricks bounced and came out of the hole and knocked over an empty whiskey bottle. Two other shirtless men cheered when it did.

Abby didn't want to stay for more than a minute, but she felt obligated to Priscilla's invite. It was a bad place that teenagers get stuck in went they want to impress their peers and don't know how to back out. Priscilla complimented Abby's hair and make-up. She told her that she wished she was as pretty as her. That was an anchor to tie Abby in for at least one drink. A compliment given so selflessly was something Abby yearned for.

Priscilla took a joint out of her purse. She lit it, inhaled, and handed it to Abby. Abby never smoked weed before. She took a drag, inhaled, and coughed viciously. To Abby's surprise, Priscilla didn't mock her. She patted her on the back. Abby took another puff, held it longer, and coughed again. The world swirled around her. A trailing end of her mother's earlier rant permeated in the back of her mind.

They stood for a moment and finished the joint, as Abby never recovered from her coughing fit; she sputtered and excused herself. Priscilla informed her that there would be some single boys here. Abby shuddered at the thought; that wasn't what she was here for.

She was dizzy but felt elated. However, an invisible bird of warning landed on her shoulder. She ignored it and followed Priscilla into the trailer on the left. The room they entered was small and filled with older men standing around drinking Schlitz beers and smoking cigarillos. When they saw Abby enter, they all stopped talking and looked at her like she had antlers growing out of her head. Each balding and oily middle-aged man was caked with the soot of the world and creased by broken endeavors; they breathed quietly as smoke rose from the orange coals of their cheap gas station cigars. Priscilla broke the tension and introduced Abagail; commented on the baseball game, that no one was watching, and pulled her into the kitchen by the hand. Mocking laughter followed as Abby left the room.

"Ignore them, they are jerks. Well, most of them are, half of them are my cousins or maybe half cousins," Priscilla said.

A large woman in a pair of pink overalls and pigtails came out of the bathroom. She was holding a baby. A cigarette hung out of the woman's mouth. She asked the girls if they wanted shots. Priscilla kissed the baby and said *yes*. Whiskey was poured into shot glasses with the word *Vegas* written on the side. The girls toasted and slammed the shots. Abby coughed and covered her mouth with her palm. Priscilla poured a second round. The woman with the baby handed Abby a can of beer as a chaser. They drank the second round and Priscilla slammed her glass on the counter. The loud noise scared the baby and it cried. The woman shushed the baby and rocked it side to side. After the third shot was done, Abby went from rebellious and uncomfortable to nauseous and flustered. She regretted coming here. Going home and dealing with unexpected outbursts was better than this.

A man with thick sideburns and a John Deere hat entered the kitchen. His eyes were dark, darker than Abby's pretended to be. His belly hung over his belt buckle. He kissed Priscilla on the lips, kissed the baby, and poured a shot for himself. They all toasted and slammed them. Abby coughed again and chased it with the beer. She wanted to leave. The man told a dirty joke and messed up the punchline. The woman with the baby called him an idiot. Abby excused herself and went out on the back porch.

Hot inebriation flooded her cognizance. She put a cigarette between her lips but did not have a lighter. A man emerged from the shadows of the awning. He held out a lighter and lit it for her. She thanked him but could not see his face. His baseball hat kept his features out of view. He told her she was pretty, but pretty in a *weird* way. Abby thanked him. The eclipsed

77

man asked her if she had a boyfriend. Abby told him that she was still in high school. He laughed and said, "So that is a *no* then?"

Abby did not answer him. She looked away and took a drag. Contemptuously, she blew smoke above her and looked at the moon. A moon that had been pelted with meteorites for eons and had craters to prove such an event. The man told her that he drove a truck and was going to start his own trucking company. Without facing the man, Abby said that was *nice*, in an overly cool tone. From inside, Priscilla laughed wildly. Abby looked through the broken Venetian blinds and saw Priscilla dancing with a lampshade on her head.

A text saying that she was *sorry* would be Abby's cover. She told her shadowy acquaintance that she would be back in a minute and stepped off the porch. She walked around the trailer and left without saying goodbye to Priscilla.

A chain link fence was in between the backyard, and an adjacent property. She ran her fingers across the fence. There was a small shack on the other property. As she passed the shack, something growled from the darkness. Looking directly into the hollow black shape, a dark silhouette scampered toward her. She backed away, but her balance was off. A dog barked in rapid fire. Then she realized it was two. In her drunken state, the dog appeared to have one body and two heads. The dogs pushed against the fence and snarled ferociously. Their attack stance caused her to stumble backward and fall into the rocky dirt.

She rolled onto her knee, got up, and ran to her car. When she got inside, a harsh reality set in, she was too impaired to drive. It was a fear she never faced before. Getting arrested for driving drunk would be bad, but getting in an accident and hurting someone else was far worse. Desperately, she contemplated her next move. Going back inside wasn't a good idea. She started her car and waited. If magic existed, like the words the famed mystic/astronomer/professor Francis Truelove spoke of, she would wish the alcohol out of her system or teleport back home.

An old man in a fedora and a dirty white tank top approached her car. He pressed his crimson face to her window; it was porous and torn like a dog chew toy.

"What the hell are you doing here you goddam freak?" he shouted.

Simultaneously, she reached into her purse and grabbed the pepper spray while putting the window down an inch.

"Is that mace? You gonna mace me on my own fucking property! You're the dumb bitch who parked in my yard!"

He kicked the driver's side door with his muddy boot and hurled more insults at her. Rapidly, Abby turned on the headlights and backed out of the man's yard. His yelling continued as he slapped the side of her window with his palm. In a panic, she sped onto the dirt road; rocks bounced off the undercarriage of her car. The main road was ahead. Without caution, she turned into traffic. Her motor functions were off. This was the first time she drove under the influence. A car slammed on the brakes ahead of her. She buried her foot into the brake pedal and the car screeched. Driving was not a safe option; she had to pull over.

Driving slowly, she spotted a gas station and parked crooked in front of a pump. It was eleven o'clock. Anxiety set in. Sleeping in the parking lot was the next best option.

"A chocolate milk will calm me down."

She went inside and staggered through the aisles, acting exactly like a newly drunk seventeen-year-old should. She purchased chocolate milk and pretzels and thought of Sutton. She texted him. In under a minute, he responded. Sipping on her chocolate milk, with shaky hands she asked if he could pick her up and apologized profusely.

He called her.

"H-hello," he stuttered. "Abby, are you okay?'

"Yes, I am now. I am so sorry. I went to a party with a girl from work, and I got drunk. Then these creepy guys got creepier. Some old man with a gangly face came after me. So, I left, and I..."

"You need a ride home," he said. There was no judgment in his voice.

"Yes." She struggled to open the bag of pretzels.

"Where are you?"

"I am at a 7/11 on the corner of 7th and Adams across from a McDonald's."

"Okay. Go sit in your passenger seat and don't put the keys in the ignition. If for any reason a cop asks what you are doing, just tell him you are waiting for your friend. You can't get in trouble that way."

"Got it."

She sat in her passenger seat and waited. In her paranoid mindset, she thought every car that pulled in was the police. She convinced herself she was getting a DUI. A half-hour passed and Sutton came as he promised. She ran and hugged him. He welcomed the attention, which was part of the reason why he came to rescue her. He parked her car across the street in the back of the McDonald's, then he took her home. He barely said a word as he drove. A country song played dimly on the radio. Abby kept her eyes closed. When he pulled up to her house, she was without words for his kindness. Even though he wasn't someone she could ever picture herself with, he was the best guy she knew.

She wanted to tell him that but after the day she had; the words couldn't be formed.

"Will you be okay tomorrow getting your car?"

"I didn't even think of that. I don't know."

"Well, if you need a ride, let me know."

"Thank you."

She put her hand on his. He kept his head forward and looked at her with his peripherals as if he were a puppy thinking it was in trouble. His awkwardness gave away how much he liked her, and she knew this even in her drunken state.

"I would have been sleeping in a parking lot, if you didn't pick me up."

He looked at her intently, "I wouldn't have let that happen."

"Thank you, again," she said. As she exited the car, she closed the door as quietly as possible.

The serenity of the warm pre-summer night was in full force. The weed and alcohol were also in effect. Crickets chirped in high song, through the humidity. She tried to shake off the grimy feeling from the party and closed her eyes, absorbing the safety of the moment. Knowing how her mother could get, Abby didn't know what to expect when she went inside. But it was certainly better than being drunk in a dangerous trailer park with Neanderthals; a lesson learned.

As quietly as she could, she unlocked the front door. To her surprise the downstairs was dark. Only the light from the kitchen stove shone faintly in the hallway. There were voices outback. Others were here. Abby didn't even notice if there were other cars on the street. Her mother cackled and it carried into the night. Then Abby heard the worship weapons: a clink of a tambourine, a half strum of an acoustic guitar, and a rattle of a maraca. She cringed and realized a private Bible study/worship service was being held. It happened every so often and usually set an awful tone.

"Oh, by the hand of Robert Smith, no," she whispered.

Dario meowed from the darkness.

"How long have they been going at it? You should have called the cops."

Dario seemed to agree, with a half twirl and a flick of his tail.

Abby walked up to the screen door and remained out of view. Tiki torches were lit around the small pavilion in the center of the backyard. Three members of the church were present, along with Richard and Nova. Two of the members were women, Stephanie Boardman, and Cindy Thurman. Both were without husbands, and they were the worship leaders of the church. They were always together. Secretly, Abby hoped they would come out as a lesbian couple. It would be beautiful if it were true, as some church members would shave their heads in protest.

Stephanie was standing and swaying, with her eyes closed. Cindy was strumming softly, in minor keys. They were as out there as Abby's mother was. The third person was Darrel Thompson, he was one of the few African Americans that attended the church. He was sweet-spirited and often just responded with a *Yes, Lord*, when the pastor preached or while someone was praying with intensity. Abby noticed her recent finds from the bookstore were on the picnic table. She could make out the shape of Charles Manson's black-and-white photo on the cover of the cult book. If bringing that into the house caused this event, then Abby underestimated her mother. It was possible that her mother could have received one of her visions and wanted to share it and make herself look extra special before tomorrow's service.

What mattered most was what was going to happen to the Francis Truelove book? It was irreplaceable. She would rather be yelled at for coming home drunk than lose it. If it weren't for the guests, Abby would march out there, not say anything, and bring it inside. With her mother already chalking up one strike across the cheek, and a razor blade to a record, Abby was scared that if she ran out to get the book, they may chase her around the yard with tiki torches, followed by a plethora of speaking in tongues.

Although Trulove didn't believe in fate, that is all that the book had going for it. If it survived the night, it would be a miracle. Thirst crept in. Abby drank a glass of water, looked in the fridge, and ate a slice of rolled-up American Cheese. With nothing else to do but wait, she crept upstairs. She washed her makeup off in the bathroom, got changed, and peeked outside her bedroom window. The small church group had broken into a rambunctious prayer service. It was common for this to happen when a few Pentecostals got together. Given the time of night, before the Sunday service, it was akin to an alcoholic having a few drinks before going on a bender.

Nova burst a banter of glossolalia, and all followed, jumped up and down, and clapped their hands, except for Richard. They enclosed Richard in a circle, by holding hands around him. One after another yelled passages from the Bible mixed with bold proclamations of faith. Stephanie claimed God told her that Richard had to be bold in his faith, in doing this, he would be a true man of God. Abby furrowed her brow.

After the Spirit spoke through Stephanie, there were shouts of praise and more clapping. The incessant clapping always tied in the praises to God, often went on to excruciating lengths. Richard with raised hands, appeared sullen. Abby looked at the clock and it was past midnight. More clapping continued. The tambourine shook, followed by the maraca and the strumming of the guitar. Abby laid down and put the pillow over her head.

If the party she left was drunken and dangerous with embers of self-destruction abound, then the midnight worship service in her backyard was a suicide bomber with a dynamite vest. She feared that their freedom in the Spirit would destroy her precious book. It was sacred to her, as its rituals and words were keeping her stable. The room spun, and she wanted to throw up. She rolled onto her stomach and fought the urge. Aside from the nausea, she was grateful to be in her bed rather than be curled around a putrid toilet in a trailer, with horrifying-looking cousins being too cousinly with each other. A slow-motion image of a shirtless man throwing a cinder block in a hole while laughing wildly was the last thing she thought of before she fell asleep.

12

The merciless blunt hammering of a firm hangover loomed over Abby, like a shovel breaking through a rusted pipe. As always, Dario was relentless about being fed and hopped on her in excess, meowing as if nothing in the world mattered but his needs. The incessant maddening of the cat's persistence forced her to awaken fully. Abby bolted upright and was sick to her stomach. It was still dark outside. Without looking at the clock, she guessed it was around six. Grumbling curses, she shuffled downstairs and told Dario she loved him as they traveled into the kitchen. He purred and yelled until she fed him. Then he purred while he ate. Sitting quietly, in regret for drinking so much, she sat at the kitchen table in post-inebriated silence.

Like a specter appearing in a haunted house, her mother stepped out of the pantry. Abby was startled. The hair stood up on her arms, and her mother appeared ghostly in her white gown. Abby pretended to remain stoic, as subduing her emotions in front of her mother was key to survival.

"I have been in prayer for your soul, as I fear it is in jeopardy." Nova's voice was strained. She had the composure as if she just ran three miles and was sweating just as much.

"How about good morning, do want some eggs?" Abby whispered.

"I assume you were out drinking last night?"

"Yes," Abby wanted to pretend her awful night was fun, to reveal to her mother there was a world outside of here that wasn't so dismal.

"Where was this place of Gomorrah?".

"At a trailer park, with a girl I know from work."

"Whom?"

"A nice girl named Priscilla."

Abby didn't know why she told her mother, as she wanted to keep her in the dark as much as possible. Priscilla would never replace Rose, and Abby could never see herself visiting her world again. It just felt good to tell her mother she had a friend. Sadly, Priscilla was the closest girlfriend she had.

"Trailer trash and drunkenness. Did you toss your virginity into the hands of the Devil's lap as well? Do you realize what could have happened to you?"

With how the events unfolded last night, Abby partially agreed with her mother. Abby thought her reason to go so far into darkness was caused by the torch of judgment her mother persistently carried in front of her. She opened the refrigerator, took out two small strawberry yogurts, and ate them quickly.

"I know how to take care of myself," she said.

"No, you don't," Nova said.

"Am I sitting in the kitchen or am I dead in a ditch?"

"I despise the way you act. I hate the way you look. You look like a witch. Worst of all your tone is putrid." Nova's arms hung at her side. Normal posturing was gone. She acted like a wisp appearing after a conjuring.

"You bring this tone out of me. Months ago, we weren't like this. I don't know what happened to you, or why you went balls deep into that stupid church."

"Language!"

"No, Mother let's have this conversation. Was it being promoted to a prophet? Is it all that end-times bullshit? The return of Christ and the battle for souls and Armageddon? Because the way you act isn't Christian. And if you want to hit me and yell from the Bible all day, I will yell hypocrite louder."

"Oh, Abagail. I have seen what the world allows to pass for goodness and what God sees and frowns upon. The wretchedness of youth, the casting away of holy things. All of the forthcoming judgment cannot be stopped, but a few can be saved."

"That's it then, no conversation? Just skip right to the doom of the world. I wish you would ground me or tell me more about how I look like a witch, but *no*. The end of the world is here and the great prophet from a fifty-person church, in Shitsville, Tennessee has all the world's answers."

Nova shook in fury. Her parenting gauge was gone. Her self-control was drained away by incessant fasting and diet pills. Nova had been on a three-day run of drinking chicken broth. It was her only sustenance while she was on a long fast. Fasting was considered crucial in biblical times. Prophets and wise men, who wanted to consecrate their bodies and lives to God would take on this taxing practice. To add to Nova's misconceptions, was the isolation from the rational world.

"Abagail Gibson, your path of iniquity will lead you to the road to hell!"

She stepped toward Abby, with her hand raised, ready to slap her. Abby stood up and braced her hand against her mother's striking arm.

"Let's not dish out anymore abuse today." Abby was surprised at how calmly she spoke. Nova was taken aback by Abby's defensive action.

"I am going back to bed before my last church service ever. Now excuse me, I need to throw up first."

As Abby left the kitchen, her mother spoke sharply, "Judgment will fall upon you."

Abby walked up the stairs and didn't hesitate with her response, "Thank you, Mother, then I will wait for it."

As Abby had promised, she did get up on time and got ready to go to her last church service. Her phone alarm woke her, and it was nearly dead. She plugged it in. There were two missed texts from Priscilla and Sutton. She would text them on the way to church. As she got ready, she made up her mind that she wanted to go out with a bang.

With grandiosity, she teased out her hair, higher and wider than it ever had been. Robert Smith himself would be jealous. A week ago, she found a black glittered crow pin at a thrift store. It was intended to be a broach. It fit neatly in her nest of hair behind her ear. The black dress had a white collar and short sleeves. Small black cat hairs were visible. There were always a few cat hairs on all of her outfits. She used the roller to try and remove them. Her black cardigan would cover it, regardless of the heat, she always brought it with her. The final touch, for the church members to enjoy on her last day of attendance was the make-up. The palette was black eye shadow with silver eyelashes and black lipstick. In the past few weeks of attendance, she kept her goth persona at fifty percent, just to steer away from drama, but today, as she was judged by her mother, nothing was holding her back.

Her phone was still charging under multiple layers of discarded outfits, and she left the house without it.

When Abby came downstairs, she stood in the front room and looked out the window. Nova looked at her and yelled *no*, not once but five times.

Richard surprisingly defended Abby calmy. "Let her go."

"I will not be embarrassed," Nova said.

"Think of this, after this week, I won't be in your presence to embarrass you anymore. And I will be paying rent here as well," Abby said.

Nova stormed outside and slammed the car door when she got in. They rode in silence. It dawned on Abby that her car was still at the McDonald's parking lot. She didn't bring it up, as it would start another fight. Richard would have to take her after the service. Maybe they could cut out early since her mother liked to linger for hours afterward and pray for everything in the world that did or didn't deserve it.

When they arrived at church it was the same two dozen cars as it had always been for the past four years of attending. The church only held around fifty parishioners and saw little growth. The head pastor, Jack Ulma was an unlikeable, hard-nosed right-wing politics person. His bloated jowls hung over his tight dress collar, with a red mark on his forehead that was mildly Gorbachevian. He put Christian values in everything and would argue to no end about how there was a certain way America must be, and he terrified Abby. With the way he acted and how her mother prophesied, Abby wondered how the outside world would react if they heard the insane things that were spoken each week.

The song service was the usual hour of torture. It was led by Stephanie Boardman, and Cindy Thurman, somehow fresh-faced, as only hours earlier they were in Abby's backyard. The jumping and the shouting and the tambourines were like bombs going off in Abby's skull. A retired accountant played the bass guitar, with as much enthusiasm as a retired accountant could do. His teenage son played the drums with as much rhythm as an unenthusiastic retired accountant's brainwashed church teen could do. Every church member had a tambourine or maraca, banging and shimmering in and off the beat with the amplified kick drum. They sang and yelped in and off key with the amplified vocals of Stephanie's voice which had the pitch of an ill mixed-breed dog.

The pastor's wife, Mildred, played the organ in between songs to keep the flow of the Spirit. She looked like a sweet old church lady but was not.

She kept tabs on people, who gave and who didn't, who stayed the whole service, and who cut out early. She was a thorn in the side of some of the families and was part of the reason why the church didn't expand. When the parishioners were ignited with the height of emotionalism, they would jump up and down, clap hands, and claim victory in the Spirit by marching up and down the aisles, yelling praises and proclamations at random. As one would do this, others would outperform another's flamboyance, as an action of showboatism, to prove who could get into the *Spirit* more than the other. Running up and down the aisles would surface near the end of the song service, which encouraged the children to partake in spiritual worship gymnastics.

By the end, most of the parishioners were in the aisles dancing and flaying and shaking in explosions of self-hysteria. As always, Pastor Ulma stood the entire song service and clapped his hands slowly and inaudibly, as he was waiting on what God had in store for the church that day. Before the pastor's time to preach, Nova would go behind the pulpit. It was only for a few minutes. She shared with the congregation, the revelations that were on her heart. Last night's faux revelation was about the doom of the young people of America.

This morning, she slowly came behind the pulpit. She didn't look well. As she spoke in cryptic banter, she looked at Abby and told the congregation that her daughter was lost. Abby wasn't paying attention until she saw everyone turn around and look at her. Nova held up Abby's book about cults, with Charles Manson smiling manically on the cover. Nova told the congregation that the Devil was tearing at her daughter's soul. As people glared at her, agreeing with everything Nova said, Abby became flush. The thought of being hit in the head by a cinderblock from a shirtless trailer park drunk seemed less painful than this. Abby smiled at everyone and waved.

Nova stretched her hands toward Abby. She told the congregation that her daughter made a claim she wasn't returning after today. Everyone shook their heads and grimaced their faces at her. Members stood up and stretched their hands towards Abby. Some called on *Jesus*, and others yelled at the *Devil*. Abby's head swirled, as she sweated profusely. Earlier, she lied, when she told her mother she was going to throw up. Because the feeling she had then was much worse now. She doubled over, holding her mouth, and retched in front of everyone. The congregation gasped in horror.

Pastor Ulma shouted, "That is a demon coming out of her system!"

The crowd agreed with him. Some rejoiced and shook tambourines, and others shouted. Abby ran to the bathroom. It was a small single-stall unit. She locked the door behind her and threw up again. As gross as it was, she felt comforted by kneeling in front of the toilet while placing her arms over the seat and let her head hang over the water. Her reflection in the vomitous bowl looked like a crow's nest peering out of the pit of hell. A woman banged on the door and asked if she was all right. Abby didn't recognize her voice.

Carefully, Abby stood up and her legs shook. She scrubbed her hands and wiped her mouth. Her makeup was smeared. She placed a wet stack of paper towels on the back of her neck. Sweat dripped from her face, smearing the silver and black and white makeup, and gave her the appearance of an angry ghost clown.

Another woman's voice was heard outside the door. She said that throwing up was a sign of possession. A third voice said that they needed to lay hands on Abby and exorcise the demon.

Abby snapped, "All of you need to shut the fuck up and leave me alone!"

It was like a gun went off. All of the clamoring outside of the door ceased. Abby placed her hand against the door like a firefighter tests a surface for heat. She unlocked it and peeked outside. A crowd was in the hallway. Pastor Ulma was standing in front. His expression was dismal. She stepped into the hallway. Each face she knew, not all by name, was in contempt for her. All that could be heard was their breathing. All that could be felt was the heat from their angry, cheap perfumed, sweaty bodies.

Pastor Ulma whispered, "Your mother met with me this morning and she confirmed that you are a witch. She told me that you burn sage and that your cat is a familiar."

It pained her to do so but Abby laughed and covered her mouth with her hand, "Are you serious?"

The pastor lifted the book, *Channeling Your Conscience Through the Unknown Universe*, and held it in front of her face.

"Channeling?" A woman yelped in the background.

"That is Satan!" A man yelled.

"This is a book of the occult. Your mother found it in your room. It has incantations within it, which is devilry, and yet you stand and mock me in God's house," Ulma said.

Abby didn't respond. She wiped water from her nose with her sleeve.

"You know..." the pastor wagged his finger, "...if our country was under the proper ruling like it was centuries ago, we would be able to burn you at the stake."

Abby looked at each of them. Her mother's gaunt, grey face was in the crowd, but Richard's was not. *He is probably hiding somewhere,* she thought.

"Well pastor, today is my last day here and I wanted to go out in style."

She took a cigarette out of her purse, placed it between her lips, and watched the members become frigid.

"Now, before you burn me at the stake, could I bum a light from one of you?"

The pastor exploded. He tore the book in half. An old woman, whom Abby barely knew shrieked. A young boy raised his hands and screamed a passage from the Bible about witches. A thin man that looked like a sick pelican, raised his hands into fists and shook. Abby thought they were going to pull her apart. She ran for the door. The pastor chased after her, calling her a jezebel, harlot, temptress, and a whore. Abby's mother followed apologizing to the pastor. Abby burst through the front doors and ran into the parking lot. She turned and saw the pastor shaking his fist with a torn half of the Truelove book in his hand. Her mother exited followed by the worship leaders, the pastor's wife, and the ushers.

Abby ran toward Richard's car and stood in front of it. She wondered how far the congregation would go. Would they strike her? Did they have no boundaries? She scanned the crowd for Richard. He was one of the last to exit the church. The congregation scampered into the parking lot and traveled toward her. The pastor's wife handed a Bible to her husband. Pastor Ulma held it in his pudgy hands. He screamed from memory, passages about iniquity, hell, and Satan. Abby watched him hobble toward her, as she kept backing away.

Stephanie Boardman led the group into a song of worship, and all followed her lead. Some held hands together and others pointed at Abby yelling words of condemnation. Behind the crowd, Abby saw Richard break his way through.

Abby backed into an old, white Cadillac. It belonged to Pastor Ulma. She wished she had more unsettled yogurt and old booze in her so she could throw up on it.

"Satan!" Pastor Ulma yelled, "We are here out of love, for Abagail Gibson, we want you to deliver her and bring her back to us. Loose her!"

The crowd made a half circle around Abby, blocking her from any way of exiting. The pastor raised his Bible and pressed it against her head.

"Mr. Ulma, you are hurting me," Abby said. She was beyond crying; she was beyond panic.

"Satan you will loose her!" he yelled. Ulma gripped the Bible firmly with both hands and held it against Abby's forehead. He pushed as hard as he could and forced her to kneel. She slid against the car and onto the pavement. Abby looked up and saw the swaying of hands in one mass, the voices of the congregation were in one song of insanity. It was then that Richard broke through the crowd. He pulled Pastor Ulma by the shoulder and forced his way in between Abby and him. Abby didn't hear what he was saying.

A blonde woman was running by the church. She saw the commotion and stopped. Her first thought was a car accident must have happened. She was trained in CPR and took boxing classes on the weekend. When she saw Pastor Ulma press the bible on Abby's head and force her to the ground, she wanted to punch the pastor and not consider resuscitating him if he passed out. As she sprinted toward the crowd, she saw Richard standing in defense of Abby. She climbed over the hood of the Cadillac and stood next to Richard.

Ulma yelled a passage from the bible about demons. His wife yelled and said that Abagail was always rebellious. A red-headed boy with a crooked bow tie said she looked like a witch since day one. Nova stood silent in the crowd. She was embarrassed by Abby and wished she had given her up for adoption long ago.

"What the hell is wrong with you assholes!" the blonde runner shouted.

Abby covered her face, she felt like birds were pecking at her flesh. She saw Richard stand up for her. Words were exchanged between him and the crowd. She didn't know what was being said. She didn't know who the blonde runner was. Since she was in running clothes, Abby assumed she was just passing by and witnessed the madness. She was surprised a bystander gave a damn.

Richard turned to Abby and put his hand on her cheek. "Honey, are you okay?"

She smiled at him but shook her head.

"I am going to get my phone. Ulma accosted you. I want to call the police; this is fucking insane," he said.

She knew what he meant when he said he was going to get his phone. There was a strict church rule that all of the phones had to be kept in the coat room. Another church of the same denomination in Tennessee had a bad prayer service that went viral. Someone videotaped a pastor not much different from Pastor Ulma saying nonsensical things. The pastor laid hands on some new members of the audience. One of the ladies fell back in her chair and twisted her wrist. The narrative of the public was that the pastor was erratic and out of control. Since then, Ulma ran a tight ship, as he was afraid of the world seeing what kind of person hid behind the walls of the East Holy Tabernacle of Blueville.

Richard's actions were going to draw a line in the sand, he was standing up for her, and Abby was proud of him for saying *fuck*.

"You are out of control, Ulma! Leave my daughter alone!" Richard yelled.

Richard had never called Abby his daughter before. She was always referred to as his stepdaughter.

"I saw you hit her with a Bible!" the blonde runner yelled.

"I never struck her!" Ulma said.

"Pastor, I think you did," said Ms. Cushing. A feeble voice came from the crowd. She was an elderly woman who came here out of curiosity after her husband died. "This young woman may be eccentric, but a devil she is not."

"I was casting a demon out of her!" Ulma screamed. His face became flushed like raw hamburger meat.

The blonde runner put her hand on Abby's shoulder, "Honey, I wish I had my phone. I don't run with one. But I will wait with you, okay?"

Abby smiled at her. She held up a bent cigarette. "You wouldn't have a lighter would you?"

"No," the woman laughed.

Richard ran into the church. Nova followed him. Abby didn't know what her mother's opinion was, on what just transpired. She assumed it was negative. The congregation began to disperse; the majority of them trailed inside. The pastor was led in by his wife and one of the elders. He walked slowly, and those close to him consoled him, by rubbing his back and telling him he was a great shepherd. Abby watched them leave. As the lot cleared, a thought ran through Abby's cluttered mind. She checked the passenger door of Ulma's Cadillac; it opened. It was mint, classic, and from the 80's. Abby pushed on the lighter and waited until it popped. She lit her cigarette. It took great restraint to not burn a hole in his seat, as she didn't want to start a fire. With her luck, it would blow up and she would have to go to jail.

"Ma'am..." Abby said to the runner. "...thank you for stopping to check on me but I am going home now."

The blonde woman beckoned to Abby, "What about an ambulance? You might have a concussion."

"I'm sorry, I don't want to wait around this place for one more minute."

Abby thanked her again and crossed the street. She blew cigarette smoke above her head disdainfully. The blonde runner watched Abby walk away in the heat, with her black cardigan, boots, and teased-out hair. She marveled at her. When she got home from her run, she told her husband about the young woman who looked like a vampire, who got hit in the head with a Bible in a church parking lot. He had a hard time comprehending the bizarre story. Later that week he saw someone local, that fit Abby's description, who ended up on national news.

13

Despite the afternoon heat, Abby's anger burned hotter. It took her thirty minutes to walk back to the house. This morning she swore she would never return to the church again, now she wanted to spit in the face of every one of its members. She wondered if her mother and Richard would be home before her. She expected Nova to be in attack mode. To Abby's surprise, Richard wore a different shade today; he defended her. Regardless, she was not going to spend the rest of the afternoon at home and needed to get her car. Work would take her mind off of things. Even though she wasn't scheduled, she would call and ask if she could just work the counter. The plan was to return and tack a hundred-dollar bill to her mother's bedroom door for the upcoming rent. It would be the *kiss-my-ass, I am an adult, leave me alone, P.S. I hope to be out soon and never see you again* money.

If Dante was cool with it, she would work every night this week, especially on her birthday. Even though she enjoyed old books and records, she had to save every dime she could, so she could be out as soon as possible.

When she got home, Dario ran through the house and yelled as loud as the Puritans she just escaped. She put food out for him; he purred as she petted him and started to cry. She went upstairs, put on her work clothes, and switched out purses. With no car, she would need a ride from Richard. The other option was to call Sutton, but she didn't have the energy to deal with his emotions now. He was an angel, that wanted much more than she had to give.

After fixing her makeup and taming down her hair, she sat at the kitchen table. Her cell phone was in front of her. Calling a cab was the next best option, but she sat in indecision and wondered if Richard would take her. It all depended on how the car ride home for him was turning out.

She texted Rose, *You aren't going to believe this shit.*

Even though Rose and she had become somewhat distant, she was the only person she could talk to about something this insane.

On the kitchen counter, four chocolate cupcakes, wrapped in plastic were tempting her. The dark chocolate powers held more allure than a book about the occult and felt stronger than blowing a contemptuous puff of smoke in the face of an angry church. She ate two, and considered eating the others, but didn't. Her reflection judged her from the silver side of the toaster; distorted and miserable. It made her want to hide, even from herself. She had a vision brought on by stress and a sugar rush, of a gold vein cracking through the yard, up to the fence. She slid her phone into her purse, the citrine geodes were still inside, and she squeezed them. The practice that was done yesterday brought her peace.

"Aaaaaaaaoooooooooooo, aaaaaaaaaaaum," she chanted. The second time she made her voice deeper.

Holding onto the geodes tightly, she walked through the backyard and headed to the tennis court. She approached the chalk circle, still intact.

"What were those words?" She closed her eyes and focused. "I will cross the stars."

It was a tragedy what happened to Francis Truelove's book. It was torn to shreds never to be admired again. She sat in the chalk circle, concentrated, and squeezed the geodes. Phonetically, she broke down the complex phrase, from how she recalled.

"Nan."

"Natcattirankalaik."

"Katappen."

A breeze blew through the branches. She felt warm inside.

"Vittu natcattirankalaik katantu celven."

The air pressure around her changed immediately. Off in the distance, rain fell, and it covered the south side of town. She watched the grey clouds move. The sky quickly became overcast. A thin mist was in the air that formed into a drizzle. It was refreshing. She looked up and the sky above her and it was thinly clouded, but red, deep red.

"Nan Natcattirankalaik Katappen," she said.

She squeezed the geodes so tight that the aching in her palms was taking the pain out of her soul.

94

A swirling in the clouds appeared directly above her, like the precursor warning of a hate-filled tornado. A faint illumination of red kissed the edges of the cumulus tufts. A reverberation was felt beneath her; shaking her insides. A thin tree in front of her went diagonal, from a sporadic tempest. Her heart pounded, and her pulse was heavy in her throat as if she were held upside down.

And before she stood up, she was gone.

14

An acid-drenched argument took place, on the car ride home between Richard and Nova. Richard was furious with the church for what had just taken place. He vowed to never return and swore that if something happened to Abby, every member would be held accountable. He wished he obtained the blonde runner's information as a witness to the chaos. But just mentioning the *blonde runner woman,* who also happened to be wearing a tank top, would send Nova into unnecessary jealous convulsions. He called Abby multiple times and texted her but there was no response. He didn't blame her for being angry and needing time to herself. But walking home in the heat could have been avoided.

Maybe she called a friend, he thought. And it dawned on him that he wasn't sure if Abby had any friends. Since Rose left, Abby never went out with anyone else. Guilt set in as he realized he was unaware of that part of her life. Today's fiasco made him realize he should have stood up to Nova sooner.

Nova was in a tirade about Abby being rebellious and obstinate. She said Abby was just like this one unruly teenager whose mother was a song leader at a church, just like theirs. The daughter admitted she was Wiccan, and the church had the girl removed.

"The witchcraft spawned from the father not being stern enough with the daughter!" Nova screamed.

"Are you kidding me?" Richard said.

It was just like Nova to turn the story around. A congregation chased after her daughter, and she pointed the finger at him.

"A real witch, like with a pointy hat and broom?" Richard laughed.

"She was into the same things that Abby is into; the dark clothes, the white sage, and the occult books!"

"I see. So, it was the clothes, sage, and books," Richard said. His tone was mocking.

"It is because you don't lift a hand to her when she gets out of control, and today you defended her."

Richard pulled the car over. He put his hands over his face. Two boys rode by on their bikes and saw Richard. They thought he was hiding from them. A German Shepherd followed them. The boys made barking noises as they passed the car. The dog barked along with them.

"Are you saying I should be hitting her? Is that what you actually think? Is that what is going on in your head right now?"

"She is unruly," Nova said. Thin veins bulged in her bottom eyelids. She had lost so much weight in the past few weeks that parts of her face, which used to hold a smooth fullness were now dehydrated and sagging.

"I will never hit her, nor should any father of that church act that way with their children. It is like that piece of real estate goes back in time, to the fucking 1500's."

"How dare you!"

"Oh, spare me the theatrics!"

It was the first time he spoke up to Nova in the four years of their being together. She glared at him, and he kept his face forward as they drove home.

Nothing else was said between them. Nova closed her eyes and acted like she went into a trance, muttering to herself. Richard kept his focus. The real problem was Pastor Ulma. If it weren't for him, Nova would not have taken this bizarre position as a prophet. Months ago, she didn't act like this. Despite her strong opinions, she used to be able to hold a normal conversation that didn't end in outbursts. She was kept and beautiful. Richard never thought he could love her more. Things changed when Stephanie Boardman, Cindy Thurman, and she went to a prophetic Bible conference. A TV preacher was on tour, whom they were enamored by, and they drove two hours to see him. He would call out things to the audience that God allegedly told him. He claimed that Nova's calling was going to come to its fullness. Afterward, she approached Ulma and told him about her calling. Then, at every Sunday service, Ulma allowed her to share with the church. All of the messages were related to the Book of Revelation, divine judgment, or the rapture.

When they pulled in front of the house, they noticed Abby's car was gone.

"She left?" he whispered. Richard called her again, and it went to voicemail.

"First, we need to get the oil and pray, then go on a fast. You will write down the things that I get in the Spirit. I am getting something now, hold on." Nova placed the back of her hand to her forehead.

Richard ignored her and went inside the house. Even though Nova ransacked Abby's room recently, Richard never stepped foot into Abby's room. Only a few times, did Abby yell out to him in passing, yet he would only stand in the archway to talk to her. He respected her privacy, and she never gave him a reason to come in and snoop. Because of her absence and phone silence, he peeked his head in. Her room was in teenage girl disarray. There was no telling if she came in a hurry and left in a flash or if it always looked like this. She never worked on Sunday, but he wondered if she went in, or perhaps went to a bookstore.

Could she have gone to replace the book that Ulma ripped in half? he wondered.

He looked around the room. There was a black plastic bag on the floor. The bag was for the bookstore in Nashville. He took out the receipt. It was from last Thursday. The store's address and phone number were on it. He knew the location by the mall. There was a Game Stop near there. A place where he used to spend a lot of time and money. He took a photo of the receipt with his phone.

Nova was in the kitchen looking out the window. She was drinking tea, still in mumbling mode. Often she would say she was just in prayer throughout the day. Normally, Richard never said a word, but he doubted that she prayed nearly every damn minute of the day.

Last November, when Nova lost her job at the insurance company, is when he saw her take a turn for the worse. They hid the reason from Abby. A Muslim family came into Nova's office. She gave them a regular home/car insurance pitch, but she didn't stop there. She stumbled into a line about a book she was reading. It was about Armageddon and Christ's return. Deeply offended, the Muslim man told the manager, who was already frustrated with Nova's overzealous ways, and he let her go.

"Richard, are you listening to me? Go get a pen and paper," she said.

It was rare for Richard to speak up. He never did in high school or college, as he never stuck out to anyone, he wasn't even bullied. In his twenties, he got an IT job and never moved out of his comfort zone. He bought the house, back in 2002, because it was a deal. When he met Nova, he took Abby in like she was his own. At best, he just appeared as someone who was supportive but stood off in the background, and easily dismissed. That part of him dissolved when he saw Pastor Ulma push on Abby's forehead with the Bible.

"Nova, I am going to look for Abby. If there is anything you should pray about, it should be that I find her and that she doesn't hate us for what that shithead Pastor did today."

"Wait, what?" she asked. A timidity immediately surfaced.

"Jack Ulma assaulted our daughter. I think she hit her head. She might have a concussion, and now she is out driving who knows where? Did she go back to that trailer park to get drunk? I don't know if she has any friends I can call. And all you care about is some vision, that you are probably making up."

"I beg your pardon!" Nova yelled.

"I beg *your* pardon!" He mimicked her with extra sass. "Yeah, yeah, I know, God told you *this* and God told you *that*. Just pray Nova, pray that nothing happens to her."

Without any direction, Richard drove aimlessly to find Abby, and in that, he felt he had a purpose. He punched the steering wheel until his hand hurt. And for the first time in his life, the pain woke him up.

15

Father Meyers walked through the aisle of his church after the morning Mass. Everyone had left except one of the maintenance workers; he was using a leaf blower in the back parking lot of St. Mary's Cathedral. The priest picked up a gold dish, which was used for serving communion wafers, and headed to his office. The door was slightly ajar. He hesitated, knowing well that the office door was always kept shut. Slowly he pushed the door open with his shoe and spoke.

"Is anyone there?"

"Yes, Father come in," a strange voice spoke to him.

Father Meyers froze; in the ten years, he had served at this church, not once had anyone ever entered his office without his say-so.

Quickly, he barged into his office, "Who are you, and what are you doing here?"

Someone was in his swivel chair and was facing the window.

"You have no right to be in here!" the priest shouted.

The man in the chair spun around. He wore a black nylon stocking over his face, squishing his features. Two drawn circles were around the eyes, made with paint. It made the stranger look like a freakish cartoon. He was wearing a thin black dress suit, a black tie, and a silver tie clip of the planet Saturn.

The priest was so alarmed his jowls shook, and he dropped the communion plate.

"Father Meyers, you look like you just shit yourself," the young man laughed.

The priest turned to the door and yelled for help. Another thin man with a nylon stocking stood in the hallway and blocked his exit. He raised his hand to stop the priest from running and shut the door. Father Meyers stared at the closed door with his arms at his side, powerless.

"Father, please take a seat. I just want to talk to you for a moment, and we will be out of your way."

"What do you want with me? We have no money here; all donations are made electronically or by check. The cash is..."

"Father, I don't believe you, nor do I give a shit about the money. The oodles and oodles of cash that the Catholic Church makes is the least of my concern."

"Then what kind of man breaks into a priest's office?"

"One who is on a quest," Jericho smiled.

"A quest? What do you mean?" The priest turned around.

Jericho walked around the desk and sat on the edge. He calmly folded his hands like a teacher sitting in front of a classroom.

"You see, like the prophets in your Bible, I am on a mission. Only mine goes beyond our realms. You can say it will exist in the next plane, or perhaps when your Christ rules when the Second Coming happens."

"What sort of blasphemy is this?" The priest started to shake; he put his hand on his forehead and sat in a small wooden chair.

"A demon spoke to me while I had a wonderful vision derived from peyote. It is a spiritual practice done by the indigenous people. You know the indigenous, the people that the Catholics massacred?"

The priest was silent; he felt defenseless and was forced to listen.

"I was promised a place to rule here on Earth when the phase of our plane changes. I knew this when I was young. But it was confirmed by my horned friend that I met in the desert this past weekend. There will be a special alignment in the stars soon, and I need to do a ritual, kind of like the one that you do with the wine and the wafers. What is that called?"

"The transubstantiation," Father Meyers said. His voice was weak.

"Now correct me if I am wrong," Jericho said, "That means that the communion wine and those bland wafers, actually turn into the body and blood of Christ during every service."

"Yes. The body and blood of Christ are integral to a Catholic person's faith and penitence, the sacrifice of the Holy Jesus on the cross..."

Jericho raised his palm. "Stop with the lecture. I was inquiring about the brazen doctrine that defies logic, not the meaningless meaning behind it."

The priest was not going to banter dialog with a man of such stature. He wasn't sure if he would leave the office alive. He knelt on the floor and yelled, "Please have mercy on me!"

Jericho slapped him across the face, "Stop your groveling! You are the bilious curds from the udders of a stench goat!"

The priest yelped and lay sideways on the floor. He held his face and moaned.

"Oh priest, I will ask you one more time to get up. I am not going to have a conversation with a slug."

Father Meyers got on his knees and crawled to the chair. He put his hands on the arms of the seat and struggled to stand.

"Are you good? Now that you got that out of your system?" Jericho asked.

"My son, God will judge you for your actions."

"Yes, yes, I have heard it before, and I don't give a damn. I am here for only one thing."

"What is that?" the priest whispered.

Jericho leaned down and picked up the gold communion tray, "This is what I came for."

"The communion tray, why?"

Jericho smiled, " I am going to eat a woman's pancreas off this."

Father Meyers had a sensitive bladder. He would often go without drinking anything all morning just to get through Mass. His other option would be to wear a diaper. After Mass, he had a tall, cool glass of water. When he heard what the communion plate would be used for, he urinated himself.

"God have mercy on the world, I pray your wickedness will be met with righteous indignation." Father Meyers made the sign of the cross and blessed himself.

"Perhaps." Jericho straightened his tie and collar arrogantly. He knelt before the priest and took a moon-shaped blade out of his jacket. He held it in front of him, "Do you know what this is?"

"It looks like a pagan blade used for sacrifice."

Jericho laughed. "Very good. You aren't as dumb as you look."

Father Meyers became angry, he wanted to fight back, but he was old and out of shape. He silently prayed to God, hoping to get out of this alive.

"Tell me, priest, before I leave you, have you ever hurt a child?"

The anger gave Father Meyers focus. He leaned close to Jericho's squished mesh face and whispered, "Never."

Jericho was hoping for a different answer; he wanted to see him struggle as he had written the priest off before he stepped into the church.

"Hmm. I believe you," Jericho said.

Jericho noticed that the priest had wet himself. He looked keenly at him, "Tell me this then, how long have you been a priest?"

"Thirty-Nine faithful years."

"Wow." Jericho soft-clapped with the blade still in his hand. "With all the awful things that have come out about the Catholic church, and all the accusations you must have heard, there had to be one instance that you knew of, where a priest hurt a child."

"Yes, I have. And it is wrong; those men should be ashamed," Father Meyers said. His knee started to twitch rapidly.

"Hmmm." Jericho rubbed his finger underneath his chin, "Did you do anything in your power to stop them?"

Father Meyers looked down at the floor. Guilt was an emotion he dealt with often, and he was tougher on himself than most priests he knew.

"I did nothing to stop them. I didn't know how."

Jericho took the priest's right hand, opened it, and sliced his palm with the blade. The priest gasped. Jericho folded his palm for him. Then he wiped the blood off the edge of the blade with his finger and drew a circle on the gold communion plate.

"Now, this is ready to do what I aim to use it for," Jericho said.

The priest held his bloody hand close to him. Blood dripped onto his robe. He doubled over and wept. Jericho leaned down and kissed him on the forehead.

"You might need stitches, Father."

Jericho left the office and shut the door, quietly. Isaac followed him. They exited through the back of the church. The groundskeeper saw two men wearing black stockings leave the church and walk across the street. They cut through a backyard of the funeral home into an adjacent parking lot, where Gentry waited for them in the van.

The groundskeeper ran inside, put gauze on the priest's hand, and called the police. By the time the police arrived, the van was already ten miles north, heading towards Kansas City.

16

Nova deserved Abby's anger, perhaps Richard did as well, and that was Richard's explanation for her not picking up the phone. Standing up to Nova made Richard feel alive. He was never a man who stood up to authority. His parents lived a timid, and mouse-like lifestyle, and he inherited their approach as well. Despite the church being a bit much at times, he just liked to sit there and let his mind wander. But today, was a different day. He was going to find Abby and tell her that he loved her. He hadn't recalled saying that to her since Christmas. With Abby's birthday approaching, he was going to get her a new pair of Doc Martens. When he saw Nova again, he would tell her that there would be changes in the house; changes for the better.

Richard drove to every place in Blueville he thought Abby would go to. The pizza place, the salon, and the library, but there was no sign of her. He drove out of town and headed to Denny's and spoke to Dante. Dante knew of Richard's name and said that Abby wasn't scheduled until tomorrow. With nowhere else to turn, Richard remembered the receipt from Above & Beyond Books and drove to Nashville.

When Richard arrived at the bookstore, he checked the parking lot for Abby's car and did not see it. He went inside and got nervous when he saw Tony and left. Realizing that giving in to social awkwardness would never solve anything, he went back inside. He introduced himself and said that his stepdaughter was really into weird books and described Abby to him.

Tony smiled, "She is an enlightened young woman, that has an incredible journey ahead of her."

"How do you know that?" Richard was puzzled at such an unwavering statement from a stranger.

"Some people are just one in a million. I know this because I am one in a million," Tony laughed.

Richard grinned at him; he looked through the shelves at random. Tony guided him to where Abby was at the last time she was here. Richard looked at a book, *The Twisted Colors of My Dreamscape: A Metaphysical Journey through the Subconscious* by Platina Dapplemeyer. The cover was a woman's face, split into a spectrum of colors. It was published in 1975 by a small press company that specialized in metaphysical books that were written in a multitude at the time. The imagery spoke to him. He knew Nova would hate it with a passion, and Abby would adore it.

"I think I just figured out what my stepdaughter likes," Richard said.

He bought it, thanked Tony, and left.

Richard sat in the car and felt his search was futile, and after two hours of driving around, he headed back home. As he passed the East Holy Tabernacle of Blueville, he wondered if Abby could have visited the church. Given her temperament, he wondered if she would return to pepper spray Pastor Ulma. He smirked and would be proud of her if she did. Then fear settled in. What if this wasn't a *fuck you all* night out, but something worse? What if someone grabbed her? It was a thought that no parent ever wanted to entertain.

During the time he was gone, he did not hear from one member of the church. For how awful the day was, he expected to hear from Pastor Ulma or at least one of the elders. Certainly, Stephanie Boardman and Cindy Thurman had no problems telling him what they thought God wanted for him last night. Now they were silent in their hypocrisy.

When he opened the back door, Nova was kneeling on the kitchen floor. She had a veil over her face and was sitting in the dark. There was only faint light remaining from the sunset kissing the edges of the windowsills.

Nova didn't acknowledge him.

He was tired of her shit. Spending most of his time with a woman who claimed she saw visions in eggs and bacon, and demons in commercials, had run its course.

Richard turned on the light and went into the pantry. He took out an old bottle of wine. They used to imbibe in the early part of their relationship. Out of the blue, Nova wanted to cut it out completely. Then, Richard just went with it, only because he didn't like the taste of red much. He uncorked the bottle. They didn't have wine glasses anymore. He took a small glass tumbler out of the cupboard and filled it. Nova just watched him.

"I didn't find her; in case you were wondering. I drove around and checked the areas that she might frequent. Then I went to her work. I spoke with the night manager, who is kind of weird. I also checked a bookstore she likes down in Nashville. After all that, she can't be found and isn't responding to any calls or texts. She can't be found now because she doesn't want to be. It is up to her to come back. And she will punish us with her silence, because of what happened at the church, today."

He drank the wine and finished the glass in nearly one gulp. "So, Ulma said that given the right place and time, Abby should be burnt at the stake, because of a book that you gave him. I am assuming you went through her room and found it?"

"She is angry. She will be back when she gets it out of her system," Nova said. She was surprised at what length Richard had gone in the search for Abby.

"Yet, no call from any church member? Not one message asked, *how is the poor girl who was chased like a dog*?"

"No," Nova whispered.

"I am thinking about getting a lawyer."

"A lawyer, why?" Nova put her hands on her chest.

"Well, Abby is still a minor. Ulma is an abusive tyrant, who thought he could beat a demon out of her with a Bible. And I partially blame him for the way you act."

"That is not what happened," Nova snapped. "Abby was testing him."

Nova stood up and lifted the veil, so only her mouth and nose were exposed. There were times during her fasting when she would eat crusts of bread and chicken broth. She never told Richard, but from time to time, she would take diet pills and only drink water. By Sunday afternoon she would resume eating small portions. The fasts always took a toll on her system. For the next day, she would resume light eating, then consume normally for the rest of the week. It would change again if she had a dream or a vision. She opened the bread box, cut off an end of pumpernickel loaf, and ate a small piece with honey butter.

Richard wiped his mouth. The buzz from the wine gave him the confidence he hadn't felt in some time. "That is what happened, and you are too damn blind to see."

"Don't you curse in our holy house! It is sanctified," Nova yelled.

"Shit, ass, fucker, balls," Richard said. "Write that down in your little tablet of special things. Those specific, cryptic things that only you can see and interpret, just you Nova, and no one else."

Her head jerked with each syllable on his run of expletives. Richard poured himself another glass.

"Maybe I am thinking too far ahead, but if Abby doesn't return tomorrow. I am going to the police."

"You are jumping to conclusions," Nova said.

"I am? But your visionsssss aren't?" he hissed. His eyes floated while he waved his arms like he was balancing on a surfboard.

She lifted the veil completely off her face. The fluorescent light shone harshly on her cheekbones. Her face looked haggard. She gazed at him intensely as if she were looking at spots of darkness in his soul.

"Your complexion used to be radiant. Your eyes used to have light in them. It was a delight coming home to you. Now I sit in the driveway and wonder what crazy thing you are going to pull. What next big ball of fire will be coming down from heaven? You turned into one of those crazy people who hold the signs up in New York and claim the end is near, and when it doesn't happen, the date gets changed and you hold up a new sign. You went from a sweet country church girl to an unappealing lunatic."

"I will fast tomorrow, Richard you will see, God will show..." Nova's chin quivered.

"I heard enough of your shit," he interrupted. "I am not going to that goddam church anymore.

You can do what you want. But I am warning you that there might be a lawsuit against the church, depending on how Abby wants to handle that asshole of a pastor."

Nova leaned against the wall. She covered her mouth with her hands. She acted like she was struck.

Richard ignored her theatrics. He was too shaken and sat down.

"When she returns..." he choked. Panic began to surface, but he believed Abby was just out in the world and pissed. He convinced himself that she would be home soon. "...I am going to make sure Ulma never preaches again. There is a catholic church by the baseball field, you can go there and be a nun if you want because you dress the same. And I bet they don't look as faded as you do."

Richard went upstairs, with his tumbler of wine. When he used to drink, all he did was just become tired. He wasn't a mean drunk or a horny drunk, alcohol in his bloodstream just gave him an edge he always wanted to have when he was sober. Unfortunately, the magic elixir only lasted so long until he had a good scare on the road one night. He swerved into another lane and almost hit a dump truck. It shook him enough that he knew he needed to change. That was before he met Nova.

He went into the spare room. The only furniture was a single bed and a small TV. He turned it on and flipped through the channels. A black and white movie was on a weird cable station. A tall busty woman with black hair was driving a race car through the desert. She was with two other pretty women, who also had fast cars. The music playing sounded like a surf song. There was a race between the tall woman and a handsome guy. It ended abruptly, and the tall busty woman killed the man by karate chopping him in the throat. The women kidnapped his girlfriend, and they fled across the desert again. Nova would think this movie was filth, and that contented Richard. He left it on, finished his glass of wine, and drifted off to sleep.

17

The next morning, Abby did not return. A tightness laid in Richard's chest. He checked her room, went downstairs, and fed Dario. He called her phone; it went to voice mail. He texted her asking if she was *okay*. He went outside to the carport and saw her car wasn't there. He looked up and down the street and called her again. Of all of the mediocre half-emotions Richard was known for displaying, panic was not one of them. One horrifying thought after another filled his mind. Was she in a car accident and hurt? Or drunk or on drugs and in jail? Was she with a man and violated? Or in a gang and stabbed? Did she get shot and was bleeding out, or was she poisoned?

The sulfites in his system were slowing his morning perception. They opened a door in his conscious that had been hindered by four years of crazy preaching from the wacky church land.

It was the first time in this relationship that he went to bed angry, while his wife slept in a separate bed. He felt guilty, because he loved Nova, although the person he loved, he hadn't seen in some time.

He poured a cup of coffee, added skim milk, and let it sit there until it went cold. He called off work and wanted to call the police. From what he understood, by the misconception of police TV shows, there had to be a twenty-four-hour time period to file a Missing Person's Report. An angry goth teenager, that hated church and her mother, and didn't come home for one night, shouldn't be the most alarming thing the police had to deal with. He decided to check at her school.

Nova was at the top of the stairs, looking flighty. It was the look she got when she claimed God spoke to her. Richard wasn't in the mood.

"I am going to Abby's school. Maybe I can talk to someone, a teacher, or a student. I don't know. I think you should come."

Nova's face was hollow. She jerked her head dramatically as if a message was just received from upon high.

"Richard, I have been in prayer, and God spoke to me. He said that our daughter will return on Wednesday. I feel she is safe, and she is angry with the pastor. I don't know what she is doing this moment, or where she is. That hasn't been revealed to me. But she will return."

He stood in the middle of the stairs and met her gaze. The guilt he was feeling for sleeping in a separate room passed. He was angry again.

"On Wednesday?" he asked.

"Yes," she whispered.

"What you are hearing is a psychotic delusion. You don't hear from God."

It was words he never said out loud and only thought a few times. They were as heavy as an anvil dropping on Nova's head. She backed away from him.

He walked passed her, showered, and dressed. He texted Bruce, from his office, asking if he knew a lawyer.

Bruce responded, *Oh shit, you call off and now you need a lawyer.*

I will explain later, Richard replied.

Quickly, he grabbed his keys and phone and went into the front room. Nova sat awkwardly on the edge of the couch, still wearing the same white gown. Her face was as bitter as a bowl of crushed lemons that a cat had pissed in.

The Price is Right was on mute. Nova hated the show because the women who hosted were too sexy, or as she put it, *homewreckers for men who stayed at home.*

"I guess I am going by myself then?" Richard rubbed his forefinger and thumb across the growing stubble on his chin.

"Wednesday," Nova said. "God told me that Abby would return on Wednesday."

Richard's face turned red. He wanted to slam the door until the hinges broke off, but he left quietly.

Bruce texted back, *Here is the contact card for the lawyer my wife used when she got into a car accident. He helped us out a lot. Let me know if you need anything else.*

The contact card was for D.L. Browning & Associates. A small firm in Nashville. Richard did not hesitate. The image of Abby running from the pastor and the congregation kept playing in his mind. He called the lawyer and articulately described yesterday's events, *aside* from Abby not returning home last night. Browning told him there was a valid case. He recommended that he refrain from contact with the pastor or any member of the church. Richard thanked him for his time and said he would get back to him soon.

When Richard arrived at Abby's school, he went straight to the principal's office. A secretary greeted him. He said who he was and waited. The Vice-Principal, Ms. Lewis, brought him to her office. She was a short, silver-haired woman, in a commanding suit, with perfect posture. He informed her that Abby had not returned home last night. He stressed that he called her multiple times but did not tell her about the incident at the church.

Ms. Lewis gave him a judging glare but smiled at the same time.

He apologized for not knowing who Abby's friends were, or where to turn. "I don't think going to the police is necessary yet. Or perhaps it is?"

His tone was easy to convey because his face matched the temperature inside of him.

"Is there a reason why Abby would stay out all night? Does she have a significant other, or was there an argument at home?" Ms. Lewis asked.

Even though Richard didn't know the woman for more than a few seconds, he wanted to blurt out everything. He searched for words, with a long pause. Describing the recent tension at home was difficult, and he wondered if what Nova was doing could be considered abuse. He didn't stop Nova the night she came up from the basement with the box cutter. Nova stomped up the stairs and cut The Cure records to shreds. *My wife is abusive.* And there he sat, in shock, as he realized this.

"Mr. Gibson?" Ms. Lewis asked. The sun shone in the window behind her. The white in her silver hair exploded with light. She was electric, and in her morning magic, she seemed like she could be trusted.

"My wife and her, are constantly at odds."

"I see."

"I am sure you are aware of the way Abby dresses. She is so dramatic with everything. That can make things volatile at home. My wife is incredibly

115

conservative." He coughed into his hand nervously. "Abby, would gather dead crickets and spray paint them black and glue them to a hat if she thought it would make it look better."

"I must comment, Abby does have a marvelous style." Ms. Lewis smiled.

Richard raised his eyebrows.

"I am assuming the arguments at home are just with Abby and your wife, and not you?"

"Yes ma'am," he responded. The last time he recalled a moment when he sat in the vice principal's office was when he drew a picture of a fish with a dick on it in science class. That was in tenth grade. His emotional intelligence had not changed much since then.

"Well, Abby will always be Abby, to the fullest," he said.

"A diva, in a small town." Ms. Lewis chuckled. "I love her and her style. I hope she is just angry and will return home soon. But I think there is someone else we can find more information from your daughter."

"Stepdaughter."

"I see," Ms. Lewis said.

He followed Ms. Lewis down the hallway to meet the guidance counselor, Ms. Coleman. As they entered her office. An attractive woman greeted them. She shook Richard's hand. Ms. Coleman was the kind of woman who purchased her dresses out of high-end catalogs. Pictures of her status and happiness were displayed around the office: diplomas, a smiling husband, and two children.

After Ms. Lewis introduced them, she left them be.

Ms. Coleman offered him coffee, and he gladly took it. As it was good for his nervous hands and kept him focused. As he sat, he knew that Nova was the reason for this, he divulged everything to Ms. Coleman before she could get a good gauge on him.

"I am concerned about Abby. She didn't come home last night. I want to go to the police, but I might be overreacting. She got into it with the pastor of our church, in front of everyone. That place is a shit show. I never really went to church much in my life, but I think that place is dangerous. I know Abby knows this. And I think that is why she is so angry. Not only is she smart, but she is smarter than her mother. I just want her to come home

116

and she hasn't responded to any calls, and I don't blame her. I think she is probably at a friend's house, only I don't know who that friend is."

Ms. Coleman put her hand on top of his. "May I call you, Richard?"

He nodded his head.

"How well do you know your stepdaughter?"

Richard thought for a moment. "Her best friend Rose went here. Then she moved to Miami. That is when things changed."

"Yes, Rose Hernandez."

"You know her?" he asked.

"I hardly spoke with her, as I don't with students who don't come to me with personal issues. But I knew when she left. I heard something happened to the family and it was a near overnight move to Florida."

"Rose's father had an affair with some woman, and the mother and her left. It was almost instantaneous.".

"Well, it had a major effect on Abby," Ms. Coleman said.

"I realize that now. I thought she was going through a phase with the clothes and stuff," he said.

"It is no secret that she took a huge change in her wardrobe and demeanor. She used to be bubbly and skipped down the hallways with Rose. I..." she refrained from her next sentence.

Richard zeroed in on her pause, "What is it?"

"...I know you are a religious family."

"My wife more than myself."

"I assumed Rose and Abby were a couple. But I don't know if it was kept from you and your wife. I think when Rose left, Abby fell into a depression. Her weight fluctuated dramatically. It is harder for a father to recognize these things and approach them."

He sipped his coffee and allowed the cluttered desk inside of his mind to be cleared off for a new folder of information that he never had. He thought he was a good stepfather, although he wished he could have stuck up for Abby more when the fights happened, and Abby's sarcasm didn't make it easy.

"I never suspected that about her and Rose," he said.

As he said this, Richard felt dumb. He thought of a handful of moments where Abby joked about being a lesbian in front of Nova. He knew Abby liked to push buttons, but the jesting could have been the truth. "I thought the whole funeral attire thing was associated with her love for that goth band she loves, The Cure."

"It could be. But all of it is for attention, even though goth kids say they don't care what anyone thinks. That type of scene tends to be melancholic. It was prominent in the 80's, not so much in a small town, though. Sometimes those kinds of kids think they are poets and others can become self-destructive."

"Have you spoken to Abby before?" Richard asked.

"I made it a point. The change she went through from last year until now is drastic. She became painfully reclusive from the students. However, her teachers liked her."

"Did she open up to you at all, because her mother...." he hesitated. He knew that if he said what he was feeling, then he would throw Nova under the bus. In his mind, he hoped Nova would turn over a new leaf, as he had stood up to her. If Abby came home today, then this trip would just be informative, "...well, they don't get along."

"Mind you this is a term Abby used. When she turned *all goth*, I was worried that she would harm herself. Sometimes kids in that circle can do things, cut themselves, just to push themselves to the edge. I asked her twice. I think I was probing too much, but she came back around."

"And?"

"And she didn't, she actually showed me her arms and legs. Then she went on this diatribe about doing hair and make-up, and how it was her obsession. She plans on moving to Nashville and then to New York City. She has a lot of ambition; it goes beyond the boundaries of what a regular high school girl from a small town thinks. I know she is young, but this is what she is saying now. The point is you need to support her decision to do this. I looked up some places for her online and she was going to approach you and your wife about heading to a place in the fall."

Richard felt like shit. A stranger knew more about the inner workings of his stepdaughter than he did. He regretted all of the church nonsense. It gave him a purpose for a time until Nova went nuclear.

"I think I might be a shitty stepdad and husband."

"You aren't," Ms. Coleman smiled. "Because you are sitting here. I will tell you that there are hardly any dads who would go this far."

He checked his phone; still no response from Abby.

"Would you recommend that I go to the police?"

"Well, you can make a report and tell them she didn't come home. They will take her description and put out an APB for her. If she is just somewhere blowing off steam, and she comes home today, then there was no harm done."

He felt helpless and put the coffee cup on the desk.

"I don't know what to do." He rubbed his forehead as a headache was forming.

"You need to do what keeps her safe," Ms. Coleman said. She looked over at the picture of her daughter on the desk.

"What would you do?" he asked.

"I can't tell you what to do, only recommend. For your next action, go with your gut, and when she comes home, hug her, and tell her you love her. Work on getting her into the school she wants to go to."

They stood up at the same time. She handed him her card.

"Please keep me up to date with her whereabouts, and when she does turn up, if she wants to come back and talk to me, tell her she can."

"Thank you."

"I will take your advice, not only talk to her, but I will listen as well."

"And I will see you this Friday at her graduation," she said.

A lump formed in his throat, for a second he wondered if Abby wouldn't be back by then.

"Of course." His voice quivered.

She shook his hand again and opened the office door.

He stepped into the hallway and turned around to face her. Ms. Coleman was just about to shut the door. She smiled at him and held it open, only partially.

"I wish my wife was as well put together as you."

He winced at the stupidity of his statement.

She nodded her head with a smile and shut the door. He hung his head low and walked with his hands in his pockets. A cloud hung over him as he made his way to the car. It only took a minute for him to make a decision and go to the police station.

18

Entering the Blueville Police Station cemented the harsh reality of Abby's absence. Richard hoped he would have heard from her by now. He had to take charge of the situation and didn't want to be negligent anymore. Coming this far, rattled him, and his hands shook. He had been to a police station only once in his life, and that was for his DUI. Since then, the police terrified him. For years he and his coworkers would go on endless rants about police brutality, and share videos of traffic stops gone wrong. All of the worst scenarios went through his mind as he stood in the front room.

He spoke with a young woman at the front desk. She had a bowl haircut and narrow yellow eyes. He told her he wanted to file a Missing Person's Report. She got up and ran out of the room. Richard scratched his head. A broad and muscular police officer returned. He had a classic cop mustache. Richard had seen him in town before. He introduced himself, as Officer Grey and they shook hands. The young woman returned to the room and apologized for exiting so abruptly and said it was her first week on the job. Just answering the phone had been taxing for her.

Richard informed the officer that Abagail had been missing for twenty-four hours. The officer told him that waiting that long was common misinformation, spread by poorly done TV cop shows. The crucial time for finding a missing person is within the first twenty-four hours. Also, it depended on the age of the person, whether they were elderly or a young child. Richard apologized and felt more stupid by the minute.

Richard gave the officer a photo of Abby and her stats. The officer quickly made a Missing Person's Report for Abby. The high-contrast photo of her was on the screen, staring intensely at Richard. It made him sick to see her as a statistic rather than his stepdaughter.

Her face couldn't be anymore pale, he thought.

Officer Grey called the state police and gave the report. He put the state policeman, Officer Janson, on the speaker phone. The distorted voice and the noise in the background drained the emotion out of the small office. Janson repeated the same information, verbatim, as Grey confirmed. Richard nodded his head and gripped the edge of the desk; watching his fingers turn red to white. He muttered curses quietly to himself and wanted a drink. It was a feeling he had not associated with on a regular weekday in a long time.

"Mr. Gibson?" Officer Grey asked.

"I am sorry. My head isn't with it."

"Did you check all of her friends and family?" Janson asked.

"Um," he cleared his throat, "Abby doesn't have many friends. In fact, she is a loner, and our family is small. Being gone this long isn't normal."

"All right," Janson said. "If there are no more doors to knock on, then I suggest you wait by the phone. An APB is being issued now, local and state will be on the lookout. Her report will be on the local news tonight and it should go wider from there."

"That's it?" Richard asked. He felt like a raisin being put in a microwave, a dehydrated fruit, shriveling into a husk.

"That's all we can do for now," Janson said.

Officer Grey lowered his eyes. The harshness of something so delicate was never handled well by anyone in any job, but it was the first time that Officer Grey had to handle a Missing Person's Report.

"Thank you." Richard's voice was strained. The state police officer hung up. Officer Grey filled out more paperwork without looking up.

Nausea kicked in. Richard ran to the bathroom and threw up. He washed his face and stared in the mirror. A *pussy* is what he thought of himself. Thick glasses, balding, skinny, with no muscle mass. Just a pale IT guy with no balls. His intelligence was his best asset but was never put to good use. For most of his life he was on autopilot, and it showed in his marriage. He hated who he was because he knew he could be better. Calling Nova now would bring out the worst in him. He wished he could be as strong as Officer Grey or as callous as Officer Janson. He went back to the office and sat down, crossing his legs. Grey looked at him and gave a tight-lipped smile. Richard wanted to tell him that he didn't know what to do with himself. He opened his mouth, then closed it; the words never formed. Hot coffee was staring at him from across the hall. Richard got up and saw there were only Styrofoam cups available. He poured a bit of coffee, sipped it then spit it back into the cup. Richard hated the smell of Styrofoam. There was nothing left for him to do but go home.

He texted Nova and said that the report was made. She texted back, informing him that Ulma reached out, and said the congregation was praying for Abby's safe return. He wanted to tell her that Ulma could go *fuck himself* but refrained. Richard considered calling the pastor himself, but he kept his emotions focused on Abby.

While sitting at a stoplight, he played with the radio. A 70's rock song came on. It was a sound that was usually unwelcome around Nova. The lyrics were about holding up a bank and getting shot; Richard sang along. There was a tavern at the end of the street, and he pulled over. A drink had been beckoning him since this morning. It was the wrong thing to do, but he would rather be anonymous in a bar than be home with his crazy wife.

The bar was mostly empty. He sat at the corner stool and ordered a Bud draft. A bearded man tried making conversation, but Richard wasn't good at small talk with strangers. When he was in college he used to frequent a sports bar. That was when peer pressure told him who he should be. Slamming pitchers of beer and pounding shots were common practices back then. A time when he never knew who he was and forgot about it when he got there.

Three beers and two and a half hours passed. Minute to minute he checked his phone, for good news; anything concerning Abby, but there was nothing. He left a twenty-dollar bill on the counter and went to the bathroom before he left.

On the wall above the urinal was a mass of layered stickers. One said, *Support Vietnam Vets and their sacrifice*. Something happened inside of him. The booze gave him courage, which had been untouched for years, it was a chemical reaction in his brain. He had to make a call to someone he respected but was terrified of. This someone was a Vietnam Vet who fixed things. He called his father-in-law. A hard ass who lived off the grid in the backwoods of Illinois.

The phone rang twice, and Jerry Beaumont answered.

"Richard." His voice was husky and already aggravated.

"Sir. Um...we might have a problem."

"What did Nova do?"

"It isn't her, at least partly it isn't. It's Abby." Richard was pacing on the sidewalk in front of the bar. He felt the effects of the beer. He didn't want his words to slur, so he focused as hard as he could and sat on the curb.

"I am listening."

"Abby didn't come home last night."

"When did you last see her?"

"There was an incident at church, she walked home, and left."

"An incident, what happened?"

"The pastor, well, he is an asshole and they got into it. He chased after Abby, and so did the congregation, calling her a witch and the pastor..." Richard paused. As he relived the moment, his strength left his voice.

"Did he hit her?" Jerry barked.

"He..." Richard coughed; anger rose in him. Something had awoken. "...the son of a bitch pushed her against a car by pressing a Bible against her head. He thought she was possessed or some bullshit."

It was uncommon for Richard to speak that way. The anger was justified. Jerry being a man who tried to keep his temper subdued, felt the fire. Jerry grabbed his hat and thermos. "Where was Nova during this? I am assuming she was on the pastor's side."

"Y-yes sir. I went to the police and filed a Missing Person's Report for Abby, I don't know if it was presumptuous to do so but..."

Jerry interrupted, "The police aren't going to do shit. Listen, I will be down there in the morning. Find out what Abby does with her life that you don't know about, and we will take it from there. I will see you when I see you."

Jerry hung up.

Richard wanted to tell him that he stood in front of the angry crowd at the church defending his granddaughter from a modern-day witch trial. He wanted to inform Jerry that had become a man of action, but he froze; that wasn't important now. Richard sat in his car and gripped the steering wheel. He shouted as loud as he could and punched the horn. Tears formed; he ran his fingers through his thinning hair. Then a hint of calm settled, as long as Jerry came here, he would fix everything.

"We will find you, Abby," he whispered.

Jerry stood in the kitchen, closed his eyes for a minute, and planned his next move. He went into the living room and kissed Margaret. She had lived with Jerry for the past two years. He told her he could never marry again. She knew his past and she was okay with that.

The grim look on his face, when he entered the TV room said all that needed to be said. Margaret got up and made him two ham sandwiches and put them in his old lunch box.

Daisy and Clegg, his two German shepherds, tripped him in the kitchen. Clegg moaned and licked Jerry's hand. He petted him and told him that he was a good boy. Margaret filled his thermos with cold black coffee, leftover from the morning. He took a sip and went into the bedroom closet. On the top shelf was his .38 revolver. He opened it, spun the chamber, and put it in his waistband. He was on the highway within twenty minutes and headed south.

19

Abby's Missing Person's Report hit the 10 o'clock local news. Richard sat cross-legged on the bare floor. Silently, he wept when he saw her picture appear on the screen. Dario rubbed his face against Richard's arm as if he knew what was going on. Nova was watching him from the other room. She was convinced what God had told her was true, that Abby would return on Wednesday. She had repeated this message to Richard when he returned home. He told her to keep her delusions to herself, and they hadn't spoken since. Richard did not tell Nova that her father would be arriving within the next few hours, as her father was the only person who seemed to keep her in line.

The phone rang. Richard was stiff from cramping muscles and hobbled to the phone. Nova watched him through the spokes of the banister. He answered, it was Mildred Ulma.

"I was expecting Nova to answer," she said.

"Perhaps she knew you were going to call and avoided you, since she has clairvoyance." He turned toward Nova as he said this.

"I don't understand," Mildred said.

"Of course, you wouldn't." He closed his eyes and rubbed his forehead. He wanted another drink but kept his composure.

"I am just calling to say that my husband and I are praying for Abby's safety."

"Ms. Ulma, I have to politely say, and you can tell your husband this, you can stick those prayers up both of your asses." Richard hung up the phone.

"Richard!" Nova screamed. She stormed into the room with her hands on her hips. "That is the pastor's wife, a woman of God."

"Who is also part of the reason why your daughter has not returned." Richard did not flinch when he said this. He did not raise his voice. It was a sign of strength that he had not shown to Nova before.

Nova's mouth hung open. She blinked rapidly. "Honestly, you couldn't think what you are saying is remotely true."

Richard pointed his finger at her. "Then where is Abby, and why has she not returned?"

That night Richard slept on the floor in front of the television. And for the first time, Dario slept next to him.

As Abby's Missing Person's Report aired, Sutton was with his older brother Simon. Simon had been driving his quad that day and broke his axle, while off-roading. They pushed the quad almost two miles through the woods and loaded it onto Simon's pickup truck. The next morning, Sutton got up at dawn and made breakfast for his brothers. It was a normal practice for him to do push-ups in the living room while they got ready for work. He would watch the news and shower after they left. The report aired again but on an affiliate station. When he saw Abby's face on the screen, with a number for the police, he fell in denial that she was missing. *She couldn't be*, he thought. He watched her go into the house on Saturday night.

He called her and it went to voicemail. Then he texted her as he left and headed to her house.

When he arrived, he saw a pickup truck, with mud spattered across the side, parked in front of Abby's house. A muscular older man with a gray ponytail was standing by the truck. He was looking in the empty carport where Abby parked her car. A cigarillo was hanging out of his mouth.

Sutton parked on the opposite side of the street. Timidly, he approached Jerry.

"Are you one of Abby's grandparents?"

"I am her grandfather. Who are you?" Jerry replied. He stood sideways while Sutton approached. It was a standard pose for Jerry to give unopen body language to offset all strangers.

"My name is Sutton, sir. I gave Abagail a ride home on Saturday night."

"You did?" Jerry looked down at the ground, adding in the information that he was already trying to piece together.

"Yes sir. She was at a party and got drunk. She called me for a ride home."

"So, you saw her *at* the party?" Jerry asked.

"No sir, I saw her *after* the party. She called me at eleven o'clock. I picked her up at a 7/11. I parked her car across the street at a McDonald's and brought here. I waited until she got in, then I went home."

Jerry turned to face him. As Sutton explained, Jerry was believing him. It was how Sutton looked him in the eye and explained himself properly.

"I texted her later, but she didn't respond."

Jerry eyed him up. "Are you in the military?"

"Leaving for the Army next month, sir."

"Not the Marines?" Jerry smirked.

"No sir."

"All right son, let's get Richard, and get Abby's car."

Richard had an extra set of car keys made for everyone's vehicles. It was a precautionary thing. He never told Nova because he was afraid she would move or lose them. The three men drove to the McDonald's in Jerry's pickup. Abby's car was still in the back parking lot. Sutton pointed across the street, showed them where he met her, and suggested they go in the 7/11 and get video footage. Jerry believed him. Sutton's account was important, but he wasn't the last person who saw Abby.

Richard told Jerry where he had searched and suggested revisiting the same places. Jerry agreed but didn't want to drive around aimlessly. He suggested they question people who saw her prior to her disappearance. Richard remembered that Abby was at a party with a girl from work, named Priscilla. Nova had told him when she spoke of Abby's trailer park drunkenness.

He called her work and asked for Priscilla. Since Abby's face had been on the TV, Priscilla had been a wreck, she picked up the phone. Richard told her who he was and that he was retracing Abby's footsteps from the previous night. Nervously, she gave him the address, which was a few doors away from where she lived. Priscilla did not disclose that.

Jerry was impressed with how he produced the information so tactfully.

They went to the trailer park and Jerry parked his truck in the ash lot in front of the two trailers. Jerry took the .38 revolver out of the glove box.

Sutton looked at him and smiled. "I didn't know you were packing, sir. I would have brought my Glock."

Jerry didn't seem impressed but nodded. He put the gun in the waistband of his pants and walked up to the trailer on the left. Two skinny cats were sitting on a burnt-out clothes dryer. Multiple cinderblocks were in and around a hole. Broken whiskey bottles littered the yard. A child with a dirty face looked through a fingerprinted window at the men. A shirtless, greasy man, holding a bowl of Rice Krispies answered the door. He held the expression of a man who was about to shit his pants. Jerry held a statuesque face of contempt. Richard and Sutton stood off the porch behind him.

"C-can I help you, sir?" the shirtless man asked.

"I understand there was a rowdy party here on Saturday. My seventeen-year-old granddaughter was here. This is her. Jerry flashed the Missing Person's Report on his phone. We are looking for her and any information regarding her disappearance, and we were wondering if you could help us. The shirtless man stepped back and pointed to the other room.

Jerry opened the broken screen door and held it open with his boot. Sutton and Richard followed.

"I was playing cards and drinking beers that night," the man said.

"So, you saw my granddaughter?" Jerry asked.

"Yes sir. Priscilla works with her." The man put his bowl of Rice Krispies on top of a stereo speaker. On the other speaker was another bowl of cereal, unfinished from a previous time.

"And who is Priscilla to you?"

"My cousin."

"I see, and who is the gentleman who lives in this establishment?"

"You might want to talk to Uncle Dennis."

The man pointed into the other room.

Jerry thanked him and went into the next room. It was a display of unpleasant filth. Not fit for anyone to visit or live in. An old Golden Labrador limped toward Jerry. It whined at him. He put out his hand for the dog to smell. The dog submitted to Jerry and licked his hand. He told him he was a good boy, and the dog sat in the kitchen by his empty bowl.

A two-year-old child in a diaper walked by with a metal socket from a socket wrench in its hand.

"Uncle Dennis!" Jerry yelled. He walked into the next room.

A man in a fedora with a squished face, and a wife beater was in a recliner. He was watching a pornographic movie on VHS. A bag of potato chips was resting on his belly. He was licking the salt and oil off his fingers.

Dennis replied, "What?"

Jerry entered the room. Sutton was a step behind him. Richard stood in the kitchen looking nervously at the greasy man, who was pouring another bowl of cereal. He had seemed to have forgotten where he put his first bowl.

On the recliner next to Dennis were stacks of TV Guide's dating back to the 80's. A rusty toolbox was on the floor. A pattern of tools: washers, bolts, and screws were on the ground, laid out in a semi-circle, a pattern that a child would make.

Jerry looked at the TV screen. He walked up to the VCR and paused the video. The screen's frame froze with a woman's face wincing in between a world of pain and pleasure.

Jerry exhaled in frustration. "Is it good to watch something like that with the little one around?"

"Who the hell are you?" Dennis asked.

"A frustrated man," Jerry said.

"Well take your frustration somewhere else and get the hell out of my trailer."

Jerry held up his finger to his lips, signaling for Dennis to hold his words. He held up Abby's photo on his phone.

"There was a party here on Saturday night. Did you see this young lady?"

"And what if I did?"

Sutton's hands were behind his back, and his posture erect. He was in pure military stance, a lean body from many sets of push-ups and pull-ups. Given the state of this place and from what Abby told him, Sutton was beginning to boil with rage. He was basing his reactions on Jerry's composure, but he felt that amping the situation might find more answers.

"I did see her. As she was parked in my yard," Dennis said, "I told her to go on and get. She told me to fuck off."

"She told you to fuck off?" Jerry asked.

"Well," he paused and cleaned out his ear with his pinky, "Maybe she didn't and someone else yelled *fuck off* from behind me, but I thought it was her. I saw she was in a foreign car, and my dad worked for Ford, years ago. I didn't like her car as well. So, I slapped my palm against her window, and she sped off."

"You did all that?" Sutton asked.

"Yes, I did. As it is my property." Dennis thumbed at his chest.

"You scared her good, then."

"I hope so."

Sutton stepped in front of Dennis and punched him in the nose. His squished face was more squished than it was when he was born.

"You hit me in the nose!" he screamed. Blood spurted onto his sweat-stained shirt.

"That's good enough son. Let him bleed out," Jerry said.

Dennis leaned forward. Blood dripped onto his bony legs and the brown shag carpet.

"Have you seen my granddaughter here before that night?"

"Never," he cried.

"How are you certain?"

"Because she looked weird. Like one of those vampire chicks. Priscilla hangs out with different girls. Not like her though."

"And after she left, you haven't seen her again?"

"No sir, I haven't"

"Should I hit him again?" Sutton asked.

"Please, don't. I swear, I am telling the truth," Dennis cried.

"Come on son," Jerry said to Sutton.

Jerry ejected the VHS tape and took it with him. The three of the men left. Dennis continuously yelled that his nose was broken until they shut the door to the trailer and his voice became muffled. They stood on the porch. Both Sutton and Richard looked at Jerry in awe. He lit a cigarillo.

"I think that piece of shit was telling the truth. He knows we would have beat it out of him. Wherever she went to on Sunday, it wasn't here. And I don't think these degenerates would have welcomed her back. Thank God."

"Thank God," Richard said.

Sutton nodded his head. "Where to next?"

"Her work."

They drove to Denny's. Jerry parked the truck in the back. A waft of bacon and hashbrowns filled the air. Jerry loved breakfast at all times of the day, but he did not want to eat until he got more answers. Dante was out back, smoking. The AM manager had called out sick and he was pulling a double. As the men approached, he held a smug look on his face.

"You the manager?" Jerry asked.

"Is this about some bad service or something?" Dante jested.

Jerry folded his muscular arms. Sutton mimicked him. Jerry trailed behind both of them.

"My granddaughter, Abagail, works here, and she happens to be missing. I am trying to retrace her steps."

"Sorry, sir. I didn't know who you were." Dante reached out his hand and shook Jerry's hand. "She is a good kid, a good worker, and all that. And she wants to work more when she turns eighteen." Dante pointed over Jerry's shoulder with his cigarette, "I believe I told that gentleman the same thing yesterday."

"That's my son-in-law. Well, as I said we are retracing. Is Priscilla around?"

"Yep, let me go get her." Dante ashed his cigarette and went inside.

Richard admired how Jerry was able to size people up. He cut through small talk, partly through intimidation. Even Dante acted differently, as if he was hiding amphetamines from a cop. His eyes were shiftier, and Richard liked him less than he did yesterday.

Priscilla came out and acted like she was caught stealing. She was visibly shaken.

"Any word on Abby?" she asked. "I saw her on the news, and I am sick over it."

"No word, ma'am," Jerry said. His tone changed; he didn't stand like he was going to punch someone. He knelt to her eye level as she sat on two milk crates.

"Were you two close?"

"Trying to be. I am not sure if she likes me though. She left my party the other night without saying a word."

"Why do you think that is?" Jerry asked. He didn't need a response to *why*.

"I don't know. Maybe because I'm trailer trash," she laughed.

Jerry wasn't amused with her attempt at humor. In his mind, she was exactly what she said she was. He looked away. But it was a statement that spoke truth. He knew that Abby wouldn't be at her place in hiding, in the transparency of what Priscilla admitted.

"The last I saw her was when she went out for a smoke on my back porch. Then she ran into my uncle in the front yard. I heard he yelled at her and kicked her car door."

"Funny-faced-looking fellow?"

She nodded as she put a cigarette in her mouth. "I take it you met him."

Jerry smiled with a nod. "Listen, may I take your number, and you take mine. Call if you hear anything."

"Yes, sir," she said.

"Thank you for your time," he said.

They got in the truck and drove back to the McDonald's. When they got on the road, Jerry called Abby's phone. He heard her voice before the beep and tears filled his eyes.

"Abby, it's your grandfather. I am in town looking for you. When you are done being angry, come back home, please. We love you."

Richard never saw his father-in-law cry before, nor say the word *love* to anyone. Richard wanted to tell him what he thought, and it was that Abby was pissed at Nova and him. Not just him, but Pastor Ulma and what happened at the church. The lack of support for Abby and her plans in the fall was the last straw. He cursed himself for agreeing with Nova about making Abby pay rent. She was taking it out on them by being silent. She was brooding somewhere, with one of her books. He hoped that if Abby got Jerry's message, she would return by the end of the evening.

In traffic, Jerry closed his eyes. He dozed for a millisecond. Sutton and Richard were unaware of this. The light turned green and the car behind them beeped. Jerry jerked his head and coughed.

"You okay, sir?" Sutton asked.

"I have been up for a bit; I think I might need to catch a bit of sleep, when we get back to the house."

"Do you want me to drive?" Richard asked.

"Nope," Jerry said. His brain wouldn't let him rest. He would fight sleep as long as possible, until Abby returned, or a clue concerning her whereabouts.

They arrived at the McDonald's. Sutton got in Abby's car and followed them. Jerry rolled down the window and threw the VHS from Dennis's VCR into the dumpster.

"That's the second time I am smelling breakfast and driving away. Do you have fixin's at the house?" Jerry asked.

"Yes sir," Richard said.

"Has Nova been behaving?"

"Nova is, um..." Richard exhaled and put his hand on his forehead.

"Just say it."

"...she isn't well. They have been at each other's throats. More so Nova flipping out; more than usual. Abby does push buttons, but Nova has become a different person, by yelling Bible verses and throwing stuff. She scares me. It's all this stuff her pastor filled her head with. Then they chased Abby out of the church on Sunday."

"Yeah, fill me in on that again?"

"The pastor got the idea that Abby was a witch and pushed the Bible up against her head. They treated her like a monster."

Jerry looked at him wild-eyed, "Are you shittin' me?"

"No sir."

"I think we are going to pay him a visit."

"Well, I called a lawyer yesterday."

"And?"

"He said if I want to sue, Abby will need to file a police report and refrain from contact with anyone from the church."

"Son of a bitch. No wonder why the poor girl went off the grid. And how is Nova with all this?"

"As I said sir, she isn't well."

Jerry looked at him again. Richard became nervous and kept his eyes forward. That was all that needed to be said.

When they got home, Jerry parked his truck in the yard, on the side of the house. Sutton parked Abby's car in the carport. A grim feeling hung over them, as the day had been unsuccessful. They went inside without saying a word.

Nova heard the men on the porch. She didn't know who would be visiting and ran downstairs. When they entered, she was startled to see her father, as Jerry had kept his visit a secret. Her complexion was sickly, and her dress made her look like a ghost. Jerry's face cringed when he saw her. She came towards him timidly, like a little girl, and hugged him. He put his arm around her and felt how thin she became.

"Nova, you look like you need a good meal."

"I can't eat right now, Dad. I am not myself."

"Well, you are going to go upstairs and take a shower and put on normal clothes. This *lone prophet on a hill* nonsense needs to stop. In the next few hours or days, depending on Abby's situation, we have to expect town folk and the police walking in here. And you do not want to carry yourself the way you have been. So, if God is telling you something. Keep it to yourself. Got it?"

Richard's mouth dropped, and it turned into a half smile. He covered his reaction with his hand and walked away. Sutton didn't know how to react, so he followed him into the kitchen.

"Dad, I just want you to know something that God..." Nova said.

"All I heard was *yes sir*," Jerry said.

Nova lowered her head and went upstairs. It was the first time in months that she was not able to tell anyone what God told her.

Jerry shook his head and went into the kitchen. Sleep was calling to him; he wanted to lay down in the back of his truck and close his eyes for an hour. A full stomach would give him proper focus. He washed his hands and went into the refrigerator. He took out eggs and bacon.

"Do you gentlemen oppose to eating breakfast now?"

"No sir," Sutton said.

Richard shook his head. He was amazed at how he handled Nova. The men ate quietly. Nova did not come back downstairs. Jerry made her a plate and covered it with a paper towel.

He took the empty plates from the kitchen table and put them in the sink. He hated seeing old ketchup on plates after eggs were made, it made him nauseous. He rinsed the plates and forks as fast as he could and let them air dry in the dish stand. Sutton was mesmerized by him and planned on staying here all night. He would only leave if he was told to. Richard enjoyed Sutton's company, and he broke the tension just by being present.

Jerry dried his hands with a dish towel and looked attentively at the men. He pulled out his flask and took a sip. His composure demanded attention. The room fell quiet. There was even a pause on the television, in between the program and the commercial, as if Jerry demanded its silence as well.

"Margaret is doing well; she sends her love. She couldn't take the time off of work, to come down and she is keeping her eye on the dogs. I would have loved to have brought them, but they would have torn up your yard."

"Dogs are like that," Richard said. Although he didn't know if that was true.

"When Abby comes back..." he choked, "...we would like for all of you to come up and visit us when you can, and it might do Nova well, to get her out of here for a while. "

"That would be good sir. I think a road trip would do us well," Richard said.

"Do you have anything to drink here?"

Richard smiled. "Nothing fancy."

Jerry grinned. "Am I the fancy type?"

The men laughed.

Richard went into the pantry, he returned with a jug of red wine. A picture of a Victorian woman with a sour-looking face was on the label. He raised his eyebrows playfully.

"We have a few bottles of this in the pantry."

"That'll do."

Richard took out three tumbler-sized glasses and poured them halfway. Sutton was proud to hold wine in front of the men. They treated him like one of them, more than his brothers did, who always rode his case, to standards which he couldn't live up to. Richard and Jerry were treating him like family, more than he expected.

The three of them sipped. The wine held a delicate flora, it was fruity, with a hint of vanilla, and had a tart kick. No one commented on how unmasculine of a flavor it had. A hard, burning drink was to be expected after a day of knocking on doors with a bitter end. Fruit vanilla was second best, with these men.

Jerry leaned against the kitchen counter and finished his glass. He winced his face in disgust as he put the empty tumbler on the stove. Quickly, Richard filled it.

Jerry looked at both men grimly.

"It was back in '74 when my wife, Helen, disappeared. We were coming back from a church revival. There was a guest preacher, his name was Grantly. I think his initials were S.W. or something stupid like that. He was a doom and gloom prophet of God and was selling his run of paperbacks; weird shit people bought into. I never understood why Bible folks go bananas over those kinds of things. Visions of the apocalypse, that only a certain man can decipher, it is just a bunch of snake oil to me."

He sipped from the glass.

"Like all people at the church, they were taken up by this fancy preacher who had too many gold rings. I only went for Helen, because if it made her happy, I suppose I should be happy, or at least pretend that I was. Church was just kind of a quiet atmosphere for me, as long as I could stand against the wall and observe, I was fine. I just hoped that when I die, even if I didn't understand it, perhaps God would cut me a break.

"But Helen wanted to get involved. She wanted to bake cookies for this preacher. My own wife didn't bake me cookies, but apparently, she marveled at Grantly's ministry. She felt that he deserved her kitchen warmth. She asked me to pull into a grocery store and get all the things needed. Then she started speaking gibberish."

"Like speaking in tongues?" Richard asked. Everyone, except for him, did that at the church. Because of this, they had always treated him like the odd man out.

Sutton sipped on the wine, each time Jerry did, mimicking his moves. He was mesmerized by Jerry's rugged persona. It made him miss his father.

Jerry put the empty glass on the counter and pushed it away.

"It wasn't like that, I heard speaking in tongues before. This was different. This particular night, it was like something happened to her mind. I know this sounds like bullshit, but it was as if she got a message or something."

138

Jerry put his hands over his face. He wanted to tell them as he had never spoken about it, in its truth, to a living soul. With Abagail's disappearance, a thought crossed his mind. He wondered if the same thing happened to her. It made him sick to his stomach. *Not twice in the same family line,* he thought.

"When I left the grocery store, Helen was gone. And the police..." he paused.

Richard and Sutton looked at each other and then to Jerry. Even in that moment, he had the fortitude to fight off tears.

"At first, they were helpful. Then the media got involved, then the narrative changed. A missing woman from a small town doesn't sell as many papers as, an ex-Vietnam vet in question for missing wife."

Jerry turned around and showed them his back. A hard minute passed.

"What happened, sir?" Sutton asked.

"She was never found, and my poor daughter Nova never recovered. I think these misfires she has, is because of what happened then."

Richard never looked at Nova like that before, that her outbursts were just misfires. As if she had the capacity to function normally but at some moments she was *off.*

"Jerry, I never knew," Richard said.

"No one has. And Sutton, I appreciate you not saying anything. I like you enough to drink with you and you are going into the Army so, I best figure..."

"Your secret is safe with me sir," Sutton said. "Perhaps it isn't my place to suggest anything but what if we start a search party? With just local folks? My brothers would help. Maybe some of those old Catholic ladies wouldn't mind knocking on doors."

Jerry coughed into his hand. He took out a cigarillo and put it behind his ear. He turned around and looked at Sutton. Although Sutton had not stood in front of a drill sergeant yet, he felt like this was as close as he was to one.

"That is a good idea, son. Better than waiting on the police," Jerry said.

Out on the street, a car door shut, followed by a second. A man and woman wearing suits and dark sunglasses climbed the stairs slowly. Sutton got up and looked out the window.

"It is an unmarked car; two suits on the porch.

"It's probably detectives or the FBI," Jerry said.

"I'll talk to them." Richard's hand shuddered as he opened the door for them.

They introduced themselves and shook hands. Detective Parker was a plain woman in her thirties, all career, no wedding ring, and had the face of someone who passed the wine and went for the whiskey. She showed her ID and took out a notepad and pen. Her partner was Detective McRaney, salt and pepper grey, goatee, also unmarried. A burn scar was on the back of his right hand. He showed his ID as well and folded his hands in front of himself, allowing the burn scar to be visible first. They stood in the living room uncomfortably. Their stoic presence sucked what little warmth was left in the room.

Nova came downstairs. A towel was around her head. She was dressed in jeans and a t-shirt. Jerry stopped her from entering the room in the hallway. He got within an earshot of her.

"With how you have been acting lately, I suggest that you let Richard do the talking," he said.

"Abagail is my daughter," she whispered.

Jerry poked her with his finger. "You could incriminate yourself, by being stupid."

As of late, Nova had only listened to one man, and that was Pastor Ulma. To the point where Richard's voice meant nothing to her because Richard did not have a line with God. But her father's presence put the fear of God in her, and in that moment, she listened to him.

The detectives greeted Nova when she came into the room. Gone were the ways of her being welcoming; Nova was just pretending to act like a housewife. She sat on the edge of the couch. Her mannerisms were distraught and fitting, but her reasons were different.

Richard asked if the detectives wanted coffee. They replied *yes,* and Jerry went into the kitchen for them.

They asked the same questions that had been asked at the police station: friends, family, and work-related. Richard gave them the same answers as he gave to the police. Only this time he told the detectives about the argument between the pastor and Abby.

Nova became visibly uncomfortable and went to say something but didn't.

"Do you have anything to add Ms. Gibson?" Detective Parker asked. Nova shook her head.

They asked to see Abby's room. In accordance with all teen girls' rooms, it was a mess. They stood in the center of clothing, book, and magazine disorder. Detective Parker took photos. She mentioned to Detective McRaney that they wanted access to her internet history and social media. Richard stood in the hallway and watched them. Richard thought that Nova would have followed him upstairs. Despite the arguments, this moment felt grave. One would assume in a time like this, that a husband and wife would cling to each other; but Nova wasn't acting as she should have been. It was obvious to the detectives as well.

Detective Parker lifted Abby's mattress. A vinyl record of *Disintegration* was underneath. Robert Smith looked at them, with a sad and beautiful glance.

"I think that is her favorite record," Richard said. He smiled because he knew Abby had replaced it, from the one that Nova destroyed.

Detective Parker picked it up, turned it around, and looked at the song titles. She never heard of The Cure before and put it back under the mattress.

They went out back and searched the yard. McRaney pointed to the gate in the back. They went to the top of the hill and examined the street. Detective Parker took pictures. They ventured to the tennis court and saw the graffiti and symbols. Two halves of citrine geodes were shell side up, on the chalk drawing which Abby had done. Parker took photos of that as well. They searched the perimeter and looked up into the windows of the houses. They went down to the garage port and looked in Abby's car. In the console was the half-torn picture of Robert Smith's face. Parker picked it up, felt the edge with her finger, and put it back. Sutton told them that he had driven it back that day and where it had been.

Detective McRaney asked Sutton probing questions. His tone was interrogative. Sutton, being hard-edged by his brothers, and his desire to be the best of the best with his future set for the Army, was aware of the psychological tactics that the detective was using. The detective needed to rule out Sutton as a suspect. Sutton was aware of all of this. He offered the information calmly and well-worded, with two-word responses. He cared about Abby and wanted her to return home safe, but he had seen enough crime shows, where police would often point the finger at the boyfriend. *Yes ma'am* and *yes sir*, was the way to go until they left.

McRaney wasn't sure what to think of Sutton, even though he passed the litmus test.

"Before we came, we checked the hospital. But there was nothing," McRaney said. "Check all friends that she has, high and low."

"I went to her school yesterday," Richard said.

"What did you discover?" the detective asked.

"That she has been reclusive this past year. Mostly because Abby's best friend moved to Miami before Christmas."

"Have you contacted this friend? It is possible she could be visiting her."

Richard froze. With all that had been going on, this didn't even cross his mind.

"I am sorry, I didn't even think of that because her car is here," he said.

Parker nodded her head in agreement. "That is true but call and see if they heard from Abby. All of these options need to be considered. Think as she would."

Richard humbly agreed.

"We are going to broadcast her photo and have the FBI contact info on tonight's news, it will become regional. In this stage, the news can be your ally," McRaney said.

"Will there be a search party?" Sutton asked.

"Tomorrow morning, we are going to work with local and state police. We will meet at the Blueville Police Station and start by knocking on doors and combing the wooded areas. Any volunteering would be helpful."

"My brothers and I will be there, we have two quads and can cover tougher terrain," Sutton said.

"Thank you, son," Jerry said.

"Also, Mr. and Ms. Gibson, use precaution, news stations may come around. At times they can be helpful, but we have seen cases where they tend to bring more unwanted tension." McRaney said.

"As in?" Richard said.

"The media has a tendency to not see people as people because they want a story. So, they might camp out front. We have seen it happen before."

"That won't do well in a small town like this," Jerry said.

"We would suggest to refrain from speaking to them and keep to yourselves in this difficult time."

The detectives shook Richard and Nova's hand and left.

Jerry didn't trust the detectives. This scenario was echoed by what he had been through in the past. He was beyond tired and needed to get some rest.

"I apologize, sir if I spoke out of line to the detectives," Sutton said to Richard.

"No, son, you are fine." Richard put his hand on his shoulder.

Richard stood on the back porch and texted Rose's mother, Anna, and informed her of everything.

Anna called him immediately. When they spoke, she was hysterical. Rose was in the kitchen and overheard the conversation. She grabbed the phone out of her mother's hands. Her voice was shaking. Richard tried calming her and told her that everything was going to be *okay*, even though those were just false words of comfort. Rose wanted to fly up and help with the search. Richard told her just to stay by the phone and that he would update her day-to-day.

Nova stood on the porch and wanted to cry. She never imagined a search party looking for Abby. Tomorrow was Wednesday. According to what she had heard from God, Abby would return. Yet, doubt was standing before her, like an obelisk cracking through ice. Her stubborn faith was slowly being chipped away.

Richard and Jerry stood on the porch with her. Richard grabbed Nova's hand. Jerry came from behind and wrapped his arms around them.

"Don't lose hope," he said.

Secretly, he was beginning to wonder if an object in the sky, that shot a ray of light, just like what happened to his wife years ago, was the same source of Abby's disappearance.

20

The next morning, Sutton and his brothers took their quads and combed the forest behind Abby's house. Dirt paths went wide on the outskirts of Blueville. They drove through each one calling out her name. They made their way through the woods and into the borders of the next town. As Sutton searched, his heart sank. His thoughts went from Abby being lost and hurt, to wondering if they would find her body. When he was miles away from her home, he started to lose hope and turned back.

Richard and Jerry went door to door in the neighborhood. Two large photos of Abby were printed out and shown to each person they met. One was the version of her before she went into her goth phase, and the other was current. Nearly everyone was helpful and encouraging, but they could not provide any additional information. Most of them knew who she was by the photo with her heavy make-up. Yet, to Richard's surprise, some didn't even know there was a missing girl from their town, as some never look outside their front door or are aware of the world they live in.

Nova stayed home and waited by the phone. People called throughout the day. Some were from the church, others were from older neighbors, just looking for updates. In between the calls, the silence became deafening to her, and she became angry with God.

Families and store owners searched in and around the neighborhood. Groups of teens from Abby's high school combed the streets with their parents. Ms. Thorne, an elderly but spry woman told her niece Cecily Streiber, who worked at a news station, in Cumberland City, that a peculiar teenager was missing and there was a huge search in town. Ms. Thorne told her that Abby was a different kind of girl, one that probably killed small animals and cast spells. Her disappearance was mistaken and was probably deliberate. Cecily thought this angle was newsworthy and came to Blueville to interview the Gibson's.

When she visited the Gibson house, Jerry and Richard were sitting out front. Both men were exhausted and emotionally drained. She asked if she could interview Richard and Nova live on camera; Jerry advised it should just be him. When the camera was on, Richard went blank, he realized that he might never see Abby again. He stuttered. Cecily caught him off guard and asked him if Abby was involved in the occult, and could her absence be considered a runaway case instead. This snapped Richard back to reality and he called Ms. Cecily Strieber a *bitch* for saying such a thing.

This clip made Abby's case cycle wider, as Richard's reaction acquired more attention than expected. Abby's face was flashed on most channels consistently, throughout the day. The story became widespread, to surrounding states, and eventually her report was aired on a national news station for just a few seconds.

Tennessee Teen Yet to be Found.

Because of Strieber's line of questioning, some said that Abby's disappearance was deliberate, and she ran away and joined a cult.

That evening, Nova drove to church on her own. Dizziness took over her better judgment, as she was on a fast. Two diet pills dissolved in her empty stomach. Her faith was at its lowest point in her life. The church prayed for Abby's safe return. Pastor Ulma did not attend that evening, just his wife Mildred. She spoke to Nova in private and said that Richard's attitude was not commendable. Nova thought her complaint was petty but said she would speak with him about it.

The following day, the police reassembled, branching further into the forest regions, in a circumference around the town. The dogs picked up no scent. The detectives had questioned students at school, only confirming Abagail's reclusiveness towards others. They found she had no romantic interests and had kept to herself for the latter part of the school year. Her grades were excellent, despite her dressing *weird* and keeping to herself. Some families discussed the possibility of suicide. An old catholic woman said that Abby was a Satanist, and her mother was a witch. Richard found a rosary on the porch, with a note saying to pray ten Hail Mary's for Abby's safe return.

What had gone unnoticed, far in the back of her home, by the unused tennis court, was a chalk circle with the astrological symbols. The catalyst for her disappearance was regarded as graffiti. The geodes that laid beside it, were just rocks to anyone who had seen them.

By Friday morning, the search was called off. The police and their dogs had dispersed. The news crews had left. Detective McRaney told Nova and Richard not to give up hope, but they didn't believe what he said. That day her senior class graduated high school. Clarice Andrews, A valedictorian girl, gave a speech concerning a better future for students. Her voice choked and added a moment of honesty, unlike all the other forced speeches that day. Clarice said that although she didn't know Abby personally, she wished for her safe return, and to *keep her in our thoughts and prayers.*

In the afternoon, the Clark family, who were the only Jehovah's Witnesses in Blueville, stopped by the Gibson's house. Ms. Clark brought a casserole with her. Her husband Judd waited in the car. Ms. Clark informed Richard that their daughter, Janessa, was holding a candlelight vigil in town on Saturday night. Some of the students were going to show up as well. Richard thought it would be nice and said he would attend. Nova was in regular clothes, sitting by the television, she was near catatonic. Her emotions were dismissed as normal for the situation, but Nova was enduring a battle with God. She had thought she heard his voice clearly. Misinterpreting was not feasible, it had to be something else. Since Abby didn't return home when God said she would, therefore Abby must have disrupted God's will. She must have been heading home on Wednesday, like Nova originally heard, but Abby somehow changed it. Whatever Abby had done, disrupted the will of God. Nova convinced herself of this and rocked back and forth slowly, ignoring Ms. Clark and her casserole.

"Did you hear us, Nova?" Richard asked.

Nova laughed to herself and did not look at them.

"It would be nice to see you tomorrow night if you are feeling up to it," Ms. Clark said.

Richard put his hand on Ms. Clark's shoulder and told her that they would be at the vigil.

As the evening came, Richard and Jerry sat under the pavilion out back. A citronella candle flickered in between them. They were beyond fatigued.

They drank whiskey sours and hardly spoke. Jerry was considering renting a helicopter to search the woods.

A car pulled up in front of the house. Richard saw through the fence that it was an old Cadillac. He got up and rushed inside. Nova opened the door and Pastor Ulma greeted them with a forced smile. The dusk light caressed his bloated crimson face, making him look like a wax statue. One of his associates Ned Swilton was with him. Ned was a recovering alcoholic. He swore that it was Pastor Ulma's words that brought him to the light, and he would jump into the fire for him.

Ulma took one step into the house and stopped.

"That's far enough," Richard said.

Nova flinched; she had never seen Richard take command of anything before. Jerry walked into the living room, rested his arm on the banister, with his drink in hand, and watched.

Pastor Ulma put his hands out, "Richard, I want you to know that we have been fasting and praying for the return of your daughter all week."

Richard cracked his knuckles like he was getting ready to fight, "Do you know my wife, who claims to be a prophet at your church, said she heard the voice of God and that my daughter would return on Wednesday?"

As Richard said this Nova acted like a puppy who was being chastised for peeing on a carpet and awkwardly sat down.

Ulma followed her with his eyes, "Well, I don't know what she heard or saw, but I can assure you that she is under much stress."

"How would you know? You weren't here to help us search this week. You just say that you are praying and kept out of sight," Richard responded.

"Richard, I know you are upset..."

"Jack, if I were to place a Bible on your forehead because I felt led to. Isn't that how you say it, you feel led to do something? And you fell over the banister of my porch, and you hit your head on the sidewalk, and it split open like a cantaloupe, could I say that it was the power of God?"

The color drained from Pastor Ulma's face. It had been a long time since someone stood up to him. He never expected it to be from a quiet parishioner, like Richard Gibson.

"Do you think you should be drinking during a time like this?" Ned interrupted. "Maybe you need to relax."

"Hey, jerk-weed, why don't you mind your business and go sit in the car," Jerry snapped.

Ned's face contorted. The mindset he had was to support the pastor, unconditionally. In his years before church, he had seen men like Jerry Beaumont put men in their place quickly. Jerry stared at him; stone-faced. Ned recognized his place, excused himself, and went back to the car.

"Richard, I think we might be thinking two different things here," Ulma said. His face returned to its regular reddened state, matching the map pattern birth bark on his forehead.

"No word salads, pastor. I won't have it."

"Richard, please," The pastor put his warm swollen hands on Richard's shoulder. "I would like to pray with you." He looked at Nova, "Nova let us grab hands together." He reached out towards her, thinking he had the ability to lift her off the couch and embrace his sweaty hand.

"Pastor, I am going to say this politely," Richard leaned through the doorframe. "Please get the fuck off of my property, before I feel led to kick your ass."

Jerry roared with laughter. He doubled over and coughed. Ulma's mouth opened in shock. He stepped backward.

"I think a charlatan like yourself, knows when he has nothing left but to leave," Jerry said.

Pastor Ulma put his head down, looked confused, and got in his car. Ned didn't say a word to him. Ulma looked up at Richard and didn't want to push the matter anymore. They left and drove to the church. Ned apologized to the pastor and went home feeling defeated. He was mad at himself for not being stronger.

Pastor Ulma didn't go into his house, which was adjacent to the church. He put the old Cadillac in reverse and headed toward the highway. After driving ten miles, he pulled off to a town called Fredonia. A small plaza was off the exit. He parked in front of a dollar store. Festive music blared through the open doors of a Mexican restaurant. In the corner of the plaza was a bar called Lucy's. He got out of his car, opened the trunk, and took off his shirt, vest, and tie. His undershirt was soaked with sweat. There was a wrinkled polo inside, and a baseball hat. A brown gravy stain remained on the shirt, from last week's buffet. He put on the shirt and hat and entered the bar.

When he walked inside, he sat on a stool and asked for a draft beer. On the television was a TV show he had never seen before. A gay man was out to lunch with his straight friend. He complained about going to a party solo. They joked about going together. The studio audience seemed to think this was funny. Normally this would have made the pastor mad, but he couldn't focus. He sat there without touching his beer and let his hands tremble.

21

The **Saturday morning** was sweet and mild. Alyssum flowers had overgrown on a hillside near the town, and a breeze carried a sweet smell in the air. When Richard awoke, he was convinced Abagail was dead. A block of ice rested frigidly in his chest. He turned to Nova and wanted to share his fear, hoping it would shake her back to reality. She was asleep, on top of the covers, in a long-sleeved gown. Her hands were folded on her stomach, her color was sickly. He thought she looked like a vampire. It was a small but defining moment where he began to hate her.

It was not the norm to give in to drinking hard liquor, but the bonding done with Jerry these past dreadful days was consoling. His head ached and he shuffled down the stairs to make coffee. Outside of the kitchen window, two squirrels chased each other around a tree. Dario yelled at them. Richard shushed him and put food in his bowl. With no other stone to overturn to find Abby, he sat in the haunting quiet of the morning and sipped on his coffee, feeling hollow. He didn't want to wake Jerry, who had been sleeping under the covered bed of his truck since he arrived, which was a very *Jerry* thing to do. Richard did not want to turn on the news or go through his phone, he just wanted to sit there. If Abby was dead, he wondered what procedure was to be done next. As he thought this, his shoulders felt like something cold had gripped them. A tightness crept around his throat.

How is a funeral done if someone is still missing? he wondered. He dumped the coffee in the sink, put his hands over his face, and wanted to cry but couldn't. In a stalemate of emotions, he decided not to move for the rest of the morning.

Nearby, at the local baseball field, a junior's game was being played. Both teams were compiled from local families. A few kids from out of the area participated. The game was of no importance, aside from town comradery, and to alleviate the mood for the recent media attention. The frenzied swarm in the town was more than anyone could handle.

During the first inning, the game was interrupted, by a single thing that multiple people saw at the same time yet had a different account of how it happened. Billy Meyers was pitching and threw a fastball, at Randolph Adams, a tall kid from Jenkins. Adams struck a home run, and the ball flew over centerfield. As the ball went over the fence, a silver flash of light appeared from above, as if it were a thin waterfall, moving as fast as lightning, Those who saw the flicker, didn't believe it happened, as their minds couldn't comprehend what appeared afterward. They claimed that Abagail was there the whole time and hadn't realized until the Adams kid hit the home run. Those who saw the flicker of light stated that in one second Abby wasn't there and the next second she was; as if she appeared out of thin air. A testimony from a young couple avowed that Abby walked out of the woods, climbed the fence, and laid in the field until she was noticed.

A boy in a faded AC/DC shirt yelled, "There is a naked woman in the field, covered in mud!"

A mother, with prescription sunglasses, in the shape of a cat's eyes, squinted, and saw muddy black bangs and a pale face. She realized it was Abby. "That's Abagail Gibson! The missing girl!"

"Abagail Gibson?" Another mother, with a lime green babushka, exclaimed, "This is an answer to our prayers."

"How in the hell did she get there? Did she drop out of the sky?" A mustached man, wearing rainbow suspenders and cut-off jean shorts yelled.

Ms. Sewell stood up and ran to her car. She was in her early sixties and ran one and a half miles every morning and had for nearly ten years. Once a year, over in Jenkins, a 5k was held on Thanksgiving. Ms. Sewell participated and was always first in her age group. She ran passed most people much younger than her. The same fire she carried during that race was with her today, and she retrieved an old fuzzy, yellow blanket from her trunk. The baseball game stopped. Apprehensively, people scattered onto the field. Abby was hunched over, covering herself with one arm and holding herself up with the other. Despite the brain fog, she was aware of where she was but didn't know how she got there.

By the time Ms. Sewell approached her with a blanket, Abby was sitting knees to chest; covered in a thick, brown substance; it was unearthly, a drippage of nightmare fuel. Abby watched everyone slowly walk toward her. Each person's face looked at her, judgingly, like she was a deformed animal in a cage. While keeping eye contact with the glances of the emerging faces, she turned to her side and retched, then attempted to wipe her mouth with her gelatinous-covered hand. She examined it in shock and curled her lip in disgust. The thick brown substance smelled like the garbage bin in the back alley behind Hooper's Deli in mid-July, only if rainbow sherbet was melting on top of rotten lunch meat. Voices spoke in blabbering harmony from the approaching crowd.

A man eating a hot pretzel dropped it on the ground and stepped on it as he advanced. A mother covered her son's eyes, as she realized Abby was without clothes. A nun blessed herself with the sign of the cross and kissed the rosary that was around her neck. A poodle wearing a blue t-shirt, that had pinstripes on it barked. Two twin red-headed girls sneered their faces at Abby, a defense mechanism they developed, to the second-glance reactions they received from others because their parents dressed them identically.

Ms. Sewell broke through the crowd, with a face of motherly concern. A face that her mother used to wear for her when she was in desperation. She held out the blanket wide. Abby recognized her face, as someone she had seen in town over the years. It was the expression worn by someone who actually gave a damn. Ms. Sewell wrapped Abby in the blanket. Even though she wasn't cold, her natural reaction was to shiver.

"It's okay honey. Let's get you somewhere safe."

Abby stood up; her legs shook. Ms. Sewell wrapped her arm around her shoulder and walked her to the car. The woman with the cat-eyeglasses called 911.

"You shouldn't move her," a platinum blonde woman, who looked like a small pig, in a purple Mumu yelled.

"This is a matter for the police," said an old man who looked like Orville Redenbacher, minus the bowtie.

"Are you taking her to the hospital?" asked Clarice Andrews. She was shocked to see Abby walk by her. She had just mentioned Abby at the graduation speech, yesterday. Clarice didn't know Abby personally, but had seen her in the hallways, and liked her because she thought Abby looked like a rock star.

"Don't pay attention to anyone Abby, just focus on walking," Ms. Sewell said.

"Ms. Sewell, you shouldn't be doing this," said Ethel Bernstein. Ethel and Ms. Sewell didn't get along. They lived across the street from each other. "You could get yourself in trouble."

"Oh Ethel, shut up. I don't mind getting in trouble for doing the right thing."

Ms. Sewell gently sat Abby in the car. People had followed, watched, gawked, and observed Abby, asking her questions about where she was and what happened.

"Is this real?" Abby asked. Her voice sounded like sandpaper.

"Yes, honey it is." Ms. Sewell said. She backed out of the parking lot and headed to her house.

"Thank you, ma'am. I don't understand what is going on."

"You just appeared in the middle of a baseball game, out of thin air."

"What?"

Abby had an image in her mind, red lights were in the sky above her; it felt like seconds ago. Her head hurt when she thought of it. She forced her mind away from the thought and imagined being at home in her room with her cat. When she focused on this thought, the pulsing her in head subsided.

"Don't talk now, just save your strength."

Ms. Sewell took the back road to avoid any commotion that would follow. She lived in Blueville her whole life and knew every road and side street. She took a turn down an alleyway behind the shops. Carefully, she drove passed dumpsters and stacked milk crates. She turned onto a side road, cut behind the fire station, and parked in the grass, behind her home.

"I feel like I am drunk," Abby said. She opened the car door and threw up in the dirt driveway. Her throat burned. "Oh God, I am sorry."

"Don't worry about that hon, let's get you inside and cleaned up before the world shows up on my porch."

"The world?"

"Yes, your face has been on the news for the past week."

Abby's head spun when she heard this. The fiasco at the church only felt like moments ago. Ms. Sewell took her by the hand and led her up the stairs. A small dog barked from inside.

"Why are you being so nice? I don't know you."

"You know my granddaughter Chelsea; she's an eleventh-grade girl, with big glasses and crutches. Her legs don't work like everyone else's."

"I know her, she is sweet," Abby said. Her words were slurring.

"When we saw you on the TV, she told me that you always held the door for her and stopped people from pushing by her. Heaven knows that a little niceness goes a long way."

Abby closed her eyes, "Thank you for helping me, ma'am."

"Call me Ms. Sewell, honey."

They entered through the kitchen. A small mixed-breed chihuahua growled at her. Abby felt threatened and stopped.

"Ramone, you go on, and get, she is our friend."

The little dog sneezed at Abby and ran into the other room.

Ms. Sewell walked her up the stairs, guided her into a small bathroom, and shut the door.

"Now take your time and clean yourself up. I will hold off whoever comes knocking on my front door as long as possible."

Abby didn't respond. She sat on the toilet, covered in the foreign substance. The last thing she remembered was meditating and chanting at the tennis court.

"The red lights," she whispered. A sharp pain entered above her right eye. A tear trickled down her cheek. She rubbed her forehead and forced herself to remember. As the pain increased, she grit her teeth.

"Yes."

She remembered levitating and seeing her house, then her mind went blank. Rubbing her temples with her fingers, she tried massaging more memories out of her bewildered mind, but that was all she could conjure.

"I think that was some sort of UFO above me."

Abby turned on the shower and let it warm up.

The rubber mat inside the tub was thick. She didn't want to get it covered in the gunk that was on her. She stepped in and let the hot water clean off the brown matter. Its consistency was like tapioca pudding. It clogged the drain, and the tub started to fill. She moved it with her hand, the drain opened, and it clogged again.

"Dammit."

She coughed, and her chest hurt. She reached outside the shower and pulled a wastebasket towards her, throwing clumps of the substance into it. It would have been easier for her to have hosed off in the yard. But that would have been too much of a sight for anyone who passed by.

"Ms. Sewell!"

"Yes, dear."

She had been sitting at the top of the stairs holding Ramone.

"I am going to need something to wear."

"Sorry, I wasn't thinking. I will get you something."

Ramone barked and followed Ms. Sewell into the bedroom. Abby scrubbed herself thoroughly. Then she sat in the shower and let the water wash over her. Her thoughts became loose; the concept of time disappeared. The bathroom door opened and then it closed. Ms. Sewell said something to her, but it was muffled.

A half-hour had passed. Ms. Sewell knocked on the door. The sound took Abby out of a stupor.

"Abagail?"

"Yes," she squeaked.

"Considering everything, are you feeling okay?"

"I think so. I just needed a minute."

Ms. Sewell opened the shower curtain, reached in, and turned off the water. She handed Abby a towel.

"No rush, and if you want me to chase them away I will."

"Are my parents here?"

"No, dear. I don't have their number. I am sorry. I can give you a ride home if they can't get you."

"I think I will..."

Abby trailed off, she wondered how her mother would have taken her disappearance. The unpredictable outbursts, ranging from anger to happiness

156

were always a coin toss. Most of it came from what her mother thought God would want her to feel. As for Richard, Abby wondered if he would mimic every move Nova did. Both of them were probably at church the entire time. Then she remembered, how Richard stood in between the ravenous church crowd and her. That was a brave side of Richard she hadn't seen before. Perhaps her stepfather was becoming less like the mindless drones that attended Ulma's church.

"I am sorry, honey, the police and paramedics are here. I told them you would come down when you are ready..."

Abby looked at her intently with weeping eyes.

"...or I can tell them to go jump in the lake," Ms. Sewell said.

"No, I will be down. Thank you for trying to protect me."

Abby dried herself. Clothes were left on the toilet seat: a large pink and blue plaid shirt, with puffy sleeves, a baggie a pair of khakis, and old ladies' white cotton underwear. Matching pink socks were in a ball on top of the pile. She held up Ms. Sewell's underwear. Even with her perception off, a bubble of laughter rose from within. Abby dressed and took a scrunchie out of the medicine cabinet for her hair. When she lifted her hair she noticed something weird on the back of her neck. She felt three raised bumps in the center. There was a small compact mirror under the cabinet. Abby lifted it behind her head and examined the bumps in the reflection of the mirror. The three of them were in the shape of a pyramid as if it was done by a machine or if she was branded by a crude device.

"Was I bitten?"

She took a fingernail file and poked at one. A shock went through her face and made her jaw momentarily numb. She dropped the mirror and file on the floor.

What the hell is going on with me, she thought.

Running her fingers over the bumps again, she pressed on them. She fell unconscious and levitated in the air toward the ceiling. Her arms and legs dangled as her head lightly touched the ceiling. She became balloon-like.

Ms. Sewell climbed the stairs and wanted to check on Abby again but felt sorry for what the poor girl must have gone through. Ramone looked out the side window and barked. Suddenly, Ms. Sewell thought of her husband. Today would have been their thirty-second anniversary. He died eighteen months ago of a brain aneurysm. Going to the baseball game kept her from being depressed. It was as if he was watching her, much different from the other times when she would speak to him. The feeling was so overwhelming she looked out the window and thought she saw an apparition levitating outside.

"Herbert, is that you?"

She placed her face close to the window and smiled as she saw something floating, wispy, and grey. Then it disappeared. Abagail slowly descended to the floor, and she awoke, unaware of what had happened. She picked up the nail file and mirror, placed them back under the sink, and left the bathroom.

Ms. Sewell was still smiling when Abby exited. "You look a bit queasy, honey, I have just the thing to fix that." She went into the kitchen.

Abby stood in the middle of the stairs and saw the crowd of reporters on the sidewalk through the thin curtains of the front window. Two stern-faced detectives were in the living room. They examined Abby scrutinously. They addressed themselves as Detective Parker and Detective McRaney. They had the pleasantries of funeral directors. A greying paramedic, with a poorly done tattoo of a wolf on his forearm was sitting on the couch. He stood up as he saw Abby enter the room and greeted her warmly. His face expressed concern as if he was worried about her well-being prior to this moment. Ramone barked at everyone. Ms. Sewell shushed him.

Detective McRaney began standard preliminary questions expressing alarm and eventually crouched in on being intimidating. Ms. Sewell put a glass of ginger ale on the coffee table next to Abby. Abby sipped it immediately. The magic effects that ginger ale held for an upset stomach took action.

The paramedic looked into Abby's eyes with a flashlight. He told her not to talk and checked her pressure and pulse. Detective Parker cleared her throat. McRaney started writing in a notepad.

"Ms. Gibson, do you know where you were in the past week?"

The paramedic put the light pen on the table and put his head down. He wanted to tell the detectives to hold their questions.

Abby smiled painfully, "I have no clue where I was. I only know what you all saw, or what Ms. Sewell saw this afternoon. It was like it was...Sunday and now it is today."

"Ms. Sewell said that you just appeared in the middle of the baseball field," McRaney said.

"Yep."

"Are you in any pain or discomfort Ms. Gibson," the paramedic asked. He took her wrist, lifted her arm, checked her forearm, and bent it. He did the same to the other.

"No, sir," she said.

"The moments leading up to your disappearance, do recall anyone, a man or woman grabbing you from behind? Or perhaps a vehicle following you, like a van or truck?" Parker asked.

"No, nothing like that at all. I walked home from church, last Sunday."

"You walked?" McRaney asked.

"Yes sir."

"Is that the normal way you get home from church?"

The paramedic raised his finger to the room. He checked Abby's pulse and blood pressure with a cuff. The room was silent, yet noise from the crowd outside could be heard. The paramedic got the reading and took the cuff off. He put on his stethoscope.

McRaney proceeded to question, unconcerned about what the paramedic was doing.

"No, there was an incident."

"An incident?"

"I went there with my mother and stepfather. The pastor, who *is* out of his mind, found a book that I had been reading and made a spectacle in front of everyone. The church got it in their head that I was a witch and chased me out into the goddam parking lot. The pastor felt empowered by God, I guess to place a Bible on my head. I was pressed up against the car by the angry mob and he forced me to the ground."

"Did you hit your head when you fell?" Parker asked.

Abby was stunned that her story didn't evoke any emotion from either detective.

"Oh my," Ms. Sewell said. "How could anyone think a sweet girl like you is a witch?"

"I don't think anyone at that church even thinks, ma'am," Abby said.

The paramedic raised his finger to the room to silence everyone and put the stethoscope on Abby's chest. He asked her to breathe in and out and hold it. She didn't want to go to the hospital, She wanted to go home and lock herself in her room. So, she gave the paramedic nothing to be concerned about. With each question he asked her, if she felt discomfort or pain or nausea, she lied and just said that she was tired.

Ms. Sewell was so concerned about how Abby's pastor thought she was a witch; that she failed to mention the brown substance that was on her.

"I didn't hit my head," Abby said. Although the whole scenario went so fast, she couldn't remember if she did or not.

"While you were gone, do you recall being sexually assaulted or violated in any way?" Detective Parker asked.

"What? No," Abby said.

"Heavens!" Ms. Sewell exclaimed.

"Did you check yourself in the shower?"

"Not more than I normally do."

Abby became defensive. Even though her mind was disjointed from a loss of time, she had expected the detectives to be more courteous.

The paramedic snapped his fingers from high left to high right and made Abby's eyes dart, to gauge reaction.

The detectives looked at each other for a moment. They whispered into each other's ears.

"Are you inclined to use narcotics, maybe a little marijuana," McRaney held his fingers up to his lips mimicking smoking, "...or alcohol?"

Abby looked at the paramedic. He shook his head and smirked.

"I just turned eighteen, so I am not old enough to drink and I don't know where I would find..." she smirked, "...marijuana."

"What was the last thing you recall before you disappeared?" McRaney grilled.

"I was in my kitchen, alone. And I wanted to go to work. I didn't want to be home." She realized that if she told them her car was missing, and that she was at the party the night before, it would have opened a door to more ridiculous questions. She omitted parts of her story and gave them a conclusion. From what she knew about the law by watching true crime

160

shows, they had no reason to detain her. They were just filling in the blanks to close their case.

"I went up to the tennis court behind my house to clear my head. It is a nice view on the hill above everything. Then I went blank."

"You just went blank? That is all you remember?" McRaney said.

Abby nodded her head.

As she said this, she remembered the geodes. The geodes were the key to the incantation. She forgot about them and wondered if they were still where she dropped them. She remembered the phrase she said.

"Katantu celven," she whispered. As the words were uttered, Abby felt a change in the room. It seemed like no one heard what she had said. No one spoke until Ramone barked and broke the silence.

"Did you say something, Abby?" Parker asked."

"No ma'am. I have nothing to add."

The paramedic fastened his bag. He stressed that Abby was dehydrated and should go to the emergency room if she felt any drastic changes in her body in the next twelve to twenty-four hours. He told her that she needed rest and should take vitamins for her immunity. Abby wanted to tell him about whatever she was covered in when she appeared on the baseball field. She wanted to tell him that she threw up and had been dizzy. But given the situation, she decided to tough it out and took heed that she might have to go to the hospital if things became worse. He stood up and passed by the detectives, giving McRaney a stern look, and excused himself. When he opened the door, the noise from the media clamored. Multiple news cameras and reporters stood as a mass, like a hungry, deranged monster. The paramedic shut the door behind him. Abby wanted to stand on the porch and give them the middle finger. She opened the curtain and watched a newswoman report a live news feed in front of a camera.

"What the hell is going on out there?" Abby asked.

"Your disappearance kind of turned our little town upside down," Ms. Sewell said.

"You don't say."

The detectives stared at Abby. Ms. Sewell watched them watch her and admired Abby for her strength.

161

"Detective Parker if you don't have any more questions, I would like to go home. And is it possible if you could give me a ride?"

"Our car is parked right across the street," Parker said.

"I will go outside and distract them and you two go around back," McRaney said.

Abby thanked Ms. Sewell for being so kind. Ms. Sewell embraced her. At that moment, warmth overwhelmed Abagail. An old woman who she hardly knew, produced more human kindness than she had experienced since Rose left. If they held any longer, tears would have been the next option, but she broke free.

"I will return your clothes."

"Don't bother. I am glad I was able to help you in this crazy time."

"Thank you again."

Ramone barked at Abby. Not a bark saying goodbye, but one that claimed that he was a dog in a living room, sitting next to its owner.

"Yes Ramone, I will come by and visit, when things calm down."

Abby scratched him behind his ears.

Parker led through the kitchen and Abby followed. They walked along the house toward the front. Parker raised her hand to Abby, stopped, and waited. McRaney stood on the porch and asked the media to step back, and he pointed to the left, to distract them from Abby's exit. A reporter interrupted him with a question. Another one listened to him and moved to the left. A blonde female reporter spotted Parker coming from the side of the house. She noticed Abby behind her. The reporter stepped on Ms. Sewell's property and her cameraman followed.

"Step back please," Parker said.

Abby followed Parker into the street. A horseshoe of bodies, cameras, and microphones formed around Abby.

"I said step back!" Parker shouted.

An oncoming police car came to a halt in the street and turned on the siren in an attempt to disperse the crowd. Abby kept her head down. A vain thought crossed her mind, with all this attention, she wished her hair and make-up were done to her standard. The outfit she was wearing, for live TV, was something she wouldn't want to be found dead in.

A young handsome man, with slicked black hair stepped out of the crowd. Eyeliner was on his bottom lids. He had a silver pin of the planet Saturn on his black tie.

"Pardon me, Ms. Gibson," he said.

He asked her a question, but it was muffled in the commotion. The blonde reporter stepped next to him. A camera was over her shoulder.

Abby was dizzy. Her throat was dry. A hot spot formed on the back of her neck.

"I am sorry, what?" She became flush and started to sweat profusely.

"Is it true that you dabbled in occult practices prior to your disappearance?" the Saturn man asked.

Immediately, the front of her head ached. A connection was made to the moment in the backyard. *How did he know?* Abby wondered.

"I don't know," she said.

"Ms. Gibson," McRaney addressed Abby. He was holding the back door of the unmarked car open.

Delicately, the handsome man put his hand on Abby's shoulder, "Any type of symbolism like that is usually connected to otherworldly, astral, or possible alien contact. Do you think your disappearance was related to something to extra-terrestrials or UFO's?"

"Are you saying my disappearance was related to UFO's?" Abby asked. Her face went from a skeptical smirk to twisted confusion. "I am one of those weird UFO abductee people now?"

"Ms. Gibson!" Detective Parker yelled.

Abby looked at the handsome man again and realized he didn't have a microphone. He was just a man on the street asking her a bizarre question.

Abby got into the car. The man in black stared calmly at her through the window, as the reporters moved around him, he disappeared. A male reporter shouted at the window, asking her if she felt her UFO claims were true. A cameraman was behind him, aiming a camera into her face. She stared into it blankly.

Minutes later, they arrived at her home. Abby thanked the detectives. She was grateful for the ride, but she didn't trust them.

When she looked at her house, a sense of dread came over her. Going inside didn't feel inviting. The last time she saw her mother was in the maniacal crowd last Sunday. She tried to open the door, but it was locked. Parker got out and opened it for her. Abby got out and stood in front of her.

Parker had a personality profile for Abby. She had been in her room, to her school, and seen her online interactions. The person she had in her mind and the one who stood before her were two different young women. Parker pitied Abby.

"You know, women in your situation will attract an unwanted amount of attention. If you lay low, it will eventually dissipate. You just have to keep a cool head."

Abby nodded her head. She kept her guard up, as any woman around her mother's age who gave advice, would be looked at as motherly.

"I think I might dig a hole in the backyard and hide there for a few weeks," Abby said.

Parker laughed. She handed Abby her card and said that she could call her if she needed anything, but the case was closed. Abby wondered how long it would take for the reporters to figure out where she lived and if they would camp outside of her house.

The detectives drove away. Abby realized that wherever she had been for the past week, her car keys and cell phone were still there.

"My fucking Doc Martens might be on a UFO," she laughed.

Richard's car wasn't in the driveway. She noticed her grandfather's truck was parked in his spot instead. Abby assumed her grandfather came down to be with them while she was gone. It excited her to know he was here. The last time she saw him was at Christmas, Margaret was with him. Then, the house felt more like a home. As Abagail went inside, she didn't know what to expect.

"Hello," she said.

Dario meowed from the other room; he came running to her.

"Dario, what is up buddy?" She picked him up and kissed him.

"Abagail!" Nova shouted.

Nova came down the stairs and stopped mid-way. While embracing Dario, Abby stared at her. It would have been a normal reaction for a mother to embrace a daughter in distress, but something stopped Nova. Abby sensed it immediately, and her guard went up.

"The angels that have spoken to me since I have been a little girl have returned. I have been silent with God, even mad at him. For God did speak to me and tell me that you were to return on Wednesday, then you didn't. But it was the angels who confirmed that you were supposed to return but veered off another path."

"Is that so?" Abby asked. Her chin quivered. Even though her mother fought with her bitterly, she expected a different reaction. "So, it was God and the angels, that told just you and only you?"

"Yes," her mother hissed. She stepped rigidly on the stairs.

Dario sensed the change in the mood, kicked out of Abby's arms, and ran off.

"No, *how are you doing* or *what's new*, but God told you *this* and *that*. That is where we are starting?"

"God does not lie to me. Meaning wherever you were, and whatever you were doing, you were ready to return on Wednesday, but you changed that." Nova gripped the banister top with her hand. She had been fasting and barely had the strength to stand for more than a few minutes at a time.

"Oh, I did? I changed God's will when I disappeared with no fucking memory! Well, I am sorry," Abby said.

"Are you mocking me?" Nova asked as she stepped closer. This time Abby didn't back away, she didn't run outside. Instead, she took a step closer to her mother. Both women glared at each other.

"Nope."

"Tell me, Abagail Gibson, daughter of mine, daughter of insolence, an outcast of the church, where were you?"

It pained Abby to have no memory of the time lost. From appearing in the center of the baseball field to going to the backyard last Sunday. It was just one moment to the next. Aside from the fog she felt in her mind, she didn't change in her small world, but the world around her did. There was no action of concern or embrace, from her mother. She was met with harsh unbelieving, as if disappearing was deliberate. The boiling point was reached, the sliver of patience was gone, Abby responded the only way she knew how, with sarcasm.

She looked her in the eyes and said, "Mother, I was doing what you expected, I was whoring about."

Nova gasped and put her hand on her chest. Abby walked by her coolly and went upstairs. She went into her room and locked the door. She was hungry, and it was a hunger she had never felt before. But to avoid conflict, food would have to wait until Richard and her grandfather came home.

It dawned on Abby that she missed her birthday and graduation. She wanted to cry but didn't have any tears left. She laid down and quickly fell asleep.

22

It was exactly three in the morning, and Abagail was sitting on her knees in the darkened hallway, in a half-circle of light that came from her bedroom. Fear gripped her heart; she couldn't get off the floor and walk to the bathroom. She had been trying to flush her system all afternoon and had to pee. But something was keeping her from standing up.

Purple and blue lights flashed from around the edges of her parent's bedroom door. A deep sound similar to a washer machine with a blanket stuck in a spin cycle came from the room.

"Yes," Richard wept. His voice was loud and shaky.

A voice spoke in a weird language. It sounded like her mother, only it was doubled with another voice, slowed down, as if it were being backmasked; maniacal and demonic.

Abby stood up slowly, with her back against the wall.

The voice spoke again, spewing foul indecipherable words that sounded like retched blasphemy. It was common for Abby's mother to think there was a satanic message hidden in forms of entertainment. Now her mother's voice was the source of the sound.

"Yes," Richard said. His voice was breaking as Abby's mother's voice grew stronger. Liquid seeped from under their door, into the hallway, and across the floor. It dripped over the edge onto the stairs. The liquid was milky-blue and sap-like.

As if she had no control over her legs, Abby moved across the floor and was standing at the doorway of their bedroom. The carpet was soaked with the bilious blue milk that continued to trickle from underneath the door. Abby called out to her mother and stepfather, but the sound that emitted from their room was drowning out her voice. Slowly, she opened the door and held her hand to shield her eyes from the blinding purple light.

What Abagail saw defied all understanding. Between the two open bedroom windows on the wall was a hole from the floor to the ceiling. Tentacles covered with large circular discs came from the hole and gripped the wall. In the center of the tentacles was a protruding bulbous mass, with a face that resembled her mother's, yet her mother's eyes were white; there were no irises.

Kneeling beneath the tentacled creature was a man in a red sheet, covering all of his features. Abagail knew this was Richard.

The creature spoke again. It was a dialect not from this Earth.

"Yesapharacalmata!" It shouted.

"I will do as you say!" Richard yelled."

A pair of black goat's legs, which were attached to the tentacled creature stepped through the hole and into the room. One hoof stepped on the floor and the other hoof pressed on top of Richard's head.

"Yesapharacalmata, Rashinayaktaiiiiiiii!" the creature yelled.

"I don't knowwwww," Richard cried.

The creature became aware of Abagail's presence and looked at her with a smile. The sound of a trumpet blared but was distorted.

"Abagail does thou writhe in the outer darkness?" the creature asked.

Abagail felt like she was going to melt into the floor, she grabbed the door handle and slammed it shut. She closed her eyes and opened them. She was standing in front of the bathroom mirror. Her breathing was frantic.

"Holy shit."

Since she came home, everything had been blurry. The paramedic should have taken her to the hospital. Nothing seemed to be functioning properly and her mother made everything worse. The only normal moment she had was when Richard and her grandfather hugged her earlier, but they still felt far away. There was a discussion concerning Abby going to the hospital when she tranced out in the kitchen again. Abby said that she would let them know tomorrow and that she just wanted to eat.

They made her dinner, a vegetarian lifestyle be damned, she wanted a hamburger. Her grandfather grilled for them, and Abby was so hungry she didn't remember eating it. After dinner, Richard and Jerry drank whiskey sours in the backyard and did not probe Abby with a million questions. Her mother stood off in the shadows. When no one was looking, Abby took a swig of whiskey from the bottle and went to her room.

A quick clip played on the TV of Abby walking out of Ms. Sewell's house with the caption below.

Missing teen returns mysteriously, town raises questions.

Witness accounts gave their testimonies. Ms. Phillips, the local gossip, said that Abby was sitting at the baseball diamond the entire time. She said Abby was covered in mud and stood up when the ball went over her head. A man with a mustache that looked like a caterpillar claimed he saw a flash of light, like a beam of lightning, hit the ground and there she sat, in front of everyone. "One second she wasn't there, and the next second she was," he said.

The phone didn't stop ringing that evening until Richard unplugged it. The reporters and nosy neighbors had parked their cars on both sides of the streets. Some just wanted to see what would happen next from the re-appearing teen, who had become a national story in a short week. Across the street, Mr. Robinson told everyone they had to leave. A reporter asked what his opinion was of Abby and if he suspected any foul play. Mr. Robinson told the reporter to go to hell and went back inside.

Always nipping at his flask, Jerry allowed the coals to burn in his furnace. He took out the garden hose and sprayed the gawkers and it dispersed the crowd and commotion.

Only once did Abagail's mother touch her, and it was for show. She put her hands on Abby's shoulders from behind, at the kitchen table. The moment was taken to bark praises to God for Abby's safe return. In any other setting, it would have been suitable, but it went from a quick prayer to loud clapping and shouts, then twirling. This was quickly shushed by Abby's grandfather, as he had zero tolerance for anything fanatical.

What stuck out to Abby the most, was the eyeliner-wearing man in the black suit, with the silver tie clip of Saturn. The bizarre question he asked meant he had been in and around this property in the past week.

"Who are you Saturn man, and how did you know about my scribblings?"

She wondered if he was watching her house now. Her imagination began to run wild, and she wondered if someone could be watching her from the other side of the mirror. Foolishly, she opened the medicine cabinet and looked inside to be certain there wasn't a camera recording her. She washed her face and dried it with a towel, and fear crept in further that if she lowered the towel, someone or something would be present in the bathroom with her. With the towel still over her eyes, she turned it off and opened the door.

"Abby." Her mother whispered from the darkness. She was in front of her bedroom.

Abby yelped and covered her mouth.

"Mother, are you trying to scare the shit out of me?"

Thankfully there were no tentacles, or a milk-soaked carpet to add to the already startling image, of her thin and haunting mother.

"I thought I heard you crying."

"No, I am fine. I just had to use the bathroom."

The streetlight cast faintly in through the front hallway window, and Abby could barely make out the shape of who she was speaking to. Her mother took a step closer, and the outside light caught her jawline. The underlight made her once attractive mother look like a floating skull.

"Did men touch you whilst you were gone? Because if you have been impregnated..."

"No," Abby interrupted.

Her mother turned around and went back to her room, like a living skeleton returning to its crypt. There was no fight, no tentacles, and no glowing lights. Perhaps it was a moment of pure concern from her mother. Or she was sleepwalking, and it was just her subconscious that cared.

Abby went to her room. She turned on the white Christmas lights that made a spiral on the ceiling, imagining it was a cluster of stars that she was traveling toward. She wondered if she really was on a UFO, or maybe in a secret government facility. She wanted to touch the mysterious bumps on the back of her neck but feared another jolt to the jaw.

The next morning, she awoke to a stillness. It was before the panic set in. It was like she was on the edge of a knife, unaware of what direction the next threat would come from. The fragile serenity of this moment reminded her of the time Rose, and she stood on a small sand bar off the coast of Virginia. They collected seashells when it was low tide. The tide would be rising within the next few hours, and they awaited her grandfather's return. That was when he had a powerful motorboat. As he said he would, he came and got them, but Abby's imagination played out that the tide came in above the bar and they drowned. That evening they ate fresh crab with Old Bay seasoning. The seashells they collected were thrown away this past Thanksgiving after Rose had left for Miami. As seashells never mean a thing, in the middle of Tennessee, when your mother thinks you are a harlot.

Like the ring of a clock, panic surfaced and knocked its heavy hand on the door of her heart and soul. Sweat came early today, as July was around the corner.

Abby checked her Myspace page. It was a unique pocket of the internet where she regrettably felt most indulgent. Posting a photo for comments and attention was becoming a thing with high school and college kids. She couldn't imagine a society being dependent on it in the future and hoped that it would run its course. On a day, where she knocked it out of the park with an outfit or makeup, she would make a post. It felt good to connect with someone across the world who was similar to her and gave a nice comment. On occasion, creeps came out of the woodwork and showed her the dark side of the internet. Blocking them was always the answer, and she wished people had that same button in real life.

Her inbox was flooded with DM's. The friend request list was overloaded. In her brief national spotlight, she had been sought out by people around the world. Some of the friend requests were women, who looked like her, in some form of gothdom, just reaching out to say *hello*. Others were men, stretching from her age to old gray-haired, faux rockers. There were messages from people who were bloggers about aliens, abductions, and UFO sightings. All of it was overwhelming, and she ignored every blinking beckon. She searched for Rose's page and sent her a message.

"Hey, I am okay. I know you might be hearing some crazy shit. Yes, I disappeared for a week. No, I don't remember anything, and I don't have my cell phone. I lost my good Doc Martens as well. My mother is a bitch as expected. However, Richard is being really cool. I think I have to go to the doctor for an evaluation. The FBI (I think) gave me a ride home yesterday. Last night there were news crews in front of the house. I don't know how to process all that is going on in my head. I might just skip town and come to Miami. I will have to

wear a head scarf and Jackie-O glasses for the summer. Should I brush up on my español? All that I remember is:

Estoy cansado de que todas ustedes, perras, ¡se interpongan en mi camino!

But I don't think that will get me far down there. I'll email you when I can. I will check back later today. I wish I was boring.

Love you. -Abby.

She turned off the monitor and buried her face in her hands. Dario always reacted to her quiet sobbing and meowed. He needed to eat. It was the stubborn struggle she had with his feeding time versus not wanting to go downstairs and face a crazy woman who lurked in the house. Would her mother be juggling knives for Jesus today, or would it be worse?

"Dammit Dario, I just want one minute of peace."

His front paws rested on the bottom of her bedframe. He purred at her and stared intently.

"No, I don't know where I was. I am trying to figure that out."

He meowed and blinked his eyes slowly.

"Do I look like I was abducted?"

She touched her nose to his.

"Well maybe, I should have taken you with me."

Quietly, she went downstairs. Richard was sitting at the kitchen table, in his robe, drinking coffee. Three wrapped packages were in front of him. The larger box was in black wrapping paper with a black bow, the other box, uniquely shaped, was with colorful wrapping paper. And the smallest object, book-sized was wrapped in the same black paper.

"Hey Abs, how are you feeling?" he asked. His tone was concerned. It was fitting for the given situation, but it was an emotion from him that she wasn't accustomed to. She had prepared herself for immediate rebuttals of spiritual warfare conversations, but the end-time prophet was still asleep.

"I am alive," she replied.

"Are you trying to be tough right now?" he grinned. A grin that she had never seen on him before. It was a supportive fatherly grin, a role he was always afraid to step into. She found it was surprisingly comforting.

"I am amazed that you know there are layers to me."

172

"You are a teenage girl."

"Not anymore. I am old enough to buy guns, and cigarettes, and fight in wars now."

"You are right." He looked out the window for a moment, his chin quivered. "I am sorry, you weren't here for some important moments in your life last week."

Abby shrugged her shoulders and half-smiled. There was nothing else to say about her mysterious disappearance. Absorbing this moment for what it was, would be the only normal moment she had in a long time.

"Well, I am glad you are home and safe, so happy birthday."

"Thank you." Her voice was soft, and her guard was lowered.

Dario headbutted her calf. She shushed him as she enjoyed a moment of peace. Abby fed Dario and he purred loudly while crunching dry cat food. She was anxious to tear into the gifts but wanted to have some coffee before she sat down. For the first time in her life, she did not add any cream or sugar. She sat down in front of her gifts and did not make eye contact with Richard.

"Before you open these, I want to go over two things with you." Richard scratched the side of his forehead with his fingernail, leaving a red mark.

Waiting for his next sentence, she sipped on her coffee.

"I called your doctor yesterday. I was surprised he called back. He had seen you on the news and suggested you go to the hospital to get looked at. I told him that you didn't want to sit in the waiting room for hours."

Abby didn't like where the conversation was headed because she hated doctors and hospitals.

"And?" she said.

"And he is willing to see you today. Which is really accommodating, considering his office is closed on Sundays. I guess he is just concerned about you."

Abby wanted to say *no*, but she was worried as well.

"*We* want to make sure that you are all right."

Abby interrupted, "*We* as in you and mom, or just you and grandpa?"

Richard ignored her question as he did not want to add to the growing rift between everyone and Nova.

"I want to make sure that everything is fine with you. Knowing the way you are, you will be back at work in a few days. I just need to make sure that you can drive and function properly."

"Okay," she nodded her head."

She picked up the smallest package, shaped like a paperback book. She assumed it was a cheesy devotional book on prayer or hope.

"Wait, aren't you guys headed to the good old Tabernacle this morning?"

"Ummm..." Richard twisted his coffee cup playfully. The side of the cup had a bold square font, with the phrase, *Even Robots need Coffee*. "...last Sunday, before you disappeared, I thought you went for a ride to cool off. When you didn't return, your friend Sutton led us to your car in the McDonald's parking lot."

"Holy shit, Sutton. I kind of forgot about him for a moment." She rubbed her temples.

"Yeah, he was here, nearly every day. He and his brothers searched the woods for you, and he gets along with your grandfather quite well."

"Where is he by the way?"

"He is sleeping in the back of his truck. You know, he has to do things his way."

"Hmmm."

Despite this update on Sutton's concern, he would not be someone she would get involved with romantically. If Sutton had his way, they would be married, and she would be pregnant and living at a military base in Afghanistan. That wouldn't do well for her vinyl record collection or her cat.

"After Pastor Ulma pushed you to the ground. I sought to take legal action. Even though I think you might have pushed his buttons, I will stick by you, as I don't think he should preach ever again. The lawyer said that we shouldn't have any contact with him or his church since the incident. And since you are a legal adult now, it is up to you to decide if you want to press charges. I would be a witness that he shoved you against the car. I don't know if other church members would agree or pretend to be blind."

Abby was shocked. These were fighting words. This would cause a rift between Richard and her mother, "Are you serious? What about...?" Abby pointed her finger to the ceiling.

"Well, all of that kind of paused when you vanished last week. I mean, people searched the woods for you. We told you that last night, but you were kind of in a daze."

Abby didn't remember them saying anything. Nothing in her mind, from the previous day, or week, and the recent past was clear. The creak of the floorboards upstairs indicated that her mother was up and about.

"With that said, *we*, as in you and I are not going there anymore."

She giggled, "Are you an atheist now?"

"No. But I never really believed in anything until I met your mother. She was different four years ago."

"She brushed her hair four years ago," Abby said.

They both laughed. In that warm exchange, she wondered if Richard would divorce her mother. She wouldn't blame him, but if that happened, would she lose him altogether?

"Open these before she comes downstairs. I want you to have a normal moment before.... well before things change."

Abby unwrapped the paper and saw the cover of an unfamiliar book on a unique subject. From a time and place where spiritualism was discussed without hell fire to pay as a punishment for imagination. *The Twisted Colors of my Dreamscape: A Metaphysical Journey through the Subconscious* by Platina Dapplemeyer.

"What? How did you know what I am into?"

The cover art had a myriad of colors and symbols, envisioned from a meditative hallucination brought on by the artist. A glorious picture of Ms. Dapplemeyer was on the back, in a pose with her hands and palms upward as if she was channeling her spirit elsewhere.

"This is wonderful." She got up and hugged him. It wasn't the normal action for her to hug anyone. But nothing seemed normal this morning.

"I found that at Tony's bookstore down in Nashville."

"You went all the way down there for a gift?"

"When I went looking for you last week. I went into your room looking for clues. I found a bag with the receipt on the floor, and the address was on it, and I ended up there."

Excitedly, she flipped through it and read the chapter titles.

"That Tony is a cool dude," he said.

"He is," Abby smiled.

"He said that you were one in a million."

"Really?" Her heart was warmed by the statement and the gesture at what length Richard had gone to.

Abby opened the thin, long box. It was from her grandfather. A small handwritten card said:

This was your grandmother's. Somehow it fits your style, today. Good to have you back.

It was a Victorian-style hand mirror, with a long brass-colored handle, patterned with ornate carvings of fleur de lis.

Abby gasped. It was beautiful. It was antique. It was perfect.

"This is unfucking real," Abby said. She covered her mouth with her hand and apologized for swearing.

Richard grinned and shrugged his shoulders. "With the week you had, I won't yell at you for swearing."

When she touched it, a jolt went through her fingers. She dropped it back in the box.

"You okay?"

"Yeah. I felt like a buzz there."

"A buzz?"

"I don't know, I am stupid."

Cautiously, Abby picked it up again and held it up to her swollen face. Looking sickly, more pale than usual.

"Abagail," A faint voice said. It went through her soul.

"What?" she asked.

"I didn't say anything," Richard said. He sipped his coffee.

She looked at herself again. dying her hair would do her well.

"I think I want to dye my..."

"Abagail." A whisper came again. Abby put the mirror down and stood up.

"Did you hear that?"

"No? You are freaking me out a little. Do you want to lie down or something?"

She shook her head, closed her eyes, and rubbed her forehead.

"No, I am good."

She put the mirror back in the box, put the lid on it, and picked up the last gift.

Abby knew that it was wrapped by Richard, as her mother would not have picked black wrapping paper and a matching bow.

She smiled at him warmly, "Good job on the paper."

Unwrapping it, showing playful impatience to enhance the appreciation, she threw the bow over her head and opened the box. It was a pair of black shoes, and they were Doc Martens.

"Damn, Richard. You kind of outdid yourself."

"Well, we felt..."

"*We*, there is no *we* in this. This was you," she scoffed.

"Yes, It was just me. Sorry. Your mother got you a gift on her own."

There was a no-shoes rule in the house but, Abby did not hesitate to put them on. She stood up and admired them.

"I knew you had the boots already, so I bought the shoes. I know they have different colors, but you don't usually wear anything but black."

"Well, these are replacing my boots now. I love them, thank you."

She reached in and hugged him again. Richard reached out and embraced her, both of them matured and they became someone different, overnight.

The card inside said *Happy Birthday*, with an image of a miserable black cat on the cover. It was signed, *Richard, Mom, and Dario*. A hundred-dollar bill was tucked inside.

"Oh my gosh. Thank you."

She wiped a tear from her eye and looked down at her shoes again.

The warm serenity was broken by a clearing of her mother's throat. Her mother was standing in a dark grey dress in the archway of the kitchen and living room.

"Those look nice, Abagail."

Calling Abby by her full name, usually meant trouble. As of late, everything to Nova was trouble.

"Thank you, mother," she said. Abby lowered her head, and her countenance changed.

"Well," Nova said excitably, "If we already had our coffee, then we can head over to church early. It only makes sense for us to go as a family, since God has returned my daughter."

That suggestion had the equivalent weight of a dump truck pouring sand in through the kitchen window.

"Um, I-I," Abby stuttered.

"No," Richard said. "Neither, Abby, your father, or I will be attending church this morning."

Richard had been clear last week when he said he wasn't returning. But it was like Nova to pretend as if things weren't said when she wanted to get her way.

Nova's face became contorted, stroke-like, and waxen. She stormed into the kitchen; Dario got in her way.

"Move!" she yelled.

He ran into the other room. Nova took a glass from the cabinet. She turned around and shouted, "So, I assume, I will be the only one praying for our family today. A literal miracle happens in this house, and you won't give thanks to God!"

"At Abby's discretion, I will precede how she wants to with legal action, concerning last Sunday's events," Richard said.

Nova held the glass tightly. Abby thought it was going to crack in her hand.

"Legal action!"

"Yes," Richard said.

"For what?"

"Because your pastor is a crazy asshole who abuses his parishioners," Richard said. He was calm. He stacked the empty boxes on top of one another.

In all of the time that this relationship existed, Abby had never seen this happen. She couldn't help but smile. A shadow passed by the back door; it was Jerry. He opened the door and came inside.

"Already yelling?" he asked.

"Father, this doesn't concern you," Nova said. Her voice lowered.

"Well, my dear, that is where you are wrong," he said. He looked at Abby and smiled. "How are you feeling birthday girl?"

"Good, Grandpa, thank you for the mirror. She moved across the kitchen and hugged him. The icy act of the goth teen had melted quickly that morning. What Antarctic breeze that was expected from her mother was stopped by two loving family members.

"Nova, I can hear you as clear as a bell out in the yard." He rubbed his hand over his stubbled chin. "I have been thinking. What Richard told me what happened at the church, and the way you have been acting, this all could have been prevented."

"What are you saying?" Nova asked. She put the empty glass in the sink.

"Can you say your actions have been normal for anyone?" her father said.

"Do you realize that God searches across the land to seek out those who are willing to do his bidding?" she said.

Jerry raised his hand to stop her. "Nova, I think you need to stop with the theatrics and consider talking to a therapist, maybe more than one."

Nova's face contorted. She picked up the empty glass and inhaled deeply. Her face reddened, and she shook.

"I am being persecuted for my calling," she said in a whispering exhale.

"Listen," he moved closer to her. "Your aunt thought these things about herself, as well. She helped raise you and was deep into religion. I thought maybe a little church would help you. But you made it into something terrifying."

Abby gave a shocked look toward Richard. He squinted his eyes at Nova, wary of her next move. This conversation was needed but there was never a right time for it. As any time to have it was igniting a powder keg.

In a flash, Nova opened the cupboard and knocked baking supplies out of her way. She retrieved a large plastic bottle of extra virgin olive oil. She uncapped it and poured it into the glass. Spreading her hands wide on the kitchen sink, she shouted, "Yes Lord!"

Paper towels were lying sideways on the counter. She unraveled a long piece and rolled it into a cone.

Nova faced her father, eyes bulging, she dipped the paper towel cone into the glass. Oil soaked in quickly.

"Prophets of old have endured such things from their adversaries," she yelled.

She took the soaked towel cone and flicked oil at her father, catching his shirt and jeans."

"What the hell Nova?" Jerry said.

"The Most High will vilify his anointed, and you are choosing the path of the golden calf. The calf of bitterness that was forged from golden trinkets and melted down into idolatry. My daughter was lost and then found, yet she returns to the path of the lost again! I am the one who has stood in the gap to bring down the strongholds. I am the one!"

"Stop it!" Jerry yelled.

She turned to Abby and flicked the cone at her. It caught Abby's face and spattered onto the linoleum floor and onto her new boots.

"I am the one who has prayed for you to come out of the pit of Sheol. The town search party was not necessary because I had a vision of you in the dark forest, with your harlotries, and you laughed. I saw you laugh at the grace that could have made you into a Godly woman."

"Mom cut it out!" Abby yelled.

Richard stood up, "Nova calm down!"

"And you! My dearest husband." She flicked the towel at him, catching his shirt and face.

"The one who has borne no children into this world, because of your sterility which you have been smote with! God never gave you children, yet you turn mine against me?"

"Mom, chill the fuck out!" Abby yelled.

"All of you!" she screamed, "have been the brazen of the brazen, the jackals who laughed at the prophet! Like Elijah who called down fire, it is I who have seen the end, yet you stand and mock, while the world is in threat of burning."

Tossing the towel at the kitchen table, Nova lifted the glass and smashed it on the floor; oil and glass scattered. Nova screamed in blood-curdling madness. She yanked her hair and spun around in circles. "Seraphim Eli, Cherubim Sarthos, Thrones of Might and Mercy!" Nova called on the imaginary angels she created back when she was a little girl. They were supposed to be warriors for the end times battle between agents of heaven and hell.

The three of them stared in astonishment as if the angels were manifested in front of her, judging her for her manic episode.

When Nova stopped spinning, she dry heaved in the sink.

"Mom?" Abby asked.

"Don't!" Her mother screamed. Spittle dripped from her mouth and hung below her chin. She turned and ran out of the kitchen. Broken glass cut her feet; blood and oil mixed on the linoleum, leaving footprints behind as she headed to the front room. Nova ignored her wounds and grabbed her shoes and burlap satchel by the door. She slammed the door behind her. Random passages from the Old Testament were uttered incoherently mixed with glossolalia, as she got in her car, and drove off.

Without saying a word, they all looked at each other, mouths agape. Dario came into the kitchen and batted at a crumbled piece of black wrapping paper that was on the floor. He meowed at it and looked up at Abby.

"Well, that went well," Richard said. As painful as it was, they all laughed, in an attempt to expel the tension. However, deep down inside of Abby, sorrow surfaced for her mother's well-being and mental health.

23

Doctor Bronson's personality was as sterile as the small, overly bright room. He had seen Abby's missing person's report on the nightly news. Although he didn't show much emotion to any of his patients, he was deeply concerned for Abby. His daughter was in college, and witnessing Abby's disappearance, made him worry for her safety, as well. When Richard called yesterday about Abby needing to see him, he was more than accommodating.

Abby laid on the examining table and checked her vitals. He asked the same questions that the paramedic did but was more concerned for her mental health. He prescribed her anxiety medication and recommended she see a therapist. An experience like this would be taxing for anyone. He stressed that she needed plenty of bed rest. Any extreme stimulus could aggravate her already fragile psyche, especially with memory loss.

As all of this was said, Abby didn't disagree, but she wondered how much more her mother needed help than she did.

Blood work was ordered to be done that week. Despite her claiming to be a vegetarian, he said she needed to eat better and had symptoms of being anemic. He told her to call if she needed anything and left. A nurse would be in to give her a B Vitamin shot.

As Abby waited for the nurse to return, she fidgeted on the examining table. Giving blood made her queasy. She had only done it once before. The room was uncomfortably bright, and she covered her face with her arm. Thinking about her last moment before she levitated, she realized that all of this was connected to the incantation from Francis Truelove. It was his words and the bizarre phrases from her vivid cosmic dreams that did this. Whether or not she left the Earth in a ship or floated about aimlessly, she had scarce recollection of anything. Every time she tried to piece something together, painful headaches would surface. The three dots on the back of her neck freaked her out and she didn't know how to tell the doctor about them. If they were placed by aliens or high-tech secret government kidnappers, what would be the next step to take?

Oh, by the way, Doc, I think an implant from an alien is in my neck. That will sound rational. she thought.

"Ms. Gibson," A man's voice addressed her.

She raised her arm and felt groggy. A micro-nap happened briefly. The disposable paper stuck to the back of her legs. She sat straight up and felt like a glass dish that came out of an oven.

"Ms. Gibson," he said, "I am sorry if I startled you."

The man smelled nice; his voice was soothing. From the back, she saw slicked dark hair that came over the collar of his white coat.

"The doctor mentioned that you are a vegetarian."

"I am sorry?" she asked. She heard what he said, but her response was delayed. And the answer would be *sometimes.*

"Yes."

The nurse turned around to face her. He became more clear as her eyes focused. His frame was trim, hair styled, with a black tie and black dress shirt that was fashionable, unexpected for this profession. She became conscious of her perspiration. He kept his eyes on the clipboard and scribbled erratically.

"Well, usually novice vegetarians do not make proper food choices. Pizza and cheese fries at the mall, versus bean salads and tofu. If not done correctly, you could end up becoming anemic. I would suggest you take iron supplements."

He took her hand quickly and looked at her fingers. "If your nails weren't painted, they would most likely appear purple underneath, as an indication of low iron."

He put the clipboard on the counter.

"Close your eyes for one second, please."

Immediately, Abby felt something was off, but she listened.

"Okay, open them."

A camera flash went off. He took a close shot of her face with a Polaroid camera.

"What the hell?" she said.

His grin became unprofessional, as if he said a joke to an audience in his head.

"Sorry, we have to do that with all of our patients, for their file."

She squinted her eyes at him. He reached for her wrist; his index finger touched her bare leg. He checked her pulse and stared into her eyes intently.

"Your heart is racing," he said.

Quickly, she snapped her hand away from him. He frowned at her as if her reaction was rude.

"Abagail, what words did you use when you did the incantation?" he asked.

"What did you just say?" she whispered. A tightness formed in her throat.

He took a step closer to her and leaned in. A reflection of her pale moon face stared back at her in his abnormally large dark eyes.

"There were chalk drawings of geodes on the concrete lot behind your house. That practice was taken from the writings of the mystic Francis Truelove, wasn't it? How did you do it? What did you chant?"

"You aren't a nurse." She slid her legs off to the side and hopped off the table, "Who the fuck are you?"

"Hold on, I just want to talk," He put his hands up like he was surrendering. "If you did make contact with something else, something alien, something not from this world, it would be good to be around like-minded people."

She snatched her purse, grabbed the pepper spray, and without faltering she sprayed him. The quick action took him by surprise. It burned his eyes and nasal passages. Tears and snot burst forth like a dirty faucet. While clutching his face, he screamed. Abby opened the door and ran down the hallway toward the entrance. At the end of the hall, blocking the exit was the man in black that she saw yesterday, in front of Ms. Sewell's house.

"She fucking maced me, get her!" Isaac yelled.

Jericho ran toward her. She pivoted and sprinted in the other direction. The new Doc Martens were not track-worthy, but she ran like hell. The hallway led to a fire exit. Shouts echoed from behind her. The pepper spray was still in her hand. Footsteps were getting closer. She crashed through the metal fire door. An alarm went off, and she was in the back parking lot. A black van was parked on the left. Panic took over. A hand grabbed her shoulder, and she yanked it off, like an unwanted spider. She was off balance and cross-stumbled sideways. Jericho grinned, his neat black hair hung loosely into his eyes. The Saturn pin gleamed on his black tie.

"Who are you people?" she said.

"Don't be afraid. If you come with me, I can show you."

"Is that why you are fucking chasing me?"

She lifted her arm to spray him in the face, but Jericho grabbed the inside of her wrist and pushed it away. A mist of pepper spray shot upward and caught the left side of his face, and an arc caught her eye. He coughed and she gagged.

"Stop, please," Jericho said.

At that moment, something snapped in Abby, she was tired of being the victim. She kicked him as hard as she could in the kneecap. Pain shot through his leg. Jericho's eyes bulged as he shrieked. She backed away from the teary-eyed crying mess. As she ran down the alley, he called out to her.

"Abagail, you need us!"

She wanted to spray him again, but he was too far away. Her right eye was dripping, and with him being immobile, she headed toward the front of the building. Richard was exiting the doctor's office and saw her run out of the alley and head into the donut shop next door.

"Abby!" he yelled, "Are you all right?"

"Some creep attacked me!"

He ran towards her. When he saw the expression on her face, he wanted to protect her. A role he felt he should have been doing long before today. He followed her into the donut shop. Immediately she went to the counter. While holding her eye, she pretended to be calm and purchased milk. Richard came up from behind her, paid for it, and retrieved his phone. He was about to call the police but hesitated.

What would Jerry want him to do? he thought.

Abby ran into the bathroom, uncapped the milk, and splashed it in her eye. The stinging subdued. Her mascara ran in black streams down her milk drenched face. With her hands placed on the sink, she contemplated not leaving the bathroom, out of fear of her pursuers.

Minutes earlier, in the waiting room of the clinic, Jerry heard a man's voice scream. He jumped out of his seat. The large double doors were locked. He snapped at the receptionist. The receptionist didn't react as fast as Jerry did. Through the window, he saw a thin man wearing all black run after a staggering man in a white lab coat. Jerry kicked open the double doors, with the heavy heel of his boot.

As Jerry ran, a flashback came to him, it was one that never left him since the war. It was a nightmare that struck at random; a 'Nam moment. While retreating into the jungle from an ambush, shots were fired around him and his closest friend Private James Tyson. James and he were inseparable. They cleaned latrines, got sick, and were shot at multiple times. They managed to survive together for a few short months. Until there was a mission, one they weren't supposed to be on, which ended in an ambush. The Viet Cong took their squad down. Jerry and Tyson returned fire. Men around them were cut to pieces. Jerry told Tyson to run. They cut through the brush and made it twenty feet before Tyson was shot in the back. Jerry continued running until he realized he was alone and turned around. Tyson was leaning against a tree, his eyes were open, but he was dead. In the clearing behind him, the Viet Cong approached. Jerry was outnumbered and alone, he continued to run. Despite the loss of his friend and the tragedies he witnessed, during that time at war, the lack of physical injuries gave him a delusion of invincibility that he carried with him for the rest of his life.

A fire alarm rang from around the corner. A woman's muffled scream was heard behind a locked closet door. Jerry kicked the door in. Doctor Bronson and a nurse were inside; faces filled with terror. Their hands were zip-tied behind their back.

"A pale man, with a ponytail locked us in here," the nurse said.

He wanted to free them, but Abby was his priority, and he pursued the running men.

Jerry continued down the hallway. The fire alarm was blaring from the arm of a metal door. He kicked open the door and saw a black van, with darkened windows to the left. The tail end was in the alleyway. The man in the doctor's coat ran around the back, to the passenger's side and was out of view. Quickly, Jerry pulled his revolver from his vest pocket and fired a round in the air. He wanted to shoot through the back window but thought Abby could be inside.

When Gentry heard the shot, he panicked and stepped on the gas, while Isaac hung on the handle and his foot on the runner guard.

Jerry ran after it and saw it had no license plate. As he chased the van, Gentry drove over a concrete parking divider and cut in front of an oncoming car. The tires squealed, it hit the main road and continued east.

"Abby!" he yelled. His stomach sank as he watched the van take off in the distance.

He was going to chase them to the ends of the Earth. And he was going to kill them. With all of his strength, he ran into the front parking lot; his chest was wheezing.

Inside the donut shop, Richard saw the black van drive over the curb and cut into traffic. He went outside. Abby came out of the bathroom and saw Richard through the front windows.

"Jerry, we are over here," Richard yelled.

A wash of relief overwhelmed Jerry when he saw Abby exit the donut shop. He doubled over and put his hands on his knees. The revolver was still in his hand. Abby and Richard came toward him.

"Holy shit, I thought I lost her," he said.

Abby ran over to him, wiping her eyes.

"You all right?" Jerry asked. He put the gun back in his coat pocket. Abby hugged him. The closeness she felt with her grandfather never changed. The world saw Jerry Beaumont as a rugged son-of-a-bitch, but Abby saw a timid bear.

"I pepper sprayed both of those bastards, but I got myself as well."

Jerry laughed, "Good girl."

He took out his flask, uncapped it, and sipped. Richard stuck out his hand and took the flask, sharing in the *holy-shit* swig. Abby took the flask out of Richard's shaking hand and took a nip as well.

Doctor Bronson rushed outside. His hands were free from the zip tie.

"The police are on their way!" he yelled.

"Good," Jerry said. "And that is our cue to leave."

"You can't. You are witnesses!"

Doctor Bronson pushed the bridge of his glasses to keep them from sliding off of his sweaty nose.

"To what?" Jerry asked. He never trusted the law. He believed the police only gathered information after the fact. When they did chase after someone, it was usually the wrong person.

"Well, I didn't see anything. All I know is my granddaughter screamed at some fake doctor. She pepper-sprayed him and ran out the door. I am not sure what kind of place you are running here."

Doctor Bronson took a step back, "This was an attempted kidnapping! My nurse and I were accosted. And did I hear gunfire in the alley?"

"Tell the police everything you just said when they get here," Jerry said.

"And you will tell them as well," the doctor snapped.

"Abby, do you feel safe here?" Jerry asked.

Abby shook her head, and stepped behind Richard, out of partial view from the doctor.

"Then we are leaving. If the police need our statement, they can come by our house. Richard give the doctor your phone number."

Richard grinned at Jerry's take-charge assertiveness.

"Now let's get the hell out of here. I want an Egg McMuffin."

As they approached the pickup truck, they slowed their steps at the same time.

"What is this?" Jerry said.

A red circle of blood was smeared across the windshield. Underneath the windshield wiper was a Polaroid picture of Jerry's truck; the edges of the photo were burnt. Disturbing etchings were drawn in red pen on the back.

Abby's head spun. She knew it was a black magic spell. The Saturn man and his cohorts had marked her family. The weirdos that were going to show up in her life now, were far more dangerous than any alien, or UFO she encountered.

Jerry took a bottle of water out of the truck and sprinkled it over the blood. He turned on the wipers. Richard examined the Polaroid.

They got in the truck and Abby sat in the back.

"Are you okay?" Jerry asked.

Abby nodded her head. "I think so."

"Let's just get out of here. I doubt they will come back, and I don't want to be around for the stupidity of the police."

Sirens were approaching in the distance. Jerry turned off the main road and made an unknown detour.

"I saw that black van on the way in. It was far behind us. I should have been more careful," Jerry said.

Abby flicked her fingernail on the edge of the burnt Polaroid.

"I recognized one of the men from yesterday. He approached me when I left Ms. Sewell's house. I thought he was a reporter at first. He came right out of the crowd and asked me if I was abducted by a UFO."

"One of those men were at Ms. Sewell's house?" Jerry asked. "How certain are you?"

"A thousand percent."

"Jerry, who do you think they are?" Richard asked.

"Cultists, Illuminati maybe? I don't know. They are all idiots. I would like to think us holding them off today, scared them."

A police car flew by on the main road. Jerry slowed down and watched them in the mirror.

"Who knows? Are they organized enough? Do they have money? And more importantly, what do they want?" he said.

Abby stared at the symbols on the back of the Polaroid. They were different from what she saw in Francis Truelove's book. She rubbed her nose with her sleeve.

"If they got to you today, and they locked up a doctor and nurse, then they have to be taken as a serious threat."

Jerry put his window down. He lit a cigarillo when they stopped at a traffic light.

"Listen, I am sorry I didn't want to wait around for the police. I just don't have faith in them. Abby, if you want to, maybe you can call those detectives. Just tell them you were scared and that is why we left."

The radio was on. An AC/DC song was playing. Jerry blew smoke out the window. A young woman with brown curly hair pedaled her bike across the intersection. Her t-shirt had a picture of a coat hanger on the inside of a circle with a line crossing it out. Jerry thought the graphic was odd, he watched her pass by and drove on. Richard side-glanced at Jerry. He wanted to break the silence and say something but remained uncomfortable. He wanted to be strong like Jerry but didn't know how to. Jerry sensed this, he took a last drag from his cigarillo, coughed, and tossed the butt out the window.

He turned the radio down.

"I want to let both of you know, I never told you the truth before. I have always held onto a lie."

"About what?" Abby asked.

Richard looked over at him, like he was a rabbit caught in a snare.

"It's about your grandmother disappearing."

Abby leaned forward and put her hand on the back of the seat.

"I have always been... terrified, that if I ever told the truth, people would just think that I am nuts. And back then it wouldn't have helped my innocence."

"Innocence?" Abby asked.

"Your grandmother disappeared because a big light in the sky took her. She levitated off the ground right in front of your mother and me."

Jerry let that soak in. He didn't say anything for a minute, and they let their silence say everything. He continued, "The ground vibrated, and I felt it in my soul. There she was moving upward, as slow as you would move on an escalator, up a few hundred feet, screaming in some weird language, and then she was gone. No one saw it, except a little girl and her uneducated truck-driving dad."

"Was it a UFO?" Jerry asked.

"In technical terms, yes."

"What do you think it was?" Abby asked.

"I know what I saw then, and I didn't believe it. Yet, my wife disappeared. I have lived with that loss my whole life. Maybe the same thing happened to you, Abby. Something unexplained like this, especially with your memory loss. It has to be more than a coincidence. A phenomenon of this kind, repeating itself in the same family, it is just so damn bizarre."

Abby looked out the window. This was hard to comprehend. She heard about her grandmother disappearing when she was little, but it was rarely spoken of. Richard didn't want to believe what he was hearing but he believed in Jerry so much, that he just nodded his head in agreement.

"And the real question is Abagail, if they did take you, why did they return you?" Jerry asked.

She reached up behind her head and delicately felt the dots on the back of her neck. *Something from another world may have done this*, she thought.

They stopped at the McDonald's drive-thru and ate in the car. Words weren't said between them, and the atmosphere lay thick.

When they returned home, Nova's car was parked diagonally in the street. The driver's side door was left open. Given Nova's history of attention-seeking drama, this would be a good move to jar her family.

Richard looked over at Jerry, "What the hell is going on here?"

Jerry bit his lip and looked like he wanted to scream but held it deep within his gut.

They got out of his truck and slowly approached the house. Jerry's cell phone rang. He looked at who was calling him, "Sorry I have to take this." And he stepped away.

Richard watched him and saw his face was heavy with concern. Richard knew whatever Jerry was being told, it would take him back home that night.

Abby and Richard opened the front door; neither of them knew what to expect. Abby's mother was kneeling on the floor in front of the TV. Only it wasn't a moment of prayer, and the TV was not displaying a religious show. Nova was wearing a faded pink t-shirt and jean shorts. It was an old form-fitting shirt, a style she used to wear. Richard realized how much weight she lost, from not taking care of herself in the past few months.

Tears rolled down her face, she looked at them and seemed coherent. As if a spell was broken.

"Pastor Ulma and I had words, and he asked me to leave the church for good," she said.

"What kind of words?" Richard never pushed the lawyer business since Abby returned, but he would go down that road again if necessary.

"He called me a false prophet and a heretic."

Richard wasn't sure what a heretic was. But any name-calling Ulma said would be ignored unless a threat was attached to it.

"Oh," he said.

"Yes. Now I am just a sheep with no shepherd."

Abby was going to chime in with sarcasm, reminding her that the Lord is her shepherd, as it says so on the plaque in the bathroom, but she abstained from her wit.

"I am sorry. I haven't been right for some time. I am sorry for this morning. I am sorry for all of it. I don't know if I am in the right place spiritually."

Richard and Abby didn't agree or disagree with her, they just stood in awe and listened.

"In some way, I thought if I acted more radical, then God could use me more for his purpose. I think I was wrong."

Something welled up within Abby. It took a moment of clarity, for her mother to break a glacier of ice off, into the ocean to melt. Abby went up to her room, lifted her mattress, and came down with The Cure's *Disintegration* in her hands.

Abby put it on the record player and fearlessly, she lowered the needle and let it play.

"Last year, I found one of your old records in the basement. I felt alone after Rose left. I didn't fit in with the kids at school anymore. I played this and something changed in me. You had to be the same age I am now when this album came out," Abby said.

The sun shone through the front door. As it filled the room, Nova's mood lifted simultaneously. The melancholy of the music and Robert Smith's swooning voice set a different tone that the front room of the house had never felt before.

"I was eighteen," her mother said.

"I am assuming, you were really into this until you had me."

"Yes, and I was scared shitless then. I was a mother that just graduated high school, and your biological father existed in my life for only mere minutes."

Abby perked up. It was the first time in a long time she wanted to hear everything her mother was saying.

"Your grandmother Ruth, who was your grandfather's oldest sister, took me under her wing. She was tough and narrow-minded, and she loved to pray and read the Bible. I adopted a lot of her ways; on how a Christian woman should act and carry herself. It was easier to go that road than to be a bitter teenager, with a kid. When I saw you start with the make-up and hair, I knew you were going down the same path. I just didn't want you to make the same mistakes I did."

Richard cringed when Nova said the last words.

Abby didn't react negatively. She was contented with the honest conversation with her mother.

"I don't mean that you were a mistake. I just don't want you to have to become an adult so quickly. And I am sorry, to both of you. I haven't been in a good mind frame lately. I think I am off."

Richard put his hand on Nova's shoulder. Abby moved in and hugged her mother. Richard wrapped his arms around both of them. The second song on the record played. Abby imagined the scene looked like a 90's Winona Ryder film. It was a picture she wanted to burn in her memory. A moment, without any context, would appear as a normal family melding together after a small misunderstanding.

Jerry walked in and saw the three of them embracing, with non-gospel music playing on the record player. For a moment, he thought he was in the wrong house.

Abby broke the hug, saw the grim look in his eyes, and knew there was something else on his mind. He had been a pillar of strength for her. The family would not have made it without him. The exceptional character that Richard was showing was partly because of what Jerry drew out of him as well.

Nova moved in and hugged her father. She didn't say a word. Jerry looked confused. He had hoped what he was experiencing would be a new change in his daughter.

Richard turned down the record player. Robert Smith was low but still audible, his angsty voice was still inspiring.

"Margaret fell off the back porch. It is my fault. The back stairs are wobbly and one of the dogs tripped her. She broke her hip and jaw," Jerry said.

"What?" Nova exclaimed.

"She cried out all night until our neighbor heard her this morning. They took her to the hospital in an ambulance. I can't believe I have to say this, but I have to head back."

Abby's heart sank.

Richard sat on the couch and put his face in his hands. "I am sorry, Jerry. This is awful."

"Yeah, well, what are you going to do?" Jerry smiled.

"I can make you a pot of coffee for the road," Nova said.

"That will be a good start."

Jerry put his hand on Nova. A gesture that Nova hadn't had from her father in a long time. His warmth was needed in this house, and it would be gone within the next half hour.

"Abby, can I see you out back for a moment?"

Abby got up and wiped tears from her face. She was proud of them, to her she had grown in front of her family. Diffusing a time bomb was something she wasn't used to. And making it a habit wasn't something she wanted to continue. For now, she would mimic whatever her grandfather would do.

"Yes sir." She followed him out back.

They stood by the shed. He took out his .38 revolver. He opened the chamber, spun it, and shut it. She was nervous, as she had never held a gun before. He showed her how to do the same; how to pull the hammer, how the bullets went in, and how they were removed. A bag of shells was in his pocket. He gave them to her. Six were in the chamber and thirteen were in the bag. One bullet was used prior as a warning shot back in the alley behind the doctor's office.

"I don't want you to take it out unless you plan on pulling the trigger. If you are pulling the trigger it is because you are afraid someone is going to seriously hurt you. You got it?" he said.

She nodded her head. The gun felt natural in her hand. She thought she would be more scared when she held it. With all the trauma she went through, she wondered if the parts of her that told her to be scared were burnt out of her psyche.

"What did I say?" Jerry said. He was firm and intense.

"Aim this at any son of a bitch that gets fresh with me, as long as there are no cameras around."

He laughed, "Seriously."

"I will only pull this out, if I am scared shitless, and hopefully scare them shitless."

"All right. I hope you don't need it. And I don't need to tell you not to mention this to your folks. So, hide it in your glove box, lock it, and keep your car locked."

"Yes sir."

He hugged her. He wanted to tell her that he believed her confusing story of events. That if she said she was taken away by an alien craft, he would accept every word of it as truth. But he didn't know how to say it. It was easier giving her a gun.

"Call me if you need anything, especially if you shoot someone."

She put the gun in her sweater pocket.

"Were those words said by the father on *Little House on the Prairie*?"

He laughed into a cough.

"I think that was a *Gunsmoke* episode."

They laughed and went inside. Jerry said his goodbyes and took a thermos of black coffee with him. An odd peace filled the room when he looked back at his daughter, son-in-law, and granddaughter. The crazy day still ended with an unwanted adventure ahead of him, but he felt he did his best, as any grandfather could hope for.

As he traveled, a memory surfaced from the night his wife was taken. He pulled over on the side of the road and put on the flashers.

"Helen knew this, even back then."

His mind recalled when Helen yelled in some sort of language, to him after she swore seeing fireflies.

"*Tan makalukum avvare ceyyvarkal!*" Helen yelled. "*Margaret is going to break her hip and jaw.*"

Jerry recalled that moment as clear as if it just happened in front of him.

"How did Helen know?" he said.

He pulled back onto the highway, scared for Margaret. How could his wife predict a detail over thirty years ago, about this exact moment? It was a little after midnight when he made it to the hospital. Margaret's sister Jackie was sleeping in the chair next to her. He relieved Jackie and held Margaret's hand. She opened her eyes and smiled. Her body was broken and swollen.

Margaret wanted to tell him that she had a dream of an angel visiting her but was unable to speak. She blinked at him slowly and cried. Without saying what was on her mind, Jerry sensed her words, as he could not tell her what was revealed to him by his wife from decades ago.

24

The overwhelming desire to eat a chocolate cupcake surpassed any type of reason. Abby wanted to indulge but didn't want to be home when she did it. Since she missed her birthday, and no party was done for her, she was going to entrust this mission to only one person. A future army man willing to bend over backward for her. She would not take advantage of Sutton's sweetness, but she would enjoy his company, as he had been so concerned for her when she was gone. Thanking him in person was the least she could do.

There was one thing that needed to be done first. Since she had a brief cycle on local news channels, she was concerned about being recognized, mostly by the wrong people. Being a sorceress with hair and make-up, she was able to conjure a quick makeover. She cut the back of her hair, layering it to her neckline. The length of her bangs was tapered into chin-length pieces. Next, she stripped all of the color out with peroxide. It saddened her but she felt it was necessary. After all, when things calmed down, she could dye it back. Heavy black eyeliner was substituted with red. Black clothes were not negotiable though. Being known as the *missing girl who returned home*, wasn't going to change her style. She checked her outfit in the standing mirror, using her grandmother's hand mirror to look at the back of her head.

With her finger, she traced a circular shape around the three mysterious red dots. She didn't realize how high she cut the back of her hair. The dots would be visible for the next couple of weeks unless she got extensions.

"Abagail," a woman's voice said. The voice was faint.

The chills formed on Abby's arms and neck. She lowered the hand mirror.

Abby was certain it was the same voice from before. She looked out her bedroom window, to see if someone was outside speaking to her. Logically, hearing the voice at that level, alone in the room, didn't make sense. Her eye twitched and she rubbed her head.

"Who is there?" she asked the voice.

"This is your grandmother, Helen," the voice said.

Abagail suspected the voice was coming through the hand mirror. If it was her grandmother's, it would only make sense because the mirror belonged to her. The odd phenomenon, with how things have been going, was slightly possible. Abby held it in front of her and stared at her reflection.

"Helen, how are you communicating with me?"

Abby watched her mouth move as she spoke. She was angry at herself for being so scared, and furious with herself for looking so stupid.

"I don't have time to explain. I can get in trouble for telling you this, but I have been able to peer into your timeline and there is someone you can protect. Someone whose life can change the fate of many. Your unawake side knows this when you drift?" the voice said.

"My what?" Abby asked.

"I am not telling awake Abby this; I am telling this to your subconscious."

Abby thought on this.

"So, my alleged alien-abducted grandmother, is telling the possible alien-abducted subconscious version of me, that I have a mission?"

Her phone lit up; Sutton was outside.

"Abagail, when you drift, just go with your instinct," the voice said. The line of communication was cut.

It was the most faint that the voice was in the conversation. Doubt took over and Abagail began to deny that the conversation happened.

Sutton texted her, *Hey I am outside.*

Abby picked up a pen and notebook and wrote down: My unawake self knows what Helen is talking about. She slid the tablet under her bed and went downstairs.

When Sutton saw Abby exit her home, he saw a different woman emerge. The week's time had felt like a month to him. The predusk haze cast a glow on her face that made her look angelic. The teenager he had dropped off a week ago, who was a drunken mess, morphed into a beautiful, composed woman. To his dismay, he was the hero that night and didn't feel like he was treated as one. He jumped out of the car and smiled at her. He held the same look a boy would, waiting in the outfield to catch a fly ball, in anticipation of receiving approval from the crowd.

Slowly, Abby came down the crooked concrete stairs. She felt elated as tonight would be the first normal evening she had with another person in a long time. Nervously, Sutton shifted his weight from one leg to the next. Flowers were in the passenger seat, awaiting her.

"Oh shit," she whispered.

All that she wanted was to get out of the house, and he was rolling out the red carpet for her.

In an awkward Frankenstein's monster stride, he walked toward her and hugged her tight. The embrace felt good, but it was too much; it was too much for him.

"H-how are you? You look great. I like what you did with your hair." he said.

He was wearing a coral-collared shirt and wore a wood-based cologne. She hesitated and saw an image of herself pregnant with a baby next to her eating Bonbons watching the *Price is Right,* while he was away on a military training exercise. That thought made her nauseous. She shrugged it off.

"I am good, I think," she grinned. "Are those flowers for me?"

Wildflowers were wrapped in tissue paper and cellophane, sitting upright, and fastened loosely in the front seat belt.

"Y-yes."

"Thank you, that is so sweet."

He opened the door for her. She slid in and held the flowers on her lap. Having never received flowers before, aside from the corsage she got when she was in eleventh grade, she was grateful. She smelled them; but there was no fragrance, as some wildflowers were just wild.

Even though Sutton gave her more attention than she wanted, it felt good to be treated well. To her surprise, he did not bring up any questions about where she had been in the past week; he just talked. His brother and he were restoring a car. His mother had to go to the doctor. Some politicians did something related to the Middle East. It trailed nowhere, yet it was a necessary buzzing of dialog that some men have while trying to maintain a mood.

He took her to a small bakery that served coffee, in town. It would be closing within an hour. They sat inside by the front window. She devoured her chocolate torte cupcake, while he continued his buzzing. She wanted to explain that she only wanted to be friends. But she couldn't form the words. As long as she dodged any conversation about them as an item or the future of their lives, she was safe. He seemed too eager to please her, but she felt no judgment come from him.

Feeling comfortable, she went to the counter and got a second cupcake. She consumed its passion like it was the last sweet thing on Earth. He watched her and sipped his coffee. It was the first time she had eaten something like this in front of a young man and didn't have the urge to throw up afterward.

Back at home, under the relief that Nova would not be returning to church anymore, Richard fell into a rare mood. Since Jerry had visited, he nipped at whiskey nightly. A bottle was hidden in the vestibule outside. Whiskey took a bite out of his uneasiness, and he had the urge. He brushed his teeth vigorously and sat by Nova who was lying on the couch, watching a sitcom. Not seeing some religious asshole on the TV made his mood soar. He laughed at the mild joke delivered by some actor phoning it in. A spark occurred in him, he put his hand on her hip. She looked over at him and they made intimate eye contact. It had been months since they caught each other's gaze. Genuinely embracing this afternoon seemed to bring the old Nova out of hibernation. He wanted to forgive her for the previous months of insane actions. As difficult as it was going to be, he knelt on the floor in front of her, touched her shoulder, and kissed her lips. To his surprise, she reacted to this. They made love for the first time since late last year. Back then Nova got it in her head that an end-time prophet shouldn't partake in sex for pleasure, tonight her guard was down; she was having a very human moment.

Afterward, they lay in bed. Richard stared at the ceiling and was concerned about things that he didn't think he would ever be concerned with. In the past couple of weeks, he wondered what his life would be like without her. Each day was becoming intolerable. Now he wondered if things could be repaired. Nova lay on her side, with her bare back facing him. She didn't want to tell Richard, but she heard a voice, deep inside of her, instructing her to start her own church. The unhappy members of Ulma's congregation would follow her, as they knew she was called by God for big things in the *last days*. The sweat of her husband was still on her, and it made her want to throw up.

25

The next morning, Abby awoke without an alarm clock. It was the first weekday out of high school, and she was without a reason to be awake so early. Dario was not in the bedroom. Richard must have let him out and fed him. Out of habit, she reached for her phone and forgot that she didn't have it anymore. Today, she would have to get a new one. With her grandfather gone, she wondered how safe she would be. He had been her bodyguard and was partly the reason why her mother had a breakthrough moment yesterday. Even though he gave Abby a handgun, she wasn't going to walk around like she was in the old West. His absence would be felt.

Picking up her grandmother's mirror again, she waited for a voice.

"Helen, it is Abby."

She heard nothing, no whispers, no beams of light.

Your unawake side knows this when you drift, her grandmother's voice echoed in her memory.

Was the voice her grandmother, or was she becoming delusional like her mother?

A bird settled on the rain gutter and chirped. In the distance, a car door slammed. She heard a man's voice. Immediately, Abby thought it was the creepy men in black from the walk-in clinic. She got on her knees, crawled to the window, and peeked outside. Up the hillside, behind her property, she could see a black suburban on Chuchi's street. It was near the tennis court. Her heart pounded heavily.

It was them, she thought.

She crawled to the closet and grabbed the handgun.

She heard the man's voice say faintly, "We can drop her off later."

Abby peeked over the window frame again. There was a blonde man in a polo picking up a little girl. A woman came around the side of the suburban and kissed her. He put the girl in the back seat, buckled her, got in, and they drove away. It was just a family who happened to be driving a black vehicle. After yesterday's encounter with the fake nurse and the Saturn man, her paranoia was going to get the best of her. She put the gun back in a box and shut the closet.

She got dressed and went downstairs. Richard was gone. He left a note on the kitchen table.

Sorry, Abby, I had to go to work today. Here is the extra car key and some money for a new phone. If you don't want to go out on your own, wait for me to come home. There are some eggs on the stove.

-Richard.

She didn't know if she had the guts to go out in public today. Waiting for him to come home, was a comforting idea. As she thought that, her mother yelled from upstairs. She was praying, without concern for noise, and it was intense. Being cast out from the church yesterday would make her unpredictable. With Abby's grandfather being gone, there would be no referee. Abby was trying to forgive her mother for some of the irrational behavior, but she would never forget the slap across the face. It was a fifty-fifty chance that the day would not have confrontation.

Dario came into the kitchen and meowed. He sat statuesque and blinked.

"Dario, I can't stay here today."

He blinked again, understanding, as he hid during Nova's times of intense prayer as well.

Abby crept back upstairs and grabbed her grandfather's handgun. She held it in her hand. It was loaded. He showed her how to open and close it; just like in a movie. This was the first time she was alone with a gun, but it didn't scare her. She aimed it out the window and looked down the site. If she was going out today, it was unlikely she would need it, but it would make her feel more safe having it. She put on her hooded sweatshirt and zipped it. The gun went in one pocket and the sack of bullets in the other. If she was going to carry it, she wanted to have fired it, at least once.

While she walked up the hill, towards the back gate, she realized how much her life had changed in such a brief time. She missed her graduation: the exit interview of high school bullshit and the transition into working-class life. The loss of memory she suffered, was like a coma patient who is only cognizant of the before and after, as the world around them changed. She wondered how she would recover, and if she would be safe living on her own.

As she approached the tennis court, she saw the chalk circle outline with the astrological symbols. The geodes were gone. Someone had taken them. A breeze rustled through the tall grass, and a dog barked in someone's backyard. She stood outside the circle and remembered what she had done. Surprisingly, her head didn't hurt.

"Aaaaaaaooooooouuuuuummmm," she chanted.

Just hearing it, freaked her out.

The sky was partially cloudy. Scanning the horizon, she looked for silver saucers; there were none. She looked to the tree line behind her and saw no green or grey large-headed beings with black eyes looking at her. She became more certain that someone, a something had found her that day. Did Francis Truelove get abducted as well? If so, he wouldn't have been able to write the book, or did she go further than he did? Regardless of what happened, if they returned her, she had to figure out what to do with the rest of her future. If she wasn't on a UFO or in a test lab somewhere, she had to work. And if she had to work, she had to protect herself.

She went back towards the treeline and followed a path used for dirt bikes and cut through the thin brush. She walked through a small clearing where local kids would hang out. Behind the clearing was nothing but forest that went on for miles. Bottles, both beer and soda were scattered on the ground, amongst fast food refuse and candy bar wrappers. A white plastic lawn chair was tipped over next to a nearly full gallon jug of water. Abby picked up two green beer bottles and carried them to a pile of rocks. She placed both bottles side by side and walked backward twenty feet. Visualizing the sneering, handsome man in black, in the hallway, she aimed.

Her grandfather informed her, all she had to do was aim and pull the trigger.

Either you pull the trigger or freeze.

She pulled the trigger. The report was loud and made her jump. She missed the bottle. Looking over the site of the barrel, closing one eye, she aimed again, held her breath, and squeezed the trigger again. She missed.

"Dammit."

Steadying her hand, she held the bottle in her sight and fired again, and the bottle exploded. A surge rushed through her, and even though she murdered a glass bottle, it made her feel powerful as if she was fighting back from being kidnapped. She aimed at the other bottle, and on the second shot, she hit it.

She pointed the gun downward, opened the chamber, took out the used shells, and put them in her jean pocket. She reloaded, the first bullet was with shaking hands, and the last was more confident. She spun the chamber, then shut it. It is a powerful thing, for a kidnapped woman, returned into her habitat, to have the confidence of using a handgun.

Hopefully, her approach to the summer would be more guarded. Now she had to take the next step out into the world as a battle-scarred young adult.

26

Abagail called **Above & Beyond Books** and asked Tony if he had any other material by Francis Truelove. He informed her that the author was published through a small press and would be hard to track down. He asked if she could wait while he did a quick search online. He checked eBay and a website that dealt with rare books and occult items, but nothing was for sale. An old sale was listed on the site. Someone had recently bought another Truelove book, but it was off the market and sold for a high price. He took her number and would call her if anything surfaced.

The ability to be enlightened by dabbling into an obscure source of knowledge, and to watch it be tossed away so carelessly, depressed her. Pastor Ulma tore the Truelove book to shreds in his vile ignorance. He was the worst of his kind, a witch-trial-making, book burner. Abby sensed the welcoming arms of despair but pushed them away. Despite being a moody goth, she did not want to wallow, as it would be unproductive.

She acquired a new cell phone and was raked over the coals into an eighteen-month contract. Thankfully, the money Richard gave her, padded the cost. It was a new flip phone, that had better internet connection than the last model; a mild improvement. The resources the smartphone had to offer kept her from going back home. Sitting in front of her computer in her room had been the norm for so long, but now she grasped another strand of independence.

She had lunch at a Chinese restaurant by the highway. Recalling old phone numbers and contacts was difficult for her over-saturated brain. The most important contact she needed in her life right now, was Rose. And for the first time in her life, she sent an email from a phone. It was a run-on sentence, that was nearly indecipherable, describing all of the events that had taken place since she last emailed her. It was a perfect email that only

Rose could interpret. Just writing it felt like therapy. And in her solitude, she valued her independence. This shone a spotlight on the harsh reality, that she needed to continue to stay busy and get on with her life, despite whatever happened in the recent weeks. Perhaps no questions of her whereabouts would ever be answered.

In her anxiousness, she called the restaurant for work. The day manager, Jeanene answered. She told Abby that if she was up to it, she could come in, even though some of the workers, had a pool betting that she was going to turn up dead. Jeanene told her that her daughter went looking for her in the woods last week with some other girls from school. Abby was surprised because she didn't know her daughter. Even more so, Abby didn't think anyone cared as much as they had shown in her absence. Jeanene stressed that if any commotion was caused by her presence, considering how sensational Abby's story had been, she would have to work in the kitchen. Abby told her that she would take anything and that staying busy would be good for her.

Abby finished her sweet and sour chicken and became hypnotized by her new phone's functions.

"Aren't you that girl who went missing?" a girl asked, from behind the counter.

Abby didn't realize she was addressing her. Like Abby, the girl spent time in front of the mirror working on her image. Her hair was long in the front and spiked in the back. A nose ring was in her nostril, and she wore two different-colored Chuck Taylor's.

"I am sorry?" Abby said.

"You're that girl who went missing! You dyed your hair though," the girl said.

"I was hoping if I dyed it, I would be mistaken for someone else."

"Oh, well you still look like you. Especially around here."

She came out from behind the counter and stood near Abby's table. "So, what happened are you okay?"

Abby was put off by the girl's forwardness. However, she searched her eyes and found a bit of sincerity.

"I think I am. And I don't remember what happened. Thank you for asking though." Abby said with a bit of frigidness. She put her napkin on her plate and pushed it to the edge of the table. One of the chopsticks slid off the plate, fell off the table, and landed on the floor. Abby didn't lean over to pick it up. The young woman ignored it, sat in the booth, and crossed her legs.

"I am Megan," the girl said.

"Abby."

"I know," Megan smiled. "We go to the same high school."

"I thought you looked familiar." Abby looked down at her phone. A habit she didn't like to do, as she thought it was rude when others did it to her, but Megan's curiosity was making Abby feel like she was in a terrarium.

Megan's eyes danced across Abby's face, taking in all of her style as if she saw color for the first time. Abby became embarrassed. If she was prone to showing color in her face, she would have.

"My family said you got caught up in a cult and ran off."

"A cult?" Abby laughed, "Is that the rumor?"

"One of them."

"What do you think?"

"I don't know. I have seen you around in school. You look like you want to kill people most of the time, so I thought it might be true."

"Well, I don't belong to a cult."

"Doesn't your family go to that weird church with the snake handling and stuff?"

Abby scoffed, "I wish, then I would want to see that shit up close."

Megan reached her hand across the table and touched Abby's arm. "Well, I am glad you are back."

Abby looked at Megan and frowned. "I can't tell if you are being real or not."

"What?"

"This exchange is off-putting."

"Sorry, if I offended you." Megan got up abruptly and went behind the counter. The phone rang on the wall and Megan ignored it.

Abby sighed. In the past year, it had become harder for her to discern if people were being genuine. And given the way she dressed, people either avoided her, by stepping away or crept in too close. Abby's defense was always rudeness, and this girl didn't deserve it.

"Hey," Abby said. "I am sorry. I don't know how to react when people I don't know come up and talk to me."

Megan addressed her without turning around. "That's okay. My mother tells me that I don't know boundaries."

The girls exchanged numbers. Megan sent a cat smiley face emoji. Abby laughed. She realized that everyone she met didn't need to be overly scrutinized.

In Abby's trunk was a spare work shirt and apron. They weren't clean but it would keep her from going back home. With nowhere else to go, she headed in for her shift at three.

When Abby arrived at Denny's she parked in front of the main windows. The employees were always instructed to park in the back, so up-front parking would be available to the customers. With her safety in mind, she wanted to keep her car in view while she worked. If the Saturn man or a wild reporter came looking for her, she could make a mad dash and get the hell out. She walked around the restaurant to the rear.

A kid with a camouflaged hat rode by on his bike. He was talking to himself in a high-pitched voice. As he passed Abby he said, "And there is one now. We can't trust her."

Abby shot him a glare, but the kid never turned his head to look at her.

From afar, she saw Dante. As she expected he was standing out back, heel against the door, smoking. He scanned her with his eyes and added a flirtatious grin. Something was different about him. His demeanor changed. As if her passage into legal adulthood put her in a different view to him. She never regarded him as a creep, at least towards her, but in the twenty steps it took to reach him, she changed her mind.

"You went blonde." He blew a cloud of smoke above him. A social signal that smokers did to draw a line in the sand when they say something they think is dramatic.

"Yeah well, I didn't want to be recognized."

"I think you'll stick out more than you did before," he grinned.

"We will see what happens tonight."

She didn't want to make him feel comfortable with her, but she wanted a cigarette, and he was always keen to give her one. "Can I borrow one?"

"Now that you are of age, you can buy your own, and you owe me at least two packs."

"If you keep me on the schedule, I can do that."

"As long as there is no drama, and you work hard, I don't care."

"Got it."

"Priscilla is out. She is not responding to any calls. Who knows with her? One week it is overtime, the next week it is time off. So, you can take her shifts this week."

"Thank you," Abby said. She wondered if Priscilla was okay. She cared about her but would never venture to her neck of the woods again. Drunk cousins, tossing cinder blocks, and dangling babies while doing shots wasn't the new family she wanted to adopt. After a long drag, she ashed the cigarette on the bricks and put the unfinished half in her apron pocket. "All right, good chat."

He nodded.

"One last thing," he looked at her intently.

His mere presence became uncomfortable. It was uncomfortable enough to make her want to get back in the car and drive home. Maybe it was the years of Dante never being put in his place by a woman, or drugs burnt out his receptors. But his next line was going to be something she would mark him by.

"I don't believe your story, the UFO's, or alien shit; none of that is real. I don't know if you are doing it for attention or ran away to have an abortion or get high or something, but it isn't my business."

She lowered her head. "Okay."

He raised his palm, deflecting anything she would say next.

"But I never had a complaint about you once. You work hard and show up when you are supposed to. Just don't talk about what happened to anyone. Given how crazy this place gets, people will eventually forget about what happened. Especially with how much you change your hair color."

She laughed nervously. "I was thinking about changing my name tag."

"Nah, that's dumb. The waitresses will call you by your real name in front of the customers and you will go by another?"

"You are right, I guess," she said. "Thanks, Dante."

"Yep." He jutted his chin, folded his arms, and looked away.

The night was busy. She made good tips. If a busy weekday was a way to gauge how much she could make monthly, she could find a studio apartment by August. A place between here and Nashville would work, cutting down on city costs while keeping a healthy distance from her unpredictable mother. She wondered if Ramen noodles were healthy.

Marcus, the head cook, asked if she was all right and complimented her hair. He was older than Dante and had grey teeth. Passing the threshold into young adulthood either changed her standing with men, or they stepped over the line all the time and she finally noticed. The fact that she never reintegrated properly back into a social setting after the disappearance didn't help. Perhaps people were being kind? Or maybe people never knew what to say, and words just fell out of their mouths, and their motives could only be told by looking into their eyes.

Gracefully, she worked into the end of the night. No customer recognized her as the *missing teen from town*. The blonde hair worked. Or they didn't see anyone different because they just wanted a plate of hot grease?

It was a half hour before her shift was over. A truck driver came in and sat in a booth. His massive shoulders were slouched from years of bad posture and held the weight of a man who lived at greasy diners. The saddened face he wore with his long brown mustache made him look like a large Bassett hound who took the form of an ex-professional wrestler.

"Evening ma'am," he said. His voice was deep like a dried-up well.

"Evening sir, what will you have?

He put the menu down and folded his hands.

"I don't know what I am looking at the damn menu for. I knew what I wanted when I smelled it cooking in the parking lot. Just give me a double breakfast. That's two eggs..." he emphasized by holding up two fingers, "...two sausages, and double bacon, with double toast."

"Sounds good. Double OJ as well?"

"Sure," he smiled.

"Well, I will charge you for one OJ though," Abby said.

"Thank you, young lady."

She walked to the kitchen and put his order in."

"Oh, and coffee too," he yelled.

"Double coffee, yes, sir."

She sipped on her Red Bull and returned to the floor, with a pot of coffee and two small glasses of Orange Juice, carefully palmed in her right hand. Abby put the OJ and a pot of coffee in front of the trucker, he thanked her.

Before returning to the kitchen, she stepped into the lady's room. It was a two-stall bathroom, that was rarely cleaned. She went into the furthest and sat on the toilet lid. Tears formed, and she fought them, but it was a useless struggle. She wiped them with thin-ply toilet paper and make-up smeared, and then she cried harder.

"What the fuck is wrong with me?"

All seemed to be going well, yet a build of unexplained emotion said otherwise. A woman came into the bathroom while talking on her cell phone. She had a strong New York accent. What she broadcasted, the events she had planned this weekend were going to be *wild*. She used the stall next to Abby, didn't flush, nor wash her hands, and left.

Abby rubbed the back of her head and felt for the three red dots. The top dot was raised. She flicked it with her fingernail and a sharp shooting pain went through the muscles of her neck. It felt like there was a wire underneath her skin as the pain electrified and traveled to the bottom of her jawline.

She felt in the center of the dots and pushed. Her eyes rolled into the back of her head, and she slouched forward. The laws of gravity did not apply, and she floated off the toilet seat, rising like a balloon to the ceiling. Her hands and feet hung lazily. Slowly she twisted, as her head touched the ceiling panel.

Miles away, Young Jeremiah Hodges woke up in his bed choking uncontrollably. His perpetual choking spells were triggered by something as simple as a dust particle inhaled in his sleep. This particular spell was more inflammatory due to a chest cold. His little face was red as his panic-stricken mother entered the room. She slapped him on the back, in an attempt to help him. Jeremiah's face turned purple. His mother tried to calm him down and hold him, but he pushed her away, as her embrace made him feel like he was suffocating. A grey shadow appeared behind his mother. It was a woman's pale face, with dark eyes. The shadow reached out and touched Jeremiah's hand. Immediately his coughing spell subsided. His mother wept as she saw Jeremiah return to a regular breathing pattern. As he gained the strength to talk, he told his mother he saw an angel standing behind her, and the angel touched his hand.

Across town, in a high rise for the elderly, a seventy-one-year-old widow, Marla Castle was watching the nightly news. The program focused on violence in America and said how women were not safe, on their own, in cities across the country. This terrified an already paranoid Marla so much that she went into the spare closet and retrieved her husband's revolver. When her husband, Alexander was alive, he told Marla not to worry about anything, as he would take care of her. This was something Alexander wanted to believe because he convinced himself that he would outlive his wife. When she would pass, he would spend the last of his days on a cruise ship, playing shuffleboard with other men his age. A variable Alexander had not predicted, was that he got sick with a bitter cough, that progressed into a painful one. Marla told him he needed rest, and he didn't listen. Two days before Christmas, he died of pneumonia.

Marla never opened the gift he left under the tree for her; it was a protest of her stubbornness to match his. She wondered if somehow he knew he was going to die so suddenly and was in denial.

As the story continued on the news, it focused on a case not far from where she lived.

The reporter said, "Even in smaller parts of the country, citizens are at risk, in the small town of Blueville, a young teen girl was abducted, and went missing for a week, then mysteriously returned in the middle of a baseball game. In the surrounding towns of Blueville, locals mention the possibility of a UFO abduction...."

Marla muted the volume with her oversized remote control. She placed her tired hand on her chest. She wanted to cry but was too old for tears. Those moments were long gone. However, coping with the dread that enveloped her, as she walked through an empty apartment was a weight she didn't want to carry anymore.

She picked up the heavy revolver and went into the kitchen. She poured herself a glass of raspberry iced tea and took two Fig Newtons out of a Tupperware container. After eating one, she left the other on a folded napkin. She wondered how funny it would look for the forensics team to come into her apartment and take a black and white photo of a Fig Newton with

216

crumbs next to it. Would forensics even show up to an old ladies' apartment with an open and shut case?

Her husband had taught her how to shoot the gun. Even though he said that in the event of a break-in, he would be the one holding it and not her. She cocked the hammer back and looked out the window of her seventh-floor apartment.

A memory of them dancing from forty years ago was the last thing she thought of. Suddenly, a grey figure with a pale face appeared before her, outside of the window. The pale face moved and appeared in the room next to her, by the small dining room table. Marla smiled at the figure and squinted her eyes. She thought of her younger sister, Francine, who died in a car accident years ago, and how much her sister loved life, even though she never married. Francine used to feed the birds on the way to work and said that life was in nature.

Marla cursed Alexander for dying so foolishly, then she told him that she loved him.

Marla placed the gun on the dining room table and realized her actions were irrational. She unplugged the television and wanted to feed birds for the rest of her days. She never picked up the gun for such an action again.

Back at the restaurant bathroom, Abagail was floating, and her hand twitched like an electric impulse shot through her. Her neck was bent like it was made of rubber and her head slouched forward. The top of her shoulders touched the ceiling and her arms and legs dangled, as if she wore a sleeping cat on the edge of the arm of a couch.

The New Yorker with the cell phone entered the bathroom again; in her own universe, in her own attention-seeking phone conversation. She did not notice the floating Abagail.

Hell yeah, and that's so cool, was her topic of conversation with an equally interesting person on the other end of the line. She fixed her lipstick, didn't wash her hands, and left.

Slowly, Abby descended to the floor. When her shoes touched the ground, she awoke, unaware of the event that happened. She washed her hands, wiped the tears from her eyes, and made a failed attempt at fixing the make-up streaks on her cheeks. The thought of scaling back on her goth make-up seemed appropriate for the remainder of the summer. *Maybe it was time to grow up a little*, she thought. After all, not all future beauticians need to overdo it on their appearance.

When she returned to the dining room, a disheveled man, wearing a baseball hat and a tan tattered suit walked in. He carried the energy of a homeless person, who had only stumbled into misfortune recently. An old brown Buick, with a torn roof, was parked out front. By deducing what vehicles had been pulling in and out all night, it was safe to assume this car was his. Abby told him that he could sit anywhere. He chose to sit in the booth directly across from the Bassett hound-looking trucker. They both looked at each other for a brief second. The trucker looked at a newspaper he had brought in with him.

She addressed the disheveled man. A foul body odor was strong. It was inevitable he was on hard times and quite possibly lived in the car that matched his appearance. Dante had a rule about tossing certain people out, who could make anyone else's dining experience unpleasant. Abby just kept as normal, as her first night back to work had been going smoothly.

"Evening sir, what can I get for you."

He flipped the coffee mug over, in front of him.

"C-coffee and th-that's all." he stuttered. He put a dollar bill in front of him. It was obvious he was making any monetary concerns she would assume he would have, very clear.

"Coffee it is sir."

Without stopping, she went to the kitchen for a pot. She took a deep breath, held it, and returned with the coffee pot, and poured it into his cup. He stared at her as if she was the only person in the restaurant.

Marcus slid the double breakfast under the heat lamp. He saw Abby walking by and tapped on the counter. She picked up the breakfast, retraced her steps, and came up from behind the trucker, so she didn't have to pass the disheveled man.

"Thank you, hon," he said.

"Sure thing," she muttered.

The trucker was aware of what effect the disheveled man was having on Abby. He was going to ask her if she was all right, but she remained the hard worker and stepped toward the disheveled man's table and asked if he needed anything else.

His face was tan and could have been mistaken for a handsome man at one point in his life. Whatever scars he received at that point, emotionally or physically, were still worn on his dirty jacket sleeve. With unblinking, and glassy eyes he held up a dollar bill, showing her the back of it. He pointed to the pyramid, the Eye of Providence; an overlooked piece of unique artwork on the back of US currency.

"Did you see this while you were on the spacecraft? Have you had visions or flashbacks since they returned you? That happens sometimes."

Abby's motions slowed as if she were hypnotized.

Nervously, he tapped at the pyramid on the dollar.

"You see, our government has been blatant about this, right in front of our faces, but Americans are too ignorant, at least a great majority of them to see it. Even way back then, in our country, secret organizations have known about aliens and their technology. It isn't a wonder to the masses anymore. It is just a wonder *how* people keep forgetting. Of all the visitations and abductions, it seems a story like yours, gets attention for just a minute, and people move on to the next thing. As if our brains can't handle any more craziness, we just seem to shut off. Or perhaps whatever engulfs news cycles to put a pretty woman's face on the news for days, then it falls out of cycle. You don't sell for their commercial breaks anymore. And here you are serving hot plates of grease to truckers when your fingertips touched alien beings and a craft from another world."

Abby took a delicate step backward.

"I am sorry, what?"

The trucker observed everything, as he stuck his fork into his sausage.

Abby heard what the man said, every word of it. She didn't know how he could speak of such wild things uninhibited. It was like he read a script from a science fiction story.

"I don't know what you are talking about," she said.

"Yes, you do," he smiled. "You can sit with me if you are allowed to, or perhaps we can meet later. I would suggest a public place. As you should for your own reservations concerning safety."

"I am not comfortable with this conversation," she said. Tears formed in her eyes. Throughout the past months, she worked hard at trying to be stoic.

But acting tough and being tough were two different things, and she didn't feel either of those.

"I am not a creep, I swear," he grinned.

"Everyone who says, *I am not a creep*, usually is a creep," she said. "That is like saying, I am not a cannibal, I don't think people are tasty."

He folded the dollar into thirds and put it in his pocket, "Well, all I want to do is ask you a few questions before you start to rewrite what you experienced."

"Sir!" The trucker raised his voice. A half of a sausage link dangled on the end of a fork.

The disheveled man winced at the assertiveness of the trucker.

"If the young lady said she ain't comfortable, then she ain't comfortable. If you address her in such a way again, I will pick you up with my left hand, while holding this sausage with my right hand, and toss you out on your ass and continue eating my sausage."

The disheveled man held up his hands and attempted to hold back the flames.

"I apologize, sir. I am just talking."

"Well, it is clear she doesn't want to talk. Drink your coffee and leave her alone."

Abby wanted to thank the trucker, but she darted into the kitchen. They were the only patrons left in her section and her shift was ending in minutes.

Dante looked at the two men, through the kitchen window.

"What the fuck is going on out there, Abs?"

"That guy, who I think lives in his car is acting weird and that trucker told him to calm down."

"Son of a bitch, I was having a good night too," Dante said. He pushed open the swinging door and stood with his hands on his hips. In his form of taking charge on the floor, he looked like an out-of-work Elvis impersonator, pretending to be a referee.

"Is everything all right out here, sir?" Dante said to the disheveled man.

"Yes sir, I am sorry sir. I know you are the man, and I don't want to offend you or your establishment in any way."

"Maybe you should leave," Dante said. He pointed his finger to the door.

220

The disheveled man took the dollar out of his pocket, unfolded it, and placed it on the table. "I can pay for the coffee."

Dante lost his temper and stepped towards him while his arm was still pointing to the door.

"What part of get the hell out didn't you hear?"

The disheveled man hopped toward the entrance like a scared cat. "Just give that to the lady as a tip and tell her I am sorry."

Abby saw this from the port in the kitchen. The disheveled man saw Abby, spun on his heel, and leaned over the counter.

"Listen if you want to talk..."

"Out!" Dante yelled.

The trucker stood abruptly, and his silverware clattered on the table, "Mister, what did I say?"

"Throw me out with the left hand, the other hand is holding sausage. Yes sir, thank you, Jesus, America *this* and America *that*, I am out." The disheveled man saluted with his left, then right hand. He went into the glass vestibule as Dante was darting towards him. Dante opened the glass door and the man jumped out onto the sidewalk. He got in his beat-up Buick and attempted to start it, but it choked. He waited a few seconds and tried again. It started and he drove off.

Dante looked at the trucker. He was still standing, chewing on his sausage.

"You all right sir?"

The trucker nodded his head.

"Do you want your meal comped?"

He shook his head, "I don't mind paying. You all served me, and your waitress was nice."

Dante rubbed the back of his head and went into the kitchen. He exited through the back door and let it shut behind him. Abby came back to the trucker and thanked him. He took out a twenty-dollar bill and handed it to her.

"That is your tip. It was probably the worst table you had in a while."

"Yep," Abby smiled,

She put the check on the table. He continued to eat his two breakfasts quietly and read the paper.

Five minutes later her shift ended. Dante came in and asked if she was okay to drive home. Even though she was shaken, she assured him she was fine. He said that he would see her tomorrow at three, and she was fine with that.

She took out her pepper spray and hid it in her fist. She checked the parking lot; no Buick, no dirty man in a suit. Her crime-show-saturated mind was extra paranoid. She took the long way home, by driving toward the highway. Car lights trailed behind her in the distance. A gas station was ahead on the right, she pulled in. The trailing car never passed. It made a turn elsewhere or pulled over on the side not to be seen by the station lights. Abby sat and waited. Five minutes passed and she got back on the highway. Again, she saw car lights behind her. They were too indistinct to tell if they belonged to the same vehicle. She drove two miles and took the exit back towards the south side of her town. She knew of another gas station, and as she approached, she saw that it was closed, as it was past eleven.

Calling the police would be stupid. Calling Sutton was a possibility. She wanted to call him and drive to his house. Then the beat-up Buick appeared. It turned into the gas station.

Abby's Honda was parked alongside the gas station entrance. The store was only lit by dim interior lights and fluorescents signifying what chips and soda it held. He pulled up behind her car, but she was not inside. He turned off the car and sat with the headlights on, flooding her interior. He waited to see if she would stick her head up from hiding. A minute passed and he rolled down his window and lit a cigarette.

Patiently, he tapped on the steering wheel. Behind him, he saw movement in the sideview mirror. From out of the shadows, Abby approached. She was holding the revolver with both hands. The disheveled man turned to look at her, as he considered shitting his pants. Without showing fear, she aimed the gun in his face. He opened his mouth and the cigarette dangled on the end of his dry lip.

"Please don't shoot."

"Why not? You are a fucking creep who follows a teenage girl home from work. I think if I blow your head off, I can get away with it in court."

"You aren't a teenager, you turned eighteen while you were abducted. I read your story."

"Why do you give a shit?"

"Tell me one thing, and I will leave you alone."

"Enlighten me."

Carefully, he took the cigarette out of his mouth. "Did they leave you with any implants? I am sure they did. If what you say is true."

She hesitated. He knew things she wanted to hear, and she had the upper hand. She took a step back, "Take your keys out of the ignition and get out."

He listened.

"Toss me the keys."

She caught them with her left hand.

"What is your name?" she asked.

"Talon."

"Like a bird's claw?"

"Yes."

"That's a stupid name. Nobody names their kid Talon."

"My mother was a drunk. She did a lot of dumb things, had three kids, one Braylon, the other Enzo."

"I like the name Braylon. Is he like you?"

"No, he is in jail."

"For what?"

"A lady was getting mugged in the street right below his apartment. He threw a hammer from the second-floor window. It hit the mugger in the skull and killed him."

"Why didn't the lady testify that he saved her?"

"She ran off."

"I think I like him better than you."

Talon grinned and nodded his head slowly.

A car stopped at the intersection; rap music was blasting, and the frame of the car vibrated. Abby lowered the gun by her waist but kept it aimed at Talon.

Talon raised his voice to compensate for the noise, "You aren't going to shoot me with the gas pumps behind me? What if you miss and blow us up?"

The light turned green, and the car drove off.

"I bet you haven't even fired..."

Abby raised the gun in the air and pulled the trigger. The report deafened her ear. She did her best to keep a straight face. Even though she scared herself, it was worth it to watch Talon shit his pants, and if he didn't, he sure smelled like he did.

"The timid waitress girl was an act. I get to play that for tips, and if shooting creeps was a job. It wouldn't be my first time doing it," she said.

She tossed Talon's keys into the bushes.

"What did you do that for?" He pointed at his car. "This is all I have!" he screamed.

"I don't give a shit, get out."

He opened the door. His face winced, like he stepped on a nail. The color drained from his gaunt face. She stared at him with a cold glare. He covered his face with his hand and his hat lifted. Abby noticed tinfoil underneath it. She popped her trunk; a box of old magazines was inside, next to a tire iron and jack. She held the gun on him and put the tire iron in her back seat.

"Get in," she said.

"In the trunk. Really? I can sit next to you in the front seat, or I can follow you in my car."

"You came to my work, and followed me around the city for what? My autograph?"

She wanted knowledge from him but after yesterday, she wasn't going to be taken advantage of by another UFO-obsessed weirdo. Any time spent with Talon, she wanted to have the upper hand.

He climbed in the trunk, begging for forgiveness and muttering curses to himself. She shut it. He yelled hysterically. She turned on the stereo, and the soothing sounds of The Cure tried to calm her nerves. She rolled down her window, lit a cigarette, and drove towards the highway heading south.

27

Talon kicked wildly in the trunk, but Abby ignored his cries. Eventually, he tired out. She never imagined herself holding someone at gunpoint and holding him against his will. Her desperation made her feel justified. This was her second encounter with a threatening situation concerning her disappearance. The people who threatened her had an ideology that went beyond her own experience. With the irrational thoughts of these strange people, she would fight them at all costs, and would not be the victim anymore.

He had information that she wanted, and she would get it from him. After she was done with him, she would drop him off at a police station, or maybe ditch him on the side of the road, and leave his ass stranded.

If her grandfather were here, he would do the same. Without realizing she was speeding, she held her focus and slowed down. If she got pulled over, she would have to explain to the police why she had a screaming tin foil hat man in her trunk, and a revolver in her sweater.

Up ahead was an outdoor carwash. The area was well-lit. She pulled around the back and drove into the bay. She turned off the car. Robert Smith would sing to her later. Carefully, she drew the revolver, held it at her side, and opened the trunk.

Talon was bug-eyed and scared shitless. His face was dripping with fear. A tractor-trailer passed on the main road; it hummed in the distance, between black trees on rounded hills. This signified how far out they were from the rural area. She checked her watch. It was almost midnight.

"I could have died from carbon monoxide poisoning," Talon said.

"I doubt it. People have been riding in trunks for years. The mafia do it all the time," Abby said.

"How do you know?"

"I am in the mafia."

"Bullshit." With much groaning, Talon slowly climbed out of the trunk.

She took the half cigarette out of her apron and lit it. Taking a long drag, she blew smoke above her. Her venture into young adulthood was accelerated dramatically by impulse. She folded her arms and kept the gun visible, with her finger off the trigger.

"Shut the trunk. Lean your ass against the car and talk."

Talon did as she commanded. "Do you have another one of those?" He pointed two fingers at her, moving them like he was playing a piano.

"No."

"Shit." He muttered and dug in his pockets. He pulled out a stick of gum, unfoiled it, and chewed, open-mouthed, like a cow. He put his thumbs in his pants pockets and looked off into the trees behind her.

"You know it was very rude to put me in the trunk like that. I could've got hurt or sick or something."

"I don't want you in my car because you smell like shit, and you are dangerous."

"I am dangerous? "he asked. "Look at you."

Abby deepened her voice, "Tonight, at eleven, an eighteen-year-old waitress is followed home by a homeless man, wearing a tin foil hat. She shot him in the kneecap and moved on with her life, after that sports!"

"Why are you such a bitch?

"Because my mother is a bigger bitch. Now talk or am leaving you here."

"You already screwed me. My car had everything in it. My maps, things I can trade. Dry rations."

She reached into her apron and tossed his keys to him.

"You didn't throw them in the bushes? Were those dummy keys?"

"I picked them up when you were in the trunk. Now, why did you follow me?"

He took the gum out of his mouth and played with it in his fingers, then put it back in his mouth.

"You want to know why I wear a tinfoil hat?"

"Enlighten me."

"Because they..." Talon pointed up, "...are monitoring us."

"And something you wrap chicken in, keeps them from scanning your body?"

Talon tapped his head with his finger, "It's brain waves, honey. Since they returned me. I have taken a special interest in other abduction cases around the country. A lot of them are bullshit. But there are a few that seem valid. I can account for nine that are probably legit out of dozens of cases that I have done research on. I think the aliens who took me, know about me. And I definitely know the government is aware of me."

He looked out into the night. In his pause, the song of crickets rose. In the distance, by tall grass, a group of lightning bugs were visible. When he was younger, his brothers and he would keep them in a jar. The top of the lid would have holes poked in it for air. He always felt like he was like them, being observed by something larger, and that something could easily squash his life.

"Part of me thinks that some aliens and the government are working together on some level," he said.

"So, there are different types of aliens? Not just green men with big eyes floating around in metal saucers?" Abby asked.

"You can mock all you want, but where the hell were you for a week? I mean you said it yourself on live television. Let me quote it, 'I am one of those weird UFO abductee people now?'"

Abby lowered her head. "I did say that."

"You did, and then you are all over the news, some whacko goth teen trying to get attention. It immediately discredits your story."

"Then why are you here asking me this shit, and following me around?"

"Because of that guy in black that was on camera with you."

"What?"

"If people like them are asking you weird questions, then they think it as well."

"I don't understand."

Talon took a step toward her.

"If other people inquiring, that look like him, are asking you questions about high strangeness, then you must not have been on drugs or a drinking bender for a week, or whatever people are saying about you."

The Saturn man and his cohorts were more than just rabid fanboys. This briefly crossed her mind before, but she hadn't had time to collect her thoughts. If only her grandfather were still here. His street smarts and strength would keep her safe. Maybe he would let her stay with him. She could leave at the crack of dawn and stay off the grid. *What about beauty school?* she thought. Would these freaks dictate her life? All of her plans would have to be put on hold.

"I had an encounter with them yesterday. I think they were going to kidnap me."

Abby leaned against the trunk of her car.

"The greasy-haired guy showed up again?" Talon asked.

"Yeah there are two of them, and there is a driver as well. They smeared blood on our windshield and put a burnt Polaroid under the wiper. I pepper-sprayed two of them. Then my grandfather chased them with a gun." She held up the revolver, "This gun."

"Holy shit."

"The guy posing to be a nurse took a Polaroid of my face, and they have my blood type, stats, address, and stuff."

"And you aren't freaking out about this!" he shouted.

"I am, but I don't know what to do. I don't know how to feel."

"You are stupid," Talon said. He pointed at her, and brown spit flew from his mouth.

"How am I stupid? What am I supposed to do?"

"Well, you don't go to work at fucking Denny's! You leave your house and go to a hotel!"

A car drove by on the highway. Talon turned around and looked at it, he put his hand above his eyes as if it could help him see further.

"They could be watching us now."

He ducked behind the car and looked up at her.

"Why are you standing there so calm?"

"What the hell has changed in the past five minutes? One car went by."

"Listen, lady, these UFO nuts might be watching you. They might kidnap you for fun, or they might be the government posing as UFO nuts trying to shake you down. And worst of all, you don't know why you were returned by the aliens! Unless..." Talon flattened his hat, as if it were coming off his head, "... they find you valuable."

"And why is that?"

"For starters, do you have any implants?"

Abby gave him an unnerved cold stare.

"You do. Did you play around with them? They hate that, be careful they might abduct you again just to fix it."

It was the first time she became afraid of anything Talon said.

"Can I see them?"

"What?"

"The markings. Every abductee has markings."

"All right, don't get too close."

She put the gun in the pocket of her sweatshirt, turned around, and lowered her head.

"I need more light to see, come under the port."

She stepped to the center of the bay, next to her car's passenger side.

Talon stepped close and examined the dots, "Can I touch the area around them?"

His body odor was vomitous. She held her breath.

"I would rather you not touch me."

"These are bizarre," he said. "I wish I had my camera with me."

His breath crept around her like a putrid fog. She had to tolerate his grossness, as he was the only person in the world who would look at these dots and agree they were alien.

"I am going to touch around the area."

"Just be careful."

Delicately, with his filthy fingers, he touched her skin on the outer sides of the dots.

He thought they could have been used to supply sustenance while on board the ship.

"Does that hurt?"

"No," she whimpered. She felt like a snake was crawling on her.

"What about here?"

He slid his finger in between the red dots.

"It is a little sensitive there. I pushed it earlier."

As she said this. Clumsily, he pushed in between the dots. Abby's body went limp.

"Whoa!" Talon yelled. "What the hell, are you all right?"

Abby did not respond. He took a step back. Her arms drooped and she leaned toward the ground as if she was doing a yoga stretch. Slowly, she raised off the ground. Her head bumped against the soap-scum-covered aluminum ceiling.

"Abby!" he yelled. "Oh shit, the fucking aliens are going to be here any minute."

He backed away and started to cry.

"Abby?"

She floated like a balloon and did not respond.

Talon turned and ran.

"No more shittin' aliens, no more damn UFO's. Oh Jesus, Allah, Satan, Bruce Lee, help me, I gotta hide!"

Fear took over. He wanted to help Abby. She was just beginning to trust him. But he was scared of what might happen next. If a UFO came, he would not save her. If a black van came, he would hide. Talon was never strong, he was never good, he just wanted to survive, even if it meant pushing someone out of the way.

Frantically, he ran to the rocky hills behind the car wash, while keeping his eyes upward. Wild brush was on the hillside. He stooped out of view, behind weeds and a conglomerate of rocks. It was foolish of him to think if a ship from another galaxy hovered over him, his tinfoil-lined hat and two-foot-tall thorn bush would spare him; fear made Talon do foolish things.

Minutes passed, as he observed the floating Abby. Her arms and legs dangled. Talon waited for something in the sky to appear. There was nothing but the infinite stars above. His mouth was agape, and he saw a meteorite pass. He covered his face with his arm to hide himself from its gamma rays. Nothing appeared from the sky and no darkened vehicles approached.

28

Today was **William Westin's** twentieth birthday. He stood in the backyard, of a place he used to call home. William left home two years ago because he told his parents he hated them. Mr. and Ms. Westin had him late in life. Now they were in their sixties. They never understood their son, as much as they tried. He had always been different from the rest of the kids his age. He used to shoot birds and squirrels with a BB gun in the backyard and impale their small heads on the spokes of the chain link fence. William claimed it warded off evil spirits, but he really wanted to scare the kids in the neighborhood. The doctors said that William had an emotional issue, or that he was *chemically imbalanced*. Also outside of any good doctor's recommendation, William was high on an overabundance of medications that pushed his already dark brain into darker regions. William returned home, not to celebrate his birthday with his parents, he came home because he wanted to kill them. A few hours ago, he purchased a long steak knife. He also bought a two-inch thick steak, meat tenderizer, and expensive steak sauce, at a grocery store on the way in. He wasn't certain if he would eat the steak at his home, or at a hotel on the way out of town while heading back east. Or perhaps he wouldn't cook it at all and eat it raw in the living room. All of those options made sense, but he had other business to attend to first.

The basement door, in the back of the house, never triggered the alarm. It was a flaw when the system was installed. William had always kept the key, he used to sneak out when he was in high school, steal alcohol, and commit random acts of cruelty in the night hours. That was back when he was in eleventh grade. He unlocked the door, took off his Van's slip-on checkered shoes, and left them at the bottom of the stairs. They were directly in the way for anyone to trip on, as his father had always said. William thought it would be funny to leave his sneakers there, in remembrance of many arguments.

Noiselessly, he crept up the stairs and passed through the kitchen. Indecision set in. He decided that eating the steak here was the best option. Carefully, he took it out of the bag and placed it on the table. He placed the tenderizer and steak sauce next to each other, like little soldiers. He moved the bottles twice and then three times. The steak knife, however, made no sound when he took it out of the bag, it was held in pure murderous silence. He wielded it warily and it caught a glimpse of blue and green light from the fish tank in the living room. His parents never had a cat or a dog, they were fish people. It was another reason why kids made fun of him because he had such old parents.

William made his way down the hallway to his parent's bedroom in vulgar silence. He pushed open the door with just enough room for him to slip in. The hinges did not creak. Silently, he stepped into the bedroom, the six-inch steak knife was in his hand. He ran his hand across the top of the bedspread on his father's side and felt nothing. His father was not there. He crawled onto the bed, slid his hand out, and felt nothing on his mother's side. Mr. and Ms. Westin were not home. In frustration, he laid on his back and cursed to himself. He took the steak knife, held it straight out, and saw the silhouette of it in the dim light. He imagined they were out having a good time, probably celebrating that he wasn't around anymore. Rage took over, and he threw the knife across the room. It slid under a large chestnut dresser and hit the wall.

William cursed again at his stupidity and laid there; his heart raced. The vein in his left arm started to pain and his pulse became erratic. The drugs he had taken earlier had fentanyl mixed within them. William had a stroke and died in the middle of where his parents slept. A place he used to come to when he was little, for comfort during a storm. Back when thoughts weren't so clouded. Back when thoughts weren't so dark.

A few miles away, Mr. and Ms. Westin left a nursing home. Mr. Westin's brother, who had dementia resided there. An hour ago, they received a call that his brother had fallen and broke his arm. Upon arrival, they learned that the information was false, and his brother was fine, as fine as he could be. The Westins were confused but relieved; they returned home.

Ms. Westin asked her husband if he thought William would enjoy the small birthday cake they had delivered to the last address where they thought he lived. Mr. Westin shrugged his shoulders and said, "Who knows, with that boy?"

Outside of the bedroom window of the Westin's home, floated a grey shadow with a white face, it looked inside and saw William's body. The grey shadow dissipated.

29

Gently, **Abby descended to the ground**. As soon as her feet hit the wet pavement, she became cognizant. She looked at her hands and felt her face. Talon saw her standing by the car. Cautiously, he came down the hill. As he approached, he weaved and bobbed his head like a curious cat looking at a mouse-shaped object on a carpet.

She saw him scurry closer into view. "What the hell just happened?" She yelled.

As he ran toward her, he ducked down, like he was dodging bullets. He put his finger to his lips, urging her to be quiet, while he was checking the night sky for large flying objects. He reminded her of a cartoon character waiting for an anvil to drop on his head.

"You floated in the air."

"Shut up."

"You went up to the ceiling like a damn balloon. Then you came down on your own. You floated for like a half hour."

She leaned over and pressed her head against the passenger window.

"What the hell is going on?"

"This is because of them; it is their technology. You have alien tech in you. Who knows what it could do?"

"Alien technology, now what?"

"I don't know. Those guys who were chasing you are probably aware and that is what they are after."

"My grandfather thought they were a UFO cult."

"A UFO cult?"

"I think he was just trying to piece things together. Maybe I will go out where he lives. I don't know what to do."

"Well, if what he says is true, you will have to be extra careful. I don't know what's worse a cult or some secret government organization. Nearly all cults have a leader. The leaders usually force an ideology that points back to them, you know? Or like above them, but only through them. They are the only answer to their followers, or the source of it."

Talon began yelling and punching his words. His eyes were wild. He twisted his hat and pushed a folded piece of tinfoil that became loose back underneath it.

"Then comes the sex and power. The people who are following you could be like that or different and more unpredictable. Maybe they are like moth God people, did you ever hear of them?"

"You are kind of losing me here," Abby said. "Like some of what you are saying makes sense then you go off again."

She opened the door and fixed her makeup in the visor mirror.

Talon stood beside her with the car door open. His body odor was overwhelming. She stopped applying make-up and closed her eyes as he continued to rant.

"You never know with UFO fanatics, like them, don't need money or sex, they don't need power, they could be like that Heaven's Gate cult. Their leader didn't need anything from his followers. They suffocated themselves and chased after a comet. All of it was on their own accord. There was no gunpoint or poison Kool-Aid."

He paused and took deep breaths. She became uncomfortable at his lack of awareness, and how close he was to her.

"There is one thing we can do. Someone did it to me before. It might reset things."

"What?" she said. She was becoming impatient with his rambling. Between Talon and the possible UFO cult, who was going to pop out of the woods tomorrow? Moving to the backwoods of Illinois with her grandfather sounded appealing.

"I would need wood and nails and a shovel," Talon said. He was snapping his fingers erratically like he was keeping a bad rhythm to a song, only he could hear.

She closed her eyes. "I don't like where you are going with this."

"Well, it worked for me. Someone else has to be the one covering the coffin with dirt."

She opened her eyes and raised her voice. "Let me get this straight, you want to build a coffin and have me lay in it, then bury me with dirt!"

"Yeah, for like ten minutes. It resets the alien tech. As soon as I dig you up and open the coffin, you put tinfoil on your head. They won't be able to pick up your signals anymore."

"Yeah, that is not going to fucking happen." She got out of the car. "Back away please, I want to get out."

Talon took a step back; he was still in close proximity to her. When she stood up, it was the closest he had been to her face. His eyes widened when he looked at her and his jaw contorted.

"What the hell?" he said.

"What?" Abby asked.

Talon shrunk away and covered his face with his hand.

"What happened to your face?" he shrieked.

Abby sat back in the car and checked her face in the mirror. She looked completely normal, as normal as her face always looked.

"What are you talking about? I just put some eyeliner on."

"No. No, it isn't your eyes. It's your mouth, it's contorted, disfigured! Like the time I ate a chicken pot pie, and I dug a hole in it with a fork to let the steam out. Your mouth is like a gaping maw of flesh."

She looked again. Felt her cheeks and got out of the car. She rested her hand on the top of the door and looked at him with concern.

"Talon, what are you talking about?"

"They did this to you! Aliens did this!" He screamed like a woman and got on the ground.

Abby stepped toward him.

"Please don't hurt me. I am sorry. I didn't mean to speak ill against you before."

"What?"

"I-I can't right now. I can't do this." Talon looked at her, started to run back toward the hills, and looked back at her again.

"I am sorry, he yelled."

She walked outside of the port and watched him run off in the distance. He climbed up the rock hill, slipped, and cursed. Like a wolf with a broken paw, he continued to climb until he was out of view.

That was the last she saw of him.

She drove back to Blueville with the windows down. No one, not Talon or a UFO cult followed her. When she got home, she parked in the carport. She sprayed Lysol on her seat and in her trunk. She used Windex on her windows. The dank odor that Talon left behind still seemed to linger. The encounter with him started with his bizarre dialog and ended on the same. She learned nothing, aside from thinking it might be best to leave Blueville altogether until people forgot who she was.

When she entered the dark kitchen, Dario greeted her, she gave him cat treats and went to her room. She checked her Myspace page. After screening out creepy stalkers, she found people who offered her support. Some of which were just like her from around the country. An old couple, in Kentucky reached out, saying they believed her story. They invited her for dinner. Abby didn't know if she could trust anyone anymore. Another message was from a bogus Illuminati page. Their icon was a symbol of the all-seeing eye on top of a pyramid. The same image that Talon pointed to on the back of the dollar.

The message said: *We are watching you.*

Her bizarre night of kidnapping a man and holding him at gunpoint ended with her being held under the threatening fear of a stalking group. But she didn't want to be afraid anymore.

Fuck you, she responded.

She laid in bed with Dario, and the gun was under her pillow.

Far off on the edges of a forest, a black Chevy G30 van was parked. Gentry, Isaac, and Jericho were sitting by a campfire. Isaac burned a concoction of sulfur and black leaves. The air smelled rancid.

"Tomorrow the stars align for the sacrifice of the destined woman. I will take her and cut out her pancreas. Both Gentry and Isaac chanted.

"We will cut a hole to get what we need, and discard what is useless, and discard what is useless, and discard what is useless, " Isaac and Gentry said in unison.

30

Pastor Ulma sat at Lucy's bar; he finished his second beer. A third was in front of him. In the few times, he frequented this establishment, his rule was two beers/two hours. It had only been a half hour since he arrived, and he was feeling it in the tips of his fingers.

The owner, Todd Jenson, a muscular, white-haired man, in his sixties, was behind the counter. The bar was named after his wife Lucy. She passed away last year from a brain aneurysm. A picture of her was above the bar, with a metal plate underneath. It said: She watches over us.

Todd had been in an off-and-on conversation with two men at the bar, Jack, and Stan. It had been going on since before Ulma arrived. Jack had a brown vest and wore a camo hat with a deer on it. Stan had a tan vest and a camo hat with a fish on it. With their confused faces and mustaches, they could have passed for brothers, but they weren't. All of these men and their conversation aggravated Ulma.

He couldn't help but listen, and he became angry at what was being said. Todd went on a long speech about being proud of his college-aged son who was gay.

Earlier, Jack told a gay joke that Todd didn't think was funny, yet all three of them were still getting along. The direction of the conversation seemed to be mild. Jack had a way of diffusing the situation, while still being friendly with his regular patrons. Ulma was frustrated with the tolerance in America. His face contorted in frustration. Without realizing it, he grew so visibly uncomfortable that the men looked at him when he huffed multiple times.

"You okay there, sir?" Todd asked.

Ulma shook his head. He wanted to speak up, but he was aware that the alcohol was affecting his judgment.

"Hey, I know you," Stan said, "You are that preacher guy from over in Blueville. I heard you came here, playing off like you're a regular."

Ulma didn't know what to say. He thought ten miles of distance would keep him anonymous.

"I am that preacher, son," Ulma said.

"Well, chime in. Being a Bible guy and all, what do you think?" Stan asked.

"About?" Ulma said.

"His son being loud and proud out in Commiefornia."

Jack laughed.

The bartender smiled. Ulma hated that he did. "Listen, pastor, I am just telling these gentlemen, that despite our similar politics and our church, we can't shake a fist at the youth and call them whatever, and not expect to be looked at as Neanderthal's."

"Why not?" Ulma said. "It's still our country, we can say what we want. The gays can't take that away."

"No one is taking away anything. They have as much of a right as we do, that's all I am saying." Todd pleasantly folded his arms and looked up at the baseball game on TV.

Silence fell between them.

"I guess, Todd. Maybe you are right," Jack said. "I just don't know what I would do if I found out my son was gay. He got my brains and his mother's looks, so no one wants to date him."

All three of the men laughed.

Ulma slammed his hand on the counter.

"It's tolerance. You just tolerate the wrong things until they become more wrong. You accept and then, we have no choice. It isn't what our nation was based on, and it isn't what God wanted either."

"Mister, maybe you need to sit the next round out, or perhaps you need to go outside for a walk," Todd said.

"Yeah, buddy, we are all friends here," Stan said.

In a fit, Ulma finished the remainder of his beer, a portion he was more than accustomed to. He pulled out his wallet and threw twenty dollars on the counter, scowled at all of them, and left.

Although he knew he was in no shape to drive, he wanted to go home. If these men wouldn't see him for what he was, at least his wife would. He regretted going to the bar, someone here had recognized him, and no one respected him. When he started the car and placed his hands firmly on the wheel. Mints were in the console. He put four of them in his mouth and drove towards the highway. As he accelerated onto the ramp his car felt off. He kept it at a slow speed and wondered if it needed to be serviced again. There was a drop at the back end of the car, and he knew his tire was flat. He pulled over and put on his flashers.

"Shit!" He slammed the steering wheel. It was ten miles from home. He did not have roadside assistance, and he hadn't changed a tire in years. He was uncertain if he had the strength to get the lug nuts off with a crowbar. Calling the police would be foolish, as he had beer on his breath and felt a little on the drunk side. If he called his wife and explained, he would have to lie and have her get someone to pick him up. He sat in a moment of inebriated indecision.

A car pulled over on the side of the road behind him. It was about five car lengths away. A tractor-trailer passed. Its vibrations shook the old Cadillac. Ulma didn't want to get out, but he was desperate. He opened the door and hurried to the back of his car. The thought occurred to him that it could be a police officer, and if it was, he hoped it would go unnoticed that he had been drinking. He stood behind the trunk of his car. The high beams from the vehicle were on. Ulma raised his hand to block the light. To his relief, the roof of the vehicle was flat; it was not a police car. Ulma felt that the owner of the vehicle was becoming more rude, as he waited. If he were himself, he would have yelled at the person in the car or flailed his arms. And his inconvenience kept him humble.

A thin man got out. He had a hood up and a four-sided tire iron in his hand. The man walked in front of his headlights, creating a long shadow cast by his silhouette.

Ulma put his hand up to his mouth, "I think the Lord has sent you!"

"I think so too," the stranger said.

As the man got closer, Ulma saw that the man had a sweater collar high up over his mouth, and a pair of sunglasses on. This alarmed Ulma.

"I was just passing," the man said, "and I saw you had a flat."

241

"Yes," Ulma said. His guard went up. The man walked passed him without looking at him directly. He looked at the tire and kicked it. "Yep, it's flat."

"It appears so," Ulma said. If the tables were turned, Ulma would have called this man a hoodlum.

"Do you mind if I pop your trunk and put the e-brake on?" the man said.

"Sunglasses at night, son?" Ulma pointed to his own eyes and tapped underneath them.

A car passed by slowly, the driver assessed the scene and accelerated.

"Yeah, I have glaucoma. These are prescription, for night driving."

Ulma smiled and nodded. He wished he had his gun with him.

The stranger put the e-brake on and popped the trunk. He took out the jack and spare and put it in front of the flat. With ease, he undid the lug nuts with his tire iron and jacked up the car. He took the flattened tire off and rolled it to the back of Ulma's car. He rolled it in the light shone from his vehicle.

"Hmmm, I don't see any nails or anything. Maybe you got a slow leak or something."

"Maybe," Ulma said. For how quickly the stranger was working, Ulma decided that the man might just be decent after all.

"You like sports, son?"

"What?" the stranger asked. He placed the flat tire in the well of the trunk and covered it with the carpeted board.

"Sports, do you like them?"

The stranger shut the trunk. He looked at Ulma for a long few seconds, "No. I have no interest in sports at all."

"You shut the trunk," Ulma said. "You still have to put the jack in."

"Well shucks sir, you started talking and I got distracted," the stranger said.

He got on his knees and spun one of the lug nuts on.

"Gosh darn it, sir. I need your help."

Cautiously Ulma approached. He stood above the man, who was holding his hand.

"My hand freezes up sometimes." He showed it to Ulma, it looked like it was going into a spasm.

"What can I do?" Ulma asked.

"Just lower the jack. I can tighten the lug nuts with my other hand and shoulder weight."

Ulma knelt next to him. His knees creaked as he got on the ground. Ulma groaned at the swaying of his aging body. He grabbed the rod and spun the jack slowly. The car lowered. At the rate Ulma was twisting, it would take an hour to get the wheel to touch the ground.

The stranger massaged his right hand. He coughed and spoke, "You know about two weeks ago, I saw a young woman, run out of your church. She was chased by the whole congregation."

Ulma's face stiffened. He stopped twisting the rod in the jack.

The stranger continued, "I saw you there too. You hit her in the head with your Bible, trying to cast out demons or some sort of shit."

"That woman you speak of has a penchant for disorder and rebellion," Ulma said.

"I don't really care what she has. I just don't think it looks right to be Christian and all, chasing a member around and hitting them, trying to cast out demons or whatever."

The man showed one of the lug nuts to Ulma, "If I were to throw the remaining three of these lug nuts over there in the bushes, you would be screwed. I know that you are a bit out of the way from your home. I know you have been drinking. And I know since you haven't called anyone yet, you either don't have your phone or you don't want anyone to know what you are doing?"

"What do you want?" Ulma said. Anger was beginning to surface.

"Let me ask you this? With what hypocrite hand of yours to you turn the pages of the Bible?"

Ulma said nothing, he just glared at the stranger. A nervous tic twitched on his cheek.

"I am no hypocrite, son. I am a man of God."

"Hmmm mmmm, I bet you are. Just tell me if it is your right or left."

"I turn the holy pages with my right hand." Ulma lifted his hand to the stranger and gave a small wave.

The stranger grabbed Ulma's wrist with his left hand. His grip was like a vice. He forced it to the ground. The speed surprised Ulma, and he felt like he was bit by a cobra. The stranger picked up his tire iron and slammed it against the top of Ulma's hand. The metacarpals broke on impact. Ulma screamed and started to cry. The stranger stood up.

"You can scream all you want, sir. Just know the next young man that comes through your doors looking for salvation might be who is under this mask. Or maybe I am the son of someone who goes to your church. Or maybe I was sent by God to get your mind straight."

"I am sorry, son." Ulma wept and rocked back and forth.

"Do you want to call a tow truck, or do you want to admit to being a bad pastor," the stranger said.

Ulma's face opened like a faucet. He cried out to God. "I am sorry Lord for my pride and my anger. I am sorry."

The stranger looked at Ulma and didn't believe a word of what he was saying. But he wondered what would happen if he left him here.

"Get your ass up and go stand in front of your car. I will have you out of here in a minute."

Ulma struggled to get up off the ground and waddled toward the front of his car.

The stranger put on all the lug nuts, tightened them, and lowered the car. He put the jack in Ulma's back seat.

Ulma leaned on the hood of his Cadillac, holding his broken right hand.

"Go, get yourself checked out in the ER. You must have hurt it while you were changing the tire. This is what happens when you hit an innocent woman."

Ulma kept his head low and stared at the ground.

The stranger left without saying anything else. He got into his classic Oldsmobile, navy colored, with silver rims, turned off his lights, and did a U-turn across the lanes. When he was out of view, he turned his lights back on. Sutton took off his hood, he looked at himself in the mirror. He wondered if Abby's grandfather found out about this, would he be proud of him?

Ulma got into his car and struggled to ride home; it took him nearly an hour. When he got home, he told his wife, who was worried sick, that he broke his hand by changing the tire. She smelled alcohol on his breath. She didn't say anything about it, as she knew his temper would emerge. But she sensed something different in him, a brokenness. As if his long night out, was a trial by God, and somehow he was humbled. She hoped that whatever happened to him tonight, would make him a better person.

31

The next night at the restaurant was normal; no raving tin-foil hat men or UFO cult members surfaced. Abby made sixty-seven dollars in tips. Dante questioned her about parking in front. She apologized and told him she wanted a clear line of sight if she needed to get out of there quickly. He shook his head in frustration and went into the kitchen. Mentioning the gun in the glove compartment nearly slipped. It wouldn't be out of the norm for a legal-aged woman of Tennessee to be proud of packing heat, but she didn't know the rules of what was allowed on company property. Dante was still management, and at times acted like it, despite having unprofessional moments of being a creep.

That night she didn't want to go home. It was the second night of working late this week and it tired her out, to the point of feeling calm. But there was nowhere to go, nothing was open, and there was nothing to do. She drove around aimlessly and smoked four cigarettes while singing to The Cure at the top of her lungs. Images formed in her mind of her future and where she hoped to end up. Thoughts that could be forged into reality or a pipedream of what could never be. But it was something to hang onto, something better than getting married, settling down, and watching cable TV.

On her return home, she passed through an unfamiliar back road, by a permanently closed factory. Barbed wire was on the outside fence. Just as she approached the train tracks, the crossing gate lowered. A slow-moving freight train passed. The red lights from the gate flashed. She put her car in park and stared off, trailing into the imaginative subconscious.

"Aaaaaaaaaaaaaaaoooooooummmm."

A meditative chant welled up from inside of her. *Whatever happened to the geodes?* She wondered.

"Aaaaaaoooooooooooo," she chanted again.

The red lights flashed. She closed her eyes. Her throat became dry. The red lights flickered, then the red lights became all. All that was around her was a circle of red light. She saw herself from her mind's eye, as a voyeur peeking in the window. Immediately she criticized her image and hated the way she looked, but a stronger emotion took over. It was for her safety. She turned away from herself to look back at the crossing lights, but she wasn't by the tracks anymore. She was at the tennis court behind her house in a circle drawn by chalk. She was levitating and rising upward toward an object in the sky.

Everything around her was dark, a darkness thicker than anything she encountered before. The ground beneath her was solid. Hesitating with her steps, she felt the sticky resistance of a substance under her Doc Martens. Red lights appeared far above her, like lights in a salon, only if the salon were on the edge of a precipice of an unseen chasm. She was indoors, and it was colosseum-sized. An uneasiness settled in, behind her familiar anxieties. It was a warning inside of her.

The lights rose dimly and illuminated the nothingness around her. In front of her, in the depths of a void was a clicking sound. It sounded like an insect, but one that stood as tall as her. A separate clicking was further to the right, and then clicking came from behind her. Like all people before her in this same position, she did the only thing she could think of; and that was to address the unknown.

"Hello?" Her voice echoed.

A click responded from behind her. It was the closest of the clicking sounds. A cold sweat formed on her back. Her greasy-smelling restaurant hair stuck to her neck.

"Wh-who is there?"

She was powerless in an arena. Something, multiple things were watching her, and they were communicating. She wanted to run, but away from the sounds. The only place she hadn't heard clicking was to the left. When the lights came back on, if they did, she would run away from whatever was watching her. And she did not want to find out the purpose of these unknown watchers. Judging from their sounds, a pleasant response, was not expected from them. The lights returned from high above, and she ran.

The hard rubber soles of her boots slammed on the metal floor. She did not slip or skid and kept on running. Ahead of her was an archway, at least what she could gather from the distance. If it was an exit out of here she would take it. At the pace she was running and the intermittent lighting, she wondered how long it would take her. Waiting for a cycle of lights again to return would require strength that she didn't think she had to not lose her mind. She didn't know where in the world she was, and for a millisecond, in between panicky breaths, she wondered if she was on her world at all.

The light dimmed again, and as reckless as the thought was, she knew she was capable of running without tripping regardless of no light. She continued to run in total darkness. Clicks came from behind her, who or whatever was clicking was pursuing her. The red lights returned to their mild dimness, and the archway became closer.

The archway was massive. It was three times her height and wide enough for two cars to drive through side by side. The door was closed; it was metal. Ornate patterns and carvings of symbols of an unknown language were on the edges of the archway. Faces of creatures, tall and robed were among the symbols. She assumed the creatures that were in the art and carvings were the same creatures that clicked behind her in the darkness.

"I am on a fucking alien spacecraft."

Others in her position had said the same thing, in other languages from across the globe, on this one and many others that harbor bipedal beings, who are mostly made of water and electric impulses, that contained life similar to hers. The worst thoughts raced through her mind. She wondered if she would be grilled for food or interrogated for information. If these creatures captured her for sport, would she have to fight other captives with spears in an arena? All of the above was caused by an amalgam of fear, from her reading diet of alien and UFO fiction and fandom.

The cryptic writings of Francis Truelove had opened a door of information to her, with old words that were scarcely spoken. Those words were intricate and beautiful. The script that he wrote, was Tamil. On Earth, it was known as a Dravidic language, one of the oldest written languages in the world. It dated back nearly five thousand years. To man's folly, it was a language that transcended beyond the grasp of Earth's wisdom and went beyond the stars. It had been one of the first written languages because it had been given to men in that region, long ago. Beings that existed in an older galaxy, who evolved further than us, by such a margin, that they found a way to travel within wormholes throughout the universe and visited Earth and spread the usage of their language and script.

The beautiful Tamil script was engraved around the archway. Abby did not understand what it meant but recognized the gorgeous intricacies. She knew there was a connection between what she saw in the book and what was before her. Did the famed mystic/astrologer/professor make it this far? Was it possible that there was a similar voyage set for an aspiring young beautician with an eating disorder who came from a small forgettable town?

She thought hard, harder than ever. Tears streamed.

"Click, click, click."

Multiple noises from approaching creatures came closer through the darkness.

"Atai tirakka ventum enral atu tirakkum," she said.

The door opened. She entered and ran straight into unknown certainty and immediately fell on her hands and knees into a thick marsh. The door closed behind her and disappeared. Around her were tall trees from a tropical region, with dense twisted roots, mangled, knotted, interwoven within black swamp grass, and orangish brown mud. The odor was of decomposing mildew and rot. Nearby, she heard a sound of a threat, only it wasn't the clicking. It was something wolf-like. It barked, in a deep-throated wretchedness. She ran as fast as she could in calf-high water. Losing her footing, she tripped again. Cuts were on her hands and knees. The animalistic sound of rabid torment was close. It remained out of view in the dense bushes and misshapen trees behind her. Her fear changed, and it turned to strength, it surged within her. At that moment she learned she was tougher than who she believed herself to be. As she ran, in haphazard steps, she spotted firmer ground ahead. It would take her out of the marsh. A bark echoed from behind. She did not turn to look at the threat and burst through long thorns in front of her. Forcing herself through the terrain, she shielded her eyes with her forearm. Sharp ends of branches tore at her, cut her arms, and pulled at her hair. Her cheek was scraped, and blood dripped off her chin. A branch pulled on her name tag, and it came off her blouse. If she survived, it would be a moment she would laugh at later, imagining the dangling brass Denny's badge brandishing her name in an evil terrascape somewhere in the universe.

As she made it out of the thorns, she stepped into a divot and stumbled. Bracing herself for impact, her hand slipped in between a hold in a tree. A popping sound came from her wrist. Pain shot through her arm like a brick was dropped on it. It was broken. She held her scream, not willing to give away her position. Nausea surfaced. Crying would have to be buried for another time.

Carefully, she pulled her arm out of the tree, held it close, like a deformed wing, and continued to run. Ahead of her, out of the dense surroundings, was flat, dry, rocky ground. She burst through the brush and dropped to her knees. Sweat dripped from her. Her breathing was labored. The regret of being a smoker haunted her with each wheeze. She had to get up and keep moving. As she looked ahead, she was amazed to see a structure that belonged in a desert. Her mouth dropped in awe. A pyramid was in the distance. It could have been hundreds of feet tall maybe even thousands. The height was hard to differentiate, considering the distance it was from her. With the unknown creature lurking in the forest, she headed towards the vast structure. She ran until she couldn't anymore, then walked, and ran again, with her eyes half closed. With each step, her broken wrist throbbed. Thirst had become its own emotion of extreme desperation.

As she traveled toward the pyramid, it seemed like she wasn't getting any closer. Her only judgment of distance was the furthering treeline behind her. When she looked back, she saw the creature that had been pursuing her. It was a wolf, not with one head, but two, and it tore across the field toward her.

Abby ran as hard as her body would allow her.

With each step, the muscles in her body cried out *no more*, but something in her brain said otherwise; it was a small fire within, that made her realize right there, she was a survivor, and she kept on running. The snarling behind her became louder. As she got closer to the edge of the pyramid, she saw an archway at the bottom. It was the only place to take refuge, and she hoped there was a door or a gate or a weapon there, or she would certainly be eaten alive.

When she approached a metal door, she said the words that somehow came easily to her.

"Atai tirakka ventum enral atu tirakkum."

The door opened and she ran through the archway and fell onto a metal floor. She turned around and the two-headed wolf barked at her ferociously. Its eyes were blood red. Its fur was silken grey. As eager as it was to rip Abby apart, it did not enter the room she was in. The door slowly shut, cutting her off from that terrain.

Exhausted, she laid on her back and held her arm.

"Abagail." A voice spoke to her. It was a mix between a growl and a hum.

Delicately, Abby rolled onto her knees and held her wounded arm. Across the room were tall, robed figures, their eyes glowed yellow. The formation they stood in was in a triangular pattern. They floated above the ground and moved forward in unison.

If she was going to die, she wanted to hurt one of them. But she had nothing to defend herself with and held her right arm. If the creatures were decent, she hoped they would have pity on her. Fatigue took over. Strength was leaving her body. All she could do was kneel on the floor. As the robed figures approached, she saw they were nearly seven feet tall. When they came closer, it was revealed that their faces were reptilian. The tall reptile in the center had a gold gem in the center of its forehead. Its hands looked humanoid, and its palms were pressed together like it was praying.

"Who are you?" she asked.

The pyramid in its forehead was hypnotizing. The reptilian looked down at her with emotionless eyes. It spoke to her, in English, "We are observers, from an old galaxy."

"An old galaxy," a reptile from behind it confirmed.

"We travel the universe and test subjects like yourself. Witness things, take notice, observe, record, contemplate, learn, and repeat in another galaxy," the reptilian said.

"Why me? I am not an athlete. I am not a scholar. I have won no awards. No one on Earth has ever heard of me except for a few people in my hometown," Abby said.

"What you said does not define you. You are exceptional. What we see in you, is not what others see."

It raised its hands upward as it spoke as if it was drawing the words from the air around it.

"Your potential and being of who you are, when things are placed in front of you and the actions on how you react, define you."

"Define you," repeated the reptile in the background.

Abby was surprised. She thought they were going to remove her arms and legs and place her on a spit over a fire.

"Thank you for those kind words. What may I call you?" Abby asked.

"My name is Kuri," the reptilian said.

"I am Abagail."

"We know."

"Of course, you do," she said. Pain shot from her wrist up through her arm. She gritted her teeth and wanted to hurl as many curses as she could think of, but she focused on what little strength she had to maintain her composure.

"Well, Kuri, I don't know how you can say those things when I have hardly done anything with my life at all."

He tilted his head and looked at her keenly.

"We can see the end as well. Your being, and your construct from before, the now, and the future is before us. It is how we see. A ray of light passes through you and connects elsewhere. You are different and unique. There have been others, but you are different than them."

"I don't understand how." She raised her broken arm, her face winced in pain. She regretted the action as soon as she had done it. "I am just a broken girl from a shithole part of Tennessee, and all I want to do is cut hair."

"We can make you well again," Kuri said.

"We can make you well," the second reptilian confirmed.

She wiped dripping blood from her eyebrow with her left hand. The strength to stand came to her, as she realized she wasn't going to be tortured by these creatures.

"Are you in pain?" Kuri asked.

She nodded and bit her lip.

"You are almost done with your test."

"Fuck you," she whispered. She didn't care if they heard. For all of the clever usages of the word *fuck*, she hoped that in reptilian it meant the same thing as it did back on Earth.

On the floor before her, two discs lit up. Unique objects were on top of the discs. The light beneath the objects was nearly blinding. The light subsided and what resembled black shimmering bars, were stacked in a neat pyramid on the disc on the left. On the right was a black glass bottle, with ornate handles on each side. The bottle was two feet in height, with a long neck and a fanned bulbous bottom. The edges of the bottle looked like dragon wings, with glass claw tips on each side.

Kuri levitated forward. His black robe hung above the ground, like a specter from a haunted house. "You have two choices. The same has been presented before a select few. You are one of the exclusive and you are fortunate."

He moved his right hand to the bottle. "Within this vessel is an elixir of longevity. Beings from around the universe have fought wars for this. They have murdered their own families and burnt countries to the ground to hold something of its equal. It is a mystery of life and the universe, and through trial and error we have conjured our own form of it."

Abby was silent. She thought for a moment about how Kuri explained it, *beings from around the universe.*

In all of her pondering and staring at the stars, they did exist. Other Abby's from around the universe. Beings with souls, from other worlds fought and killed each other for things that were bigger than her understanding and it was presented before her so freely.

"Or..." Kuri raised his other hand and waved it towards the neatly stacked black shimmering bars. "... infinite wealth."

The second reptilian behind Kuri confirmed, "Life or wealth."

Abby went on impulse. The pain was winning its grip, but she said her piece.

"I don't want money. If I had it here, it would serve no purpose. If I had it on Earth, it wouldn't buy me happiness. My mother is awful and if I bought her something nice, she would make an excuse to throw it away. And my stepfather, who isn't so bad, has money and he doesn't buy anything aside from video games. They don't even go on vacation. You see my mother isn't well. She is probably the equivalent of some sort of sage or wise man that you have here. I am certain you have religion. If you could comprehend someone

254

who did it so poorly that they were an embarrassment and you kicked them out for doing it, yet they continued to do it elsewhere and hurt others."

Either Abby's hand completely went numb or the part of the brain she utilized for her rant, lessened the throbbing in her arm.

"Plus, I want to work. I don't really like being with people, but being around them is okay. I think I will always work. If you gave me endless wealth, I would probably find out how shitty people really are. They would lie and say things they didn't mean, just expecting me to give them money. I think having that much money could break people, maybe even break good people. A lot of movie stars seem miserable, and they kill each other and cheat on each other because they are bored. I would see the shitty side of people that I don't want to see, and I don't want to see that in myself."

Kuri slowly nodded his head. Perhaps he was impressed or maybe her response was expected.

"So, it is life then, live for centuries. See the glaciers of humankind shift?" Kuri asked.

"Life then?" the other reptilian confirmed.

Abby thought on this, and it didn't seem too pleasing either.

"I don't know, for what? To watch people, I care about die around me. No. That doesn't sound good. That sounds awful. If I did have longevity, I would want that to be somewhere where other people had it as well."

As she completed her speech, the throbbing shot like lightning from her forearm to underneath her armpit, and the side of her neck, in pulsing waves. She wondered if they were going to have to amputate it.

A young woman, unimpressive by most people's standards, writhing in her own fashion, figured out her purpose in life. It was that she could not be bribed, even with all the turmoil at home, there was something more to Abby compared to girls just like her around the world. The conclusion she came to concerning these choices, was that she didn't give a damn.

"I don't want either of these things," she said. "Go give them to someone else, smarter than me, who can use the money for good, or use their lifetime for something related to curing diseases. Maybe you could just give me medicine or something to make sure sick people aren't sick anymore or whatever would keep society from killing each other."

The reptilians murmured. Abby raised her unbroken hand, "Or if you want, you should just jettison me out into space and find a better person."

The reptilians made a wide circle around her. They all spoke to each other. Judging from the tone, some seemed upset; others seemed pleased. One hissed at the other. Just like elders in a church, people in government, or hippies in a commune, their thoughts and ideas clashed. Kuri raised his right hand. He spoke to them. They all mumbled, then came to an agreement.

The gold gem in Kuri's forehead glowed brightly.

"We learned from you, Abagail. Your selflessness has unmatched many. Is it your coding, your wiring, or is it just who you are inside? Your ability to question yourself honestly, in front of two great temptations, that many have broken themselves upon, is admirable."

"Admirable," the other reptilian said.

"To answer such questions yet come up with more questions is wisdom in itself," Kuri said.

"Great, can you fix my arm now?" she asked. "I don't even remember half of what I said because of the pain. You could have fixed me, and we could have had this conversation in a better setting."

One reptilian hissed at her. Abby wished she didn't say anything, but sarcasm was her best and worst gift.

The reptilians looked upward, and a large clear capsule was lowered from above her. It shook, clumsily. It was supported by small, cables and tubes. Kuri moved toward her in towering dominance.

"Know this, that most people did not hesitate to take wealth, only a few took life, on this planet and others. Some are now gone, and we have lost contact with them, and others have taken their own lives. We will use our medicine to fix you. And we will reward you with something else. But this moment will be in your mind only temporarily."

The capsule covered her like a cheap ride at a carnival. She was encased within it. Judging from what the reptilians have motioned towards, being pleased with her, she assumed this next phase of her adventure would be less taxing. A drill-like whirring noise buzzed from behind her head. Before she could turn around, something pierced the back of her neck.

"What are you doing to me? I thought I passed your stupid test?"

A flood of warmth entered into her body. Her eyes fluttered; she became tired. Her arm became fibrous, her stomach became marshmallowy.

And she slept.

WHEN ABAGAIL AWOKE, she was in a white robe, sitting in a cozy white chair, that felt like synthetic leather. In front of her was a white glass table. On the table was a white coffee mug and a large clear flask of liquid was next to it. The room she was in was as large as an underground cavern. A place like this was in her mind from a TV documentary about Alaskan caves. The entire room was white and glassy, textured with dripping stalactites, running down the walls in frozen waterfalls, but the temperature was comfortable. The first impulse she had was to check her make-up and hair, but there was no need because she was alone, and that didn't matter anymore.

Her arm was well again. There was no swelling or scarring. Whatever the reptilians had done was miraculous. She looked down at her feet and was astonished to see fuzzy bedroom slippers. Above all things in the universe, the comfort of slippers was figured out by lizard people.

"They took my damn Doc Martens."

She stood up and walked around the room.

"Hello." Abby's voice echoed. There were no doors or windows in the cavernous room, just the furniture in the center.

"Make yourself comfortable. Relax, Abagail," a woman's voice said.

"Who are you?" Abby asked.

"I will wait to disclose that. First, I want to say how proud I am of you."

"That's nice, um... what the hell is going on here?"

A melon-sized, white bulb lowered into the room, dangling from a clear cable. Inside the cable was a twisted wire, that resembled a curled phone cord. On the front of the bulb were two glowing panels. To Abby, it looked like a skull of a robot, or droid.

"Hello, Abagail. It is nice to meet you," it said. The panels lit up with each syllabic pattern.

"Um, hi," Abby said. She was startled, the voice sounded like a young woman from Earth.

"Please sit. They specifically designed that seat for you. I had to explain the comfort of human posture to them. It was made in one of their 3-D production chambers, just for you."

Abby sat.

"What do you mean, our posture? Were you human?" Abby asked.

"You see, we are from the same DNA coding. There are some of my cells left here on the ship, in an encasing room. Not too long ago I got sick and sadly, even with Tolkanaytian technology, my body rapidly decayed. My conscience was uploaded into the drive here on the ship. I live here amongst others who had a similar fate and who also reside within libraries of data. There are some games and their versions of movies that I watch. Some of the footage is time changes of naturescapes back on Earth. There are rapid declines within the poles of our planet, as the Earth is heating up. It is a marvel how back in the 1800's, the Earth only had a billion people, yet in the span of 100 or so years, we reached seven billion. No wonder why the Earth is warmer?"

Abby's eyebrows raised. "I kind of missed everything you said after the *same DNA coding.*"

"Abagail, I don't know how much your mother told you, about the night that I disappeared, years ago."

"Disappeared? Wait a minute? Are you..."

"Your grandmother." The orb moved closer to Abby as it said this.

Despite it being mechanical, Abby wondered if it was programmed to exude emotions. Suddenly a warmth surfaced within her when she heard this.

"And you are a machine?"

"My conscience still exists, and a bit of my body. Actually, just fractions of it."

"By the hand of Robert Smith! Is it okay if I call you Grandma?"

"Yes, or you can call me Helen."

"Wow!" Abby's face brightened. She wiped tears from her eyes and expected to see mascara, but there was none, "How long have I been out?"

"On Earth? It is Thursday."

"Oh, man. I am eighteen now! Woo hoo!" Abby jumped and spun around. "I am going to buy cigarettes and get a credit card and buy a nudie mag!"

"Abagail," Helen interrupted. "They are impressed with you."

"You mean, the tall guys in the robes with the lizard faces? What are they called?"

"They are the Tolkanaytu. They are from an old part of the universe, much more advanced than any planet within our galaxy. The means of travel, that the Tolkanaytu use is not by light speed. They travel through wormholes in space, by the utilization of gemstones, and the bending of gravity."

Abagail was interested in what her grandmother was telling her. She loved science and always excelled in it. However, as her brain went into learning mode, a well of anxiety surfaced. If today was Thursday, back on Earth, then she was supposed to be graduating from high school tomorrow. The fact that Abby cared about something so small, while she remained on an alien craft, with reptilians from across the universe, showed how her mind couldn't comprehend the grand scope of what was happening before her. As real as it was, it seemed too surreal to meet with her long-lost grandmother's essence, which was uploaded to a hard drive on a ship, conversing about the means of space travel.

Abby stood up, "So, wait? There isn't going to be an alien invasion with lasers and ships and that tall lizard guy meeting the President?"

Helen laughed, "No. This is a science ship, and their missions go beyond the concept of brutish infiltration. How would a race of beings learn from the universe, if they are set out to destroy it?"

"Well, that's a relief, because as much as Earthlings bother me, I would hate to see them used as food. So, what is going to happen now?"

"They have made their decision. It is a result of how you answered their questions. Others felt a certain way about you, but the head sage, Kuri has the final say. Only it has to happen according to his plan, and how they like to do things."

"I hope I have a say in it for myself, and I would like to add, I just got a crazy craving for Doritos. I don't know if they can make some or if we can stop somewhere."

"They can make most things with the DNA splicer and the 3-D builder. Those slippers you are wearing were the first of its kind. I had told them about the design from my memory."

"Wow, Grandma Helen, you rock."

"All right, Abagail, I need to explain to you something first."

The white orb lowered itself across the table from Abby and rested at her eyeline.

"Drink some milk tea," Helen said.

Abby never liked milk tea before. Complaining wouldn't make sense because there were no waitresses around to get anything else. She poured the white, milky fluid into the coffee mug and sipped. It was warm and sweet.

"You are going back to Earth," Helen said.

"No way! I thought the lizards were going to use me for some sort of experiment?" Abby yawned and covered her mouth with her hand.

"There is something that you need to do for them, but it will be disclosed to your unawake side."

"My unawake side?"

"Yes, it is hard to explain, but your subconscious will understand."

"Well, that's good." Abby yawned again.

The orb moved across the table toward Abby. "And Abagail, it was wonderful to meet you."

Abby felt flooded with warmth. Her eyelids drooped, and she became incredibly tired.

"Grandma, did the lizards roofie me?"

"Just relax," her grandmother said. Her voice trailed into echoes.

Abagail rested her head on her freshly fixed arm and slept.

32

A heated argument transpired between Nova and Richard. It was one that was needed, but the feelings that came afterward, if allowed to take place, would permanently dismantle their lives, and Abby's as well.

Nova was on another fast and was drinking chicken broth in the kitchen. When she used to do this, it was usually in accordance with Pastor Ulma. Now, she was on her own. She was hearing from God directly and writing things down again.

When Richard saw her back in the gown and veil, he wanted to cry. He thought the worst was behind them. It was like watching a heroin addict; shoot up in the kitchen. Whatever words she was going to say to him would top all that he had heard before. Despite what was going on with Abby, Jerry was not here to keep Nova in line.

Richard saw her sip and put the bowl down. Nova went to speak, he put his finger up and remained stoic. He went into the pantry and took out a bottle of wine. It was the wine that he shared with his beloved father-in-law. He filled a tall glass to the brim.

"Go ahead with your nonsense," he said. He sat down in front of her.

She ignored his comment and went into a long diatribe like their interaction was a comfortable scenario. He took a large sip of wine and stared at her but did not hear a word she said. He didn't want to argue, it was pointless. The energy wasn't there. As the alcohol took effect, his eyes welled up and he thought of a good day with Nova. *Was it last Christmas?* Dinner was prepared by Jerry and Nova together. Playful arguments happened in the kitchen. Dario jumped on the counter multiple times and had to be put in Abby's room. Abby kept letting him out because he wouldn't stop scratching the door. That was before Abby became fascinated with The Cure. That was before Nova went to that conference and lost her mind.

"...And that is why I feel that God has called me to start my own church. One that will be bigger and better than Pastor Ulma's ever was," Nova said. Her chest was rising and falling with excited breaths. Her smile looked like it belonged on a wax sculpture. She waited for Richard's response.

The words that followed, weren't meant to come out of Richard's mouth the way they did, but like all arguments between frustrated couples, they were a shotgun blast to the face. He was in pain and wanted to let her know. Sadly, it was a common thing to happen amongst married couples.

"I want a divorce," he said. As the words were verbalized, he realized if it took place, he would lose Abby and Jerry as well. Then Richard would have no one. His parents died when he was young and he was raised by his grandparents, who were long gone. The time before Abby and Nova, his adopted family were just drunks at a bar, until they weren't friends anymore, just drunks who moved on to hang out with other drunks.

"A divorce? But God hates divorce," Nova said. She placed her cold, clammy hands on top of his. As he wiped his eyes with his sleeve, he hoped it would have snapped her out of it. He imagined them kissing and making up, as she renounced all the heavy doctrines and archaic ways of schizoid emotions and odd teachings that she had allowed to take hold of her psyche.

She responded like any person with delusions of grandeur would. All the responses blamed outward.

"The Devil is in you now and he is deceiving you."

"Goddam you and your Devil," he said. He got up, kissed her on the forehead, and went to bed.

"Richard?" she beckoned as he climbed the stairs.

"No!" he yelled.

Tonight, he would sleep in the spare bedroom. The room was stuffy. He opened the windows. Outside someone was using a gas-powered weedwhacker. It would be too noisy to watch TV, even though he wouldn't be able to focus on anything. He shut the window, stripped down to his boxers, and sat on the floor with his glass of wine. After flipping through the channels, he found a movie starring Cristina Raines. She lived in a creepy apartment building and was invited to a cat's birthday party with weird people singing to it. He dozed off and woke up to her screaming. She was in a short nightie and wielded a knife. An old grey-skinned man attacked her, she

262

stabbed him and cut off his nose. It made Richard's nose itch. He scratched it and remembered that Nova and he were going to get a divorce. It made his heart hurt. He finished the remainder of the wine, laid there for a moment, and decided to sleep on the hardwood floor with no pillow. What would he tell Abby? She was old enough to move out on her own. It is what she wanted for some time. She wasn't his real daughter, and without Nova, he would be alone. At best, he would only see Abby a few times a year. Would she even visit him if a divorce happened?

Nova sat in the kitchen. Her palms were flat on the table. She did believe that the Devil was in Richard. The Devil always had a way to rob God's blessings. To fortify herself against the Devil, she had to fast more and pray harder. This would keep her focused on what God called her to do.

An aid in what she had taken during all of her fasts this year was diet pills. She knew they were man-made and prophets from the Bible didn't take them, but it was time for her to get earnest with God. The suggested dosage was once a day. She had already taken two. However, God had to know how serious she was about starting her own church. So, she took three more. If it kept her up tonight, she would speak in tongues until morning.

Nova made a list of who she would approach at Ulma's church, so they could leave and come with her. She also needed a place of worship. This puzzled her. If God wanted her to start her own church, where would that be? She would have to rent a place. She smiled and wondered what this new place of worship should be called.

After an hour she went to bed. Light from the TV flickered from the spare room. She peeked in and saw Richard asleep on the floor in his underwear. On the TV, was a woman being chased by deformed people in a hellish nightmare. An old man who looked like the coach from Rocky was yelling.

"Filth," she muttered. She turned the TV off and let Richard lay there. She hit the empty glass with her foot, and it tipped over. Richard did not move.

She went into the bedroom and laid down. She pulled the veil over her face and prayed softly. Her heart raced. Pain shot from her neck up to her throat. It traveled down underneath her arm. A strong tingling formed in her hands, like her circulation was being cut off. She thought she was having a

263

vision, from God. On the ceiling, holly berries grew. They spread across the ceiling and moved at an accelerated rate. The holly climbed down the walls and touched the carpet. Berries dropped from the ceiling, bounced on the bed, and onto the floor.

She giggled but it hurt her throat to laugh.

Noise from downstairs took her out of her trance. Abby was home, only it sounded like she brought company. The kitchen table was moved. There was low talking. It was a man's voice. Heavy footsteps climbed the stairs; it sounded like more than one man. Nova sat up, she gripped at the tightness in her chest. The bedroom door opened. A man in a black robe, with a hood pulled over his head walked in. Only his bottom jawline could be seen, he turned and looked at Nova.

Nova shrieked, clutching her throat and chest. "Jesus help me!" she cried.

A second black-robed man entered and then a third.

"Ms. Gibson, this is a special night. There is an extraordinary alignment in the stars tonight. What you will be part of is an epoch. A time in which something was, and something that will come. I understand that you are a prophet of the Christian God. That makes you the perfect lamb for our sacrifice," Jericho said.

Nova slammed her hand on the bed and retched.

Gentry realized that Nova's reactions were much graver than fright. She was going into cardiac arrest.

"Richard!" Nova yelled. It was a welp of terror, a cry of pain. For all the times that Nova had screamed at imaginary demons and made broad proclamations to God, this moment was not crying wolf.

Richard sat up and knew something was not right. It was not the cry, because an angel had spoken to her or the Spirit caused her to have a prophecy, this was a scream of terror. He rushed down the hallway, pushed open the bedroom door, and saw the three black-robed men standing at all edges of the bed. Nova, in her red gown and covered face, was writhing in pain.

Richard had never been in a fight once in his life. He had never lifted weights or taken karate. The heaviest thing he ever lifted was the furniture in this house, and that was only once. In his inebriated stupor, pale with bewilderment, as he witnessed his wife clinging to life, he climbed on the bed and held her.

"You fucking assholes! She is going into cardiac shock! Call the paramedics!"

He embraced Nova. She buried her face into his chest. Her eyes fluttered like a moth's wings delicately balancing on the precipice of the eternal void of darkness.

Jericho pulled the moon-shaped curved blade from the inside of his robe. He raised it above his head.

"She will be the blood sacrifice we require for the beings of the future world. They will hone in on us and visit as they have done to your daughter."

"She will be the blood sacrifice!" Isaac said. He confirmed in an adoring shout.

"Fuck you, you fucking freaks!" Richard spit.

Jericho spoke in Tamil, "Pattirattil iruntu vetti, atu portal tirakkum!"

Isaac confirmed this chant in English, "Cut from the vessel, it will open the portal!"

The moon-blade came down in a diagonal slash. Richard blocked it with his left arm as he embraced his dying wife with his right. The blade cut the meat of his forearm. He screamed. Both windows were open. He hoped that the Robinsons heard the commotion and were calling the police.

Isaac grabbed Nova by the ankles and pulled her toward him. Richard backhanded him with his bloody, wounded arm, and clung to his wife. He wished he was a fighter like his idol, Jerry Beaumont. He hoped these weren't the last moments that Nova and he would have together.

Witnessing the violence was more than Gentry could handle. He was always the more grounded of the three. But watching Richard cling to his wife desperately made him want to love someone like that. Gentry realized that was what he needed in his life. As he recognized the error of his ways, he knew that the goodness in his conscience was always buried under the thick weight of inebriation. This was Gentry's sobering moment.

He snapped and swung at Isaac, making contact with the side of his head. Isaac slammed up against the wall.

"What are you doing you fool? You are breaking the spell!" Jericho screamed.

Gentry stepped toward Jericho, grabbed his knife-wielding wrist, and pushed it against the dresser. He punched Jericho in the stomach and struggled to get the knife out of his hand. Isaac grabbed Gentry around the midsection. His hood came off in the struggle. Gentry swung his elbow back and hit Isaac in the jaw. Jericho slashed at Gentry and caught him in the throat. Blood spurt onto the floor. Gentry panicked and grabbed his bleeding throat. Uncertain of whether his wounds were fatal or not, he ran out of the room and downstairs.

"I will get him!" Isaac said.

"No! We must continue with the sacrifice; it is integral that we do it this night! For the cosmos are in alignment! Light the Candle of Enceladus!"

A trail of blood dripped through the house. With each step, Gentry wondered whose life was more important. He didn't know if he would survive driving to the hospital and die in transit. If he had only minutes to live, he wanted to spend it doing something heroic.

He picked up the phone in the kitchen and called 911. In a strained, bleeding voice, he said that a couple was being murdered by two lunatics, gave the address, and ran out the front door. He left the phone off the hook, hoping that if they didn't hear him clearly, they could trace the call.

The van was parked in shadow at the edge of the road. As he struggled to get the keys with his left hand, he was surprised he hadn't passed out by the loss of blood.

He got in, switched hands on his throat, turned the ignition, and sped off. The world was growing dim, his vision was blurred.

Abagail made a turn down the same road. Her mind was firing at full capacity, she had a total recall of all of the events since she left Earth. The red lights at the train tracks triggered everything. Whether the Tolkanaytu planned to send her back with no memory, or it was intended to come back at another time, she did not know.

A black Chevy G30 van nearly side-swiped her and she swerved onto the grass to avoid a collision.

"What the hell!"

The van continued to speed away. It took a second for her to realize that it was the same van that was in the back alley at the clinic on Sunday.

"They fucking found us!"

Abby floored it and pushed her car as hard as it would go. She slammed on the brakes in front of her home and parked crooked in the street. Richard's scream could be heard from outside.

The Robinsons were on their porch and their light was on.

"Abagail is everything all right?" Ms. Robinson asked.

Abby didn't answer her. In the four years she knew Richard, she never heard him scream once.

In a maddened frenzy, she ran up the stairs, following the trail of blood to the bedroom. She entered and saw Jericho who was entranced in the incantation, wielding the knife. He was at the bottom of the bed. Isaac was next to him holding a lit black candle in his hands.

When Jericho saw Abby, his face lit up with bizarre excitement, as if she were a friend visiting.

"At last, the queen of the cosmos has returned. The one who has left this Earth and came back again. Please enlighten us with your wisdom, oh Queen!"

Abby saw her mother's state and Richard's bloody arm. All her life, she felt like she hadn't been in the moment, it was always afterward when she gained her courage. Courage is something she felt she lacked more than any quality and when it counted, it was too late. But this was different, this was survival. She withdrew her revolver and shot Jericho in the stomach. He stumbled back and fell on the floor. The moon-blade fell out of his hand and slid underneath the bed. Abby aimed the gun at Isaac.

He yelled, "Please don't!"

She shot at him twice. The first shot hit the frame of the window, the second hit him in the chest. The force pushed him against the window screen, and he fell out onto the slanted roof.

Ms. Robinson saw this from her porch and screamed. Abby climbed onto the bed with her mother and Richard. She held her mother's face in her hands.

"Mother, please don't go!" Abby sobbed.

"Abby," Nova whispered.

"Mother, I love you. I am sorry."

"It's okay, Abby," Nova said.

Nova exhaled in a strained rattle. The light dimmed in her clear blue eyes; the corners of her mouth held a faint smile. Abby wondered if the things her mother believed about eternity were true. Did angels carry her off to the pearly gates of Heaven, or did she pass away quietly into a peaceful sleep, guided by nothing? Was the Jesus that her mother preached about with such vehemence present for her at her last dying moment?

Richard howled in anguish, with his bloody arm curled up like a torn wing off a bird. Abagail cried, but a root of strength sprung up from within, and she held her composure. The emotional bomb buried deep inside her would go off at another time. She found a t-shirt on the floor and wrapped Richard's arm with it. He put his hand around the back of Abby's neck and touched her forehead with his. He wept in small yelps like a puppy demanding to be let out of its crate. Abby sat on the floor with her back against the bed.

A hollowness opened in her heart. She did not listen to the gurgling of the blood in the lungs of Jericho, who was dying on the floor behind her. Nor was she concerned about Isaac, who lay upside down on the slanted roof, in front of her house. As he stared into the void of the cosmos, the peristalsis of his esophageal flap kept his last meal within his stomach. He had eaten crackers earlier that day, mixed with a quart of barrel-aged whiskey. He wanted to remain light as he infiltrated a family's home.

Abagail pulled her knees to her chest and wrapped her arms around them tight, so tight that she began to vibrate like a spinning top. Far off in the distance, sirens approached.

33

The events that took place at Abagail's home that night shocked the town. A teen abduction, a bizarre cult, and three deaths all within the span of a few weeks were more than the quiet town could handle. The police ascertained that the deaths of Jericho and Isaac were an act of self-defense by Abagail. The phone call left by Gentry were integral to the case, and the Robinsons confirmed that he left at the time of the call.

In his final moments, Gentry did find his purpose and that was being a hero. He bled out on the side of the road next to a closed-down laundromat.

Underneath the back seat of his van was a copy of *Channeling Your Conscience Through the Unknown Universe* by famed mystic/astronomer/professor Francis Truelove. It was a second-edition paperback copy. When the van was impounded and eventually sold off at an auction. The book was found by someone else, much more curious, and much more sensitive.

Since Nova wasn't considered a member of Ulma's church anymore, she had no religious affiliation. She was cremated. A small gathering was held for her in the backyard. A few metal chairs were lined up in a half circle around a photo of her, glued to a foam-core board, and placed on an easel. Abby lit white sage in a mason jar to clear the air from negative energy. Jerry and Margaret came down for the service, as well as Jerry's youngest sister Jude. Margaret had a hell of a time traveling with her broken hip. But she was a tough woman and made the ride. As she recalled there was a pleasant time with Nova last Christmas, that was before she was deemed a prophet. Only Jerry spoke, he said that he wished he was a better father to her. Richard cried the whole evening. Abby sat next to him until the sun went down and the moon came to its fullness.

Richard heard from a recent ex-church member that Ulma did a "Beware of the False Prophet" sermon the Sunday after Nova passed. A portion of the congregation thought it was in such poor taste, that nearly a third of them vowed never to return. Even though Richard was thrilled to hear of Ulma's flock dwindling, he was still angry. He wondered what would have happened to Ulma if he had hired that lawyer. The fasting that was preached upon, was connected to the diet pills that Nova took. And it would be a great thing if that bastard lost all credibility.

Afterward, Richard told Jerry why Nova took the diet pills. And how they were connected with her heart attack. Richard wanted to ruin Ulma's career. He dwelled on how Abby was pushed and how the lawyer wanted to get involved. But in the end, Jerry felt revenge was not the best road to go. He surprised himself by saying it. He didn't want Abby to undergo scrutiny again. Her word versus a twisted pastor's would not be pleasant for anyone.

"We could shoot him in the ass or something," Richard said. This made Jerry laugh heartily. Richard loved that he made a man of Jerry's stature crack up.

"If we went by that measure, I fear that I would run out of bullets," Jerry said.

Jerry took Nova's ashes back home with him. The place she grew up in was no longer around. It only made sense for Jerry to take her remains to the woods on his property. He placed Nova's ashes by a triple cluster of white birch trees. Even though Nova lost touch at the end, Jerry thought she would have liked that, at least the younger version of her would have.

Richard put the house on the market; he couldn't bear to live in it anymore. The market was at a low point, and he made less than what he bought it for. This didn't concern him, as the house would only remind him of the nightmares that unfolded that tragic evening. The couple who bought it called it a deal. Sadly, it only took a few nights for them to say the vibe of the house was off. They tried to sell it but could not, and it sat vacant.

Abby saw Sutton one last time before he left for boot camp. He wanted her to be in his life. She knew he was going to say something along those lines, and his sincerity was what made him special. She told him he was a good man and should find another woman, not just anyone, but a good one. After the past month she had, Abby didn't feel good about anything at all. He didn't agree, he said she was the *only* one for him. This statement pushed her further away. He moved in to kiss her, and she dodged it. Sloppily, he kissed her on the cheek. They hugged. And that was the last moment in their friendship. He never told her about what he had done to Ulma on the side of the highway, it was a secret he kept from the family forever.

Sutton made a career out of the Army and did nearly twenty years of service. He did find a good woman and had two kids with her. He bought a home in Blueville, and the wife stayed there, mostly alone, and waited for him to return, only when the Army would allow it.

When Abby finally spoke to Rose on the phone, they became hysterical. Rose didn't want to believe all the things she had missed in such a short time. She cursed at Abby, wept for her, told her she loved her, and asked her to move to Miami. Abby agreed and took the proposition. She had some money, that Richard gave her. And she felt that moving would be a fresh start. Richard was saddened by this, and he expected it as well. He urged her to get her radiator checked because an old car with that many miles could have issues. It would be tougher to get something fixed in an unknown state, while no job was set. But her desire to leave was too great. Abby didn't want to be in Blueville anymore.

When the house sold, Richard downsized into an apartment in Nashville. He got a different IT job and played video games to pass the time. He never did remarry but kept in contact with Jerry as much as possible. But Jerry was tough to pull more than one-word answers out of, so phone conversations were difficult. Richard made a point to drive up to Illinois for Thanksgiving and Christmas. It was kind of Jerry to consider Richard still part of the family, even though the women who connected them were gone.

As for Abby, she faced the bitter irony of clinging to the darkness of being a goth girl because of how her mother treated her, and since her mother's passing, the world seemed a bit more dim. While holding her mother's dying face, and looking into her fading eye-light, Abagail forgave her mother for everything. She hoped her mother knew that wherever she was.

34

A fire was before Abagail; dry leaves crackled in the flames. She was in a cave. Her hands were dirty, her nails were long and unkempt. Her attire was made of fur from a dead animal. She smelled like rawhide and wet earth. At the entrance of the cave, shadows of a threat passed by. Instinctively, she picked up a thick branch, with a sharpened stone at the top, to defend herself. The threat did not enter the cave. Her stomach growled, but she knew to stay inside until daylight. Water rippled from an underground source, from the far wall, and escaped at a crevice on the other side. The pool was deep enough to put both hands in. She drank from her palms. The extracellular protozoa did not have a negative effect on her as her biome became accustomed; in this was her sustenance, in this was her strength. Tomorrow she would hunt, she knew this because she would not be prey anymore.

Abby awoke in her car in a truck stop parking lot. Only a few hours earlier, her eyes were heavy, and the car's radiator had been overheating. Hopefully, the mixed gallon of water and antifreeze would keep it stable, until she could get it fixed. It was some hundred miles from home and some hundred miles from Miami. Rose was her destination. Rose was someone who kept her stable. Perhaps Rose was built up in her mind so much that Rose wasn't even aware of how important she had been to Abby's sanity.

In the backseat, Dario cried in his cat cage. She let him out and put him on a lease. He relieved himself and tried covering his waste with dry grass. She picked him up and kissed him. She got back in the car and drove on a secluded state road. Endless tall trees spread across a vast mountainscape. As the sun set, ribbons of crimson shot across the sky like stab wounds in the belly of a shot deer. She drove in the darkness; her travels were only lit by the headlights of her car and sporadic traffic passing in the opposite lane. Then it appeared in the sky above her, it was as large as three football stadiums. She slammed on the brakes. Her car skid. She wanted to take a picture with her phone but was in awe of the massive structure that hung over the Earth. Nearly all photos of UFO's were blurry, often the photographer being criticized as an amateur or doctoring the photo, although this was true in some instances. But in most cases, the photographer was too dumbfounded to react quickly enough. The resulting photo would always be blurred, as a cheetah catching a gazelle is an act of force so great, that just witnessing it, and telling the tale afterward, should be more than enough.

Somehow she knew it was her time. She got out of the car. It was inevitable that the Tolkanaytu would find her again. As if the consciousness of her grandmother spoke to her, assuring her it was the right time and place. Abby's legs shook. A beam of red light appeared from the center of the ship and hit the road directly in front of her. It was more beautiful than a rainbow, more terrifying than an atomic bomb explosion. Abagail wasn't made for this world. And she knew her car wouldn't make it to Miami anyway. She reached inside the car, picked up the cat cage, and opened her trunk. In a recyclable grocery bag was a record with Robert Smith's face on it. The album was *Disintegration*, it came out in 1989. It was the year her mother went to see The Cure on tour. In a parking lot outside of the concert is where Abby was conceived. A nameless man was her father. Abby picked up the record, held it in one hand, and the cat cage in the other, and walked under the immense structure in the sky.

Dario meowed to her.

As she walked toward the light, she chanted, "Aaaaaaaaaaaaooo, aaaaaaaaaaaummm."

The moment she stood underneath the light that shone from the center of the massive ship, she slowly lifted off the ground. For the eighteen years, she had on this Earth, must have forged her mind, body, and soul, into something admirable, like a geode as a conduit of transcendence, because the aliens from an older part of our universe came back for her. Abagail said *goodbye* to the world she barely knew, and she ascended.